Wildflowers and Butterflies

A novel by

Peggy Poe Stern

Moody Valley
Boone, North Carolina

Published by
Moody Valley
475 Church Hollow Road
Boone, N C 28607
moodyvalley@skybest.com

Cover painting by Peggy Poe Stern
Cover design by David K. Stern
First published 12-09-2024
Edited

ISBN: 978-1-59513-076-1

Dedicated to Our
Friends and Family
Past, Present, and Future

Chapter 1

*

I didn't want to think what I was thinking, but I couldn't stop myself. My mother, my beautiful mother, who had spent time dancing on stage before she met my father was now dancing with deadly cancer as her partner. Her partner was causing her to lose everything – including her life. What it had not taken from her was her iron will to stay alive long enough for me to grow up. She wanted me to get straight A's in school so I could get a scholarship to a good college. It would be the only chance I had to further my education. There was no doubt that we were destitute.

"Don't do as I did," she often told me. "Don't give up your dreams in order to get married before you're old enough to realize what you're doing to your future. At least I got you out of my mistake, and you're worth more to me than anything else in this entire world."

Mom stopped dancing after she married my father. When he discovered Mom was pregnant with me, he decided he didn't want to be tied down with a wife and a baby. He took off to the good Lord only knows where. Mom accepted the fact that he didn't want the responsibility of having a wife and baby. It was obvious she had loved him enough to allow him his freedom. She never tried to find him or even divorce him. There were times when I would catch her taking a picture of them on their wedding day from her nightstand and staring at it with tears in her eyes.

"She's still in love with that no account," Aunt Mary would tell me often. "She ought to have divorced him a long time ago for desertion and found herself a good man. One that would love her and take care of her and you. She deserves a good man. Not only that, but she should also sue him for back child support. It would be enough to help out with all her medical expenses."

I agreed with Aunt Mary. Any man who would run out on my beautiful mother had to be no-account and crazy as a bed bug. My sweet, wonderful mother deserved a good man, but I knew it was too late.

As the days passed, I would hear her crying at night when she thought I was sleeping. She didn't know that I saw her looking at the stack of bills she was no longer able to pay.

We had to eat. Had to pay the mortgage on the house and on the restaurant. Needed an unimaginable amount of money to pay the ever-increasing doctor bills. Not to mention the medicine needed to help my mother fight the cancer that ravaged her body. I watched her grow pale, lose weight, lose hair, and become unable to work in the restaurant with Aunt Mary. I did everything I could to help out, but I was only twelve years old. Aunt Mary and I couldn't possibly work enough to keep up with the cost of running a household, a restaurant and fighting cancer.

Mom had been the backbone of the restaurant. She was the one who was up at five o'clock in the morning and didn't go to bed until after midnight. How she'd managed to keep going for all these years was beyond me. Now, the cancer had almost stopped her in her tracks. Two hours in the restaurant and she had to spend the rest of the day in bed.

Aunt Mary had to hire two women to take Mom's place. There was no money left over to pay Aunt Mary or Mother. I never got paid for what I did. The only payment I wanted was for Mother to get well. I wanted the mother who was able to take care of me instead of the other way around.

I learned what the word foreclosure meant when our mortgage came due. It meant we would be put out on the street – literally. I also learned what repossessed meant. We had ten days to pay for the van mother hauled restaurant supplies in or it would be taken away for us.

I walked the streets in turmoil. I saw people going into stores buying all sorts of expensive things when my sweet, hardworking mother had not a dollar to pay bills with. Not to mention pay for medicine to ease her pain and keep her alive. Playing by the rules, as Mother had done all her life, didn't add up to a thing other than poverty and desperation.

I watched men in suits and ties carrying briefcases, who obviously had money in their billfolds, walk about town. Their wives and girlfriends strutted about flashing diamonds on their fingers, in their ears, on their wrists and around their necks. I didn't know how they managed to have so much of everything when my mother was dying because she had so little. But I wanted to find out.

I cut across a little park that had one bench. Green grass was growing along with a few spindly flowers someone had been kind enough to plant. An old man with snowy-white hair was sitting on the bench. He nodded his head at me as a greeting. His hair was the whitest I had ever seen on anybody. His face was full of wrinkles. His blue eyes were filled with kindness.

"Come over here, child," he said. "What's your name?"

I hesitated. Mother had warned me to stay away from strangers. Why I disregarded her warning, I had no idea.

"Millie James," I told him my name as I cautiously eased closer. There was something about this man that drew me to him. I think it was the kindness I saw within him. Or perhaps it was simply that I needed someone to befriend me.

"I see a sadness in your pretty eyes, Millie James," he said as I drew nearer "My name is Jimbo. Oh, yes, I can see why you're sad." He reached his hand out and touched my hair. Pulled his hand back and opened his hand. "You had a fifty-cent piece stuck behind your ear. I bet that will buy you an ice-cream cone."

"Ice-cream cones cost a dollar," I told him.

Mother had also warned me about taking things from strangers, but I took the money anyway. When you had nothing, everything was a temptation.

"How did you do that?"

"Simple," he held out empty hands for me to see, and then touched my other ear. "I'll be a monkey's uncle. You have another fifty-cent peace behind that ear."

"Where did you learn such a trick?" I asked as I took the other coin from his hand when he held it toward me. "Do it again," I said.

He laughed. "One ice-cream cone is enough for today."

"One ice cream cone is never enough," I said.

"I suspect you're right about that," he grinned, but didn't offer me more ice cream money.

"Where did you learn to do that?" I asked again without offering to return the money.

"I used to run a magic show," he said with a touch of pride. "I was very good at it if I do say so myself."

He then opened his other hand and held out the cheap dime-store necklace I had been wearing around my neck since I was six years old.

"I was so good at sleight of hand that I could just about take the underwear off a person without them knowing it," he told me with sincerity.

I grabbed my necklace back. "How did you learn to do that?" I questioned again, more than a little envious.

"It becomes simple once you know how and practice a lot," the old man said, seeming to know how desperate I was feeling. "There is one thing I've discovered during my many years on this earth. It's that most rich folks get rich by taking away from poor people," he told me. "I believe in the Robin Hood theory. Taking from the rich to help those in desperate need."

I realized my desperate need was showing.

That was how I met the man who called himself Jimbo.

Several times a week I would go by the little park just to see if the old man was there.

I wondered if he could teach me his magical *sleight of hand.*

*

Mother had spent a lot of time teaching me right from wrong. Somehow the wrong took on a different meaning as I watched her puking in the bathroom commode after her chemo. What she was going through was wrong.

Wrong applied as I watched her take every item of value to the pawn shop trying to get by for one more month before we lost everything. Fear and uncertainty had a way of shooting their painful darts into me both day and night. I could only imagine what it was doing to my mother.

Mother knew the pawn shop man was cheating the socks off her by what little he offered. She had no choice other than give up her few valuables. The pawn shop man knew desperation when he saw it. I was also desperate to make everything alright again, but what could a twelve-year-old possibly do to help financially?

It was on a Saturday, and we made another trip to the pawn shop. Mother watched tearfully as the man put her gold wedding band in a display case he set on the counter when his arm accidentally bumped into the case, spilling everything over the countertop and at my bare feet.

"Don't touch anything," he demanded as though we were going to steal something. "Leave right now," he shouted as he ran around the counter to rush us out of the pawn shop.

Mother and I left. Neither he nor Mother knew I had clamped my toes around a diamond ring. Once we were a little way from the pawn shop, I bent down to rub my bare foot, took the ring in my hand, and slipped the ring into my pocket. Considering how much the man always cheated Mother, I didn't feel the least bit guilty about what I did. I planned on finding another pawn shop after I figured out the approximate value of the ring. I didn't want to get cheated the way mother was being cheated.

That evening while Mother lay in bed crying over her pawned wedding band, I paid a visit to the old man sitting on the bench.

"Can I ask you something in confidence?" I stood before him with my hand in my pocket, while Mother's warning made me stay far enough away from him until he couldn't touch me.

"Every word, every action between us is confidential," he assured me.

I took my hand out of my pocket and showed him the ring on my finger. "What's the value of this?"

He lifted his bushy white eyebrows. "Where did you get that? That's not your mother's, is it?"

"It's not Mother's. I went with Mother to pawn her wedding band. The man cheated her again, so I picked this up off the floor."

"Did he see you?"

"No one saw me."

"Most likely he'll search for it and then notify all the other pawn shops to be on the lookout. "Did you think about returning it to the crooked pawn shop owner?"

"We need it more than he does. Besides, he cheats Mother every time she takes something to him. He makes Mother cry."

"I see. Why did your mother pawn her things?"

"She's got cancer. We don't have money for food, rent or her medicine."

"And your daddy?"

"He took off before I was born.

"I see."

He obviously saw my desperation from the very beginning, otherwise he wouldn't have given me a dollar for ice cream.

"Come with me," he said. "We'll go to a jewelry store and get an estimate. I've got a little experience with diamond rings but not enough to place today's value on one."

The estimate surprised us both. It was an antique ring with a unique cut diamond stone in a platinum setting.

"Where did you get this?" the jewelry store man asked.

"It belonged to my mother," Jimbo said. "I gave it to my wife. She died a while back. I decided I might sell it as I need the money more than I need the ring."

"Say you want to sell it?" the man's eyes brightened, although he was trying to seem uninterested.

"I would if I can get that much money out of it."

"I'll buy it from you, but I'll have to give you ten percent less than its value. I need to make a little on it."

"I'll think on it. I'd like to get a few more estimates before I make a final decision to sell it. It does have a lot of sentimental value for me."

"Five percent less, and that's my top offer," the jewelry man said.

"What do you think, little one?" he said to me.

"You know what's best, Grandpa."

He grinned and patted me on the head. "I guess we could take it. It'll save us walking all over town."

Once we were a good distance from the store, he stuffed the full amount of money in my worn pants pocket. "Hope this will tide you over for a little while."

"It'll help catch things up, but I'll need more than that. Bills are overdue and Mother's medicine is outrageous."

"Outrageous," he repeated. "Big word for a little girl. Does your mother talk about her outrageous bills?"

Mother and Aunt Mary talk about them all the time."

"In front of you?"

"I listen without them knowing it."

"You're very intelligent, aren't you?"

"If I was intelligent, I'd figure out a way to pay the bills so Mother can stay alive. I don't want my mother to die," I told him. "Maybe I can get other rings from the pawn shop."

"Not a good idea. You would get caught. There are other, safer options," he assured me. "My hands are so twisted with arthritis they've become old and slow. Yours are not. There are many things I can teach someone who is intelligent enough to learn," he told me with a furrowed brow along with a slight hesitancy.

"Can you teach me how to pay Mother's bills. I've never paid a bill before," I told him. "Do you think the bank will let me do it."

"Don't know of a bank that refuses to take people's money. However, some teller might question how a young girl came to have that much cash. They might even go so far as to call your mother since they'll have her information. It might be best if I go with you. That is if you want me to. I'll show you how making payments are done."

He was right. The bank took money for Mother's mortgage payment along with her van payment without calling Mother or asking questions since an adult was with me.

"My granddaughter will be coming in to pay from now on being her mother and I aren't in the best of health. I don't expect there will be any problem with that being she is a child, will there be?"

"Of course not," the teller said. "It would be better if she brought a check for the payments instead of cash. A child carrying cash is risky."

"Make sure you always give her a receipt of payment," he told the teller, and we left the bank.

"That wasn't so bad," I told him.

"The bad part will be obtaining enough money to pay the bills each month, but you already know that. I've got an idea you'll figure that out on your own. A kid won't be punished the way an old man would if he got caught lifting a few things. The trick is not to get caught," he made a point of telling me.

"Can you teach me how to do your sleight of hands?" I asked with a touch of hopefulness. He looked down at me for a few long moments.

"You're feeling desperate, aren't you, little one?"

I nodded.

He hesitated for long moments before he spoke. "Okay. I'll teach you that along with other tricks," he assured me and let out a long breath of air. "May the good Lord forgive me," he added in a whispered breath I almost didn't hear.

*

He started teaching me every Wednesday how to do his sleight of hand trick. I practiced with him and without him.

"Speed, illusion and pure innocence, is what you've got plenty of," is what he told me.

I was a nervous wreck the first time I bumped into a rich-looking man in a suit as he walked down the street.

"Watch where you're going kid," he said angrily as he pushed me aside while giving me a hateful look.

The way he did that made me not the least bit sorry I'd slipped his billfold into my sweater pocket. "Sorry," I called out in my most innocent voice as I rushed away. I really was sorry for being the kind of person who was taking his billfold, but I didn't know of any other way to pay our bills. I figured his suit cost as much as our house payment.

Although we were desperate for money, I didn't look like a little beggar. Mother managed to buy me nice enough clothes at the secondhand stores, even though they looked slightly worn. She also taught me how to iron my clothes and fix my golden hair in curls, since she could no longer do either one for me. When I looked in the mirror, I resembled an older Shirley Temple with dimples and innocent blue eyes. No one would believe I was a thief in training by looking at me.

"This Shirley Temple is a modern day Robin Hood," I whispered to myself as I ran as fast as my legs would carry me back to the house and into the bathroom before I took the billfold out of my sweater. Five one-hundred-dollar bills, plus a twenty, and five ones were in the billfold. It wasn't enough to get by on for another month, but it was a good start.

I worked at the restaurant from the time I got out of school until midnight. I was too young to be put on payroll, not that it mattered. I never would be on payroll. Not being paid, plus being the owner's daughter got me by with working all the hours I could squeeze in.

It was obvious when some wealthy person had too much to drink, or when someone was being extra mean to the waitstaff. I really liked the drunks because they thought they bumped into me. Not only that, but they couldn't remember how much they spent or where they might have lost their billfolds.

I wasn't good at lifting jewelry off woman. Jimbo would have to work more on that talent with me, but I was sure I could learn. My hands did become slick as grease when women got too busy texting on their phones to mind their purses. I made a point of never taking money from someone who needed money more than my mother did. People who spent money to eat expensive meals away from home made good targets. The drawback was that Mother's restaurant didn't have expensive meals the way some restaurants did. People who ate at her restaurant were the hard-working type who were hungry and looking for a cheap meal.

Fortunately, a Shirley Temple look-alike with an innocent face was never suspected of being a thief. I didn't like to use the word thief or even think it. Instead, I assured myself that I was a Robin Hood. I had sewn deep pockets inside my dress where I could slip my ill-gotten gains. Plus, at the restaurant, I wore too large aprons over my clothes.

Those eating at the restaurant weren't the only people I focused on. I discovered I could do best when I was in the middle of a crowd of people. Crowds were always bumping into each other without giving it a second thought. After a lot of practice, I didn't have to bump into people. Getting within touching distance was enough.

"You're quick as lightning with a light touch," Jimbo assured me. "Plus, you're a fast learner."

He meant it as a compliment. I think he was proud of me in his own sort of way. I wasn't proud of me. I always had a bad feeling deep inside about what I was doing. The good part was Mother wasn't crying as often.

"A person has to survive the best way they can," Jimbo said as he patted me on the head. "Sometimes being a Robin Hood is the only solution in a life and death situation. Mind you, I'm here to tell you it isn't the best way. You end up paying in ways you never expect."

I feared he was right, but I was willing to pay whatever the price might be if it meant I still had a mother.

*

There were times when I caught Aunt Mary watching me with a puzzled frown on her face, but she never questioned me about anything. Never once did she ask how I got the money to pay for groceries when I was to bring supplies from the local grocery store when we got behind on paying the suppliers. Not one time did she offer to go to the grocery store or give me money when she sent me to get something.

I still managed to keep up my school grades with all the hours I was working at the restaurant. Mother made a point of telling me how proud she was of me for all the work I was doing, plus going to school. At first, I felt ashamed of myself every time they bragged on me, but things were looking up. I figured out Mother surely thought Aunt Mary was managing to pay all the bills, while Aunt Mary believed

Mother was somehow managing by pawning off everything she owned to keep the wolves from our door.

It seemed no one suspected me of anything.

And then a miracle happened. Mother started getting better. Her oncologist told her she was in remission. Although she was still pale and thin as a stick, she tied a scarf over her bald head and started back to work at the restaurant.

"We're going to make ends meet after all," Mother told Aunt Mary. "Now that I can work again, Millie can take some time off to be a young girl. She shouldn't be forced to become an adult while she's still a child."

"You're right about that," Aunt Mary said. "It's been tough, especially on her. I shudder to think what would have happened without her helping out."

If they only knew. I hoped they never would.

Things got a little less tight, but I didn't stop my newly found talent. I just didn't do it as often. I did save up enough money to buy myself a set of lock picks. I was also able to take an hour's break after school to go to the library where I pulled up everything I could find on locks and security systems. I feared I would need to know about such things in the future and I was going to be prepared in case the worst happened. I also learned the best way to shoplift without being caught on a camera. I justified what I was doing by telling myself stores charged customers extra to cover such losses. I knew I was a horrible person, but my mother's life was more important than my conscious.

There was still a mountain of back bills to be paid off, but at least, we weren't living on the streets or doing without food and transportation. Even the restaurant was doing better than just breaking even since Mother came back to help out in the kitchen. She was great at the preparation of good food. Her specialty was desserts. Drinks and desserts were a money maker. The food itself was little more than break-even at best.

Time passed, and I went from Shirley Temple to a skinny girl who dressed in boots, pants, and bulky sweatshirts similar to all the other kids in school. All my things were bought from secondhand stores. We wanted to become unique individuals. At the same time, we wanted to be just like everyone else.

Just when I thought Mother had finally become healed, the cancer hit her again. Like before, she could no longer work, and bills started piling up. I needed to find a better and faster way to pay bills other than being a pickpocket and shoplifter.

It was the richest girl in class who instigated me to take a bigger step than I'd ever imagined. She was a high-class bully who suddenly started making fun of me about pretty much everything. She and her groupies started calling me trashcan Millie. It started when my mother bought me a nice winter coat along with a pair of slightly used Niki shoes at the Salvation Army store. Sara McKay recognized them right away as being her cast-offs her mother donated. Sara couldn't take someone such as me was wearing clothes she once wore. She decided to make my life as close to a living hell as possible.

Sara always wore expensive clothes with a real gold necklace hanging around her neck. She bragged about how it was a solid gold nugget her uncle had gifted her dangling near her nubbins of breasts. She was proud of what protruded beneath her shirts.

I saw her with her mother a few times. Her mother was always dressed to the nines in designer clothes while glittering with what Jimbo had taught me to recognize as real diamonds instead of glass or paste. Sara's mother had everything my mother didn't have, plus she was a snob who was raising a spoiled brat of a daughter.

It was a mixture of anger, jealousy and need that made me do what I decided to do. I was going to break into their house and get at least one valuable. Jimbo had drilled into me an amateur thief should only take one valuable at a time, even when there were a number of easy pickings available. "It allows folks think they misplaced it and would likely not call the cops," he said. "A successful burglar should always wear surgical gloves and cover your head and mouth with something. Hair and slobber were an excellent source for DNA. Dirt is another thing you should be aware of. It can give away the location you came from as well as the tread on your shoes. Both can be traced back to the wearer. It's good to wear plastic grocery bags held on by rubber bands over your shoes. Make sure you never leave a grocery bag behind."

I slipped and practiced with my lock pick every chance I got until I knew I was good at it. I also waited for the right time. I eavesdropped while Sara bragged to her friends about all the things she did with her parents.

I found myself envying she had a healthy mother and a live-in father when I didn't have either one. Knowing such gave me incentive to take a little of what she and her parents freely flaunted.

Sara bragged she and her parents were taking a week's skiing vacation to Aspen during the school's Christmas Holidays. She even told the day and time they would be leaving home. Her bragging gave me the opportunity I longed for.

During the time they were leaving home on their skiing vacation, my mother was home vomiting her insides out as she suffered from a day's round of chemotherapy. I was working at the restaurant as usual. I told Aunt Mary I was going to take a break and look around for something Mother might like as a Christmas gift, and I could afford.

"Okay," she said relunctly suspecting I didn't have money to buy a bar of candy much less a gift. "You deserve a break. We've been crazy busy, but it's slowed down a little. Mind you, I'm not complaining. With luck and the Christmas spirit, we might be able to cover expenses for this month without having overdue charges."

That was good news, but covering one month's bills at the restaurant didn't pay for Mother's cancer treatment, the mortgage, electricity, telephone, and van payments. As for food, I took what leftovers customers didn't eat home every night to feed Mother and me.

I waited until midnight to climb out the window. I made sure I was wearing black boots, pants, shirt, and coat. I also had a black ski mask from the secondhand store along with a pair of surgical gloves from the restaurant and grocery bags in my pocket. I ran all the way to Sara's house. Once I got near, I hid in the shrubbery and bent nearly double to catch my breath and ease the stabbing pain in my side.

"A cat burglar has to have nerves of steel while never getting overly confident about anything," Jimbo once told me. "They need to be little more than a shadow in the dark. Coming and going in the blink of an eye."

I certainly wasn't overly confident. My nerves were a total wreck, and my psyche was keyed to the point I could feel my heart throbbing in my throat. I realized the chance I was taking and hoped it would be worth it – not only in profit but in revenge. What if I failed in my mission and got caught? The stress along with the cancer would surely be enough to kill my mother. Aunt Mary would lose everything along with never being able to live down the disgrace of having everyone know her only niece was a thief.

Once my breath returned, and I convinced myself to continue, I put plastic bags on my feet and gloves on my hands, took out my lock pick kit and went down their house's basement steps. I started working on the door and was surprised when it unlocked. I put the kit back in my backpack and entered the basement. There was a large glass aquarium built into a wall filled with exotic fish and giving off enough light for me to see the room. It was decked out as a rec-room for their spoiled rotten daughter.

I looked about to see if there was anything of value Jimbo and I could hock. There was an almost endless supply of electronics, games, and many other things a girl could want. There were also a few stuffed animals sitting on fancy velvet couches. I made sure I didn't touch anything and went up the stairs. I gripped the doorknob and turned it. A shiver ran up my back. My breath caught. I felt a mixture of fear and excitement.

The door led into what I took to be a mud room and a laundry room. There was no dirty laundry or clean laundry. Sara bragged about having a cleaning lady who came in twice a week to do laundry and clean up after them.

My mother was almost too weak to stand on her own two feet and yet there was no cleaning lady to come in and help. I considered myself the only help available for my mother.

I went into the modern, immaculate kitchen and then into the living room. I stood there gasping with open-mouth wonder. Sara wasn't exaggerating when she bragged about how fancy her house was. I saw nothing of value that could be put in my backpack and carried off. I felt another chill creep over me. I didn't want to admit it was fear of being caught. Sara never mentioned any security system, but it didn't mean there wasn't one. For all I knew, the police could be on their way right now.

Hurriedly, I went up the circular staircase to search for her parents' bedroom. That's where I thought women would keep their valuables. Jimbo said the most expensive jewelry would always be locked in a hidden safe somewhere, but jewelry of lesser value could be kept in the bedroom either in a jewelry box or hidden in a drawer.

The first door I opened belonged to Sara. It wasn't the room I wanted, but I couldn't resist entering, although I knew time was essential. "Get in, get out," Jimbo said. "Speed means safety. Lollygagging puts you in the slammer."

I stopped lollygagging, but I couldn't stop myself from taking time to look at the canopy bed and expensive Persian rug on the gleaming wood flooring. The bedspread and curtains were of the same lacy material. They matched the touches of pale pink in the rug. It was a girl's room whose every wish came true. I envied that.

I saw a small jewelry box sitting on a white dresser trimmed with gold ornamentation. I opened it to see it was filled with jewelry, and not the cheap dime store kind I was wearing around my neck. These were real gold necklaces. A gold tennis bracelet with tiny diamonds caught my attention. I thought it was the most expensive thing in the jewelry box. I slipped it into the lining of my jacket along with the gold necklace with the gold nugget and left the room.

I opened another door and concluded it was a guest room as its furnishings were lovely, but its furnishings were showroom perfect with only the essentials. The next door opened to her parents' bedroom. Luxury. Pure expensive luxury was how I described this room. There was a California king size bed with carved posts reaching eight-foot toward a vaulted ceiling. The room smelled of expensive perfume. Just like in their daughter's room, a larger and more ornate jewelry box was sitting on top of a gleaming, cherry wood dresser.

I went straight to it and found it locked. I took out my lock pick kit and open it in seconds. If this was the cheap jewelry inside the box, I longed to get at what was in their safe. Unfortunately, Jimbo hadn't taught me how to crack a safe. I'd have to talk to him about that in the near future. I made a point of meeting him once a week at the little park. He'd sell what I'd gotten or tell me where I should take it to pawn.

In the fancy jewelry box, everything was very orderly arranged in velvet slits. Whatever I took would leave an empty space. Moving the rings around wouldn't hide the empty spot. I rushed back to Sara's room and found a ring and rushed back to her parents' bedroom. I took the most valuable looking ring and replaced the ring with Sara's and relocked the box.

I slipped the ring in the lining of my jacket and almost ran to the basement, went outside, and relocked the basement door. Never in my entire life was I as relieved to breathe fresh air that wasn't tainted with expensive perfume.

Chapter 2

*

There was no other choice than to take the ring to Jimbo. I knew better than to try to sell it on my own. A young girl pawning such a ring would be a dead give-away that it was stolen.

"Can you do something for me?" I asked him as I sat down on the bench beside him.

"I can try," he told me. "What is it?"

I took the ring from my pocket and showed it to him. "Do you know of anyone who would be willing to buy this?"

"Humph," he grunted as he took the ring and studied it for a minute. "Where did you get this?"

I told him.

His eyebrows lifted. "Why them?" he questioned.

"Mother has gotten worse."

"And?" he questioned.

I hung my head and lowered my voice to a whisper. "Sara McKay makes fun of me. She calls me trashcan Millie."

"Why does she do that?"

"Because I wear clothes from secondhand stores. She has her friends make fun of me too."

"I believe I know someone who will buy it, but you can't go with me to sell it."

"Why not?" I thought I might need to know who this person was just in case I got more to sell.

"He's not a nice man, especially where children are concerned."

Our conversation ended as Jimbo put the ring in his pocket and stood up. "Meet me here tomorrow," I heard him say as he walked away.

Jimbo was able to sell the ring for enough to pay that month's bills plus a little left over for hiring a cab to take Mother and me for her cancer treatment and back home again. I wasn't old enough to drive, Aunt Mary couldn't afford to take off work, and Mother would be too sick to drive the van back home. I don't know if Mother was too sick to wonder about the cab, or if she was too thankful to question it.

Seemed to me nothing changed, and I feared things would only get worse.

Mom was pretending to be in a happy state of mind, although I knew she wasn't. Her face grew paler every day as the purple beneath her sunken eyes increased.

"Doing this is what will make me well again," she said in her artificial happy voice as she tied her pink scarf around her bald head in preparation for the trip to get her treatment. She'd given up on wearing a cheap wig. Pretending she was healthy took more strength than was left in her.

She'd once had beautiful auburn hair that laid in waves down her back. I envied her hair thinking it was much prettier than my blond locks. I could only imagine how sad she felt when the first chunk came out in her hand. Her beautiful hair and strong muscled, dancing body had once been her pride and joy. Now . . .

Mother kept her eyes closed every time the machine pumped medicines into her body. I knew those medicines were pure poison that were supposed to kill the fast-growing cancer cells. The problem was that it wasn't discretionary. It also kills good cells as well, like hair, and skin, along with the good intestinal things that kept her from being on her knees puking in the bathroom commode for hours on end.

I knew Mother was praying that this time the medicine would work, but we both knew it was little more than wishful thinking. I often wondered if the attempt at curing her cancer was worse than the cancer itself. Perhaps, without the treatments, she would spend her last days without suffering so much, but I wasn't sure about that, and neither was Mother. I knew in my heart she would eventually succumb to the unrelenting beast, but the chemotherapy provided one little, painful drop of hope for us to cling to.

I'd gone on the internet at the school library to study cancer and what it did to people and pulled up pictures. What I saw scared the living daylights out of me. It brought on nightmares about rotting flesh and organs that were being eaten up by an invisible monster that couldn't be stopped. The monster was inside my mother taking her away from me a little bit with every tick of the clock. Being alone scared me almost as bad as knowing the monster was real and inside mother.

I overheard Mother talking to Aunt Mary. "Thankfully, poor little Millie doesn't realize what's going on with the cancer. She believes I'm going to get well," she said as though I was still a naive little girl with Shirley Temple innocence. "The seriousness of my condition hasn't really hit her yet, and I'm glad of it. I want her to live a normal childhood going to school and having fun with her friends. I hate that she has to help out in the restaurant the way she does, but she never complains about the work or anything else."

"She always has a smile on her face," Aunt Mary told Mother. "She can do just about everything that needs doing in the restaurant. It's good for her to keep busy."

"Thank goodness she's not the rebellious kind. I'm proud of my daughter. I pray she will never change from the way she is right now. The death of a parent can have disturbing effects on a child, especially when the child is as young as my Millie. I'm not sure how to prepare her for when I'm not here. I'm not as much afraid of dying as I'm afraid of leaving her behind without her mother's love and protection. Promise you'll take care of her and raise her up right."

"You know I will," Aunt Mary told her. Her words sounding slightly insulted. "She's always been like my very own daughter, and you know it, but you're not going to leave her behind. You're going to beat this cancer."

"I thought the same thing when I first went into remission. Now I realize I will never be cured. All I can hope for is managing to stay alive until Millie gets old enough to survive without me."

Mother and Aunt Mary cried and so did I as I slipped away before they caught me eavesdropping. They had no idea I was already old enough to know exactly what was going on. They would be shocked beyond belief if they knew Mother's cancer had turned me into a thief.

So far, they surely believe the other one was coming up with enough money to pay bills. Either that or they were intentionally ignoring how the bills were being paid. Perhaps they were hoping a wealthy benefactor had miraculously shown up and was helping out. I'd heard them both say many times over that God would provide a way. Did that mean I was that way – me and Jimbo?

*

Christmas came and went without anyone getting gifts. I ended up giving Mother and Aunt Mary cards I drew and signed with an *I love you* written inside it. Mother wiped at unshed tears, and Aunt Mary gave me a hug. I got warm socks and nice underwear from a secondhand store. I knew their hearts hurt because there wasn't enough money to give me the gifts other children at school would be getting. Admittedly, even my heart hurt because Santa Clause could no longer bring me the gifts I longed for, or the gifts I longed to give Mother and Aunt Mary.

I had fantasized about giving Mother the beautiful tennis bracelet and Aunt Mary the gold necklace with the gold nugget, but I realized such as that wasn't possible. I would never be able to explain where they came from without giving myself away. If that happened, all would be lost. I took those items to Jimbo. He took care of things the way he always did.

When school started again, Sara wasn't as happy as she usually was.

"What are you pouting about? Didn't you get everything you wanted?" I heard one of her friends ask while I sat on the toilet in a bathroom stall. When they came in, I lifted my feet up so they wouldn't know I was there.

"One of Momma's favorite rings disappeared. She thought I took it."

"Why would she think a thing like that?"

"Because they didn't get me everything I wanted for Christmas."

"That's not reason enough to think you took her ring."

"One of my rings was in its place," Sara said. "I told her I wasn't that stupid, but she didn't believe me. I couldn't find my bracelet and favorite necklace either. Mother accused me of losing them and taking her ring so that I could claim someone stole them."

I almost laughed out loud.

Finally, Sara knew what it was like not to be idolized by her parents. She deserved a dose of reality. It was tough on a child to be spoiled rotten all her life. Made her grow up thinking she was better than everybody else. I convinced myself what I did was a good lesson for her so I could keep myself from feeling any guilt.

*

It was a new year, and I thought our circumstances were better with all the holiday diners eating out over Christmas and new year's. I was wrong. I got the mail for Mother only to find a bill. I opened it. It was a bill from a collection agency for her last Chemo treatment. I never realized how much those treatments cost. I needed to do something fast before the agency placed a telephone call to Mother.

I headed straight to the little park where I knew Jimbo would be on a Wednesday afternoon. He called Wednesdays his mid-week tranquility treatment. It was also the time when I could unload my burden on him.

"Now, what's gotten you in the dumps? As though I need to ask," he added as I sat down beside him. "You're in need of more money, aren't you?"

I nodded.

"You do realize bills come due every month regardless if you're bringing in money or not."

"I'm learning that lesson really well," I told him.

"Has your mother applied for disability? She might be able to get government assistance. The government is mighty free with money someone else earns."

"I don't know anything about such things," I told him. I'd overheard Mother and Aunt Mary saying something about her being denied assistance because she owned a business.

"I'm not surprised. A girl your age can't be expected to know everything. Did you do any good over the holidays?"

"Not good enough. People are using credit cards instead of carrying cash."

"You're right about that. Seems the rich always have their cards handy. They've learned not to trust. Only the poor carry a little cash but remember you're never to take from those who are struggling to keep body and soul together."

"I remember," I assured him.

"Did I ever tell you I was a cat burglar before I became a magician?"

I shook my head.

"Probably didn't. I was a lot of things back then that I've never admitted to. Was forced to live by my wits. My own mother was thrown in jail for prostitution and drug trafficking when I was eight years old. The police and social workers came after me, but I climbed out the top floor window of a whore house where my mother worked and hid on the roof until they were gone. Didn't like what those social workers or mother's pimp had in mind for me, so I hid out in the streets.

"I wasn't in the same fix you find yourself in. I had only myself to look after. I figured out how to do right well for myself even back then. Instead of staying the little beggar that I was, I figured out how to convince everyone I was one of the rich kids," he chuckled a little without any real humor. "I started sleeping in crawl spaces of rich people's houses. It got to the point where I learned how to slip into their houses and take whatever I needed.

"I was an intelligent little fart if I do say so myself. I went through a rich man's files and found information on his son who – conveniently for me – died the year before from childhood leukemia. I stole his name, his birth certificate, some of his clothes along with the money from his piggy bank, which was nothing short of a godsend for me. His parents were so devastated by his death they hadn't touched a thing in his room since his death.

"I convinced one of my mother's street walker friends to dress rather proper and take me to one of the schools nearby. She used the dead boy's name but changed the address when she put me in school. Whenever I needed a parent's signature for something, I had her sign for me. I learned a few things right off. The first thing was you need a thinking brain capable of outsmarting everybody else. The key to that is the ability to get a mighty fine education, which includes a formal education to go along with an education on street smarts. Another thing is to learn how to find, or fake, documents as needed.

"I lived in crawl spaces for years, stealing the things required to stay alive. In a way you're luckier than I was as you have a house to live in and a mother who isn't locked up in prison somewhere. On one hand, you're unlucky that you're a girl. A boy has more freedom, and no one thinks about them being vulnerable. On the other hand, folks always think the best of a pretty girl. You can get away with a lot by acting innocent. You can cover up that pretty hair and face of yours in a ski mask while learning how to move and walk like a boy and folks won't know the difference if you're ever caught on camera.

"The secret to being a successful cat burglar is doing your research along with proper timing. You must learn everything about a building, its security system, the occupants, along with the neighborhood. Most houses and businesses have security systems and cameras. You learn how to defuse them or work with them. Taking pictures and then slipping the pictures in front of cameras can work as well as using black pieces of paper. Always approach behind cameras never to the sides and definitely not from the front."

That made sense. It was only a matter of logic, but I needed to pay bills right now, not after I became educated on everything I was now dumb about.

"You must promise me you'll never do or become what my mother was. A drug addict and a whore. There are men out there who will take a young girl and ruin her for the rest of her life.

He eased his old bones up off the bench, grunting a little. I heard his knees pop as his face wrinkles deepened for a moment.

"Let's take a walk downtown a little way. I want you to see what a pimp looks like along with the house he provides for his victims and clients. They'll have a certain look in their eyes, not to mention their appearance. I call it a hungry-cat look. They're always looking for an easy target to assuage their hunger. They never get enough victims regardless of their bank account balance."

I followed him to the edge of town where he pointed out the nicest apartment building of any around. I had passed by it several times and noticed it was better maintained than most apartments. I'd never seen people going in or out, but there were beautiful Christmas lights still up and decorations in the windows.

"The elites, the big shots, frequent this place in the middle of the night. There's an underground garage in the back with a stairway to the main lobby. You must know somebody or be recommended by somebody to get inside. There are also places of ill repute that look like garbage dumps. Not everyone can afford high-priced whores."

I wondered how he knew all this and why he was informing me of such things. I had no intention of ever going near any of those places.

"I despise the man who runs the places, along with what he makes those women do, most of which are against their will. Mind you, some of them are beautiful women who are either desperate for money or hooked on drugs the way my own mother was. Once the pimps get their hold on such women, they might never be free again."

"Who is he," I asked.

"His name is Baxter Rainey. He owns the Rainey funeral home. He uses the place to launder his illegal money, but, like I said, it's not the only place he owns. Not to mention that he's raking in a killing from people's loss of their loved ones. Folks spend a fortune to give their deceased a last farewell in order to impress others by showing how much they loved the departed by the money they're willing to spend."

I knew of the two funeral homes in town. I cringed at the thought of my mother going to one. Somehow, I needed a way of keeping her alive.

"I've been watching him and his operation for a while now," Jimbo said. "I learned he has one of his flunky's collect money from his whore house each morning at daylight and bring it to him at the funeral home. I assisted in one of his flunkies getting inebriated one night and stagger out behind Holligan's bar. I recognized an opportunity when I saw one. He was more than willing to tell a stranger all he knew about Baxter Rainey and his operation, which included the location of his safe in the funeral home basement."

He turned around and started walking back toward the little park. He was silent for a while as though he was in deep thought.

"I reckon you're not too young to see a bit of the unpleasant side of life. Not that you already haven't," he added. "There are evil folks out there, Millie. Wolves who are wearing sheep's clothing so to speak. A man by the name of Oliver McKay is Baxter Rainey's silent partner."

I tripped one foot over the other and dang near fell flat of my face. Jimbo caught me by the arm to keep me from face-planting on the pavement.

"Sara McKay's father," I choked out.

"That's right. Oliver McKay is her daddy."

Why hadn't he told me that when I brought the ring and necklace to him. For a moment, I almost felt sorry for Sara. "Does Sara and her mother know?"

"I suspect her mother knows since Baxter Rainey is her brother. It's my guess their girl doesn't know a thing."

I wasn't so sure about that. Even the youngest kids knew more than adults realized they knew.

Jimbo hadn't told me about him when I told him where I'd gotten the ring he hocked. "Why didn't you tell me?" I questioned.

"No need for you to know until now."

"Why is there need now and not then?" I all but demanded an answer.

"Because you are going to acquire a right smart of money. I don't want you to struggle every month when bills come due. You're bound to get caught sooner or later."

"I was in need of a right smart then too," I told him.

"I gave you a chance to see what you could do on your own. What you *were* willing to do on your own," he added.

"I only believe in helping a person who's willing to help themselves. You did the best you could."

"I'm willing to do whatever is necessary to keep my mother alive," I informed him in arrogant bravado.

"Good excuse, Might as well admit you're getting used to having easy money, because you and I are going after a big haul. Don't reckon I've gotten too old to flex my stiff fingers for a good cause. I suspect it'll be safe for me to come out of retirement for one night when only you and I know about it."

"We're going for a big haul?" I said in surprise. I thought he was too old and arthritic to do more than sit on a park bench and give me instructions on how I could ease the money-pinch my mother was in. However, I did wonder about him knowing how and where to sell things.

"You do want to learn how to crack a safe, don't you?"

"Yes," I told him.

"Then I'm going to show you how it's done."

Chapter 3

*

I got the willies thinking of robbing a funeral home. I
wondered if the spirits of all those dead people lingered in
the bowels of a funeral home. I'd heard stories how the dead
left their bodies to rise up after three days. It was what the
Bible said Jesus did, so it should be true. I wished I knew
more about such things. A funeral home could be the place
for me to learn more insight – regardless if I wanted to learn
it or not.

"What do you know about funeral homes?" Jimbo asked
me.

"That I don't want Mother to go to one."

"Other than that?"

"Nothing," I told him. "I do know it's a place where no
one wants to be. Aunt Mary says everybody wants to go to
heaven, but nobody wants to die."

He almost grinned. "Taking care of the dead is one of the
most unpleasant jobs a person can have. I worked in a funeral
home when I was a teenager. Did you know people's bowels
and bladders release themselves when they die?"

"No," I told him as I thought how unpleasant it sounded.
"That's sad," was the only words I thought fitting.

"It's not so bad on the dead person. They can no longer
be embarrassed by it. It is unpleasant on the person who
cleans them up. I was the person who did that job. It was also
my job to drain their blood out and replace it with embalming
fluid. Makes a once pliable body feel hard to the touch."

"Gross," I said and tried not to shiver.

"I've been in worse jobs, but I won't go into that. I'm only warning you of what goes on in the basement of a funeral home."

"Thanks," I said with a lot of sarcasm.

"Life isn't always pleasant, Millie girl. You might as well learn that early on."

Like I hadn't learned that already. The necessity of being a thief wasn't pleasant either, but I was ready to become better at it. "When do we rob the funeral home?" I asked.

"We won't be robbing a funeral home. Most folks pay with checks or with credit cards. What money we'll be taking is the ill-gotten gains from the suffering and degrading of women." He almost grinned. "I'm thinking of it at retribution for the suffering such men caused my mother."

"Then shouldn't we be giving the money back to those women?" I questioned.

"No, because they're not allowed to have money. Pimps can't control the women if they get enough money to run away on, not that many of them would run away. They're hooked on one thing or another for life. It's nothing other than imprisonment and slavery. That is why I'm willing to come out of retirement for a humane cause." He grinned down at me in a tolerant way. "I'm not a crook," as President Nixon once claimed of himself. "And neither are you. We're simply redistributing ill-gotten gains where they can better help those who can't help themselves at this time."

"I don't like being a thief," I told him.

"In that case you better take my earlier suggestion and think of yourself as a modern day Robin Hood. One with a lopsided kind of honor who can redeem themselves in time."

"Is that how you think of yourself?"

"Can't say I ever was honorable, lopsided, or not. Don't suspect I ever will be."

I disagreed. Helping me keep my mother alive was an honorable thing. "When are we going to do it?" I asked.

"Tonight. I take it you'll be able to slip out your bedroom window without your mother waking up,"

I nodded. Mother took medicine to ease her pain and allow her to sleep during the night. She seldom woke up after ten o'clock when she made her last bathroom visit.

"Why tonight," I asked, wishing there was a little more time to get my mindset right.

"Because I've been observing their operation for some time now. Once a month they take their haul of money out of the safe and transfer it elsewhere. They'll be moving it out tomorrow sometime. That's why we'll take it tonight or we'll have to wait for it to build up for another month. If I'm going to crack a safe, I want to get the maximum amount for my ability and effort."

I couldn't argue with that. "Do you think it'll be enough to pay several months of bills after we split it?"

"We'll not be splitting it. You're going to get it all. The law keeps a close eye on my activities along with my spending and bank account. You see, I've been living under police protection, better known as the witness protection program, for years. Me being a petty thief allowed me to cut a deal if I squealed on some really bad criminals. I've been a perfect, law-abiding citizen ever since."

"I don't want you to get in trouble because of me," I told him in all sincerity.

He chuckled. "There comes a time when an old man has the need to do more than relive old memories."

I was as nervous and apprehensive as all get-out as I worked at the restaurant and waited until it was time to go home and take action. It wasn't a busy night, much to Aunt Mary's regret. She told me I might as well go home an hour early. I found Mother sitting up in bed looking pale and exhausted. I knew she'd gone through a bout of vomiting in the bathroom, because her face was freshly washed, and she wore a clean gown. There was also the strong smell of Lysol. Looking at her made me more determined to do what Jimbo and I were about to do. I kept telling myself all it would take to heal my mother was a lot of money, and I was determined to get it.

"I'll get your medicine if you think you can keep it down," I told her. She never took the pain medication that made her fall asleep until she knew I was safely home. I fussed at her about waiting. She gave me her loving smile and said, "You'll understand someday when you're a mother."

I wasn't altogether sure I wanted to become a mother after seeing what my mother was going through. Working day and night to give your child a good life was one thing, but dying and leaving that child behind was another thing entirely. I never wanted to do that to a child of my own. As for having a husband, I knew nothing about such things. Neither Mother nor Aunt Mary had one. I'd come to think of husbands as being useless objects, even during the times I longed for a father.

I waited until Mother was sleeping soundly before I went to my own room. I hurriedly stripped off my school clothes, hung them up so I could wear them again, and put on the black outfit I kept under my mattress. I stuck two pairs of vinyl gloves, grocery bags and the ski mask in my pockets, lifted the window as silently as possible and climbed out. I closed the window leaving enough of a crack for me to get my fingers in when I returned. It was cold as all get out, but thankfully the sun came out during the day long enough to melt away the snow until we wouldn't be leaving tracks. One good thing was all the paved area around the funeral home. We wouldn't leave tracks in the mud or in the grass.

I almost squealed when someone stepped out of the shadows. It was seeing the snowy white head of hair that kept me from doing it.

"You scared the shit out of me," I whispered my one bad word as he came to my side.

"I hope not," he whispered near my ear. "Never did care for the smell."

Oh, great. He was joking when I was petrified of what we were about to do.

"Don't be nervous," he whispered again. "And don't worry. I made sure the morgue was empty tonight except for the two dead bodies stuffed in the coolers."

Just what I wanted to hear. I hoped two dead bodies would be the only witnesses to what we were about to do. Jimbo kept to the dark shadows, alleys, and empty lots as we walked our way to the funeral home, which took over an hour. I didn't know if Jimbo owned a vehicle or not. I'd never seen him driving one.

"Once we're closer, we can't say anything even after I've blacked out the cameras. I'll be using spray paint as there'll not be any publicity about the money going missing. They won't be going to the police to report a robbery about their ill-gotten gains, but we can be assured they'll be searching for who did it. I'll be giving you hand signals to stay put, get down, come, or run."

"Okay," I whispered back. We hid in darker corners as we neared the place. He pulled out his ski cap and put it on, covering his hair and his face. I did the same. We both put on gloves and grocery bags.

He gave me a get down and stay put signal as we came to the funeral home. I squatted down making myself as small as possible as he rushed forward making sure he stayed behind each of the cameras. It took only seconds for him to black out every camera. I knew he spotted every one of them before we arrived. He motioned for me to come, and I did.

The seconds it took for him to pick the lock made me feel like an inadequate amateur. The door to the morgue was also locked, which was a good indication there was more value in there than two dead bodies. I was surprised when we entered. It was colder inside the morgue as it was outside. Such a revelation reminded me of how cold I already was.

Jimbo pointed to a metal cabinet and indicated for me to help him move it aside. I did. Sure enough, there was a panel in the wall. He used his lock pick to open the panel and motioned for me to ease down beside him. He took two stethoscopes out of his pocket, put one in his ears, and handed me the other. I put it in my ears. He placed the bell of the stethoscope where the diaphragm was on the lock and motioned for me to do the same. I listened to the sound the tumblers made as he turned the lock. There was a slight difference in the sound. He stopped turning, nodded to me, and started turning in the other direction until I heard that sound again. After turning in several directions and hearing the sound, the safe swung open. His whole body appeared pleased.

I had never seen so many bundles of cash in my entire life. There were hundred-dollar bills, fifty-dollar bills, and a huge pile of twenties with rubber bands around them. Jimbo took a black sack from the neck of his shirt and stuffed every bit of the money in the sack and placed the huge bulk back in his shirt making him look like an extremely fat man. He relocked the safe and put the stethoscopes back in his pocket and nodded for us to leave.

It took less than three minutes for us to be in and out. The time Jimbo allowed for being a successful thief. We took a different path going home.

"Can't believe the lock to the safe was that simple. It tells me he thought no one would ever discover his undercover operation. He'll no doubt put in a better safe tomorrow," I told Jimbo.

"I'll say he will, but don't get an idea cracking a safe is easy because it's not. It takes many years of experience and knowledge to do what I just accomplished."

"You made it look easy."

"Looks are deceiving, and don't you ever forget that bit of intelligence. Now, get yourself to bed," he whispered. "Meet me at the park after school tomorrow. You'll need to open a bank account with all this money. Having this much cash is a problem waiting to happen."

With those words he left me alone to traverse the last hundred feet to my bedroom window. I climbed in, closed the window, re-hid my nighttime uniform, put my nightgown on and shook a while from nerves and cold. Once I settled down, I went to the bathroom, washed my still cold hands in hot water, and went to check on Mother. Thankfully, she was sleeping peacefully. She had no idea her daughter was a big-time safe robber.

I went back to my bedroom and took a look at myself in the mirror. I looked the same as always, except for the trace of fear that remained in my eyes. Evidently, it wasn't easy to spot a big-time robber by simply looking at them.

At breakfast the next morning, I told Mother to let Aunt Mary know I would be a little late getting to work after school. I told her I needed to stay after school to study for a test I was to take the next day.

I met Jimbo at the park. He stood up and started walking. I followed by his side.

"I took the liberty to give you a new identity for your own benefit. You'll need to open a checking and savings account. I also have a different name and social security number for you. If anyone should ask, I'm your benevolent grandfather, George Anerson. You are Alona Georgette Anderson. You're eighteen years old. Your eighteenth birthday was on April 1st. It'll be easy to remember April fool's day. Got it?

"Got it," I said, wondering why I would need a different name and social security number. I could see needing a checking account.

"I'm putting thirty-five thousand dollars in your account. That should give you a thousand dollars a month for the several months. I'm putting the rest in your savings account. Only draw it out if necessary."

"Thirty-five thousand dollars," I said in astonishment. I'd never dreamed of having that much money in my entire life.

"Money doesn't go far these days," he advised. "Spend it carefully. Don't buy a thing you don't absolutely need to have. Pay only bills that are in the rear. Don't pay your mother's medical expenses. Go to the hospital and beg for them to drop or at least discount her bills. Hospital receives incentives for indigent people without insurance who have little to no income."

"Okay," I told him.

"I've arranged for checks and a debit card to arrive at a post office box. I'll give them to you when they arrive. I don't want you to be seen at the post office or the bank again. They have cameras. If you should get more income in large amounts, I'll deposit it for you. I've also taken the liberty of a fake ID driver's license for you, so you'll be able to draw cash out of the bank if it becomes necessary. Otherwise, checks and debit card should do the trick without you being identified."

I gave him a questioning look.

"I plan on keeping you safe, in case something does go wrong. I'm old. I can take responsibility if it comes to such as that. You want to always keep a spotless reputation. A girl always needs a spotless reputation, understand?"

I understood.

I was surprised when he handed me my fake driver's license. The picture on it actually looked like a slightly older version of me. "How did you do that?" I asked in astonishment.

"Tricks of the trade. There is little that can't be accomplished be it legal or otherwise if you know the right people. Remember illegal can do anything. Doing things legal has rules a person must go by. Dishonesty has no limitations."

I thought about what he'd just said. It made perfect sense, although it wasn't the least bit fair or just. But then, what was?

One week later, the first thing I did was pay off Mother's eighteen-thousand-dollar house mortgage. I then paid off the three thousand dollars she owed for her van.

That left me fourteen thousand in the bank for necessities. To me it seemed like a fortune, but I knew it wouldn't last long once I started spending it.

I also went to the hospital and spilled my guts out to the administrator and financial officers. I think they took pity on a girl whose mother was dying of cancer and yet with too much pride to plead for herself. At least I didn't intercept any more hospital bills from a collection agency.

Things seemed to settle down, and oddly enough Mother got better - again.

Chapter 4

*

Two years passed with me being thankful I still had a
mother. She wasn't cured or even well by a long shot. She
was simply doing a little better and managed to work half a
day at the restaurant before she return home to spend time in
bed. I kept the same hours working after school.

Several times on Wednesdays I went by the little park on
my way to the restaurant, but Jimbo wasn't there. I was
becoming increasingly worried. Finally, on a warm sunny
day, I found him sitting there as though he was never missing.

"Where have you been?" I demanded to know.

"Waiting for warm weather," he said with a light grin.
"My old bones have started to rebel when it's too cold for me
to sit on a hard bench."

I put some credit to what he said, even though I'd found
him there when it was much colder. I didn't point that out
because he did look a bit peaked at the gills, as Aunt Mary
often said about Mother. I feared he might have cancer too,
considering his age, but I didn't point out such as that.

"How have you been fairing?" he asked.

"Okay. Mother is a little better."

"How's your money holding out?" was his next question.

"I've still got several thousand. I paid off the mortgage
and the van to save interest. Plus, I've used a lot to pay
restaurant bills and living expenses."

"What did your folks think about that?"

"Oddly enough, they didn't seem to notice or comment
about not getting those monthly bills. I think they've been so

distressed any relief comes without question. I've not needed to spend anything lately. Mother and I both eat leftovers from the restaurant. There are only the electric and phone bills to pay. Mother gets that much in tips when she's able to waitress.

"You need to become a waitress," he told me. "You're pretty enough to get a lot of tips from hungry men."

"I will as soon as I'm of legal age. So far, I'm mainly work in the kitchen and after hours cleaning up."

"Do you get paid?"

"Neither Aunt Mary, Mother, or I get paid. We're lucky to bring in enough to pay the current bills."

"Then why run a restaurant if you're not making money? Looks to me like the three of you would make more working for someone else."

I wondered that same thing myself, but I tried to give a reasonable explanation. "Aunt Mary believes things will pick up. She claims people have to eat. Besides, I'm still too young, and Mother isn't strong enough to keep to a regular schedule of work."

"That may be true, but eating is something people have to do two or three times a day, so they skimp on prices. It's the luxuries that make you money. People will pay more when they feel the need to treat themselves. Start selling wine and charging through the nose for it. Put fancy white tablecloths on for the evening meals along with flowers and candles on each table. Serve steaks and potatoes while charging an arm and leg for the ambiance."

He had a point if I could convince Aunt Mary of doing such a thing. "Aunt Mary doesn't have the money to buy tablecloths, flowers or candles, much less wine and steak."

"She might not, but you do."

"How would I explain getting the money? I don't get paid anything."

"Uh-hum," he grunted. "You've made your point. Tell your mother and Aunt you've entered an essay contest online. The winner will win two thousand dollars. You'll win and use the money for a trial run."

I gave him a skeptical look.

"I'll make a brochure on the contest for you to show to your mother," he told me.

I shrugged. "It might work," but I doubted it. It would take a lot more than two thousand dollars.

The next Wednesday wasn't as warm, but Jimbo was at the park waiting on me. He handed me several brochures. "You can put them on display," he told me. "By the way, I'm thinking of giving a no-account scum of a man a dose of his own medicine. Are you interested in helping me?"

"Is it anything like the morgue thing?"

"Close without the morgue, but with dead bodies."

"Dead bodies?" I questioned with skepticism. Not being a thief for all this time felt good.

"Drug dealer. Laces everything with fentanyl. He's killing young people intentionally."

"Sounds dangerous."

"It is for the kids and young adults he sells to. If it was dangerous for us, I wouldn't get you into it now that your Mother and Aunt are doing a little better financially. This is a way for you to have some backup if your mother's remission doesn't continue."

His point hit home with a vengeance. I knew without him saying what he did there would come a time when everything became overwhelming again. Aunt Mary wasn't a whiz at finances, and Mother was hanging on by the skin of her teeth. What Jimbo suggested suited me better than becoming a pick pocket again.

"Give me the details," I said.

He nodded. "Crawl out your window about midnight tonight."

"It's not something that can be done in the light of day?" I questioned needlessly.

"Hardly. I've set up surveillance for a while now. Money changes hands at one o'clock in the morning. We'll intercept this dirt-bag at twelve-forty sharp."

"And do what?" I questioned.

"Obviously we'll be relieving him of his cash."

"Sounds too easy."

He grinned. "Are you losing you nerve in your old age?"

"Only feeling a little rusty," I reassured him without admitting my apprehension.

"Then build up your confidence by realizing we're ridding the world of one more no-account who is killing people."

"You plan on getting *rid* of him? I was quick to question.

"When he doesn't hand over the money, his suppliers might do the good deed themselves."

"Okay," I agreed. It was better to have what you needed when you needed it, than trying desperately to find a way once it was too late for a solution.

I didn't jump out of my skin this time when Jimbo met me at my window. I was expecting him to be there.

"Follow me," he needlessly whispered. I followed him to the street where a beat-up Chevrolet was parked. This time I wasn't freezing. It was early April, and the weather had turned mild. I was thankful we were riding in the car as we traveled a longer distance than the funeral home. Plus, we were all the way into a heavily wooded area in what appeared to be a section of deserted, creepy forest.

He stopped, turned the Chevrolet around, parked, got out, and then we walked until we came to a large rock outcropping in the middle of nowhere. He led me to a crevice in the rocks hidden by trees and underbrush where we both hunkered down with our gloves and ski masks on. No bags on our feet this time.

It was less than five minutes when we heard the sound of a motorcycle arriving. The man on the motorcycle came within a few feet of us, shut the machine off, but left the headlight on. He removed his helmet from his head with one hand, and rubbed his long, greasy looking hair back with the other hand.

Jimbo rose up. Much to my surprise he had a slingshot in his hands. He fitted a small marble in the leather saddle, pulled the leather saddle back and let fly. The man turned his head at the slightly buzzing noise as the marble hit him dead center of his forehead. From the reflection of the motorcycle lights, I saw his eyes roll back as he dropped his helmet. His body hit the ground.

"Get the money out of his saddle bags while I make sure he stays out cold in case I didn't pull back hard enough. I only wanted to addle him instead of killing him."

I got a bag of cash out of each saddle bag. The bags were just as heavy as the bag from the morgue. Jimbo reached down and picked up the marble he shot and motioned for me to keep up with him. For an old man, he did a good job of running. I was slowed down by the weight of the saddle bags. By the time we reached his Chevrolet, we could hear the sound of another motorcycle in the distance. We were in the car and heading in the opposite direction toward a paved road before he spoke.

"Learned to do that as a boy. We called them gravel shooters. I made my own back then. Couldn't afford anything store bought. Since then, I've discovered that marbles shoot straighter than rocks. When he comes around, he won't know what hit him and neither will the other no-accounts because we left no evidence."

"What about our footprints. Can't they track us to the car?"

The ground was rocky and there's been a dry spell. It's also dark as pitch out there. Don't think those guys know how to track or will want to. Most likely they'll either snuff him out or leave him where he's lying. Either way he'll not be dealing fentanyl laced drugs for a long time if ever again.

Problem is that's only one down while there's hundreds, if not thousands, to go."

"You plan on taking them all out?" I questioned with a touch of sarcasm.

"Would if I could. I'll have to be satisfied in doing my part while hoping others will do their part."

"I'm curious. You didn't need me to help do what you just did, so why did you bring me along."

"Back up," he said. "Plus, I wanted you to help earn the money your loving grandfather is going to deposit in your account."

"Why are you making life easy for me?" I questioned.

"Because I know what it's like when things aren't easy. Plus, you were a cute little girl with a sad face. I couldn't resist lending you a hand."

"That's some kind of excuse," I told him.

"Would it sound better if I told you I've already got everything I need," he hesitated a few moments before he added, "and you have a long way to go?"

How did I respond to that?

*

There wasn't as much money in those bags as there was at the funeral home. There were more twenties and tens in the bag and very few hundreds. It went to show that sex paid more than drug addiction.

That very day Jimbo deposited the money into my account. Regardless of where it came from, it was stealing. There was some consolation knowing the money would go to better use with me than if it remained in the clutches of drug cartels.

I showed Mother and Aunt Mary the check saying I won the essay contest. Mother cried tears of joy and Aunt Mary's eyes glowed.

"I can use that money to pay off the restaurant's food bills for this month," Aunt Mary said.

"No way," I told her and stood my ground. She looked shocked at my unexpected defiance. "I'm going to use it for a trial run on making this place bring in more income," I told her and Mother. "I'm going to buy nice tablecloths, cheap vases, flowers, and candles. With the rest I'm going to Walmart and buy the best steaks and wine they have." I didn't intend to buy the best wine and steaks Walmart had available, but Mother and Aunt Mary didn't need to know what I bought or how much I would spend. I would be taking Jimbo's advice on where and what to order. However, Walmart steak and wine would be a step up from hamburger and frozen mixed vegetables.

"You'll be throwing money away that's needed desperately," Aunt Mary argued as her face flushed red.

"You're wrong. I plan on bringing in more money by making this place a little classier. Folks refer to this place as a greasy spoon. I'm glad they're not referring to it as the *green fly* restaurant," I said what I knew would hit home.

My insult hit Aunt Mary hard, but I could tell Mother silently agreed with me. Aunt Mary was not Mother. Since Mother's illness, Aunt Mary way of management allowed what Mother built up to slowly go downhill.

"Millie has a point," Mother said. "She earned the money. It's only right to allow her to spend it the way she sees fit."

"But . . ." Aunt Mary started to object.

"Not another word, Mary. You won't have lost a dime out of your own pocket or the restaurant's if it doesn't work out."

I used the two thousand plus a large chunk of what was in my account to buy a month's supply of steaks along with the best and most expensive wine that Jimbo placed an order for. He used my debit card to pay for everything since I supposedly turned eighteen on the first of April. He gave me the two thousand dollars in cash for me to buy things he thought I needed like nice clothes and shoes.

*

I did as he suggested to improve my appearance along with my self-esteem. Sara still made fun of me to her friends, but it no longer bothered me. I felt sorry for her. If she ever found out what kind of man her father was, she'd fall off her high-horse and land hard. I wondered why Jimbo didn't informed the police about Baxter Rainey's and Oliver McKay's illegal activities.

Jimbo changed my thoughts about Sara when he said: "You might even get your hair professionally done. You're going to start looking at boys before long. I want you to pick the best available. Your happiness in life will depend on who you marry," he surprised me by saying. A no-account man makes a no-account life. I want the best for my granddaughter."

I laughed at that remark. "I'm not the least bit interested in pimply faced boys that are immature for their age," I told him. The thought repulsed me. There were better things to do with my life, like keeping Mother alive and me from worrying myself to death. I'd endured enough poverty and begging hospitals to forgive bills.

"I'll fix myself up a little," I told him with a touch of humor. "What I really want to know is why you've not informed the police about evil people who are hurting others by running drugs and sex?"

"It's likely they already know. Without enough evidence for an arrest, they can do nothing. Plus, it's not my job. Not only that, but it would draw attention to myself. If you remember I wasn't exactly a shining example of virtue back in the day. Can't claim to be now and neither can you. The thing for you to remember is you and I aren't hurting one single decent person. What we're doing is helping those who need to be protected from bad people. Always be a Robin Hood. Never take from those whose needs are greater than yours," he repeated again as though I might not have heard him all the other times. He then smiled in a reminiscent kind of way. "But feel free to have at the rich who do wrong while considering themselves better than everyone else."

"Is that the kind of advice a loving grandfather should be giving to his favorite granddaughter?" I said only halfway joking.

"Yes," he was quick to answer. "I believe it serves the purpose until my granddaughter is old enough and wise enough to decide things for herself."

I nodded and said, "Thank you." I meant it, and he knew it.

Chapter 5

*

Jimbo's suggestion was working. The ambiance along with good food and good wine was bringing in customers willing to pay a higher price for a meal. The crystal glasses of fine wine were what really brought in the profit. The crystal was fake, but the wine wasn't. Jimbo had taught me where and what kind of wine I should buy. I also had to fight Aunt Mary on serving wine as well as the prices charged for wine and steak.

"I hope God forgives us for serving wine," Aunt Mary said in a complaining voice as she glared accusingly at me. She sure hated that I had proven her wrong, even though she was now paying bills on time.

"Jesus turned water into wine," Mother pointed out. "I think he'll understand us exchanging weak tea for wine in order to pay our bills."

Aunt Mary snapped her mouth shut and said no more. Mother was still the one who owned the restaurant.

I found there was a problem with wine and fine dining. It drew a different crowd than those wanting a good cheap meal such as we served during lunch time. I had put in a food bar for lunch where people could serve themselves. It cut out two employees, which saved us money on their salaries. It wasn't an extravagant amount considering tips were also part of their pay, but every dollar helped when you were close to going broke.

Lunch people seldom left good tips. Dinner tips were different, a good waitress could make money. Thing was the waitresses had to deal with more elitest assholes.

My mother served two of the worst people I'd ever seen in a long while. The man's name was Joe Nimble and his wife Johanna. His wife was an anesthetist at the local hospital. She insisted everyone refer to her as Dr. Nimble.

"I know you," Dr. Nimble said as my mother took their order. You've been receiving cancer treatment for years. I thought you would have succumbed to it before now."

The way she said that was a degrading insult to Mother rather than a kind remark she could have given.

"You look sick," her husband added. "We don't want a diseased person waiting on us. We want a different waitress," he demanded.

Such a remark caused even more sadness to come to Mother's eyes.

"Of course, I'll send someone else to take your order," my mother said sweetly as she fought back tears. She caught my arm and dragged me into the kitchen with her before I dumped the pot of hot coffee I was carrying on both of them.

"Ignore them," Mother said to me.

"I'll not ignore them. I'll set them on fire with their *flame on an iceberg* desert. I'll teach them to insult my mother."

"No, you won't say a word or go out there until they're gone. Mavis can wait on them."

Mavis waited on them, but I had the pleasure of spitting in their food before she took it out. I didn't tell Mother or Aunt Mary what I did. I looked out the kitchen door and grinned every time they took a bite. Too bad I didn't have a contagious disease.

I still wasn't satisfied with only spitting on their food. I wanted to hit them where it hurt in a much worse way than they hurt my mother. I knew exactly what I was going to do. I would go to Jimbo and ask if he would give me further guidance in how to crack their safe.

*

Ah, yes," Jimbo acknowledged. "I am familiar with Joe Nimble and his better-than-thou wife. He's a politician and a crook who takes advantage of everyone. It's true if his wife got caught outside in a rainstorm her nose is held so high in the air she has a fair chance of drowning. What have you got in mind?" he asked.

"I want to crack their safe and clean it out."

Jimbo shook his head. "No can do. He has more security at his place than there is at Fort Knox. Even I couldn't break into that specially fabricated safe of his."

"I don't believe that for one minute. I've got an idea there's never been a safe you couldn't crack."

"Thanks for the compliment, but it's a no-go for me and you both."

I pouted a little, but I knew it was a *no go* with Jimbo. I decided it must be his age that was making him content to sit on the park bench and absorb the warm summer sunshine instead of helping me deliver a blow to a scumbag. That meant I would have to think of another way to get even with Joe Nimble and his obnoxious wife.

"Did you know both of them are having extramarital affairs? I'm putting what they do in a somewhat less insulting term for a young girl's ears."

"I didn't know that" I told him. How would I? But such goings-on didn't surprise me. I might not be experienced in any kind of romancing, but I'd read a few explicitly hot and steamy novels that did not leave out many details of what couples could do to and with each other. Seemed to me the best-selling novels detailed porn in the guise of making love. I wouldn't be rioting for the burning of such books. They did serve the purpose of letting ignorant teenagers know what they had never experienced. From what I had observed, what the birds and bees did happened quick and was for the purpose of sustaining reproduction. But then, what did I know about such things?

"Joe Nimble has a taste for underage girls. The younger, the better. Pimps make good money bringing young girls to the cheap motel room he visits, especially if they are virgins," Jimbo told me. "Such as that doesn't settle well with me," he added. "Makes me want to violent things that I'm no longer allowed to indulge in."

I cringed at the thoughts of such a man defiling young girls. He was beyond disgusting. Someone ought to take him out – as they say in crime novels, or at least allow Lorraine Bobbitt to have a go at him.

Jimbo's next words got my renewed attention. "His wife has a taste for her gardener. She's into getting down and dirty with him, literally. She's a big fan of sweat and body fluids."

More than I wanted to know. Yet, the image of a woman who worked in a sanitized, almost germ-free operating room, getting down and dirty with her gardener was forming in my imagination. Unlike the sickening image of what her husband did, the image of her and her gardener in a pile of organic fertilizer was somewhat entertaining.

"So? It wouldn't be surprising news that half the people in the world are having a fling with the other half," I said as though I knew what I was talking about.

"Exposing their habits would be a far greater punishment than breaking into their safe. The wealthy can always find a way to acquire more money, but a ruined reputation has a way of sticking it to a person forever. Especially when they're into politics."

I feared that applied to being a thief as well. "Just how am I supposed to expose them?" Thing was, exposing them wouldn't add anything to my bank account. Admittedly, I was becoming a little greedy. The more money in Alona Anderson's bank account, the safer I felt.

"The answer to that is easy. We can buy a good camera with a long-distance lens, but that would take a lot of stalking and time off from more pleasant endeavors. "Or" he hesitated as though another idea was developing before he continued, "He could walk into a setup with an underage girl."

A feeling of excitement edged with fear came over me. I was beginning to suspect what he had in mind. "Care to go into more detail?" I said like I was interested, which I was.

"Not yet. Just kind of thinking out loud. I need to converse with an acquaintance in law enforcement before I come to a final conclusion. I should have more details by this coming Wednesday."

Was he thinking about using me as a plant? What if I agreed and then couldn't get away from the horrible man? What would I do then? My facial expression must have told him what I was thinking.

"Don't worry. I would never put you in a situation where you would be in danger."

I grinned. He'd already put me in such situations. Safe cracking wasn't exactly him singing lullabies to a baby, and neither was stealing from a pimp or drug dealer.

"As you've most likely realized by now, I have this thing about those who take advantage of others, be it drug dealers, pimps or those who misbehave by considering themselves superior to others. What little I manage to do about it doesn't amount to much, but it does do my soul a tad of good."

"I'm taking advantage of others as well as you," I told him. Aunt Mary would certainly condemn me for what I was doing. She wasn't exactly obsessed with religion, but she came close.

"I don't see it that way. You're in desperate need. Desperate needs requires desperate solutions. I'm sure you get tired of me saying this, but you and I are merely Robin Hoods. We only take from those who have taken from others. Never, and I repeat, Never from the needy or the honest."

"I agree with that," I told him, although I had grown tired of listening to him saying it.

The needy were easily spotted. The honest were a different matter and more difficult to determine. I knew without doubt that Aunt Mary and my mother were honest, but I could no longer use the term to describe myself.

"See you next Wednesday, same place, same time," I said as I hurried off to work.

*

Wednesday arrived with another warm and sunny day. As usual, Jimbo was sitting on the bench much like an old person who had replaced a porch and rocking chair with a tiny garden and public bench. I wondered if he even had a porch and rocking chair since he was in witness protection. He never looked like a homeless person, but he certainly didn't look affluent. Thankfully, he always had a clean-soap smell about him, and his white head of hair was never greasy.

"What did you and your acquaintance in law enforcement come up with? I asked more out of curiosity than anything else.

"Being granted immunity from using my previous talents, along with being given a new identity, doesn't come without payback," he said with a grin. "Although I readily admit I'm more than willing to be of assistance in seeing dangerous criminals get their just payback. In other words, I've become a snitch in return for not being convicted for what I did during my more youthful exuberance."

Odd statement coming from a man who was, and still is, a safe cracker.

"Now, mind you, I don't consider being a Robin Hood as criminal activity."

I wasn't going to argue with him, but I knew Aunt Mary and Mother would disagree. If either of them knew what I was doing to keep Mother and Aunt Mary's bills paid and the wolves from our doors, they would never get over it. There was no doubt knowing would be worse on Mother than the chemo treatment. Aunt Mary might even think it was her duty to report me to the police.

"What non-criminal activity have you and the law enforcement come up with?"

"They have been working on a plan to put Joe Nimble in prison for a long time to come."

"Good for them," I said as a warning shiver brought goose bumps to my arms.

"The only reason they haven't put their plan into action is because they haven't found the perfect accomplice who could pull it off."

Ut-oh, I thought here it comes, and I was right.

"I assured them I had the perfect girl who was capable of pull off something so difficult. Not only that, but you would be willing and able of never letting your own identity be known. You do realize you are underage. Law enforcement would be in the middle of an ocean of crap if it ever came out that they actually used an underage girl instead of an undercover agent."

"Why don't they use an undercover agent?" I couldn't resist asking.

"It would be difficult for an agent over eighteen to pass as a young virgin. They want everything to be more authentic, including a show of innocence and fear that can't be faked."

"Are you saying they want to put me in a motel room with a pedophile set on raping me, and you agreed?"

"I told them I knew a girl who was able to pull off such a setup, but I also told them it would be up to you whether you did it or not. First of all, you won't be in danger. You'll only be waiting in a motel room long enough for him to verify his intent with you. There will be two or three video cameras in the room along with tape recorders. There will also be four officers waiting to burst into the room to arrest him. I will be waiting outside to take you home."

"How will putting myself in such a situation benefit me other than seeing Joe Nimble put in the slammer?"

He grinned at my question. "You're learning fast, my little protégé. The police department will owe you. It could come in handy if you're ever in an uh . . . unpleasant situation," he added. "Law enforcement have blind eyes for those who help them do things that aren't legal."

I thought about that. He was right. I did need to be owed a favor in case I was ever caught with sticky fingers. "How can I be sure of them having a blind eye?" I questioned.

"You have the option of telling on them for using an underage girl in such a sting. It would result in heads rolling with jobs and pensions lost," Jimbo said with a grin. "I assure you neither the officers nor the department would want such as that. All you have to do is dress like a young girl and wait in a motel room for him to show up," he assured me.

"Okay," I said. "I'll do it on one condition."

"And?" he said hesitantly.

"Once he's in jail, you'll help me crack his safe."

"Dad blast it, girl. I already told you it would be easier to break into Fort Knox."

"Then they will have to find someone else. Shouldn't be difficult to find a young girl to wait in a motel room – being she will be perfectly safe and well protected."

"Dang if you haven't learned how to dicker like a pro."

"That's my price. Take it or leave it."

"I'll take it, but there's one condition. You'll let me do the safe cracking my way."

"What is your way?"

"I don't know yet. It'll take some time for me to do research on their security system along with the kind of safe they're using."

"Give me your word you and I will do the safe cracking."

"I'll give you my word I'll give my best go at it."

"And you'll take me along?"

"I'll take you along."

"Okay then, I'll do it."

"Good girl. I'm positive it will be to your benefit in the long run. I'll get back with you on the three W's."

"The three W's?" I questioned.

"When where and how."

"How isn't a W," I told him.

"Spelled backward, it is.

*

I had to grin at the way Jimbo turned things around to fit the results he wanted – including me.

"Have you ever had protégés other than me?" I asked the next Wednesday when I met with him.

"Not exactly since I've been put under squealer protection. There have been a few good people I needed to give expert guidance on occasion."

"Then why me?"

"As I told you before, you were such a cute kid with a sad face. I even like the idea of having you as a granddaughter. Regrettably, I'm too old to claim you as my daughter."

"How old are you?" I couldn't resist asking.

"Old enough to know better but bored enough to need a little excitement for the pure pleasure of it."

"You're not going to tell me, are you?"

"Nope. Age is irrelevant. It's the spirit left inside you that counts. That's why I'm confident you're the one to take Joe Nimble down. This is the plan that's been worked out. I'll go over it with you step by step. I don't want one single thing to go wrong."

And neither did I.

Since Jimbo mentioned me doing such a thing, I'd been thinking of the ways I could defend myself against a grown man. I'd even pulled up all the self-defense videos I could find on the school computer. A swift strike to the groin held first place. Second place was a strike to the Adam's apple.

Third place was fingers to the eyes along with the other two in rapid succession. However, nothing would be as good as staying away from grabbing hands and running like the monsters of hell were after you.

I did my best not to show Mother my nervousness as I watched her take her evening medication. It was all I could do not to hug her extra tight and cling to her out of fear and dread of what I was about to do. At the same time, I wanted to kick, scream, and yell out my anger at having a mother who was slowly dying from a disease that couldn't be cured. Again, I felt a longing for a normal, stable family the way many of the kids I went to school with had. I even wanted a father but not a stepfather. I'd also heard a few of the kids talk about how awful a stepfather or stepmother was. They even told stories about having to endure cruel stepchildren.

Not a single one of them mentioned having to steal things in order to survive, but I knew some of them did take things that didn't belong to them. None of them appeared to have a Jimbo who had taken them in as a protégé, but appearances didn't mean much. And yet, appearances were often what survival was about.

"You're being unusually quiet," Mother surprised me by saying.

"Really? I didn't realize that."

"What's wrong? Didn't school go well?"

"School is school," I told her. "Nothing out of the ordinary."

"How about at the restaurant? Did Mary give you a tough time after I left? You have to tolerate her eccentricities. She's always believed her way was the only way. She's not gotten over you proving the change in the evening menu proved to be the right thing to do."

I already understood that. "I'd think she should be grateful to be paying the bills regardless of whose idea it was."

"She is grateful, but Mary is and always will be, Mary. Her bossiness comes from being the older sister. Now that I'm not in a domination position, she's trying to take control because she thinks it's for the best."

"But it's your restaurant. You're the one who started it and worked your fingers to the bone in order to make it successful."

"That is part of Mary's problems. You might say the restaurant is my baby instead of hers."

Could that be was why I felt as though she sometimes resented me? Both the restaurant and I were Mother's baby instead of hers.

"Don't get Mary wrong," Mother told me in her understanding way. "She loves me and you with every fiber of her body. The main problem with Mary is that she has never accomplished much on her own. She wants to be more of a success than she believes she is."

"I can understand that" I told Mother. "I want to be a big success too."

Mother chuckled. "Honey, you might not know it yet, but you're already a big success. I can't begin to tell you how proud of you I am. You've managed to be a straight A student while working like a slave at the restaurant as well as here at home. You're doing all the things I can no longer do."

I saw that tears were threatening her eyes. Neither of us needed more emotion right now.

"It's the least I can do," I told her. "I think it's time for us both to go to bed and get some rest. As you always say, tomorrow will be a beautiful day." But I wasn't sure what tonight would be.

I checked on Mother about an hour before I was supposed to meet Jimbo. Thankfully, she was sleeping soundly. I hoped she wouldn't wake up to use the bathroom while I was gone. I went into the kitchen and took a small kitchen knife out of the cutlery drawer and slipped it into my jeans pocket.

I wasn't sure if I would be able to use it, but having it made me feel slightly more secure.

Jimbo assured me a policewoman would dress me up in a little girl dress instead of jeans because that was what turned Joe Nimble on. I didn't think such a dress would have a pocket. I found a roll of extra strong tape and taped the knife to my stomach underneath my panties, and assured myself I could use my weapon if necessary.

I said every prayer I could imagine as I watched the clock. Although I didn't think a girl like me deserved God's protection. At the same time, I was hoping He would protect the sinner as well as the righteous.

My prayers were interrupted by a faint tap on my window. Jimbo threw a small twig to let me know he was waiting. I took a deep breath and lifted the window. I eased out the same as I had done before. Neither of us spoke until we were in the beat-up Chevrolet.

"When you hesitated on crawling out the window, I was beginning to think you weren't going to go through with it," Jimbo said.

"I needed a minute to gear up more determination."

"You've always had enough of that. You're one heck of a tough kid."

"Your protégé has a good teacher."

"Uhhh," he grunted without further comment. "I'll take you near the motel where the pimp takes the girls. I'll warn you it's not much of a motel. You'll be dressed up to look even younger than you already look."

"The pimp has turned against Joe Nimble?" I questioned how the authorities had managed such a setup.

"Let's just say he has been detained and replaced."

"Won't Joe Nimble be suspicious when the regular pimp doesn't show up?"

"The new guy will be arriving in the same vehicle the pimp drives. If Nimble questions him, he'll say the other guy has developed a need to lay low for a while."

"If he doesn't believe the new pimp?"

"He will. He's never had a reason to question his secrecy before. Plus, it's been a while since he's indulged in his uh . . .pleasure."

"I hope it works, and I'm not hurt." I told him while trying to sound brave.

"It will."

"If it doesn't?" I dared question.

"Then I'll slit his throat myself. Nobody harms my granddaughter," he told me with assurance.

I thought about telling him about the knife I had taped to my belly, but I didn't. He stopped the Chevrolet about half a block from the motel. A well-dressed middle-aged man got out of a gray SUV and came toward us.

"That's the new pimp. He's going to take you to the motel room," he turned to look at me. "Don't be apprehensive. I know him. He works undercover."

I got out of the seat when the pimp opened the door for me to get out. He looked me over and then bent down and nodded to Jimbo. "She's good," he said.

A cold chill ran over my body. I'd heard too many stories about young girls being abducted and used in horrible ways. What if I was one of these girls? Would Jimbo set me up? I didn't think so, but somebody could be setting him up. I was going to find out soon enough.

The new pimp took hold of my hand. I jerked away. He grinned and took hold of my hand again. "In case he's watching," he whispered in a deep voice. "Act afraid."

There was no acting involved. I was becoming more afraid with each step I took. Instinct told me to jerk my hand free and run for my life.

"Easy," he whispered. "Don't run. You're safe."

I would have laughed if I could have.

"Stumble a little. Like you've been drugged."

His hand tightened on mine, and I stumbled. He jerked me closer to his side. My heart was in my throat when he inserted a key in the door of a rundown dump of a motel and pushed me inside where a woman was waiting on me.

The woman looked professional. The room and furnishings were worse than I expected. Bedbugs, among other things, would surely be beneath the stained bedspread. I would have though a meticulous man such as Joe Nimble would demand the best instead of a dump.

"Don't be afraid," she said. "Everything is going according to our plan. Come into the bathroom. I'll dress you."

"This place is disgusting," I managed to say.

"He gets off on disgusting," she said. "He's used this room many times before."

"Then why didn't you bust him before now?" I asked.

"We didn't have sufficient evidence of what he was doing."

"Now you will?"

"We will, thanks to you. Don't worry. We have everything under control. You'll be safe."

Her assurance didn't ease my fears in the least.

"I was told you would be leery which is good. Joe Nimble likes his girls to be young and afraid. Actually, he likes for his girls to be younger than you, but we'll take care of that."

Less than five minutes later, I was wearing a pale pink dress, a long, curly auburn wig, pale, almost white face makeup along with artificial freckles dotted across my nose. She had left my panties undisturbed but wrapped a tight cloth around my chest to flatten my breasts. She was in such a hurry to transform my looks she didn't notice my knife, thankfully.

"If you wore contacts lenses, I'd put green colored contacts in your eyes to further disguise you, but your blue eyes will have to do. Look at yourself in the mirror."

I looked and drew in a breath. I didn't look anything like myself. "That's me?" I said in surprise. "I look different."

She chuckled. "Amazing what a lot of stage makeup can do if you're in a dimly lit room. We don't want you to be recognizable by him now or ever. I was told this man, and his wife, could have seen you before. We're taking no chances with you being recognized or with your safety."

I wasn't sure if what Jimbo told her was a good thing or not. I preferred them knowing nothing about me. Something inside her pocket dinged. She grabbed her makeup bag and my clothes and turned off the bathroom light.

"They're almost here. Don't turn on the overhead lights. He only likes the lamp on, which is good. You look even younger in a darker room. I've got to go but don't be concerned. We're in both rooms on either side of this one. He'll lock the door, but we have a key. We want you to talk to him. Get him to tell you what he's planning on doing to you. Once he admits what he's going to do, we'll come in."

She said all this as she hurried toward the door and shut me inside. Less than a minute later the sound of a vehicle stopped in front of the motel room. Its headlights shinned through the faded curtains for a moment before the lights were turned off. I backed up against the far side of the wall as the door opened and Joe Nimble walked in.

I have never been so afraid in my life. What I felt was even worse than I felt when I discovered Mother had cancer.

"Well, well. Look at you. He said you were young and a virgin. Appears he was telling the truth."

"Wh-what do you want with me. What are you going to do to me," I mumbled in a scared whisper, which I was not faking.

He made a sound that was close to laughter. "Why do you think you are here for?"

"He said you'd give me money if I'd let you take pictures of me."

"He told you that, did he?"

"How much money will you give me?" I managed to ask.

"Depends on what you're willing to do," he said as he moved toward me. "Girls like you can earn a lot if they're smart enough to do as they're told."

I instinctively pressed my back harder up against the wall. "I... I've never done this before," I said in a shaky voice. "Will I have to take any of my clothes off?"

"The more you take off the better."

"I don't want to take them off," I whined.

"There's always the first time for everybody," he told me. "You'll might even come to enjoy what's going to happen."

"What's going to happen?" I asked trying to sound more innocent than I was.

"Fucking," he said, as he looked at my face for my reaction. The woman had told me he got off by seeing fear. He should be on high right now.

I drew in a breath when he said that. "Fucking?" I whispered. "I'm only twelve. You can't do that to me. It's against the law."

"I'm certainly going to do more than that, and I don't want you to make a sound while I'm doing it if you know what's good for you." He had a knowing smirk on his face as he took a roll of duct tape from his pocket and held it up for me to get a good look.

"I... I've changed my mind. I don't want to do that with you. It'll be rape."

"Doesn't matter what you want. It's what I want that going to happen, and you've not got a choice in the matter," he taunted for his pleasure.

He got a sinister look on his face as he moved toward me real slow like. "Touch me and I'll scream my head off," I told him a minute before he closed the short distance between us and grabbed hold of me with the hand that still held the duct tape while his other hand clamped over my mouth. His body pressed me against the wall to keep me from squirming away. His hold on me loosened as he ripped off a strip of duct tape with his teeth and tried to stick it over my mouth. I bit his hand and screamed. Why weren't the cops rushing into the room to save me like they promised?

I twisted my head trying to bite his hand again. He laughed. "I like a girl who fights. They didn't drug you too much this time the way they did the last girl. Keep up the fighting. I like a little challenge. Makes it more exciting for me."

I tried to knee him in the groin, but he was pressed too tightly against me. I scratched at him with both hands. He pressed the duct tape over my mouth so hard my teeth were cutting my lips. He couldn't hold both my hands although he was trying too. I quickly moved my hand up my dress to my stomach. His knee had already lifted the skirt of the dress. I managed to get hold of the knife handle and jerked it free from the tape. His body was so close to mine I didn't get as much force as I wanted as I jabbed the blade into his side.

"Hell fire," he shouted as I continued stabbing as fast as I could.

There was a loud sound as the door flew open and three men rushed into the room. I made a dive for the open door and ran into the parking lot. I almost stabbed Jimbo when he grabbed hold of me.

"Easy," he said. "Let's get out of here."

I jerked at the duct tape as I ran with him to where he had parked the Chevrolet. My first instinct was to throw it on the ground, but good sense took over. I didn't want to leave any DNA behind that might be used to identify me.

"Get in. I've got your clothes in the front seat. Put them on and take off that stupid wig and dress. I almost didn't recognize you."

"They didn't come in like they promised," I said, trying not to let hysteria get a hold on me. I got in the front seat and slammed the door shut. He stared the engine and took off at a regular speed.

"They wanted to get all the proof they could without any question about his intent."

There was no question about his intent. He'd made clear what he intended to do to me. "I've got his blood all over me," I said.

"You've got what?" His eyes left the road long enough to glair at me in the dark car.

"He pinned me against the wall. I had to stab him to get away," I said as I held out the bloody knife for him to see.

"Holy shit," that wasn't part of their plan.

"They didn't come in like they promised. He was hurting me," I told him.

"Did he . . .?" he begin.

"I stabbed him when he tried to tape up my mouth."

"Shit," he said again. "Are you sure you're okay? Did you cut yourself?"

How could I be okay? "I didn't cut myself, but I've never been through anything like that before. I was fighting for my life."

"No doubt," he said. "Where did you get the knife?"

"I taped it to my belly as a precaution."

"That's my smart girl," he said. "I should have thought of that. Where is the duct tape he tried to put on your mouth?" he asked with a touch of concern.

"I've got it in my hand."

"Good. I'll take care of it along with your clothes."

"Don't ever put me in that kind of situation again," I told him as I finished ripping the dress off and pulled on my black shirt and jeans while still holding the knife.

"Give me that knife?"

"No way. This knife is going to be my permanent companion."

He didn't argue or try to take the knife from me.

"Once you get home, take a shower with your clothes on and make sure you use a lot of soap on your body along with the knife. Make sure there's not a trace of blood left on the window or floor."

"They already know who I am. They have me on their cameras."

"You looked nothing like yourself. Even I wouldn't have recognized you."

"But you did."

"Only because you came flying out the door."

I felt the tiniest speck of relief at that, but it wasn't enough to ease the hysteria that was threatening to take over.

Chapter 6

*

I left the bloody clothes and wig with Jimbo, but not the cloth that bound my chest. I certainly wasn't going to take that off in front of him or anyone else. Once I got home, I took a bath in my clothes even though I didn't want to take a chance on Mother waking up to hear the shower running at such an hour. She would know something was wrong. I even washed the cloth that bound my chest. After the scrubbing, I took my clothes off and washed my body and hair again.

The hot water warmed me, but I was still shaking both inside and outside. I didn't think I would ever be the same again. I had a whole new attitude about the young girls, and women, who were forced to endure what men did to them. I wished I could give every one of the men a knife to the gut, or better, give them a handgun slug. Law enforcement should be doing a better job of *serve and protect.*

It suddenly occurred to me that they *had* done at least one better job thanks to me – and Jimbo.

*

It took a full two days before my insides stopped shaking. I expected to see the cops come through the door at any moment, but they didn't.

To find out what had come down was another reason for me to meet with Jimbo on Wednesday.

"Wasn't sure you'd show up today. You okay?" he asked as I sat down beside him.

I nodded, still feeling too shaky to stand on my own two feet while we talked.

"What happened?" I questioned.

"He was arrested for the attempted rape of a minor."

"They won't try to make me testify, will they?"

"No. They have the videos."

"I didn't think videos were allowed. Especially when there was a setup."

"Depends on how they were presented. Law enforcement is claiming someone heard a young girl screaming and called the police. They broke the door down and entered the room to save the screaming girl. Joe Nimble was filming what was happening in order to sell it to other pedophiles. They got a judge to give a search warrant to search his house. They found pictures of young girls being raped and other things that will put him away for a long while, thanks to you."

What about his wife."

"Naturally, his wife is claiming innocence. He claims she knew nothing of his activities."

"And?"

"His devoted wife wasted no time in taking herself out of the country."

"She was allowed to leave?"

"They had no proof she was ever involved. The arresting officers claimed the girl in the motel room ran away without them being able to discover who she was. The cameras showed the girl darting out the door."

"The door of the motel?"

"Yes, but they didn't have a camera showing anything outside."

Relief sure felt good.

"They really don't know who I am?"

"They don't have any idea who you are. That was part of the agreement. It's a grandfather's job to protect his granddaughter," he added.

"It'll be easier to crack their safe when no one is home."

"You're still determined to do that?"

"Yes." I wasn't going to allow him to get away with not doing what he promised considering what he had put me through.

"You do realize she wouldn't leave the country without taking all the money and other valuables with her. That would include the contents of the safe."

"Wouldn't she be afraid to travel out of the country with a lot of cash and jewelry? She'd be checked at the airport."

"I've never flown with a lot of cash and jewelry," he said. "Don't know how such as that would work. Got an idea they have overseas accounts."

"Then let's give it a try."

"Flying out of the country?"

"Don't be silly. You know I mean cracking the safe."

"I did promise, but we need to let things settle down first."

"Did the police open his safe to see what was inside?" It suddenly occurred to me a search warrant would include something such as that.

"According to my inside information, the safe is well hidden. They didn't know about it."

"How do you know about it?" I asked.

"Knowing things is what I do best. Like I told you, I'm a snitch and I'd been spying on him."

I did think it was best to let things settle down for a while – including myself. I never again wanted to feel such fear and helplessness as I felt inside that motel room.

"I want to learn how to shoot a gun," I suddenly told him.

"Okay," he said. "I think you already know how to handle a knife." '

I didn't respond.

"I think it would be wise if you also took some kind of self-defense training.," he told me. "Is there anything that strikes your fancy?"

"I've never thought about such a thing."

"Then I would suggest you train in the American style of karate. You'll be taught the traditional style of self-defense, plus street fighting. Personally, I like the idea of you learning about street fighting."

"Will it help me protect myself?"

"It'll help, but not as much as a well delivered monkey wrench – or a hidden knife or pistol."

Chapter 7

*

"I want to take a self-defense classes," I told Mother.

Her eyes widened as she gave me a fearful look. "Why?" she asked with concern. "Are you being bullied at school? I know there's nothing at home or in the restaurant that would make you want to do such a thing. Mary isn't that vicious," she added with a forced grin.

I grinned back at her attempt at humor. Aunt Mary wasn't exactly vicious, but she certainly could be demanding and depressing.

"I don't really have a reason. It just occurred to me as something I'd like to do."

"When would you have time to take something like that? Looks to me like you're running yourself ragged the way things are now."

"It would only be twice a week for one hour. Surely, I can take that much time off to do something I really want to do."

"You're right. You deserve some time for yourself. Both Mary and I have been selfish where you're concerned. It's been . . . well just so difficult here lately. You should take all the time off you want even if it's something ridiculous like – whatever," Mother flipped her hand in the air as she tried to sound optimistic. At the same time, I knew she didn't approve of what I wanted to do.

*

When I met Jimbo that Wednesday, I told him Mother had agreed for me to take Karate lessons.

"Good," he said. "I signed you up with the best instructor I know of. You'll start taking your first-class tomorrow evening at six o'clock. Here is the payment receipt. You need to take this with you when you show up."

"That soon?" I said in surprise as I took the receipt from his hand. I would have liked to wait a few days to get used to the idea. Not to mention finding out what was involved.

"If you are going to do something, you need to do it instead of pussyfooting about."

"Did you ever take it?"

"For many years. I had to stop when I was put in the witness protection program. Had to change everything about myself."

"Did you ever use it?"

"More times than I can count. I wasn't exactly a pacifist."

"Were you any good at it?"

"Need you ask?" he grinned in remembrance. "Not to brag, but I was a natural. The best of the best. Regrettably, I've had to become someone else and lay low for the rest of my life. But I still have my memories," he said with an old man's longing.

It didn't appear to me he was laying low. Not only was he a police snitch, but he also had contacts with a slew of people who weren't exactly on the straight and narrow. Which I was grateful. Without his knowledge of pawn shops and jewelry store owners I wouldn't be able to move the trinkets I obtained. Suddenly, a new fear came over me. Would there come a time when I would also have to become somebody else for the rest of my life?

"Got any plans for midnight tonight?" he interrupted my thoughts by asking.

The way he asked that question instantly got my attention. "What have you got in mind?"

"Cracking a safe."

"Yes," I couldn't hold in my excitement. "I can hardly wait to see what old Joe and creepy Johanna has stashed in there."

"You'll have to wait a while longer for that. His safe was specially made for security. I've not been able to discover enough about it to know how to crack it. However, I've discovered another safe built by the same manufacturer that's not as complicated to crack. I'm considering this one as practice for the more difficult one."

My face must have shown my disappointment. "Oh, well. Okay," I said.

"No need to be so disappointed. Cracking this safe should pad your bank account for a long time to come." He grinned. "I've been wanting to get back at this man for years. He's a snake in the grass and I want to run over him with a lawnmower while I still can."

"Sounds good," I told him, but I wasn't sure if it was for the best to keep stealing when Mother and Aunt Mary's bills were finally being paid. Desperation was one thing, but greed didn't cut it.

"Revenge," Jimbo said. "You got your revenge on Joe by getting him arrested. You want to break into the safe to get your revenge on Johanna Nimble for what she said to your mother. I want to get my revenge on this man. Plus, cracking this safe will show you how difficult and risky safe cracking can be."

"Risky?" I questioned.

"I'm not sure you realize the consequences if we're caught. I'd be rotting in jail right now if I hadn't turned snitch. You have no one to snitch on. Cracking this safe will be the last for me and for you. I want my granddaughter to remain happy and free. Agreed?"

"Agreed," I said before the realization of what he'd just said hit me.

"I've always liked the challenge that came with safe cracking," he confessed. Taking what isn't yours is like gambling, it doesn't take much for it to become addictive. I don't want that to happen to you. That's one of the reasons what we're doing has to stop."

*

Again, I checked on Mother to make sure she was sleeping soundly. I went back to my room and put on black clothes, stuffed my ski mask in my pocket along with vinyl gloves and grocery bags, yet I didn't crawl out the window. I was feeling unsettled like something was sure to go wrong. When the tap came on my bedroom window, I drew in a determined breath, opened the window, and crawled out. Jimbo was waiting.

He didn't say a word as we made our way down the street to where his Chevrolet was parked. After he had driven several miles in silence, he spoke as he reached under the seat and took out a brown paper bag that came from a grocery store.

"Put that wig and glasses on," he told me. "In case we happen to encounter cameras somewhere along the way. Technology has become invasive since I was your age."

He then put on a greasy looking cap that was large enough to cover up his white head of hair. He also put on a pair of glasses. He didn't look like himself.

"If we get caught, I'll do my best to provide a distraction long enough for you to escape. You'll have to run like the hounds of hell are biting your heels. Don't look back and don't try to help me out in any way. I've taken care of myself for years. I can still do it, but not if I have to deal with saving you. Got it."

"Got it," I said. His words made an icy knot of fear start to develop in my stomach.

"Can you drive?" he questioned.

"I've taken driver's education in school. Mother let me get a learners permit in case . . ." I didn't finish the sentence.

"If the need arises, you can drive my old Chevrolet, but you will be taking a chance on being pulled over by a cop. I suggest you keep to dark areas and back roads as you get to a safe place."

"Don't talk like that. It scares me."

"Good. You need to be scared. What we're doing isn't a walk in the park."

He drove a little further and left the car in a far corner of a Walmart parking lot. We got out and he took hold of my hand as though we were strolling along. "Smile," he said. "Don't look scared or nervus just in case. Don't want to look like an old man abducting a young girl. I parked in a spot where the cameras don't reach, but I'm not taking a chance on being wrong. When we get to that tree, I'm going to turn loose of your hand and walk behind the tree as though I'm looking for something. Hesitate a moment and then follow me."

Anyone with any intelligence would be safely tucked in their beds this time of night. The fact that we were out walking was enough reason for us to be suspected of something. I did as he said, relieved to be hidden by landscaping.

He led me to an office building instead of a house, which surprised me as well as scared me. I knew nothing about office buildings. At least they should not be occupied at one o'clock in the morning. He took off the cap and covered his snowy head of hair with a black ski mask, pulling it over his face. He then slipped on his gloves. I did the same.

I was surprised when he took out a key and unlocked the door. He closed it and left it unlocked. The entire place was dark with no security lights on anywhere. He opened another door that went straight to a basement as though he knew exactly where he was going, which he evidently did.

The only illumination was from a tiny pin light he clicked on when we went down the stairs to keep us from tripping over things. He went straight to a wall even though the basement was as dark as pitch. He shined the pin light and carefully moved a section of a file cabinet aside to expose the wall behind it. He took a knife from his pocket, opened it, stuck the blade between two planks and pried a hidden panel open. He kneeled in front of a safe and motioned for me to kneel beside him. I knew he never wanted either of us to say a word. Voice was another way to identify a person.

He surprised me by taking the glove off his right hand and stuffed it into a pocket. Was he not worried about fingerprints or leaving DNA behind? He then took the stethoscope from a pocket and placed the bell near the dial and motioned for me to do the same. I knew he first needed to find the combination length. He turned the dial clockwise several times to make sure the wheels disengaged. He then turned the dial counterclockwise. After the first two clicks, he stopped, nodded to me to take note of the number on the dial. He nodded at me and repeated the movement of the dial two more times.

I knew he was noting the location of each click. The four clicks indicated the combination had four numbers. I thought that was rather standard instead of being as complicated as I'd imagined.

Jimbo closed his eyes as he did his mental calculations. After a minute or so, he reset the lock and put it on zero. He worked in silence as we both listened to those clicks. He worked the dial slowly, patiently. Never once did he rush. I thought cracking the safe would be fast. Perhaps in two or three minutes. I was surprised when it took him thirty-five nerve-racking minutes of precise, painstaking turning of the dial as we listened to each click.

I watched his movement, trying to learn by everything he did. I had determined it had a four number combination. It dawned on me that a four number combination could have about two thousand variables. No wonder it was taking him so long. Each movement was more than simply turning the dial.

A few minutes later, he pulled the lever, and the door opened smoothly and silently. Just like that, I thought, as I noticed the trembling of his hands. I realized what intense stress he had been under. He quickly pulled the vinyl glove back on his hand and took a plastic bag from his pocket. He withdrew a small cloth from the bag and wiped the dial along with the front of the safe to get rid of prints and DNA.

I paid attention to his movements although my eyes were focused on the bundles of hundred-dollar bills. I had never seen so much money. It had to be more than the other two halls put together. He placed his stethoscope in his pocket and so did I. He then took out two bags and crammed them full with the bundles. And then, to my surprise, he took three manila folders and put them inside his shirt next to his skin. He put both bags of money inside his black coveralls and strapped them securely to his chest with a halter type sling. He closed the safe and spun the dial. After putting the section of wall and file cabinet back in place, he headed to the stairs followed by me. He used the key to lock the door he'd left unlocked.

I never knew of an old man being able to move as fast as he did. I was running full out to keep up with him. In two minutes, we were at the tree at Walmart where we took off our ski masks and put on our other disguise and, in less than a minute, we were in the Chevrolet with him slowly driving away.

"That was close," he said.

"Close?" I questioned. "I thought it was perfect."

"If I had locked the front door instead of leaving it open an alarm would have gone off at the police station. I managed to disconnect the security system by scrambling the code to give us a forty-five-minute window. Once I locked the door the alarm went off at the police station, plus the security system came on about the time we drove out of the parking lot. I'll have to make my Chevrolet disappear for a while just in case my timing was off. I took the liberty to put fake license plates on it. I'll have to stash the Chevrolet and drive you home in a different car.

"How did you manage all that?" I wanted to know.

"Trade secret along with knowing the right people who owe me. Your lesson for tonight is to realize that you aren't the one who knows the right people or have those who owe you. It would be impossible for you to do what I just did. I want you to promise me you'll never try it. I'm going to put this money into your account over a period of time. I don't want a large deposit to draw attention."

"Okay," I told him. "You need to keep most of it for yourself."

"Told you before I can't do that. I've been given a limited amount to live on. Anything extra would draw attention. Even spending a few more dollars than I'm allowed would trigger an investigation of me."

"Depositing money in my account doesn't?" I asked.

"Not when I do it right."

It was then I heard sirens going off about two miles away.

"They're heading to the office building," he said. "We'll be taking backroads from here."

About thirty minutes later, he took an almost non-existing road through a thickly wooded area and came to a shed.

"Stay put," he said.

I watched him unlock the wooden door, open it, and get back into the Chevrolet and drive into the darkness of the shed.

"Get out," he told me. I did as shivers ran up my backbone. This dark, derelict place was starting to spook me.

He turned on his penlight, locked the door and guided me to a plank in the wall and pushed it sideways for us to exit the shed. He took me to another spot in the woods where an old Volkswagen was parked. He unlocked it and we got in.

"I hope you realize what precautions must be taken when you rob a safe. You don't have the means to do any of the leg work. Don't even try. Hear me?" he said again emphatically.

"I hear you," I told him.

"You'll have enough money in your bank account to last for years if you're frugal. Take your karate classes and live like a girl your age should live."

"What about cracking Joe Nimule's safe?"

"No need. After a good deal of snooping, I've learned Johanna emptied out everything of value in the safe, the house, as well as their bank accounts. It appears she was intelligent enough to set up her get-away plans some time back. Appears she had some kind of inkling, or perhaps forewarning of what could happen with her husband."

"Shit," I said, and he chuckled.

"I want you to crawl back inside your window, rip your dark clothes to shreds putting a strip into different trash bins, and be content and safe from now on, my little protégé."

I got out of the Volkswagen, crawled in the window, and listened to him drive away. I got in the tub, turned on the water and washed my clothes and myself with good smelling soap I had indulged in buying a few days ago. I wanted to wash away any kind of trace of the heist that might have stuck to my clothes.

Once I got over the after-shakes, I calmed down and did some thinking. Jimbo was right. If and when he put all that money in my account, I would feel like the richest girl in existence. I wouldn't need to steal ever again. I felt both relief and disappointment. Being a Robin Hood *was* starting to become addictive.

Chapter 8

*

Six o'clock Thursday arrived and I made my way to the dojo without having any idea what I should expect. I pushed a door open and walked into a large room with mirrors covering one wall. Several men in white baggy pants and sweat stained tops were taking turns kicking a canvas punching bag. Sweat ran down their faces as they did squats, jumping jacks, and pushups as they waited in line for their turn at the punching bag.

Many of the men had different colored belts tied around their waists. Occasionally, they would take a swipe at each other as they ran a circle around the room before they lined back up. A couple of them glanced my way but appeared to pay little attention to me. I stood there for a few minutes feeling out of place and not knowing what to do next or where I should go. I must have looked like a deer in the headlights. I had the strongest urge to run out the door and forget about taking self-defense classes. Why I continued standing glued to the spot was beyond me.

A slender man wearing a gee and black belt tied around his waist came out a door that had an office sign above it. He came over to me.

"Can I help you?" he asked politely.

"I'm Alona Anderson," I told him the name Jimbo had signed me up under. "I'm here to take karate lessons."

I recalled what Jimbo had told me. "Not everybody has the luxury of choosing who they're going to be for a day or longer," Jimbo had told me. "The Lone Ranger and Bat Man have the privilege of living two different lives. I see no reason why you can't do likewise."

The man's eyebrows shot up to his hair line as his gray eyes widened in irritation as though I was wasting his time. "I don't have a women's karate class," he informed me. "There is a women's class another instructor is teaching on Saturdays. That's probably what you're looking for."

I didn't think so. Jimbo hadn't mentioned anything about a Saturday class. I pulled out the receipt Jimbo had given me and handed it to him. It had my fake name, fake address, and fake age, plus the amount paid and by whom. It also said if I was underage a guardian had to sign for me. Jimbo had put my age as being eighteen on April first. I wasn't going to correct a thing, although I thought it odd that someone underage would be taking a class with grown men, but the classes were through Parks and Recreation, which meant they should be for everyone and safe. They weren't allowed to discriminate. Again, his eyes widened as he read the receipt. He frowned and appeared to be irritated if not downright angry. He slowly shook his head in bewilderment.

"Looks like your classes have already been paid for the coming year, and I can't do anything about it being it's though Parks and Recreation. Do you realize there are only men in this class?"

I wasn't the one who signed me up for a year, so how was I to know there were only men in the class? I was beyond apprehensive when the realization of what he said hit me. My guts tightened as an icy feeling gripped my chest. I just stared at him wide eyed. I think I nodded my head as though I understood. I was wondering why Jimbo would sign me up in a men's karate class for a year in advance. Did he not realize there were only men in the class? Was it his way of pulling a joke on me? Did I turn tail and run like a coward?

"It says James Boden paid cash for this class," he said with a touch of disbelief to his tone of voice. "How do you know him?"

For some reason I continued the lie Jimbo and I had told the bank. "He's my grandfather," I said.

"You're shitting me," he said in disbelief.

I shrugged. What was I to say to that.

The instructor shook his head seemingly as bewildered as I was.

"He was my instructor for a while. Beat the hell out of me every night. I learned a lot from him. Never took him to be a grandfatherly type." He lowered his voice and mumbled, "Must have sold his stuff to a sperm bank years ago," as though he didn't care if I heard what he said.

I didn't know if he meant it as a good thing or a bad thing, but I didn't question it.

"You tell your *grandpa* after this, we're even."

He let out a breath and kind of nodded as he looked me over, closer this time. "If you want to attend this class, you'll be doing everything the men do. There will be no exception or special treatment for a young woman, regardless of who your grandpa is," he told me in an unpleasant tone of voice. He obviously thought I was nothing more than an aggravation sent to him by his former instructor.

I did my best to smile instead of showing my anger at his attitude toward me. "Okay," I said. "I can do that."

"Take off your shoes and get in line with the men. You'll need to warm up before class starts. By the looks of you, you'll pull every muscle in your body if you don't."

He turned his back to me and marched back through the door with the *office* sign above it. I got the idea whoever had taken Jimbo's money and signed me up for his classes would hear about it.

I went to a corner and slipped off my shoes and made my way to the line of men without knowing what I should be doing. Several of them were grinning. One man with a head full of curly black hair turned to me. "Overheard your conversation with Sensei York. Personally, it'll be nice to smell a little perfume in here instead of sweat and farts."

I didn't know what to say or think about that remark. Instead, I said, "He doesn't want me here."

He chuckled slightly. "He all but feeds us raw meat and gun powder to keep up his killer reputation of having the toughest fighters in existence. He's afraid having a woman in here will weaken that reputation. Not to mention interrupt his style of hard-hitting training. It's not unusual for one of us to go to the ER during each workout. Broke my pinky finger a few weeks back. Damn if I didn't pass out cold," he said with a chuckle. "Hulk threw me over his shoulder and carried me into the ER. Told the receptionist three men beat me up, and he fought them off and saved me."

I nodded. I didn't know if he was joking or telling the truth.

"Sensei York doesn't think we've had a good workout if we don't go out the door bleeding and heaving for air. He feels it's his duty to make the weak strong and the strong exhausted."

I could understand a man as rude as Sensei York having such an attitude. I fought the urge to gather my pride and walk out the door. It was also a matter of pride that I didn't.

"Have you ever kicked a punching bag before?"

"No," I'd never come into contact with one.

"I'll show you how when it's our turn."

The words *our turn* made me feel a little better.

"When doing a front kick, you don't want to kick the bag with your toes. You could break them. You turn up your toes like this," he showed me on his foot, "and kick with the pad of your foot."

I tried to turn up my toes the way he did.

"Good," he said as he patted the ball of my foot beneath my toes with his callused hand. "That's what you make contact with – unless you're attacked while you're wearing steel-toed boots. Ever wear them?"

I shook my head.

"Too bad. It's our turn. Watch how I do it and follow my example."

What the heck did steel toed boots have to do with karate, I wondered? I watched him take a stance and kick the bag with one foot and then the other foot. He was impressive.

"Show off," another man called out to him. "Moved in on the girl fast, didn't you?"

"Shut your pie hole, Richard," he called back. "It's your turn," he said to me.

I tried to kick with one foot and then the other the same as he had done. I felt embarrassed with my pitiful attempt. I was also surprised at how solid and rough the canvas bag felt. I didn't move the canvas bag at all, plus its roughness hurt my foot.

"You did good for your first try," he told me, as we moved to the back of the line where he began doing squats and stretching his legs.

I watched wide eyed as the men took their turns. One man built like a Mack truck took a run-a-go and kicked the bag so hard it flew into the air.

"Dang!" I mumbled. The Mack truck man heard me and seemed pleased.

"Show off," Richard called out again in reference to the Mack truck man.

"Richard's stupid," my rescuer bent his head to whisper near my ear. "The Hulk just might break Richard in half if he doesn't watch his mouth."

The Hulk. The name fit.

"By the way, I'm Malone, and you are?"

"Alona," I said, continuing to use the name Jimbo signed me up under.

"Going to school here?"

"Yes, I am."

"Straight A student, no doubt?"

"So far, but I'm not too good in algebra. I'm afraid I might need a tutor."

"I'm not so good in algebra either," he admitted. "Junior or senior?" he asked.

"Junior," I told him.

"Good. Means you can be around here for a couple of years. If you work hard, you can earn your black belt by the time you graduate."

Sensei York came out of the office and called for everyone to line up in front of him. I stood next to Malone.

Sensei York gave me a bewildered look. "Anderson," he had obviously gotten that name from my receipt. "You're at the end of the line. Line up is according to rank."

I quickly moved to the back, noticing that the brown belts were on the left side of the room then blue, green, orange, yellow and white belts fell in behind those with rank. I was in sweatpants, a T-shirt, and no belt. I felt as out of place as the preverbal petunia in an onion patch. Sensei York's attitude was making me feel beyond unwanted as did the looks he cast my way.

I watched the men and tried to mimic every move they made. I could imagine how ridiculous I looked as I tried to throw kicks and punches in midair.

An hour later Sensei York called "Line up." As though we weren't already lined up. He then bowed us out, which was all of us bowing back to him. I was wet with sweat and a total wreck. As the men broke line and scattered about, I headed for my shoes. Malone followed me and made a point of placing his hand on my shoulder in a comforting manner.

"You did great for your first time," he assured me. "Sensei York believes in pushing everybody to the limit. He mopped up the floor with me when I first started. Every night as I rubbed pain liniment on my body, I promised myself I'd never come back, but I'm thankful I did. Took a while for me to earn his respect, but I managed as did the rest of the men. He always puts newcomers through hell. Doubt he'll make an exception of you. Tonight was a tough workout even for those of us who has been here a while. Glad you stuck it out. See you Tuesday, okay?"

His question sounded like he wanted me to come back, but he wasn't sure if I would. "I'll be back," I told him.

"Good," he said with a wide grin. "I like a girl with grit. Having you here will make all of us fellows perk up a little, including our Sensei."

I held my head high as I walked down the street imagining that someone could be watching me. I certainly didn't want to appear defeated, but I was. I had made a total fool of myself trying to mimic what the men did. I even saw humor in Sensei York's face as he watched me. His expression told me plainly that I didn't belong there, and never would. The only reason I was here was because his former instructor signed me up.

"How was your karate class?" Mother asked when I entered the restaurant.

"Okay," I said. "It was a lot of exercise."

"I can tell that. You look sweaty and exhausted. You can't work looking the way you do. You smell like . . . like sweaty men. Go upstairs to Mary's apartment and take a quick shower and change clothes. It'll be faster than going home. We've been busy. Looks like it's going to continue for a while." Mother told me even though Mary gave her a disapproving frown.

I did as Mother suggested knowing Aunt Mary didn't like anyone in her apartment. She was extremely peculiar about everything. I suspected that was why she had never married. She'd not met a man who would put up with her ways. Not to mention live up to the fact that she wanted everything her way.

Once I was under the warm shower, I broke down and cried for a full five minutes before I got myself under control. Considering what Jimbo and I had gone through; I could surely survive karate and Sensei York – not to mention the vigorous workout he demanded from the men and me. Plus,

Sensei York had presented a personal challenge where my self-esteem was concerned. I had no intention of allowing him to make me feel like a failure let alone be one.

"Did you use your towel to wipe the shower dry?" Aunt Mary ask in an accusing way when I returned to the kitchen.

"Yes, I did,"

"Did you hang the towel over the shower rod to dry? I don't like putting wet towels in the laundry hamper. Smells up the bathroom. Not to mention mold, which I'm allergic to."

I thought that was an amusing comment. Her apartment always smelled like whatever food was cooking in the restaurant. Mother had often told me we should ignore Aunt Mary and her ways. There were times when it wasn't easy not to talk back to her, but I tried to take Mother's advice.

"Now that you're here to help out, I think I'll go home early," Mother told me. "Things have slowed down while you showered. We're finally out of the weeds, and I need to do laundry."

I knew laundry was just Mother's excuse to go home and rest. She had been pushing herself hard lately

Chapter 9

*

Never for a moment did I doubt Aunt Mary's love for Mother or Mother's love for Aunt Mary. I also knew both had an undying love for me. The stress of Mother's condition was taking its toll on all three of us, even when we didn't want to admit it.

Mother claimed she was cured of cancer, and it would never return. I hoped she was right, but something inside me didn't believe in such good luck. Everything I read from the research I did gave a small chance of Mother's type of cancer not returning.

Five years was about the time a person was given to live after discovering such cancer. If Mother had gone for regular checkups, her cancer could have been caught earlier. The earlier caught, the better her chance of survival.

I was twelve when it was found. That could mean I would only be seventeen when I lost Mother. The thought was almost more than my mind could take. Losing her made me want to scream, to fight, to do something to relieve the fear and tension that was constant in my body. I needed to tell someone about my fears, but who could I confide in? Perhaps Jimbo would understand.

I met him as usual on Wednesday, but I found I couldn't talk about cancer. Instead, I said, "I went to karate class."

"Karate will be good for you," Jimbo told me. "It'll give you self-confidence along with keeping you trim and fit. Plus, you never know when it will come in handy."

I noticed how gaunt his face looked. His cheeks had sunken in, and he appeared to have lost weight.

"Have you been sick?" I asked, ignoring his comment.

"Why do you ask such a thing?"

"You look tired," I told him.

He grinned. "My dear granddaughter, it's time you realized that being tired is a permanent condition of those who are my age."

"You're not old," I fibbed a little.

"I was old a long time before you were born. Now, forget about me. I'm doing great considering. Tell me how karate went with you?"

"Sensei York doesn't like me."

"Why do you say that?"

"He obviously thinks having a girl in his all-male class will hurt his reputation as an instructor. He told me I should take women's classes on Saturdays."

"That doesn't mean he doesn't like you. It means he's concerned about you being injured. The men in his class aren't wimps. They sweat testosterone. Are you going to switch classes to Saturday?"

"No."

"Why not?" he asked. "You might be more comfortable in a group of women."

"If I'm ever attacked, it will most likely be from a man. Besides, he deliberately hurt my pride. I'm going to show him that I'm not a quitter."

"It's your choice," he assured me. "I wouldn't want you to take a class where you're not comfortable."

"You signed me up with him for a reason, didn't you?"

"I did. The reason is that he'll teach you how to street fight. Women tend to scratch and slap when they fight. They don't know how to hurt a man. Lee York can teach you how."

He said you were his instructor."

His brows lifted. "He told you that?"

"He did."

"Did he say anything else?"

"He said you beat the hell out of him every class, and that you weren't the grandfatherly type." I chose not to tell him about Sensi York saying he must have donated his stuff to a sperm bank back when he was young.

His grin returned. "You told him I was your grandfather?"

"It just slipped out when he asked why you signed me up for his classes and paid for them. I couldn't exactly tell him we were partners in crime."

"We're not partners in crime," he was quick to correct me. "I'm a person who tries to correct injustices, and you are my incentive. You and I are nothing more than Robin Hoods. Remember that."

I started to argue that point but decided against it. I cringed at where my small family would be without him helping correct injustices. It seemed to me that my family were the only ones who benefited from what he and I had done. In my opinion that wasn't exactly being a Robin Hood.

"Think of the people who have been saved from becoming victims of these lowlifes," he told me as though he knew my thoughts. "By the way, what name are you using in class?"

I assured myself he made a good point as I sat down on the bench beside him. "Alona Anderson. It's the name you put on the receipt."

"It is, isn't it. You might also take note that you're supposed to be of age. He wouldn't allow you to take the class if he knew your real age. Let me give you some advice I learned a long time ago. You'll never be able to change what happened in the past. But you can alter what happens in the future."

"I already I know I can't change the past or the future, but I wish I could do both."

"You already have altered it. Where would your mother be right now if she hadn't been able to pay for her treatment and medication? You have altered her future in the only way you knew how. In my opinion, you deserve a lot of admiration for doing what you've done."

"I'm afraid of being without my mother." I confessed.

"I understand that all too well, but you'll survive regardless of what happens. You're tough. You'll be able to handle whatever situation that's thrown at you. I hope I've helped you in being able to do that."

He had certainly helped me out financially, but I was learning money didn't last long. There was always bills coming due regardless of how little came in.

"In a year or so, you will be graduating high school. Do you have plans for the rest of your life."

Plans? How could I ever have plans when all I'd had was worry? "I suspect I'll have to work at the restaurant full time." I told him, while trying to keep the disappointment out of my voice.

"Is that what you want to do?"

"If it will help Mother, it's what I want to do."

"What about college?"

I had thought a lot about that, but it seemed a hopeless dream for me. Mother said when she was growing up college was only for doctor's, lawyer's, and teacher's kids. The rest of us had to work for a living. I knew there was no money for me to seek higher education at a college. There had been barely enough money for me to attend regular schooling. It took away a child's pride to be the poorest kid in class.

"There's plenty of time for you to decide on such as that," he said encouragingly. "A college education is a good thing to have. What I want you to understand is that you should always seek wisdom not knowledge. Knowledge is the past. Wisdom is the future."

Good advice, but I knew not to get my hopes up. I'd rather be surprised than disappointed.

"Tell Lee York your grandpa said hello, and that he best treat my only granddaughter right or I'll have to pay him a visit."

"Think that will help?" I asked not knowing if he was being humorous or serious.

"No," he said with a grin. "Lee York is his own man with his own opinions. Are you in need of more money? It takes a lot to go to college."

"Do I?" I asked. He was the one who kept up with what money was in my bank account. I couldn't take a chance on anything from the bank coming to me. Didn't he tell me I had enough money in the bank to last a very long time?

"In my opinion, a person never has enough money. Probably pay us to do one more heist before we both retire."

"I thought you said we retired when you cracked the last safe."

"Right, but something came up that I need to avenge."

Oddly enough the thought of retiring left me feeling rather sad. I didn't want to give up the possibility of having money when and if it was needed. I had discovered not having money to do what was needed was a horrible situation to be in.

"When?" I asked.

"Don't know for sure yet. I'm waiting to see what happens. Have fun at karate."

Chapter 10

*

Fun? Since when was karate fun? It was hard work, painful and embarrassing. It made me feel inadequate and out of place. That was probably why I was determined to stick it out. I had to prove something to myself as well as to Sensei York as well as Jimbo.

"You're back?" Sensei York said with lifted brows when I came in the door.

"I'm back," I told him and lifted my chin higher. We were standing face to face looking into each other's eyes.

"I'm surprised," he said with a slight shake of his head. "Most girls would have turned tail and run after coming into contact with the sweat and blood of these men."

"I'm not a quitter," I told him.

He smiled slightly. "James Boden's granddaughter wouldn't be."

I saw some kind of emotion flicker in his eyes that I couldn't describe. For a moment I thought he was going to say more, but Malone rushed over interrupting us.

"Glad you came in early," he said as he put his arm around my shoulders. "Come on. We'll work on the bag to warm us up."

Sensei York never said a word as he turned around and walked off as if he wasn't pleased by Malone's interruption.

"What did he say to you?" Malone whispered near my ear as though he didn't want the other students to hear him.

"He was surprised I returned instead of being a quitter."

"Is that all?"

"That's all. Why do you ask?"

"Just wanting to make sure he's not trying to run you off."

"Hey, Malone. Get with it or get outta the way," Richard hollered at Malone. "It's your turn at the bag not at the girl."

Malone attacked the bag with fury. I had an idea he was pretending it was Richard. I didn't blame him. I wondered why Richard was so rude and why the others allowed it. Next was my turn at warming up on the bag. Malone guided me through it. Telling me what I needed to do and why.

"Hit straight in with your fists. Making contact with your first two knuckles, and don't let your hand slide over the canvas bag or you'll skin your knuckles. Keep your elbows close to your side or you'll telegraph your punch. You don't want your opponent to know what is coming next."

Malone continued telling me what I needed to do. I never realized karate had so many things to remember. There was a reason behind every move.

"Try your front kick one more time."

I took a stance, curled up my toes and kicked.

"Good," he said you're getting the hang of it."

"Hurry it up," Richard called out as I kicked and punched the bag. "You can't kick worth a shit. Plus, you're taking up too much time being prissy."

I saw Sensei York come out of the office door and walk up behind Richard, tap him on the shoulder and then nod toward the office. Richard silently followed him. As Malone and I got back in line, I noticed that every man was grinning, including Malone.

"I predict Richard will be fighting the Hulk tonight," he whispered near my ear. "No one is allowed to belittle one of Sensi York's students."

Except Sensi York, I thought.

His prediction was right. Sensei York put Richard and the Hulk together. "Go easy on him," Sensei York told the hulk. "Don't send him to the hospital. I've got other things to do tonight that are more important." That night the Hulk mopped the floor with Richard. Thankfully, he didn't send him to the hospital, although he did draw a little blood from his nose and mouth not to mention both black eyes.

"Lesson learned," Malone whispered to me. "He had it coming. The only thing worse is fighting with Sensei York. He's deadly."

Sensei York bowed us out as usual. As I was putting my shoes on to leave, I felt a touch on my shoulder. I turned, expecting to see Malone. It was Sensei York. He nodded toward the office. I hung my head and dragged my feet as I followed him. I noticed the remaining men were giving me that *you poor thing* look. I tried to prepare myself for a tongue lashing or worse. I faced Sensei York wide eyed with apprehension.

"What did I do wrong?" I asked him.

"Other than taking this class, nothing?"

He gave me that almost grinned. "Do you plan on quitting any time soon?" he asked.

"No," I told him. "I'm not a quitter. Plus, I'm paid up for a year." I had no intention of wasting that much money regardless of how bad I was at karate.

"I see. You'll be okay in kata. You have good form. There's grace in your movements that these men don't have. However, classes are not going to get any easier. You've had warm-up time. I'll expect you to start fighting next week."

"With whom?" I questioned. "The Hulk?"

This time he did grin. "He has killer instincts. Even his love-pats are painful. When he first started, I asked him why he chose to take karate. He said he only knew of one man he couldn't beat in a fight, and he wanted to beat him."

I thought that was a good enough answer.

"Who do you want to beat?" he looked me in the eyes as he questioned me.

"Cancer," I said the first thing that popped into my mind.

"You have cancer?" he asked as a frown of concern came to his face.

"My mother does," I told him.

"I'm sorry about that."

"So am I."

He nodded as though he had decided. "I have something for you." He reached behind him and picked up a folded gee off a shelf. "I found this in the supply closet. It's been in there for a few years collecting dirt and dust. You ought to wash it good and iron it before wearing it to the next class."

"I tentatively looked at the gee. "How much is it?"

"Nothing. I was cleaning out the supply closet. If you don't want it, throw it in the trash."

I took the gee. Thank you," I told him. He nodded and opened the door for me to leave. I was surprised to find that Malone was waiting on me.

"I'll drive you home," he said. "Don't like the idea of you walking the streets in the dark."

I grinned. I had never heard of anyone being attacked anywhere near here. "No need. I take karate," I told him as an attempt at humor.

"So do I, but you never know what might come at you. Like a monkey wrench."

I now knew why Malone took karate. He was afraid of a monkey wrench. "Thanks," I said and followed him to his car, although I would have enjoyed walking to cool off some. My clothes were wet with sweat. Sensei York didn't that he was doing his job unless students could wring sweat from their belts. I enjoyed the physical workout. It helped eased the tension I was always feeling lately.

I hesitated to accept Malone's offer, but he was right. It was late and I didn't look forward to the long walk home.

He seemed surprised when I asked him to drop me off at the restaurant.

"Why there?" he asked.

"I work there."

"No shit?"

"Why are you surprised?"

"Since you've paid up for a year, I thought you didn't need to work."

"A year of classes was a gift from my grandfather," I found myself saying. "I've worked at the restaurant a long time." Odd, how referring to Jimbo as my grandfather was beginning to feel natural.

"I thought you were in school."

"I am. I work here after I get out of class."

"Oh," he said. "Have to admire a working girl."

"See you next time," I said as I got out of the car and went inside. Suddenly it hit me. What had I done? There was a possibility I'd just allowed him a way of finding out my name wasn't Alona and that I wasn't as old as I claimed.

"Who was that?" Mother asked as soon as I walked in the door. She had been looking out the window.

"One of the karate students gave me a ride."

"You do know not to get into cars with strangers," Mother made a point of telling me again.

I had to smile at that. I wasn't exactly a child. "I know," I said and gave Mother a brief hug. "He's not a stranger."

"What have you got?" she asked as she looked at the gee I was carrying.

"Sensei York was cleaning out the closet and asked if I wanted this. He said if I didn't to throw it in the trash. He said it's rather old and needs to be washed and ironed before I wear it." I knew she was worried that I'd have to pay for it. She still worried about the lack of money to buy the things we needed. It made me think of Jimbo and what he might have in mind.

"I don't know about you taking those classes, Aunt Mary told me with her usual tone of disapproval. "You should be here at the restaurant so your mother can go home to get some rest. She's been working too hard."

"Nonsense," Mother told Aunt Mary. "Millie deserves a break. The good Lord knows she's spending her youthful years washing dishes and cleaning up as it is."

Aunt Mary snorted and said no more, but it was easy to tell she didn't like Mother contradicting her.

*

Karate was good for me in more ways than one. The few hours of time it got me away from the drama of Mother's illness, along with the demands of working at the restaurant, were nothing short of a blessing. I'd heard the hard physical workout, the sweating, the comradery developed during karate was a bond that would never be broken. I hoped that was true. I longed to be accepted as part of the team. There was one thing I learned right off, if I was to continue taking lessons, I was certainly expected to earn my place. Sensei York made me earn every accomplishment I achieved during every workout in the dojo. He watched every move I made. Corrected every mistake. His only praise might be a nod of his head, which was a rare and fleeting thing.

He bowed us out at the end of a brutal workout. I was exhausted. Sensi York had fought two rounds with me. I went to the corner of the room and sank down on the floor to catch my breath. He came over, took my hand, and pulled me to my feet.

Aren't you through beating me to death?" I asked, aching all over. I knew I would have bruises by tomorrow.

He grinned "No," he told me firmly. "I'm nowhere close to stop beating on you, as you put it. You've proved you're good. I intend making you better."

"Better? You're trying to kill me," I told him as we stood inches apart.

His grin increased. "Don't let the men know, but I feel I owe you a coke and pizza. Stick around until I get dressed. By the way, the gee looks good on you."

I was so shocked by his words I stood there speechless. I had worn the gee for weeks and this was the first time he mentioned it. If I didn't know better, I'd think he'd been hit in the head hard enough to make him say something nice. Malone was watching and wasted no time as he rushed up to me.

"Can I drop you off tonight?"

"No," Sensei York was quick to answer him. "I'll see she gets home after we're through here. Class is over. You can leave now Malone."

Malone looked shocked. It was obvious he hadn't expected Sensei York to say such a thing.

"Uhh, I'll see you next class," Malone said to me.

I nodded.

"Come into the office," Sensei York told me.

I lowered my head and followed him into the office.

"Wait in here on me. Did you bring clothes to change into?"

"No," I told him. I'd put the gee on at the restaurant the same as I always did. I was still shy about going into the dressing room to change with all the men around.

"Doesn't matter. What you're wearing will be good enough," he assured me as he closed the office door.

I sat down in a comfortable chair as I looked out the window. It suddenly occurred to me that I was looking through a one-way mirror. People could sit in the office and watch what was going on in the dojo without being seen. I had not noticed before since one wall was covered in mirrors so the people who took part in a variety of activities could watch themselves. I knew a lot of students took dance classes there, plus the women's self-defense classes that took place on Saturdays.

He was back within minutes dressed in pants and shirt.

"Let's go," he said as he turned off the office light. I followed him out of the office into the dojo and then stood on the sidewalk while he locked the outside door. He placed his hand on my back and guided me to a car parked on the street. He opened the door for me to get in the passenger seat I got in feeling apprehensive. "I can't stay long," I told him.

"We won't be long. I've already ordered a takeout pizza and drinks. We'll pick it up at the drive-in window."

"Okay," I told him, wondering if I should have him drop me off at the restaurant. I didn't want to explain anything to him. Having Malone know where I worked was enough to make me uneasy.

I hadn't expected to feel comfortable as we sat in the parking lot eating the pizza. I couldn't remember the last time I ate pizza. It was too expensive. However, it was a treat from eating restaurant leftovers.

"Do you see your grandfather often?" he surprised me by asking.

"Not often enough," I answered while trying to be evasive.

"I've not seen him in about seven years. I was eighteen when I took private lessons with him."

"Seven years ago," I said in surprise. "He was old to be teaching karate." In my mind only the young could endure what Sensei York put us through.

A soft chuckle came from Sensei York. "Took him a while to become a tenth-degree black belt. You're unlikely to see a young man who deserves such an honor. James Bowman was and will always be a master. Did he not tell you that?"

"No. He seldom talks about himself. He only said you were his student."

"He was the best, but I suppose even a man such as James Bowman can get too old to teach any longer. What does he spend his time doing?" he surprised me by asking.

I didn't want to tell him that I didn't know. "He enjoys sitting in the sunshine with me," I told him. "We don't get together as much as I'd like," I repeated what I'd told him before.

"Is he still in good health?"

"I hope so, but I worry about him at times. He seems to be tired lately, but he claims it comes from old age."

"Tell him I send my best regards, and that I believe his granddaughter has the capability to become as talented and capable as he has always been."

"Thanks," I said, not feeling comfortable with a compliment from him, especially when I'd never heard him spread many compliments around. "Did you know him before you took his class?" I asked. I would like to know more about Jimbo. It was obvious he never wanted to talk about himself when we were together. He considered the tricks-of-trade he taught me more important.

"I'd heard of him, but I never met him until he became my instructor for about a year. I was a cocky brown belt when I started taking his classes." A glow of remembrance came to Sensei York's face, causing me to have the strangest urge to reach out and touch him.

"You're still cocky," I surprised myself by saying.

"Not cocky," he told me. "Confident. I have to be confident in myself and my abilities in order to gain the respect of the men I teach. I had to earn respect from men such as the Hulk."

"How?" I asked. The Hulk was huge and mean looking, while Sensei York was a small man with a tranquil appearance that was deceiving.

"The same way your grandfather earned respect. He wiped the floor with anyone who questioned his ability. He was a fighter, Alona. One hell of a mighty fighter."

"I'll tell him you said that."

"He knows," Sensei York said.

*

Malone was giving me strange looks the next time we were in class. He wasn't nearly as helpful and attentive as he had been. He was giving me the cold shoulder.

"What's wrong?" I asked him. "You seem standoffish."

"Not standoffish. Just being cautious while wondering what's going on between you and Sensei York."

"Nothing is between us," I told him, surprised at his tone if not his accusation.

"Could have fooled me."

"He only wanted to ask me about my grandfather. My grandfather was his sensei for a while."

Malone's eyes widened. "No shit. I've always wondered about the man who he'd trained under. Somewhere, along the line Sensei York became a . . . a hardnosed kind of man.

*

Mother started planting flowers all over our backyard. Her favorite was knockout roses. I thought I understood her action. She wanted to leave something of beauty behind. Something that Aunt Mary and I would remember her for. What better legacy than beautiful roses that would bloom each spring.

"Those things are expensive." Aunt Mary told her. "We don't have money to waste on plants."

I saw the sadness come to mother's face. Aunt Mary's words reminded Mother that her condition was the main contributor to our poverty. I could see the stain of guilt reddening Mother's normally pale face. I longed to say something scathing to Aunt Mary, but I knew anything I said would make the situation worse.

"You're right," Mother said in her attempt at an agreeable tone of voice. "I don't know what I was thinking spending money on plants."

I longed to remind Aunt Mary that Mother was the one who started the restaurant that provided Aunt Mary with a job and a place to stay. Not only that, but Mother was right there working while she was struggling to keep standing on her feet. If she wanted to buy flowers, she had the right to do so, even when money was scarce. Instead, I said nothing while wondering what had gotten into Aunt Mary to make her so disagreeable?

Instead of getting angry at Aunt Mary, Mother put her arm around her and gave her a hug.

A guilty look came to Aunt Mary's face.

"I don't mean to be grouchy," Aunt Mary said. "I don't want you to go bankrupt and lose everything you've worked for all these years. You know only too well what a tight pinch we're in."

"I understand," Mother told her soothingly. The restaurant is doing a little better now, thanks to Millie and her ideas after winning the contest."

"We're having to spend a lot more on food and wine as well. Seems like all we can do is keep breaking even."

"At least we're not going in the hole the way we were for a while."

I didn't want them to keep talking about finances. If they did, they might figure out neither one of them had been paying the bills. I didn't know how I would explain that. And then it hit me. I wouldn't have to explain it. I could play dumb – unless one of them went to the bank and asked who had been making the payments. Jimbo had been smart enough to have me use a fake name with fake ID.

I thought I had plenty of money in the bank, but I feared it wasn't enough to last as long as Jimbo indicated. He had put money in a savings account for me with directives that I wasn't to touch it without his approval. I didn't know the amount as I wasn't the one who got the bank statements.

If the cancer stayed in remission, we might make it without any more midnight heists. But then Jimbo did say something about going for it one more time. The thought of taking a chance on getting caught had started to concern me. Odds were that our luck had to run out sooner or later. Plus, I was getting older. Jimbo wouldn't be able to take all the blame for my actions if we were caught. I hoped Jimbo didn't decide to avenge anything or anyone.

Chapter 11

*

Malone became more possessive of me the longer I attended karate classes. At first, I had appreciated it, but now I wasn't so sure. The way he tried to accidently touch me in class, along with the way he tried to monopolize my time, was making me uncomfortable. I kept trying to avoid him and flat out refused to allow him to drop me off at the restaurant. Malone's attention toward me was so obvious that the men were starting to think it amusing.

Richard was always making unpleasant jokes about Malone and me, while Richard was a lot more handsy with my body than was proper. Sense York wore a continuous frown when he watched Malone and Richard in action. Every time Sensei York heard Richard make a joke, he would partner with Richard and rough him up a bit. Oddly enough, Richard appeared to like it. I decided Richard was a fruitcake. A fruitcake that scared me in a way I couldn't define.

Sense York had gotten into the habit of calling me into the office after class until Malone and Richard left. Sometimes he would take me for pizza which was a treat for me. He always went through the drive-through window instead of going inside, which was okay with me.

"What's going on with you and Sensei York?" Malone demanded to know one evening as everyone was warming up.

"What do you mean?" I asked, surprised at the accusation in his voice.

"You've been brushing me off and hanging out with him after class."

I didn't know how I should respond because what he said did hold some truth. At the same time, he deserved an explanation. "I value our friendship, but I don't want a closer relationship with anyone. As for Sensei York, I already told you my grandfather was his instructor. He wants Sensei York to look after me, which is what he's doing."

"Sensei York isn't trustworthy. There's a lot of talk going around about him," Malone said with a touch of defiance in his tone of voice.

"Talk?" I questioned.

"He's living with a fourteen-year-old girl," Malone whispered.

That shocked me. "What do you mean by *living with*?" I wanted him to explain further.

"You can put two and two together and come up with your own answer."

"Suppose you tell me the answer you've come up with."

As if on cue, Sensei York came out the door and lined us up. I was the last person in the back row, which showed I was the lowliest person in class, but I didn't mind. I was able to watch the advance belts make their moves. There was no question that both Malone and Richard were good in their own way. Malone was rather jerky in his movements, while Richard was fluid but was not as powerful.

Once we were warmed up, Sensei York announced it was time for kumite. This was my least favorite part of karate. I loved kata but I had an in-born dislike of fighting. Everyone sat against the wall while two people were put in the middle of floor with Sensei York as the referee.

The first to fight were Malone and Richard. Sensei York bowed them in and said "Kumite."

The fight was on. Each man was determined to do bodily damage to the other. It became more street fighting than using karate technique without Sensei York stopping it. Two of the men, Hulk and Weezie, were grinning, while most of the others had dread on their faces. It was well known that Hulk and Weezie loved to draw blood, even if it was their own. That was why these two men got to fight each other most of the time.

Malone and Richard were now head locked in a bear hug with each of them using their feet trying to knock their opponent's legs out from under them.

"Break," Sensei York called. "Break!"

Neither broke their hold. It was then I saw the power that a slender man could develop. He grabbed both of them by the back of their gees and literally jerked them apart. Both men staggered backward a moment before they started at each other again. Sensei York stepped between them. "Break," he demanded again in no uncertain terms. Both men were angry at the other, but they stopped. "Bow out," Sensei York said in a softer tone.

The two faced each other and bowed to each other and then to Sensei York, but the fury was still in their eyes as they looked at each other.

"This is a dojo not a back alley. If any one of you are not capable of using correct karate technique in this class, then leave right now." He looked each student in the eyes including me. When everyone remained seated and silent, he continued class.

Each person had their turn in fighting, including me. Much to everyone's surprise, Sensei York paired me with the Hulk. Never once did Hulk hit me with his fist. He used his open hand and grinned every time I blocked his slap. Much to his surprise, and mine, I got him with a front kick to the groin. He grunted and bent double.

"Damn," he groaned. "She … got… my family jewels." He sucked in air and let it out a couple of times. "You have to rub the pain away now. It's a rule."

The men laughed. Even Sensei York grinned. "Not tonight," Sensei York said jokingly. "Line up."

After we cooled down with slow exercises, Sensei York bowed us out, caught my eye and gave a slight nod for me to wait for him in the office.

"Damn him," Malone whispered to me as he took my arm. "He wanted me and Richard to kill each other."

I didn't argue with him on that. It was obvious Sensei York allowed them to bloody each other's noses and split lips. Of course, there were also times when someone went to the ER. Karate was a combative sport with a better-than-thou fighting spirit.

"I going to drop you off tonight," Malone told me firmly.

"No," I said as gentle as I could manage, but my refusal enraged Malone.

"You're going with him, aren't you?" he said with gritted teeth. "Even after what I told you about him."

I didn't know what to say to Malone. Neither did I know what he meant by *going* with Sensei York.

"He drops me off at the restaurant as a courtesy to my Grandfather. That's all there is to it."

"Like you expect me to believe that."

"Yes, Malone. I do expect you to believe that" I said as I turned my back to him and went into the office.

"Are you trying to get rid of Malone and Richard?" I dared ask Sensei York after I got in his car.

"No. I'm not trying to get rid of either of them. I'm giving them a lesson in self-control as well as respect for their teammates and their instructor."

"By having them beat each other up?"

He shook his head and kind of grinned in a disbelieving way. "What do you think we do to each other in karate? Kiss and make up?"

"Don't insult me. You know what I mean."

"Yes," his voice gentled. "I do know what you mean. I hope you know what I mean when I tell you it never has been a good idea to have a lone female in an all-men's karate class. Young bucks like Malone and Richard get their blood pumping hot and go after a beautiful young woman. It's to be expected."

"They're not after me," I almost screeched.

"They sure enough are."

"But I . . ."

He stopped my next words by putting his fingers over my lips. "I know. You're not interested in having a relationship with either of them."

"Right," I said as he touched his fingers to my lips again to keep me for saying more.

"You only wanted Malone as a friend. A big brother type, but you need to understand that's not enough for him. As for Richard. He wants to better Malone at everything, and that includes going after you."

I shook my head at the stupidity of such a remark.

"I see two options for you. One, you stop taking karate lessons on your own accord and ask your grandfather not to get offended."

"I don't want to stop taking lessons," I told him.

"I was afraid you'd make things more difficult on me by saying that."

"You're going to kick me out, aren't you?" I said, trying to keep my words from trembling.

"No, I'm not going to kick you out if you want to continue."

"I want to continue," I said as a stubborn streak hit me. I didn't want to be run off as a failure. I wanted to reach my goal of becoming a black belt, the same thing the other students wanted to achieve.

"In that case what I'm going to do is explain a couple of things. First thing, I am living with a fourteen-year-old girl."

I kind of froze up with disappointment when he said that.

"She is my sister. She is a deaf mute. She and I both know sign language and can read lips. I know what Malone said to you earlier."

"Why don't you tell him she's your sister?"

"I owe no one an explanation about my sister or anything else."

"But . . ." He touched my lips again. "I'm telling you about my sister for one reason only. You could say that I owe your grandfather more than I'll ever be able to repay. Therefore, I am willing to allow you to stay in karate class on one condition."

I lifted my brows, dreading the condition.

"You'll have to belong to me."

Those words shocked me. They were something I never expected to hear. "What do you mean – *belong to you?*" I asked in complete bewilderment.

"You'll have to pretend to be my girlfriend. And I repeat *pretend*. That way they'll know you're hands off and show you similar respect as they show to me."

"Are you serious?"

"I am. Think on it for a day or two. If you show up for the next class, then you agree to the farce. Right now, let's eat pizza. I'm starved."

We ate pizza in silence. I kept glancing at him. I couldn't wrap my mind around what he had just suggested. Obviously neither he nor the others realized my age. How could they when Jimbo and I had both made me older. I'd never had a boyfriend and certainly wasn't looking for one – and older one at that.

I thought about it continuously. I wanted to continue taking karate classes. I couldn't exactly figure out why other than I was determined not to be a quitter. I also wanted Jimbo to be proud of me. At the same time, taking karate was the only thing I was allowed to do other than working at the restaurant and going to school. I didn't want to give up my few hours of freedom.

When it was time for the next class, I walked into the dojo a few minutes late wearing my gee. The men were busy warming up, including both Malone and Richard. Sensei

York came out of the office, came straight to me, put his arm around me, bent down and kissed the top of my head.

"Good girl," he whispered.

*

When I showed up for the next class, Sensi York came to me with a grin on his face. He gave me a possessive hug as he grinned in welcome. His lips touched my hair near my ear. "Good girl," he whispered.

It worked. Malone wasn't as friendly to me in the same way as he had always been. I could tell he was disappointed that I hadn't reciprocated his advances. He had become way too pushy and handsy with me. I wasn't ready for what he had in mind, Although I did like Malone as a friend.

As for Richard, he kept his distance and didn't make caustic jabs about me. He did give me eyerolls from a distance when he was sure Sensei York wouldn't see him.

Hulk and the other men acted like me having a relationship with Sensei York was an expected thing. They treated me the same as they always treated me – with respect along with a big-brother kind of tolerance.

"Ready for a pizza?" Sensei York asked low enough for the others not to hear after he bowed everyone out and came to the back of the room where I was standing.

"If it comes with a quart of water," I told him as I used a napkin to wipe sweat from my face.

He smiled and pushed my sweaty hair back from where it had fallen in my eyes. "You're beautiful," he whispered so low I almost didn't hear him.

I must have looked as surprised as I felt because he grinned. I wasn't sure if this compliment was part of his 'belonging' game or if he really meant it. My bet would be on his game. The mirrors on one wall of the dojo and they didn't lie.

"Maybe, compared to Hulk," I couldn't stop myself from saying.

He gave a soft chuckle and touched my face with callused hands. Hands that he'd toughened up by beating on things, if not on people. For a moment, his eyes softened as he looked at me.

"Wait in the office on me," he said as he followed the men into the men's dressing room. Most of the men changed out of their gee before they left the dojo. I never did.

*

That Wednesday I met Jimbo at the park. He sat on the bench enjoying the warmth of the sun. I hadn't seen him for several weeks. I was surprised at how feeble he was starting to look.

"Well, lookie who's here," he said with a big smile on his face. "I was beginning to think you weren't going to show up."

"I could say the same thing about you. Where have you been?" I sat down beside him. I could almost feel the weight he'd lost.

"I had a few things to take care of," he said without elaborating as his heavy-lidded eyes looked me over. "My little protégée has grown into a beautiful young woman," he said. "Seems like yesterday you were a twelve-year-old kid with a sad face."

"And you were teaching me tricks of trade," I added with remembrance. Neither of us needed to go into further detail.

"You've still got a sad face. Care to tell me why?"

"Mother isn't doing so good."

"I'm sorry to hear that."

"Five years is the magic time. If she is still in remission after five years, she has a good chance of surviving. If the cancer return, then the prognoses is discouraging, to say the least."

"And?" he encourages as I went silent.

"It has returned, although she tries to pretend it hasn't for my sake. She's getting weaker each day. She's trying her best to make me believe she's only tired instead of getting worse."

"Is there anything I can do? Have you got enough money for her treatments? If not I can go ahead and pull off that other heist."

I caught how he said that. "I and not we?" I questioned.

"You're not an innocent kid any longer. I wouldn't be able to take all the blame."

"We're doing okay," I told him. Besides, I was sure he knew exactly how much I had in my Alona Georgette Anderson bank and savings account. I hadn't been drawing anything out of it, since Mother and I were both working, plus the steak and wine menu was bringing in more money.

"That's good to know. How about the karate classes? What belt are you now?"

"It's okay. All the physical exercise is a relief factor from worrying about Mother. I'm getting promoted the same as the men."

"How are you getting along with Lee York?"

"Okay, I guess. He's kind of standoffish."

"He's supposed to be. A sensei needs to hold himself above his students."

"Did you know he has a deaf-mute sister?"

"I know of her, but I'd never pried into her condition. I knew that Lee York was very protective of his sister. Just between the two of us, his mother was never sure who either of their dads were. She took off after the girl was born. Lee and his sister were living with an old woman. He paid her bills in return for her looking after his sister. Lee managed to keep a roof over their heads by scrape and scratch."

It seemed a lot of people had bad mothers. Thankfully mine was one of the best. "Did you teach him tricks of the trade?" I couldn't keep myself from asking.

"That kid taught me a few," he said with a shake of his head. "He was nothing more than bone covered with hide back then, but he was as rangy as a feral dog. Fight, my gracious, how that boy would fight. Always remember a hungry dog runs faster and fights harder."

"He said he owed you."

"Don't know about that. I did teach him to respect me and himself."

"How?" I asked.

"That's too long of a story to go into, even if I wanted to do it. Kind of like the tricks of trade I subjected you to, there are things best left to be forgotten."

"Why did you want me to take karate lessons with him?" I knew there had to be a reason.

"Thought I already told you why. Anyway, it's a fact that a girl needs to know how to take care of herself. No better way than to learn how to fight with a bunch of men."

Chapter 12

*

Just as I feared, Mother couldn't pretend to be her normal self any longer. The cancer had started to spread though her body. She was losing more weight as the dark circles surrounding her eyes deepened. It was all she could do to get herself out of bed, much less work at the restaurant. Still yet she got up every morning and left for the restaurant the same time I left for school. When I arrived for work after school, she wouldn't be there.

"She's getting worse," Aunt Mary needlessly told me. "Her medical bills are going to skyrocket again. Not only that, but I'll have to hire someone to replace her."

"I'll be graduating soon," I told her. "I'll be able to work full time then."

"We'll go down the tube before that happens," Aunt Mary complained.

I tried my best to ignore Aunt Mary. She had always been a worrier, while Mother was the upbeat one in our family.

When I finally got home that night, I went to check on Mother. She was in bed, but still awake.

"Are you okay?" I asked. "Has the Cancer come back?" I asked what I already knew had occurred.

"I'm alright. It wasn't too busy after the lunch rush was over, so I decided to come home to catch up on a few things here. Besides, if the cancer does come back, chemo will take care of it," Mother assured me. "You know how tough I am. There are all kinds of way to cure cancer now adays."

I knew it was only wishful thinking on Mother's part – and mine. She could no longer able to take chemo. It hadn't cured her so far. How could she expect me to believe there would be some sort of cure this time?

"I am going to be around long enough to watch you graduate high school, go to college, get married and have my grandchildren," Mother voiced what she hoped would happen.

"I'm counting on it," I told her, although I knew it wouldn't happen even if she lived to be a hundred years old. There would be no college for me. I would always be stuck working in the restaurant with Aunt Mary. What a depressing thought. Not only that, but I never wanted a husband who would run off and leave me destitute the way my father had done my mother. As for children, I would need a husband for such as that. I never had a father, but I knew the value of having one from the kids I went to school with. I had seen the love and pride in fathers' eyes when they looked at their sons or gave their daughters a quick hug. It was something I envied, but I would never admit to. I even tried to convince myself at times that Jimbo really was my grandpa, or perhaps even my father.

And then it hit me hard. Neither a decent father nor a grandfather would willingly teach his child what Jimbo had taught me. At the same time, I realized it was the only way to have enough money for my Mother's survival. I couldn't condemn Jimbo when I was a willing and thankful accomplice.

Not only was my mother in need of money, I was in need also. I had come to think of money as security that would keep people alive. I wasn't altogether sure Aunt Mary would have been able to take care of me if something had happened to Mother when I was twelve.

*

It had been five years since Jimbo and I had met. I would soon graduate from high school. Time had changed very little. Cancer was still taking Mother away from me with each day that passed, and there wasn't one thing that could be done about it. All the money in the world wasn't going to keep my mother alive.

I had convinced myself that the money Jimbo and I took would have gone to continue illegal and immoral operations if we I hadn't intervened. At the money had gone to the better purpose, which helped to ease my guilt of being a thief.

The weather had turned unbearably hot, and Mother was suffering. Her body had dropped to bone covered in a layer of transparent skin. Her face was pale with blue veins showing. Her pulse could be seen beating in her neck. There was no question her time with me was coming to an end.

"What are we going to do?" Aunt Mary moaned when she caught me alone at the restaurant. We have nothing left to pawn and I know your mother's bills have piled up and she's trying to keep them hidden from me. Not only that, but there will also be thousands of dollars in funeral expenses."

Aunt Mary's words hit me hard. This was the first time I'd ever heard her speak of funeral expenses.

"She's not going to die," I told Aunt Mary.

"We can't ignore it any longer, Millie. You might as well know nothing has cured her. The doctors want to try an experimental medicine that hasn't been approved by the insurance company. She won't be able to get it because she can't pay for it out of pocket."

I knew what I had to do.

The next day I went to the park in the hopes Jimbo would be there. He'd gotten to the point where he only showed up on occasion. Much to my relief, Jimbo was sitting on the bench in his usual place.

"You look like your dog ran away from home," he said right off. "What's troubling you?"

"It's Mother," I told him.

He nodded. "She's gotten worse again."

"Right. Her doctor's wants to try a different medicine."

"And the insurance won't pay," he said right off.

"Right." There was no insurance.

"And you're needing money to cover it," he added.

This time I nodded.

"Okay," he said. "As you know, I've been thinking on something for some time now. It's risky, and I didn't want to take a chance as long as we were both doing okay. By the way, I signed you up for another year of karate."

"Thank you," I said, but I wasn't interested in karate right now. I wanted to keep my mother alive. "When do we do it?" I asked, wanting to get at it.

"It'll take me a while to set it up. I'll let you know when I'm ready."

"Make it soon," I told him. "Mother can't wait."

He nodded in understanding. "It will be soon," he told me. "Go on home and don't worry about a thing. Your grandpa will take care of things."

I wanted to be the one who took care of my mother. I needed to feel like I was capable of accomplishing life over death. If there was a will there had to be a way, but it seemed no one had found a way to cure Mother's kind of advanced cancer.

The next week I found Jimbo waiting for me on the bench.

"What have you got in mind?" I asked him right off.

"Nothing," he told me.

"But you said . . ." I began before he interrupted me.

"I know what I said, and I also know what I did. I put more money in your Alona Georgette Anderson account. You don't realize how much money you've got in your checking and savings account since I'm the one getting your statements."

"But. . ."

He held up his hand stopping what I was about to say. "I succeeded in my plan without your help," he told me.

I felt instant disappointment. "Why without me?"

"Because you're through with doing what I should never have taught a young girl to do. If I let you continue, you'd end up in jail for life."

What he said made a lot of sense. The same thing had occurred to me, but my desperation would make me take the risk. I was willing to do anything that would have kept my mother alive for a while longer even if it was risking my own future.

A new kind of depression came over me as I dressed in my gee. Everything in my life was changing when I didn't want it to change. I wished I could have still been a happy ten-year-old girl. Up until Mother's cancer, I was happy and safe in my own little world.

I hoped going to karate would relieve some of my stress. Exhaustion along with lots of sweat allowed me a small amount of reprieve from the unhappiness I was feeling, along with sleep once I got in bed.

I put every ounce of energy I had into the workout. I beat on the bag until the skin on my knuckles curled up and bled. After that happened, I kicked the bag so hard I felt the impact through my legs and into my hips. After I put myself through a brutal warmup, I did everything Sensei York had us do with determination and precision. Every man in class was looking at me with questions on their faces. Even Sensei York lifted his brows as he watched me. I was disappointed when he had us work on technique and kata instead of kumite. I wanted to fight. Oh, how badly I wanted to fight everything.

"Okay," Sensei York said after class ended and I was seated in the office. "What's your problem tonight?"

"Nothing," I snapped at him.

How was I to answer that question? Did I tell him my world was falling apart because my mother was dying? That soon I would be left alone with Aunt Mary? Did I tell him how desperately I wanted to feel safe and cared for instead of being the one who was tried to fix things?

He reached out and took my hands in his as though he understood their pain. He opened a desk drawer and took out a tube.

"This will help the pain in your skinned knuckles. There have been times in my life when I welcomed pain. It overrode other kinds of pain."

The feel of his rough hands caressing the cream into my knuckles made me feel cared for, like finally someone was taking into consideration what I needed. Much to my embarrassment, tears escaped my eyes and slid down my cheeks. He lifted his hand and rubbed my tears away with a callused thumb.

"What is it, honey? You can confide in me."

The caring kindness in his words was what broke me. I clutched the shirt he had just changed into and buried my face against his chest as I sobbed out loud. I was so embarrassed at my weakness I wanted to drop right through the floor never to be seen again.

"It's okay. You're okay," he said in the most soothing voice I'd ever heard. "I'm here. I've got you. You're safe. I'll keep you safe."

His words made me cry even harder. His arms tightened around me. His hands rubbing over my back, rubbing my arms. The feel of his fingers caressing along my neck sent chills of pleasure over my body. I wanted those fingers to caress more of me. Wanted my body to press against his. Become part of him, his strength, his existence.

"Oh, babe, don't cry. I can't stand to see you crying like this," he whispered as his lips brushed through my hair until he was nuzzling my ear and the side of my face.

How his mouth met with mine I didn't know. I trembled with unexpected pleasure. He was giving me something I desperately needed. My mouth, my entire body was responding to his in a way I had only dreamed about. Finally,

I was experiencing the fire of passion – the unbelievable need of having his mouth claim mine.

Realization hit me. This was what I wanted every time I looked at Sensei York – every time I watched him take a bite of pizza. Every time his hands touched me.

"Easy, if you want me to stop," Sensei York managed to get his mouth away from mine long enough to whisper a warning to me.

But there was no *easy* any longer. No wanting him to stop. I wanted far more than I was getting, and I was determined to go after it. Sensei York was capable and willing. His mouth never left mine as his hands caressed up my back and then over my body. Somehow, before I realized it, those hands had moved until they were untying the string that held up my gee bottom. I welcomed the cool air on my bare legs as I stepped out of my shoes. I heard the sound of his pants being unzipped and realized they had dropped to the floor with my gee bottoms. I clung to him tighter. Kissed him with such a fervor that a desperate sound escaped my throat, encouraging him to continue.

It seemed only natural as he eased my body down to the floor without our lips ever parting. The feel of his knees spreading my legs apart also felt natural. The pain that came next wasn't. I groaned and jerked.

"Easy," he whispered against my lips. "Let me make love to you."

I let him.

Chapter 13

*

Talk about an emotional roller coaster of feelings I had on the day I graduated from high school. I was both excited and dreading what was to come next. At least mother had gotten her wish to see me graduate. She sat in the bleachers wearing a wig and a lot of face makeup pretending to be her normal happy self. All the makeup couldn't hide the pallor of her skin or the shakiness of her hands she clutched together. Wearing the wig made her less self-conscious. The treatment she had endured took away every hair, including her eyebrows and eyelashes. Not once did she complain in front of me or admit she was weak and getting worse by the minute.

Aunt Mary wasn't able to attend my graduation ceremony. She claimed she needed to stay at the restaurant. The restaurant couldn't afford to be without her for a couple of hours even though there were two employees there. She was also excited that I would now be able to work full-time. That was where the dreaded part of my graduation came in. Working with Aunt Mary had become a form of torture for me, but I would do it if it meant my Mother wouldn't have to spend her remaining time trying to help out.

"I'm proud of you," Mother gave me a frail hug as I took off my rented gown. I hugged her back feeling her bones like they were pointed sticks. She couldn't weigh more than eighty pounds. How she managed to do all the things she still did was beyond me.

"Hey everyone," someone called out. We're all going out to celebrate."

"Go with them," Mother told me. "You've earned a celebration."

How could she even think such a thing when she was standing there with tears of pride shining in her eyes while her body shook from her effort.

"I don't want to," I told her. "I want to go home and celebrate with you."

"You don't have to say such as that," she told me.

"I'm not just saying it. I mean it."

Her tears almost spilled over. What I had said was difficult for her to believe, but I could tell she hoped it was true. She was far too weak to drive the van back home.

"Would you like to go somewhere and get something to eat on the way home?"

She grinned. "Wouldn't Mary have a fit at such a suggestion. She'd claim we were wasting much needed money when we could eat leftovers at the restaurant."

"I get tired of hearing what Aunt Mary thinks," I found myself bold enough to tell her the truth.

"So do I," Mother admitted. "She means well."

"I know," I said as I put my arms around her and guided her outside to the van and helped her get inside.

"Talking about Mary," she continued a bit sadly. "I've been thinking, and I don't want you working at the restaurant when I'm no longer here. She would make a servant out of you while depriving you of your own ambitions. I went to see a lawyer and made out my will. I'm leaving her the restaurant and van. I'm leaving you the house. When you feel ready, I want you to sell the house and use the money to further your education. Go to college. Accomplish your dream life. Do whatever makes you happy."

"Were you ever happy?" I couldn't stop myself from asking.

"Oh, my darling daughter. You have no idea of the happiness I've had. First came my dancing. My very soul absolutely came alive when I danced to the music. It was like I was drifting away on a cloud of dreams."

"And you gave it up for my father," I said with a touch of bitterness.

"It wasn't like that. I didn't give it up. I replaced it with something of greater value. Your father and I shared a love that was beyond description. Beyond any words in the English language. I was happy – truly happy. And then I discovered my and your father's love had created you. The joy I felt was overwhelming. And then all that multiplied a million time over when I held you in my arms for the very first time. I couldn't believe how lucky I was to have more than I'd ever dreamed about having."

But he left you, I managed to keep myself from saying.

"Unfortunately, your father didn't feel the same way I felt. He didn't want the responsibility of being tied down with a wife and baby. He was more of a free spirit who needed to soar high with his freedom. Much like the eagles."

Eagles mate for life. They share the responsibility of keeping each other safe along with rearing their young. I wanted to tell Mother, but I didn't.

"I could have kept him with me. I could have clipped his wings and made him support me and our baby, but he would have resented me for tying him down. In time I'm sure he would have come to hate me, blamed his unhappiness on me and perhaps even on you. I couldn't allow that to happen. I told him to leave because I could make it on my own. I also assured him if he ever wanted to return, I would be waiting right here for him."

"He never returned," I said a bit more hateful than I intended.

"No, he never returned. To this day I don't know where he went or what happened to him."

"Did you ever try to find out?"

"No, I never wanted to know the truth."

"Why not?"

"I was afraid of what the truth might be. I didn't want to find out that he found another woman to love. Other children to be a father to."

"But you never divorced."

"We never got an official divorce, but a piece of paper mattered little to him. Truthfully, it mattered little to me. The love I had for your father could not be erased by signing our names on a piece of paper. I was his wife, and he was my husband from the moment we met. Nothing has changed that."

I wanted to argue with her. Tell her she had wasted her love, her life, on a man who didn't deserve the time of day from her. Surely, she knew the kind of man it took to be willing to walk out on his wife and baby without ever knowing what happened to them.

"Don't hate him," she told me in her loving voice. "If anything, feel sorry for him. He was never able to share the kind of love and happiness I have known."

For the first time ever, I realized what huge blinders Mother had worn all these years. Surely, she realized how difficult his desertion had made her life. How hard my life had been. There for a few minutes I was tempted to tell her how I had allowed a strange man to help a child of twelve steal enough money to keep her alive and to continue doing it for five long, sad years. Did she truly not realize money that kept a roof over our heads, the electric, heat, water, and phone bills paid, and the restaurant from going under didn't fall like mana from heaven?

She smiled that dreamy smile of hers as her eyes glazed over as though she was seeing something I couldn't see.

"He didn't desert us the way Mary claims. He has always watched over us. I know he suffered greatly for leaving and has tried his best to make up for it. He was the kind of man who never wanted credit for what he did. I knew he was the one who was paying our bills after I got cancer and could no longer do it for myself. I didn't tell you or Mary how he paid off the mortgage on our house, the loan on the van, along with all the bills the restaurant incurred. He didn't desert us in our time of need. He saved us, Millie. My husband, your father saved us."

Perhaps it was the shock of what she'd just said that kept me from screaming. Or maybe it was the fact that I couldn't take away her last spark of hope that the no-account man she married wasn't worth a snap of her fingers. Mostly, it was the realization that her only child could not destroy her dream of a love that never existed. Her unrealistic scenario was her way of having her last dance with the man she loved. What right did I have to take that away from a dying woman?

Mother wanted pizza. It was something the restaurant didn't serve, and I knew she hadn't indulged in eating it for years. We ordered takeout pizza from the same place Sensei York always went to. Never did he suggest I take leftovers home. I knew he took what we didn't eat to his sister.

Mother insisted on paying. Sadness filled me as I watched her take out her worn billfold from her purse and count out the one-dollar bills along with the exact change the pizza cost. My heart broke and shattered into pieces as I realized how my mother's life would end. I certainly didn't want that for myself, and I didn't think Mother wanted such a life for me either.

For a few moments, I wanted to tell her about what happened between me and Sensei York. I wanted to ask her about love, passion and even lust. Ask her for the mother daughter *talk* she never had with me. What she'd just told me wiped away the validity of any advice she might have given me. I had no intention of spending the rest of my life pretending I had a love that didn't exist. I knew without a doubt that Sensei York wasn't in love with me. He did have the passion. He did have the lust. And so did I. That was all. I feared it was all there would ever be.

*

Mother's determination to stay alive faded after my graduation. The dark circles that haunted Mother's eyes became darker as her eyes sunk deeper into a colorless face. The unseeing glaze was now a continuous stare. It was as though her mind had gone to a place neither Aunt Mary nor I could reach. She stopped eating and drinking unless I spooned food into her mouth and held the cup to her lips.

"Drink, Mother - eat Mother became phrases I continuously uttered. There was pain in every move she made as the mother I had once known faded to a skeleton of non-existence. I sat on the edge of the bed as I watched her lay there propped up by pillows. The wig was gone. The makeup was only a memory. My mother was gone although she drew in enough breaths to keep her heart beating.

Suddenly, without warning, her eyes cleared, and she looked me in the eyes.

"I don't have much longer," she said. "I've fought leaving you, but it's inevitable. It's happening many years sooner than I planned. Put the house up for sale the day you have me cremated. Keep my ashes near so you'll know I'll always be with you. Promise me you won't stay here for Mary's sake. I won't leave until you promise you'll move on without Mary and her leaching ways. My will is in my purse. My lawyer has a copy," she added.

"I'll do exactly as you say. You have my promise." There was no way I would allow Aunt Mary to weigh me down once Mother was gone. It was time Aunt Mary lived her own life just as it was time for me to live mine.

"You've always been my pride and joy."

I held her hand in mine as she managed to draw in a shaky breath in order to utter her last words.

"When you meet your father, tell him I never stopped loving him."

If I ever met my father, I would kick him in the balls so hard his private would stick out of his mouth.

Mother had no idea what I thought. She had left me alone sitting on the side of her bed as she wasted her last breath on a man who had not deserved her.

*

Aunt Mary was relieved that Mother wanted to be cremated instead of wanting a more expensive burial. We even opted out of a memorial service. Our devastating loss was ours alone. Neither Aunt Mary nor I had need to share it with anyone else.

That was to anyone else other than Jimbo. Wednesday after Mother's cremation I found Jimbo sitting on the bench waiting for me.

"It's over," he said as he took my hand in his.

"It's over," I repeated. "How did you know?"

"Newspapers have obituaries," he told me.

I hadn't thought of that, but then few people knew Mother.

"Are you going to attend college?" he surprised me by asking.

"Maybe later."

"You have enough for college in your bank account, not to mention what I've put into your savings account."

"There wasn't enough to keep Mother alive."

"All the money in the world can't keep a person alive when God decides it's their time to leave."

I knew that, but it didn't ease the hurt I felt. "Mother left a will. Aunt Mary is furious."

"Why? Did she get left out?"

"No. She got the restaurant and the van free and clear. I got the house."

"Then why is your Aunt furious?"

"She wants the house along with me working the rest of my life in what's now her restaurant."

"Are you going to relent to either?"

"No."

"Good girl. It's time for the fledging bird to fly away."

"Then you agree with what mother did."

"I certainly do."

"I'm putting the house up for sale."

"Do you know the value of it? I wouldn't want you to get cheated. I know a good real estate appraiser. I'll have him get in contact with you."

"Thank you. It would make me feel better. Can I impose further on you?"

"You never have and never will impose on me. What do you need?"

"Could you find me a good used car. Since Aunt Mary got the van, I have nothing to drive."

"Will do." And then he surprised me by saying, "Are you still attending karate class?"

"Not since Mother died."

"Does Lee know why you missed classes?"

"Only if he read the obituaries." But then he wouldn't know even if he did read them. To him I was Alona Georgetta Anderson instead of Millie James, the surviving daughter of Doris James.

*

Ten days later I had an offer on the house at the appraisal price Jimbo's friend set as its value. There was little of value inside the house. What little furniture was next to worthless. I planned on taking what little belonged to me along with Mother's vase of ashes and start driving. Jimbo had found me a used 1988 Mercedes SEL at a reasonable price.

"It has some years on it, but it's still the best car that was ever made," he told me. "I'd feel better if you were driving a dependable vehicle," he said as he patted me on the head like I was still a twelve-year-old girl. "I envy you. You've got your entire life ahead of you."

"And I've still got you," I said suddenly without intending too.

He kind of grinned. "You'll always have me – an old faker who no longer has tricks of trade to teach a little girl."

"You've been my salvation," I told him.

"You've been your own salvation."

"Why?" I suddenly asked, surprising even me.

"Why what?"

"Why did you do all you've done for me?"

He didn't miss a beat. "You were the only good thing I ever had in my life. The only innocent thing until I started corrupting you. Looking back, I should have helped you without involving you, but I thought I could teach you something you could resort to using if I was no longer around."

"I don't know what would have happened without you," I told him.

"Water under the bridge. I hope I didn't corrupt you too badly."

"I prefer to think I'm not corrupted."

"I prefer to think I've aided you in learning two survival skills if the need ever arises. Self-defense and tricks of trade."

He reached out and for the first time ever gave me a hug. Much to my shock, his body felt as weak and bony as my mother's had. A feeling of fear came over me, but I dared not admit it.

I left the little park feeling like the world I had always known was coming to an end. It was all I could do not to cry as I walked back to my mother's house. Tomorrow I would meet with a real estate attorney who would handle the closing of Mother's house. Afterwards, I planned on getting in the car and driving away, going wherever the road took me.

A man who looked to be in his mid-fifties got out of a beat-up looking car as I walked up the driveway. He caught up with me before I could unlock the front door.

"Millie James?" he questioned.

"I am. Who are you?"

"I'm your father," he said.

The unexpected shock of what he'd just said enabled me to react the way I had threatened. My sharp-toed shoe hit him in his jewels with everything my sensei had taught me to deliver. I stood there watching as he doubled over, hit the ground, moaned, rolled, and puked over and over again. After too short a time, the puking and moaning eased up and his body shakily got to his knees. I considered another front kick to his chin. I wanted nothing more than to break both of his jaw bones.

He shakily pulled a cell phone from his pocket and pushed buttons. "Send the police and an ambulance," he muttered my address. "I've been attacked."

"Attacked nothing. I've got a notion to kill you right where you're squatting," I told him through gritted teeth.

"Why?" he moaned.

"Because you're a no-good dribble of pond scum. You're no more my father than that rock over there. You're a shyster trying to take advantage of me. When the police arrive, I'll have you arrested for attempted assault. If you're not put in jail, I'll finish you off."

"You're crazy," he said, and puked a little more as he tried to stand and failed. "I'm still married to Doris James."

Those were more powerful fighting words than him claiming to be my father. His body moved as I kicked. I got him in the shoulder instead of his chin. He screamed as his arm hung useless. The sound of police sirens kept me from serving him with another kick.

Two police cars pulled in front of the house and stopped. Four men got out with guns at ready. The boldest one walked up to me after he decided it was safe to do so.

"What happened here?" he asked.

"This man attacked me as I was unlocking the door," I told him.

"That's a lie," he moaned as he got enough breath to talk. "I never attacked her. I'm her father."

If I hadn't been surrounded by officers, I would have knocked his lying teeth down his throat.

"You're claiming this little woman did this to a grown man your size?" The brave officer questioned.

"It was a surprise attack?" he moaned as the ambulance siren sounded in the distance.

One of the officers came up to us as the others held back. "I know her," he said. "My brother takes karate lessons with her. He says she's a tough one. Appears he chose the wrong girl to attack."

The first officer looked at me and I nodded. "It was self-defense. I kicked him where it would hurt when he grabbed hold of my arm."

"You kicked high enough to break his arm?" the officer questioned.

"Got him in the arm as he went down. Got him in his jewels with the first kick."

"You did this by kicking him twice?"

"It was all it took to disable him."

"Yet, he was the one to call 911?"

"He wanted protection."

I saw the officers trying not to laugh at my words.

"Let's get him to the ambulance. One of you can get his statement of what happened. I'll get Miss James' statement.

*

The closing of the house didn't occur the next day because Timmons James claimed he now owned my mother's house since he was still married to my mother. He also wanted me arrested for attacking him without what he claimed to have been without provocation.

I had to hire an attorney to represent me. Fortunately, the judge was sympathetic to a young girl who claimed she was defending herself from what she thought was a stranger attacking her.

His attorney claimed I was a dangerous person who should not be allowed to walk the streets. His mistake was trying to convince the judge that I was a trained deadly weapon, which the judge thought was a ridiculous statement about a hundred- and five-pound girl.

However, he and I both had to have a DNA test to prove he was or was not my father. He claimed everything mother left behind, including the house, van, and restaurant now belonged to him since he was Mother's legal husband.

Aunt Mary was beside herself to put it mildly. Fortunately, she was allowed to continue running the restaurant until the lawsuit against Mother's estate was settled.

"He can't do this to us," I told my attorney.

"Unfortunately, at this time, he can. As the old saying goes, a person is allowed to sue a ham sandwich, but it doesn't mean he will be able to eat it. However, we must go through the proper procedures to prove our case."

I had to spend more money to pay for the attorney and living expenses. Fortunately, all the publicity was drawing curiosity seekers to eat at the restaurant enabling Aunt Mary to pay her own bills.

"Don't draw money out of your account," Jimbo advised me. "I'm going to pay for your attorney as well as your living expenses. I don't want to take a chance on this so-called Timmons James to claim any money you have." He shook his head. "Unfortunately, your mother never filed for a divorce or claimed desertion."

"He did desert her after I was born."

"I'm sure a judge and jury will take that into consideration," Jimbo assured me.

"He's claiming he has the right to move into my mother's house. Not only that, he's suing me for a dislocated shoulder and kicked balls."

"Knew karate would come in handy," Jimbo said.

"I should have kicked him in the Adams Apple. A man like him doesn't deserve the air he breathes," I said with anger.

"I agree with you on that. I'm assuming he discovered your mother's death from her obituary. That could also mean he was keeping track of your mother. Wonder what kind of life he's led for the past nineteen years? I know a private investigator who could dig up dirt on the pope. I'll have him check things out."

"I owe you," I told Jimbo.

"I'm the one who owes you. You've kept me from dying from boredom during my old age."

I wasn't sure that was a compliment.

*

I couldn't believe the judge agreed that such a man had the right to move into what was now my house.

"Mother left a will," I told my attorney. "Doesn't it mean anything?"

"It certainly does. Also, the fact that it was your mother who bought the house and restaurant and made all the payments count."

"Then why does he have the right to move into what's now my house?"

"His attorney is pulling every trick of the law."

Suddenly an idea hit me. "Does it mean I can't still live there, or that I can't move my friends in?"

"You can certainly remain in the home you now own. I'm not sure about your friends, but he would have to take a lawsuit against you to prevent you from allowing anyone else to live there."

That was all I needed to know. That evening I attended my first karate class since Mother's death, but I didn't wear my gee. Sensei York took me straight into his office before he begin class.

"You owe me a long explanation," he said.

"It's a long story."

"Your real name isn't Alona Anderson. Begin there."

"My grandfather gave me that name so he could put money into a bank account for me without my mother and aunt knowing."

"He's not your real grandfather. I checked it out."

"He's the only grandfather I've ever known. I met him when I was twelve."

"Why would he put money in your account using a fake name?"

I had no intention of telling him about the tricks of trade. "Mother was dying of cancer. It was his way of helping pay her bills without anyone knowing."

"Why would he do that?"

"It was what he wanted to do."

"Doesn't make sense."

"It never made sense to me either, but you could say we connected with each other."

"You're not wearing a gee," he pointed out suddenly.

"I didn't come to work out."

He looked concerned. "Then why are you here?"

I told him about Mother's death, the pending sell of the house, and about the man who showed up claiming to be my father and suing me for everything my mother left behind.

"No shit," he said in surprise.

"No shit," I repeated. "He's now moving into Mother's house with me."

His eyebrows raised. "Not good," he said. "Sounds like he plans on putting you through hell."

"Feels like it too."

He frowned again. "Why are you here?"

"I want to see if the Hulk and Weezie would be willing to live in my house for a while."

"While this so-called entitled man is there?"

"Right."

Sensei York nodded. "Let me put the idea to them. I'd move in myself if it wasn't for my little sister."

"I know," I said.

"You don't know the half of it," he said. "When you didn't show up . . . Never mind," he added quickly as he stood up and went to the door to the dojo. "Hulk, Weezie come in the office for a minute."

I sat there as Sensei York laid out my story for Hulk and Weezie.

"You're not shittin' us?" Hulk said to me.

"No, you know I'm not."

"We'll take him out," Weezie said.

"No, you won't," Sensei York told them. "You'll both move in the house and give the man hell. Looking at the two of you ought to scare the hell out of him."

"Thanks," both men said at the same time. It was obvious they took his words as a compliment.

"You'll also offer protection for Alona. Also known as Millie."

"Who?" Weezie questioned.

"Alona is her nickname like Weezie and Hulk are yours."

Weezie shrugged. "Right."

"What do we get out of it?" Hulk asked.

"Free rent from Alona. Free karate classes from me as long as you're staying in her house.

"I'm in," Weezie said.

"Me too," Hulk agreed reluctantly. "Do I get to beat the shit out of the man?"

"Only Alona is allowed to do that," Sensei York told them and then added "Again."

"Again?" Weezie questioned.

"She busted his balls," Sensei York told them.

"Glad mine's not the only pair she got at," Hulk said.

*

Hulk and Weezie arrived before Timmons did. It took them only minutes to haul their backpacks into Mother's bedroom claiming the area for themselves. That left the living room couch and my bedroom. I wasn't about to give up my bedroom. I didn't think he would try putting Hulk or Weezie out of Mother's bedroom.

His attorney had succeeded in getting the judge to give him the keys to my house. He unlocked the door and entered the house like he owned the place with a suitcase in his uninjured hand. I took great delight when Hulk and Weezie walked out of the bedroom.

"Who's this bitch?" Weezie asked as though he didn't already know.

"Beats the hell out of me," Hulk said. "Let's have a little fun out of him," he grinned in anticipation. "I get the first go."

"I'm going to call the police," Timmons said to me.

"Go ahead. Since I can't finish the sale of the house, I'm forced to rent it to these two friends. My attorney made sure it was legal with a signed lease and all."

"But . . ." he began.

"Butt," Weezie grinned from ear to ear. "He's got a cute enough butt. You said you wanted to take a go at it first, or do you want me to loosen it up a bit?"

"You're not getting away with this," he told me as he took out his phone and punched 911. "I'm being sexually threatened by two crazy men. Can you send law enforcement to . . ." he continued to give my address and then called his attorney and asked him to come to my home.

Both Hulk and Weezie crossed their arms, leaned against the wall, and waited with anticipation. Minutes later there was a knock on the door. Timmons answered it before I could.

"There they are. Arrest them for threatening my safety," he demanded of the officer I recognized from before.

"What's going on here?" Another officer asked me.

"This stranger claims he has the right to move into my house. I think finding my renters here has scared him."

"Does he have the right to move in?" The officer asked.

"I do. The judge acknowledged it."

"Is that true?" the officer asked me.

"I believe it is. However, he'll have to sleep on the couch since I've already rented the only other bedroom out to these two men."

"According to his 911 call, he claimed he'd being sexually threatened."

"By whom?" I asked.

"By both of those gay men," he claimed as he pointed at both men.

The first officer let out a snort. "Jack there is my brother. I know for a fact he's not gay. I also know he's friends with Millie. They take karate with each other."

The second officer turned to Timmons. "What else are you claiming happened to warrant a second call to 911?"

"I'm claiming a right to this house, and I don't want them here."

At that time, his attorney stepped through the open door. "What's going on here?" he questioned.

This first officer held up his hand to silence Timmons when he started with his spill. "Who are you?" he questioned the attorney.

"I'm Mr. James' attorney."

"In that case, you and your client will need to step out of the house to brief each other on matters of the law," the Hulk said. As a practicing attorney myself, you're not allowed to come into contact with Miss James without her attorney present."

It was all I could do to keep my mouth from dropping open. Never would I have guessed the Hulk was an attorney. I wasn't sure he was telling the truth.

"You're a real estate attorney," Weezie whispered.

"I still know the law," the Hulk whispered back.

Anger flashed over Timmons' attorney's face as he took his client outside.

The two officers looked at each other contemplating what they should do.

"I was here. I can testify that stranger was never threatened sexually or any other way by these two men. He was simply in a rage because he'll have to sleep on the couch instead of the only other bedroom."

"Good enough," the officer who wasn't Weezie's brother said. "I think we can leave now."

A few minutes after the officers left, Timmons came back inside without his attorney. "Your little ploy isn't going to run me off," he told me. "As Doris' husband and your father, I have a right to this house and the restaurant."

It was then that Aunt Mary arrived. She marched in the open door in what had become her normal tizzy.

"Well, well," Timmons said. The crazy sister has joined us."

"I had to get a look at you for myself. You're still the slimeball poor Doris was foolish enough to take up with," Aunt Mary said as her hands went to her hips.

I felt my heart fall to my feet. This was the first time Aunt Mary hadn't kept herself in hiding at the restaurant. It was the first time she had come face to face with this man since he'd shown up. If she recognized him, then what he claimed was true.

"How dare you show up after Doris died? You were and still are nothing but a no-account opportunist. If you think you're going to benefit by Doris' death, you're badly mistaken."

"Still all bluster and stupidity," he said. "Get out of my house."

"You get out. If you don't, I'll turn over Doris' diary to the police."

"What diary?" I asked Aunt Mary.

"The one I found after her death. She documented everything this man was into that was against the law."

Timmons laughed. "Nice try, crazy Mary, but you can't pull a bluff on me."

Much to my surprise and amazement, Aunt Mary swung a right hook that was powerful enough to bloody Timmons' nose. He swung at her, but Weezie was fast enough to block his swing.

"I do declare, old man. You'll have to be more careful. All four of us saw you fall down and hit your nose on your suitcase," Hulk said with the kind of grin only he could deliver.

Timmons cursed as he opened doors to find which one led to the bathroom.

I hugged Aunt Mary. I was prouder of her than I'd ever been.

"Are you really a real estate attorney?" I asked the Hulk after I turned Aunt Mary loose.

"Thought everybody knew that" he said.

"I didn't."

"You do now," he gave what was close to a normal grin.

"Who are these two people?" Aunt Mary asked.

"Two men I take karate with."

"I do declare. Why are they here?"

"They've rented the house for as long as *he's* here," I told her.

"Well, well. Looks like all that time you wasted has come in handy."

*

If all the craziness wasn't enough, I was woken up by a knock on the door the next morning before it was good and daylight. I stumbled to the door trying not to trip over the open suitcase Timmons had left in the middle of the floor. I pulled the door open to another surprise. Jimbo was standing there. He looked past me to the suitcase in the floor and Timmons sleeping on the couch.

"What are you doing here?" I asked in astonishment as Timmons' raised his head to look at Jimbo.

"Go back to bed. I've got this under control," he said as he entered the room and looked down on Timmons.

"What's this about?" I asked.

"You're going back to bed. You'll be surprised when you wake up in another hour to find that Timmons and his luggage are gone. He's decided to disappear similar to the way he did nineteen years ago. He never bothered your mother during that time, and he'll never bother you again."

"What the hell?" he demanded as he sat up in defiance.

It was then two burley men entered the room. One grabbed hold of Timmons and the other stuffed his clothes back into the suitcase, closed it and carried it out the door. The other man dragged Timmons out.

"What's going on?" I demanded of Jimbo.

"The private investigator uncovered a few things. You'll never be bothered by him again," Jimbo repeated.

"But. . ." I began.

"Remember, you woke up and found him gone," as he went out the door without further explanation. Did he really think I could go back to bed after this?

Two hours later Hulk and Weezie made their sluggish way into the kitchen.

"I smell coffee," the Hulk said.

"I want bacon and eggs," Weezie announced.

"Where's he at?" the Hulk asked as he looked at the couch with only a pillow and blanket on it.

"I haven't the foggiest idea. When I got up a few minutes ago, he was gone." Both statements were true.

"No shit," Weezie said. "Does that mean we can't stay for breakfast?"

"I'll be delighted to cook you all the breakfast you can eat," I told them.

After the two men left, it dawned on me that it was Wednesday. I cleaned the kitchen and removed every sign that Timmons had been there. I was bidding my time to go by the little park to confront Jimbo when the phone rang.

I answered it to discover it was from my attorney.

"We have the results from your DNA tests," my attorney informed me. "I know you are anxious to get the results."

"Yes, I am," I managed to say as I prepared myself. Aunt Mary had already recognized him. I didn't need confirmation on what the DNA tests were about to tell me.

"Are you sitting down. If not, I suggest you do so."

I took his advice and sat down.

"Your DNAs showed to be similar, showing a close kindship. However, it was not close enough for him to be your father. It did show that he was likely your father's twin brother."

"Say that again."

"The DNA showed that this man was likely your father's twin brother. His DNA was close to yours, but he is definitely not your father."

"Are you sure?" I had to ask.

"According to the information I received."

"Thank you," I managed to say. I hung up the phone and sank my face into my hands. The relief I felt was overwhelming, and yet this man was my father's twin. That was as close to being my father as a person could get. I wondered if Mother knew about him. If she did, why hadn't she told me. Obviously, Aunt Mary didn't know either.

It was hours before I was able to stand on my two feet and make my way to the little park.

"I expected you sooner than this," he told me as I sat down beside him.

"Why didn't you tell me?" I demanded to know.

"Didn't have proof earlier today," he said, knowing exactly what I was talking about.

"Where is he?"

"Don't know. His uhh friends took him away."

"Away to where?"

"Don't know. Got an idea his uhh friends will keep him from coming back."

"Did you find out anything about my real father?"

"Not a thing."

"Is he dead?"

"Don't know. The investigator found no trace of him after he left your mother."

"Could he have changed his name? Married another woman and maybe even had more children?"

"Anything is possible."

I wasn't sure if I was relieved or disappointed. There was no question I was glad that awful man was my uncle instead of my father and that he was gone to wherever. Mother couldn't possibly have loved such a man for all these years. Now, I knew for a fact there could be an evil twin along with an eviler twin.

Chapter 14

*

Once my attorney got everything settled, I was legally able to finish the closing on the sale of my mother's house. When Aunt Mary found out I was selling the house she was beside herself.

"Doris wanted me to have the house," she kept ranting at me. "She didn't want me to live in that small apartment above the restaurant forever. I should have known you would try to sell the house from under me. You have no appreciation of how I've sacrificed for my sickly sister all the years not to mention all I have done for you. I gave up my entire life for the two of you and look at what kind of thanks I'm getting."

"Mother left you the restaurant and the van," I told her as calmly as I could manage. I hadn't expected her to turn on me the way she was doing. "Mother left me the house because that was what she wanted."

"Doris wasn't in her right mind when she made out her will and you know it," Aunt Mary declared.

Her words about Mother not being in her right mind stunned me. If that was what she believed, why did she wait until now to go on such a rampage? I had always known Aunt Mary was the selfish type, but I didn't think she would claim Mother was not competent enough to make out her own will.

"I'm going to contest her will. You're too young to own anything," she surprised me by saying. "You are the one who should be living in the little apartment. I deserve the house. I'm her sister. I've taken care of her and you all these years," she repeated.

While she confronted me with anger and indignation, it was all I could do to hold back the words I wanted to say to her. After all I had been through to keep both the house and restaurant from being repossessed caused me to want to tell Aunt Mary that she was lucky I was allowing her to keep the restaurant. I wondered if there was any way I could show that I was the one who had a lawful claim on the property that I made payments on, not to mention I was Mother's only child. But Mother had made out her will as she wanted. I would uphold her wishes.

"Have your attorney check with mine," I told her sharply. "I'm not going to fight with you or allow you to bully me into giving you what you want. If you can prove Mother was not competent enough to make a will, then as her daughter and her closest of kin, I will inherit everything, including the restaurant and van."

"As her sister, I'm her closest of kin. I can prove I took care of her all these years. Doris would have wanted me to have everything," she insisted as though I was the one being selfish and unfair.

"Not according to her will," I reminded her again, and made my way to the front door of what was now my house. I opened the door and looked her straight in the eyes. "Now that you've made it clear that you want to cheat me out of what rightfully belongs to me, I suggest you leave."

She stormed out of the house in a huff. "I'll show you," I heard her grumble as she left.

It was all I could do not to slam the door behind her.

I called my attorney and explained the situation to him.

"You're right," he said. "If your aunt contests your mother's will, she will most likely lose. However, she might be able to prolong the sale of your house. I would suggest you go ahead and finish the closure before she finds an attorney to represent her."

I didn't think Aunt Mary had the money to hire an attorney. I knew exactly how much money was in the restaurant's account. I also knew without Mother and me working for free, the restaurant might not survive long.

"What about the lease you signed with the two renters?" My attorney questioned.

"No problem there. We tore up the lease."

"Good. Then I see no problem with you closing on the sale if that is what you choose to do."

"It is," I told him.

When I hung up the phone, I made my way to the little park in hopes Jimbo would be there. He was. I noticed his surprise at seeing me.

"What has upset you?" he asked as though he knew something had to be wrong.

I told him about Aunt Mary and my conversation with my attorney.

"Like I always say, people can sue, but that doesn't mean they will win their suit. She might have a slight claim of taking care of your mother during her cancer treatments."

"But she didn't," I was quick to tell him. "As you already know, I took care of Mother. Mother owned the restaurant. It's in her name. She and I worked there since I was able to hold a broom and dishcloth in my hands."

He nodded in understanding. "You want my advice, then I'll tell you the same thing I told you the last time you were here. Close on the house right away. She can't sue you over something that is no longer available, but she might be able to stop you from using money from the sale until a judgement is made. You have valid identification showing you are Alona Georgette Anderson. I suggest you leave here as Millie James and start using Alona Anderson's name once you're gone. Of course, Lee York and the other karate students knows you as Alona but that shouldn't be a problem."

"He knows me as Millie James too." I pointed out.

"Right, but I'll have a word with him. He'll make sure neither he nor his students will ever tell."

"Weezie's brother knows of me," I pointed out.

"I'll take care of things if something arises. If it does, you'll be long gone."

I don't know why I said what I did, but I opened my mouth and blurted out. "Go with me. I don't want to leave behind the only grandfather I've ever known."

He looked shocked for a moment before he regained his composure. "My dear child, that is by far the nicest thing anyone has ever said to me. Unfortunately, I'm not allowed to go anywhere. Have you forgotten I'm under the witness protection program? My real name isn't Jimbo."

"James Boden," I told him.

"It's not that either. Besides, I don't want to take off. I'm content to stay right where I'm at until . . . well, until I move on the way your mother has."

"If I leave, I might never see you again."

"That's just as it should be. Every little bird must spread their wings and leave their nest. Otherwise, they'll never be able to make a life of their own. You don't want to be working the rest of your life for your aunt, do you?"

He was right about that.

"Again, my advice is to sell your house. Stash the cash in a large money belt worn under bulky clothes and leave here. Once you've settled somewhere open another account in the name I've given you and transfer your checking and savings account into it."

He handed me a folder with my bank statements in it. Then he surprised me by reaching out and hugging me close to his bony body for several moments.

"Go now," he said as he turned me loose.

"I'll come back after the closing to make sure you haven't changed you mind about leaving with me."

"No need. I've just pushed you out of the nest baby bird. Go fly away."

*

After the house closing, I did exactly as Jimbo told me. I bought two large money belts. Stuffed both of them to the limit with hundred-dollar bills and then duct taped them to my stomach. Once all that cash was secured to my satisfaction, I looked fat if not in the family way. I didn't say scat to Aunt Mary. I drove my car to the little park. The bench was vacant.

I knew it would be a long time before I returned, if ever.

"Good-by, Grandpa," I whispered, and drove away.

It was time for the karate students to be in the dojo warming up. I made one last stop at the dojo long enough to thank the Hulk and Weezie for what they did for me.

"Why aren't you working out?" the Hulk wanted to know.

"I'm moving," I told him. "The sale of Mother's house was finalized today."

"Where are you going to live? Will you have two bedrooms," Weezie asked. "I'll agree to be your roommate permanently. You cook a good breakfast."

"When you find a place to buy, I'll handle your transaction for free," the Hulk told me before I could respond to Weezie.

I was touched by both of their offers. Sensei York came out of his office. He put his hand on my back and guided me into his office.

"About what happened between us," he began.

I hurriedly put my hand over his mouth. I didn't want to hear what he had to say.

"It's okay," I told him. "What happened is my treasure to hold close to my heart forever. If I allow myself to think about it, I'll never be able to leave, and I know I can no longer stay here without my mother."

He surprised me by taking me into his arms and kissing me with the same fire and passion as he had that night. For a few moments I responded with equal fire and passion before I pulled away from the arms that were holding me.

"I can't stay even though you're make me want to," I told him.

"Wonderful has never lasted long where I'm concerned. I'll be right here if you change your mind."

I rubbed my hand over the beard stubble on his handsome face. If he took me in his arms again, I didn't know if I would be able to walk out the door. He didn't.

I left the dojo with tears in my eyes.

*

Morning found me in a hotel room two hundred miles from the place I once called home. I was traveling with a few valued trinkets, my clothes, and my mother's ashes. I didn't know where I was going. I only knew I was traveling south hoping I would arrive at a place where I felt I belonged. Regardless of where I landed, I knew I was on the greatest adventure of my life.

What Jimbo had put in Alona Georgette Anderson's checking and savings account stunned me. I had more money than I ever dreamed about. It would be enough to last me for a long time if I was frugal, but it wouldn't last forever. Nether would the money I had in the money belts. I didn't plan on spending a penny of that money. I was going to use it to buy myself a house once I found where I belonged. It was what Mother would have wanted me to do.

I'd have to settle somewhere and find a good paying job. In the meantime, I wanted to find out more about what I actually wanted to accomplish with the remainder of my life. I knew one thing for certain. I didn't want to end up like my mother by spending my life grieving over a man who was lost to me. I had an idea that was exactly what I would have gotten if I'd stayed so I could be with Sensei York. There was fire and there was passion between us, but there had not been what I imagined true love should feel like.

Until I found that kind of love, I would keep my freedom.

*

I was beginning to think I would never find a hotel that looked safe and open. I knew nothing about hotels as I'd never stayed in one. When I did find one, the price I had been quoted was shocking, but I was exhausted and afraid I might run out of gas on the side of some road if I continued to drive without a destination. I had stopped at a fairly decent hotel being it was one o'clock in the morning.

I woke up at five o'clock that morning and took a quick shower and dressed before I put my suitcase and mother's ashes back to my car. Having Mother's ashes in the room with me made me feel less alone but filled me with sadness. She said she'd always be with me, and her ashes were the closest I could come to having her physically present. I took the hotel key to the office to get my five-dollar key deposit back. I had no intention of wasting money regardless of how much was in my accounts. Being desperate for money was something I never wanted to go through again. People who said money wasn't everything had never been known desperation.

I discovered the hotel offered a free continental breakfast. I ate as much as I could possibly hold, hoping it would keep me from getting hungry for a long while. I slipped an apple, a banana, and an orange in my pocket. At the price I had paid for half a night's sleep, I had over-paid for the fruit. I got in my car and drove to a service station, went inside and left money for a deposit on gas. I had money coming back from the deposit. When I went back after it, I bought an atlas map showing all the states. Looking at it made me feel like a tiny speck in a huge world. A speck that was all alone and lonely.

A sudden spell of homesickness came over me bringing tears to my eyes. I wanted my mother. I wanted to go back home. But I no longer had a home. I no longer had Mother. What I had of her was sitting in the passenger seat.

You jumped out of the nest. I thought I heard Mother's voice. *Continue on, my darling. You're doing the right thing. Fly carefully and land safely.*

I wiped the tears from my eyes and continued on. I pulled into the first shopping center I came to, parked, peeled an orange, and ate it as I scanned the map. The fact that I could take any road I wanted scared me. At the same time, it also excited me. I didn't want to go north. That was the direction I was driving away from. That left south, east, and west. I looked down at the orange peel. South, I thought. I had always wanted to know what it was like to live in a warm place – a sub-tropical place where it never froze solid during a long cold winter. A place where oranges grew. I wondered if the entire state of Florida would smell like the orange peelings lying next to Mother's urn.

I ran my finger over the roads that led south, got a pen and paper from my purse, and wrote the road numbers down that I was supposed to take. Finally, I had a direction to be driving in. I drove until I stopped for gas, ate the banana, and drove on. The sun was setting when I stopped to fill up again with gas. I ate the apple and debated how much further I wanted to drive. I had started out early and drove all day long. Did I want to drive on into the night like I did last night? I preferred to drive during daylight so I could see the places I was driving through. Who knows, I just might find the place I was searching for before I reached the state of Florida.

I stopped at a fast-food drive-through and ordered a cheeseburger, fries, and cup of water. They charged me ten cents for water. I wouldn't make that mistake again. The next time I stopped for gas, I would buy water and a large drink along with enough junk food to keep me going.

Twilight was settling in by the time I found a motel that advertised a low price. I checked in, drove around the building to the room number I'd been given, parked, got my mother, the map, along with the supply of junk food and went inside.

I checked the map to figure out exactly where I was at. It was a little town near Savannah Georgia. I had spent most of the day traveling through South Carolina without paying much attention to what state I was in. I had been in a somewhat state of coma brought on by fear and confusion.

"Good going," I sarcastically said out loud. "You should pay more attention to where you're at. You could get lost." I laughed at myself. How could I get lost if I didn't know where I was going? I scanned the map – wrote down road numbers again and what places they would take me through. It suddenly dawned on me that I needed a cell phone. A lot of the girls I went to school with had their own cell phones. I never got one because of the cost, even when Jimbo had put extra money in my account. A phone might be a good idea since I was traveling alone. I could at least call a garage if my car broke down. Plus, it might keep me from feeling helpless and less alone to know I was able to call someone. Why hadn't I asked Jimbo if he had a phone? I could have talked to him.

Tears came to my eyes. I wiped them away, got in the shower that night instead of waiting until morning and went to bed early. My plan was to leave at the crack of dawn. I would stop somewhere and buy myself a cell phone when the shops opened.

*

Georgia, the land of pine trees, turpentine, and peat swamps. It appeared to be a never-ending roadside view for miles upon miles. Occasionally there would be smoke rising from where the peat bogs had caught on fire. I was fascinated and wanted to learn a lot more about those fires and pine swamps. Seemed to me that the water in the swamps would put out the fires, but it evidently hadn't.

I was in Florida by the time ten o'clock arrived. I pulled into the first mall I came to. An hour and a half later, I had a cell phone – with no one to call. At least I was able to get some information on it, which would be a help if not some sort of company.

I had debated if I wanted to travel the east coast of Florida toward Miami or the west coast toward Naples. I had read about Ocala and horse farms on the west coast. I thought I might like going through horse country. Plus, I preferred a small place to a large city like Miami.

The next time I stopped for gas, I could smell the difference in the air. There was a salty crispness to it. Black colored birds that I'd never seen before squawked loudly as they flew about the gas station parking lot searching for food. Even a few sea gulls were flying about. Most of all, I noticed things were green with a profusion of flowers in full bloom along with different kinds of trees. I was fascinated.

I bought more snacks and drove on.

I ended up getting on interstate 40, with people driving way above the speed limit, going faster than I had ever driven. Much to my amazement, most of the speeders had gray hair with a touch of blue added. I instantly thought of the song "Blue Hairs Driving in My Lane." Interstate 40 took me to an exit that read Naples. I remembered seeing the name on the map and took an exit leading to it. I was surprised at how well maintained everything was. There was mown grass everywhere, even in the median and beside the highways. Many of the places had sprinklers on. All types of flowers were blooming in profusion. There were even vines in different shades of red, pink, orange, purple, and white climbing on buildings and fences. I rolled down my window. Smells, along with a wave of heat, hit me in the face with a strong scent of salty air. I wanted to stop in this place for a while and experience everything that was different from where I grew up.

I stopped at a 7-eleven convenience store and filled my tank again in the ninety-five-degree heat. Went inside and bought a large drink with a lot of ice in it along with a cream cheese filled cake. I asked a woman at check-out where I could find inexpensive lodging for a few days.

She laughed. "Honey, there's nothing inexpensive in Naples. You might find a vacancy off Tamiami Trail about a half mile from here is a trailer park that rents short term if you're not too particular. It's nothing fancy, but it's cheap. It's six hundred dollars a month for a two-room trailer with a bathroom. I think you can rent it for a week for two hundred, or so I've been told. It most likely has a vacancy since this is the off season. The temperature reaches over a hundred degrees later in the day, and it will only get hotter as the days go by. The good part about one-hundred-and-ten-degree heat is it drives the snowbirds back north."

"Snowbirds?" I questioned. I'd never heard the term before.

"Oh, honey, you really aren't from here. Snowbirds are the people who head to warmer climate when it snows up north. Then when the weather gets too hot here, they head back north. You know, like birds do."

"I see what you mean," I told her.

"Soon this entire place is going to be overrun with outsiders all year around," she chuckled mainly to herself. "By the time summer is over most businesses are delighted to have the money the snowbirds bring back with them. How long are you planning to stay in town?"

"I'm not sure. It depends on if I can find a job."

"There's a lot of jobs, but few that pay much unless you can get into real estate or some other kind of high-end marketing. This place is booming in the housing market. There's a big developer who showed up from the Midwest who has developed a lot of land near the beach. He's building condos and high-rises. I've heard each of those high-rise units sell for a million dollars apiece. There's thirty units per high-rise. Talk about raking in the dough. Let me tell you this place sure has changed from the sleepy little fishing village I grew up in."

I was surprised because she didn't look that old.

"This land was once dirt cheap," she continued. "I've been told it was General John S Williams and Walter Haldeman who were the villains slash good guys who turned this place around. It all started in the late 1800s when this Williams guy took a fancy to this quaint little fishing village. He knew right away that he had found paradise. I've got an idea he also thought he'd discovered the fountain of youth when he saw all the beautiful young women who lived here. Anyway, he bought huge acreages of land, over three-thousand acres, and started developing a fancy place for the rich snowbirds to come during the winter months. Things sure do change in a couple of hundred years."

I stood there looking at her and nodding my head like the information she had told me was helpful.

She chuckled. "I knew you wanted me to tell you all that. You see, I'm a native cracker who listened to my grandpa tell stories about the good ole' days."

"I had a grandpa," I told her, grabbed my purchases, and headed out the door.

According to the map I'd looked at earlier, the southern part of Naples was surrounded by the Gulf of Mexico. If I traveled further east, I would drive over a highway that was called Alligator Alley to Miami and the east coast. I decided to find the trailer park and stay for a week, while I decided where else I might go.

I drove through town before I stopped at the trailer park. Two hundred for a week was sure a lot cheaper than what a motel room cost for a couple of nights. There was traffic but not bumper to bumper traffic. I saw Walmart, Lowes Hardware, Marshalls, a mall with Belk's and Pennys and a few other stores listed on the sign. There were also signs pointing to a hospital and another pointing to a school. I saw another building with a sign that read The Clock Diner. It was nearing lunch time and my stomach rumbled at the thought of some good food. I pulled into the parking lot and stopped.

The smell of freshly perked coffee along with the hot greasy smell of frying meat hit me as I walked in the door. It was a reminder of just how hungry I was. A good meal would perk me up. I'd been surviving on junk food for too long.

"Grab yourself a seat." The lady behind the cash register called out to me as she rang up customers. "Someone will be with you shortly."

"Thank you," I said as I looked about. There weren't many tables vacant. I took that as a sign the food was good. I found one next to a window and sat down. A waitress carrying a pitcher of water was refilling glasses.

"Good day," she said as she turned the glass on my table up and filled it with water without me asking. "There's the menu," she said as she pointed to a laminated sheet in a holder next to the salt, pepper, and napkin holder. "Someone will take your order shortly."

I got the menu and looked it over as I waited on the waitress to show up.

"What can I get for you, honey?" a waitress who reminded me of Flo on the television program asked. Her hair was piled on top of her head with several pens stuck in the sloppy, hairnet covered bun. I wasn't sure if the pens helped hold her hair up or if they were for decoration.

I ordered the daily special, which was meatloaf, mashed potatoes, green beans, along with a roll.

"Want coffee? It comes with the meal?"

"Yes, please."

"Coming right up," she said and hurried to the next table to take orders from a couple that had just arrived.

I wasn't disappointed. The food was delicious, the service good, and not too expensive. As I was finishing my meal, an older man was sitting with a younger man at a table not more than four feet across from mine. I could hear every word the older man was saying. The younger man spoke in a softer tone, but I could hear most of what he said.

"This place has good food. A lot of locals eat here."

"At these prices I don't doubt it. This place has no class. Can't believe my own son brought me to a place like this when you know my culinary preferences."

"Thought it would be a new experience for you. It's a franchise. The Clock Diners are scattered throughout the south."

"So is Burger King, but it doesn't mean they are a fit place to eat."

"Stop grumbling. If it's not expensive enough, you can tip the waitress a hundred bucks."

"Depends on if she is Hooter's material. You know I like big boobs and a cushy hind end on my waitresses."

"Since when do you go to Hooter's?"

"I've been to a lot of places you don't know about. Not that I intend to make where I've been public knowledge."

"I'm sure that is a true statement. I brought you here so we could case out the locals. It's a good place for hard working people to eat, and we're looking to find a couple of employees who are willing to work instead of only wanting to draw a paycheck."

"You might have a point," the grumpy man agreed. "Most people eating here look as if they need a job."

How I ever got brave enough to stand up and take the few steps to their table, I don't know. But I did.

"Don't mean to intrude," I told them, feeling my face turn red. "I'm looking for a job," I was quick to add.

The young man looked interested. The older man looked amused.

"Have any kind of job experience?" the young man asked respectfully.

"I've worked in a restaurant since I was ten years old," I told him.

"About six years ago I take it," the older man said with a grin.

"I've not been sixteen for quite a while," I told him.

"What is your name?" the older man asked.

"Alona Anderson." I intended to apply for jobs as Alona Anderson.

"Why aren't you working there now?" the younger man asked.

"My mother died, and I wanted to spread my wings a little."

"Your mother owned the restaurant?" The older man asked.

"She did, but it now belongs to my Aunt."

"Unfortunately, we're into real estate instead of the restaurant business," the older man pointed out. "You might get a job in this restaurant. I'm sure they are always looking for waitstaff. With your looks you should be able to get good tips."

"Oh," I said, not sure if I should take his comment as an insult or a compliment. "Sorry to bother you." I started to walk away.

"Wait a minute," the younger man said. "Would you be willing to start out at minimum wages and work your way up to a better salary as you learn the ropes?"

"I certainly would," I told him.

"Then consider yourself hired," he told me as he handed me a card with his name and address on it.

"Thank you," I said with gratitude, and went back to my seat.

"Hope you don't regret that," the older man told him. "Oh, well, if she can't handle the job, she'll be worth minimum wages just to look at."

"Sorry," the younger man glared at the older man, and then turned to me and said, "You'll soon learn this is my father's normal insulting way of acting. He means nothing by it. Show up to work at seven o'clock sharp in the morning."

"The hell I don't," the older man returned. "I say what I mean and mean what I say."

I forced a wan smile, nodded, and said no more as the waitress bough me my bill. I left a more than reasonable tip and stood up to leave.

"I'll take that," the younger man said as he held out his hand for the bill.

"Oh, no, you don't have to do that," I assured him as I held onto the bill.

"I insist," he told me as he stood up and took the bill from my hand. "Besides, my father is paying," he added as he sat back down.

"You brought me here. You're paying, plus you can be the one leaving a hundred-dollar tip," the older man informed him. "Besides, you might just have hit the jackpot in your new employee. She's young enough not to be set in her ways. Much less expect too much."

"Thank you," I said hesitantly and hurried up to the pay station anyway to let them know I wasn't skipping out on my bill.

"It's okay. I overheard the conversation," the older woman at the cash register told me. "Honey, those two are big in real estate, but you should keep an eye on the old fart. Landon Fitzgearld has a reputation," she whispered. "He's all hands where pretty girls are concerned."

I simply nodded and left. I had no intention of getting close enough to the old man for his hands to touch me. I couldn't believe my good luck. I had a job in real estate as soon as I arrived in town. I got in my car and drove back to the trailer park the 7- eleven lady had told me about. They had a vacancy. I paid for a whole month in cash while telling the man I might stay longer if my job offer worked out.

Chapter 15

*

The sixty-some year-old man who ran the trailer rental place looked me over and shook his head as though I was nothing but an inconvenience to him.

"Young renters don't last long," he said as though I was nothing more than an aggravation to him. "A month. Two months at the most."

"Why don't they last?" I found myself asking from pure curiosity.

"Move on to something better – or worse," he said. "I'll rent to you if you have the money, but if you bring a boyfriend or anybody else in, you're out. Got that?"

"I don't have a boyfriend. Don't want one either," I told him with conviction. "I just arrived. A lady at the 7-eleven told me about this place," I added for good measure.

"If the snowbirds were still here, I wouldn't have a vacancy. Like I just said, I'll rent to you, but if you cause any kind of problem, you're evicted without a refund. Got that?" he continued, ignoring what I had just said.

"Got it," I told him. At least the 7-eleven lady was friendly. This man was overweight, sweating, and grouchy as heck. I took the key attached to a leather fob and went in search of the trailer with the right number on the door.

The small trailer was furnished. It had a kitchenette, couch, and TV in one room, and a bed and dresser in the other room. There was a tiny bathroom between the two rooms with a shower. Sheets and towels came with the rental. Actually, it was little more than a travel trailer made stationary. There wasn't much room in it, but it was a place to stay, and that was all I needed. From what I saw so far, the trailer park appeared to be a place for older people with perhaps a few short time renters such as me.

I wasn't sure if I would be staying in the trailer or even in Florida for long. I supposed it would depend on the job I had just gotten, as well as the feeling I got from this place. So far, I felt like I had landed in alien territory, which was an apt feeling. Never in my life had I been in an area this warm. I had spent my entire life where four seasons came and went.

I cringed at the memory of the older man. He was rude and didn't seem to care who knew it. As for the younger man, he was nice and somewhat attractive in his own way. He had the bluest eyes and a nice smile with good teeth. His drawback was that he was too short in height and with too pale of a complexion for my preference. The good part was that he gave me a job the first day I arrived, which could be a good omen.

I placed my suitcases in the bedroom, but I couldn't make myself unpack more than a few outfits so the wrinkles would settle out. It felt more like I was still in a motel room other than in a place I would be staying for at least a month. I wondered if it was possible to feel more alone than I was feeling right now. I was an eighteen-year-old girl who had never been on her own before. I no longer had a home or a mother. I didn't even have an Aunt Mary or a Jimbo nearby. Not only that, but I was also pretending to be someone else – an older someone else.

Why? I asked myself. Was I afraid Aunt Mary would come after me for some reason? What about the uncle who had pretended to be my father? Was he gone forever never to come back to haunt me? Could there be a chance my own father would come after me? After all, he and my mother were never divorced. Did that mean he had a claim on what little Mother left behind? I had no doubt he would be able to tie me up in legal action of one sort or another. Such possibilities would keep me using the identity Jimbo had set up for me.

*

I spent a restless night. I assured myself my inability to fall asleep was because I was nervous about going to a job that I knew nothing about, and not because of the desperate aloneness that came over me. I tried to make myself feel better by thinking I was on a lifetime adventure where I was going to find myself along with finding my lifetime passion.

I got up early, showered, dried my hair, and put on makeup in hopes it would make me look more mature. I put on my best skirt, blouse, and thin jacket in an attempt to look professional. I had no idea what kind of job I would have or how to dress for it When I had done the best I could with myself, I locked the trailer door, got in my car, and took out the card the man had given me. I had no idea where the address was located or in which direction to go. I considered going to the office and asking the trailer park man for directions, but I simply couldn't face the likes of him this early in the morning. Instead, I drove to the 7-eleven where I could ask directions of the friendly, talkative woman.

She wasn't there, but a middle-aged man was at the cash register. I bought chocolate milk and a bear claw nab for my breakfast.

"Can you give me directions?" I ask as I paid for the junk food.

"Sure. What are you looking for?"

I showed him the card the man had given me with the business address on it.

He looked up at me and lifted his brows. "Samuel Fitzgerald's office building. I can give you directions, but it might not do you much good."

"Why not?"

"It's a gated business area. Private, if you know what I mean."

"I'm supposed to start working there today," I told him.

He looked me over. "Really?" he said as though he didn't believe me.

"Yes. At least I was given this card and told to show up at 7:00 o'clock this morning."

"By Samuel Fitzgerald?" he asked with a slight grin.

"That's right. His father's name was Landon Fitzgerald."

"That old man does like pretty, young girls," he said with a touch of humor along with a shake of his head.

"Thank you for the directions," I told him.

I left the 7-Eleven and drove for ten more minutes as I tried to follow the directions the man had given me. Finally, after circling several times, I found the place. The gate was closed but there was a call box. I pushed buttons on a voice box and a man's voice sounded. "State your name and business, please."

"I'm supposed to show up at 7:00 o'clock this morning for a job."

"What's your name?"

"Alona Anderson."

"Just a few moments, please."

After waiting for five minutes, I pushed the buttons again.

"State your name and business, please," the same man's voice said.

"This is Alona Anderson, again. As I said before, I'm supposed to be here at 7:00 o'clock for a job and I can't get in the gate."

"I'm waiting for confirmation to allow you to enter," he said. "As an employee, you should have received and entry code."

"Samuel Fitgerald gave me his card yesterday, but there was no entry code on it," I tried to explain over the speaker.

"Where were you when he gave you the card?" he asked with a touch of disbelief.

I didn't think that was any of his concern, but I answered him anyway.

"He and his father were eating at The Clock Restaurant the same time I was. I overheard them talking about hiring two new employees, so I approached them about a job. Samuel Fitgerald hired me and gave me his card with this address on it."

"You're surely mistaken. That's hardly a place either of the Fitzgeralds would dine at. I suggest you leave now."

"They were both there," I assured him. "If you don't believe me, can you call Samuel Fitzgerald to verify that he hired me?"

"I contacted the reception desk and verified that you have not been hired. Please leave at once. You are blocking legitimate employees who are waiting to enter."

I didn't know what to do or say. I didn't want to give in and leave, but what choice did I have? "Can you at least look at the card he gave me?"

"Leave immediately or I'll send out security."

"Please send out security. Maybe they will look at the card and believe me."

It was then that a shiny new Porsche sports car pulled up to the private entry gate next to the employee gate to be let in. The car stopped as the private entry gate was being lifted. The tinted window rolled down. Samuel Fitzgearld was looking out the window at me. He motioned for me to roll down the passenger window.

"What's holding things up here?" he demanded.

"The guard won't let me in," I told him. "He doesn't believe you hired me yesterday."

"I hired you?" he questioned as though he had no memory of doing so.

"Yes. At The clock restaurant. You said to arrive at 7:00 o'clock sharp."

"It's almost 7:00," he said as he took a closer look at me. "I've been waiting here for a while."

"Right. Now I remember. Pull in behind my car and follow me."

I pulled out and followed him through the private entry gate to a private parking area about three hundred yards from the gate. I parked beside him. I got out of my car and went to the driver's side window.

"Sorry," he said after he rolled his window down. "My mind has been preoccupied. It appears I forgot to give you the entry code yesterday." He took out another card from his pocket and wrote a number on it. "This will get you in and out. You'll need to drive behind the building to the employee parking lot."

"Okay. Thank you."

"Check in with my receptionist. She'll give you instructions," he said hurriedly, as he pushed a button on a key fob that made the Porsha beep. A door opened to a lower-level garage, and drove inside, leaving me standing there.

I got back in my car and drove behind the building to the designated employee parking lot. All the parking spaces near the entrance were full. I didn't mind parking in the very back and walking to the door that read 'employee entry.' The early morning warmth felt good, even when I wasn't used to the Florida heat. The sound of sea gulls flying overhead squawking loudly was to become part of a new life for me, as was the strong smell of salt in the air. I welcomed the early morning scents of a new place I had not become accustomed to yet. I took it as a good omen for a new life I was beginning to encounter.

The first thing that caught my attention was how pristine everything was to the point of being sterile bareness. Even the few buildings that made up the offices were plain and utilitarian. A few small shrubs were growing in concrete urns in an effort to add landscaping to the place. The abundance of flowers growing everywhere else was lacking here.

Another thing that caught my attention was that water was surrounding the offices and parking lot. I had an urge to walk to the edge of the parking lot to discover what kept the water from washing everything away. But it would have to wait until later. I was already five minutes late from showing up at 7 0'clock sharp.

When I reached the entrance door, I found it locked. I fought an urge to scream out loud. How was a person supposed to show up at work when they couldn't enter the gate or even a door? I beat on the door as hard as I could with my fist. Nothing. I started to take off my shoe and beat on it harder when I saw a fancy kind of ornament with what looked like a button in the center. I gave the button a hard jab.

"State your business, please," came a woman's voice over a speaker. At least she had added please.

"The employee entry door is locked."

"Who are you?"

"Alona Anderson."

"How did you get through the gate? I informed the guard that you were not an employee."

I wanted to scream again, but I held it inside. "I met Mr. Fitzgerald at the gate. He had me follow him to this building. He told me to park in the employee parking lot and come inside. He said to check in with his receptionist and she would give me instructions."

"Just what I need," I heard her mumble a moment before the door buzzed.

I pulled on the door handle again and it opened. I entered a brightly lit room with windows too high up for anyone to look out. I assumed it was designed to let in light without allowing employees the opportunity to become engrossed in the outside world. A woman I took to be in her thirties sat behind a desk. She was groomed to perfection while giving off an air of snobbery. It was obvious she was not pleased with my presence.

"By chance, did Mr. Fitzgerald tell you what kind of job you are to perform for us?" she asked as she lifted her painted-on brows at me.

"No, he didn't," I told her. I certainly didn't want to have a prolonged conversation with such an impatient person.

"Fine," she said with exasperation as he opened a drawer and took out several sheets of paper and a pen and placed them on the end of her desk. "Find a place to sit down out of the way and fill out this job application."

I picked up the pen and paper and took a seat in one of the two navy blue leather chairs against a wall a distance from her desk. I wrote the name Alona Anderson, but I didn't know the address of where I was staying, so I simply wrote in Tamiami Trail, Naples, Fla. When it came to the name of the high school and college I attended, I was stumped. There would be no Alona Anderson at my high school or any college I might put down. I chose the only other high school near the actual one I had attended along with a college in the state. I put down three years for the time I attended college so I wouldn't be expected to write what I majored and minored in. As for work experience, I wrote that I had worked as a waitress.

My driver's license would show that Alona Anderson was twenty-two years old, which was four years more than my actual age of eighteen as far as employment was concerned. When I'd finished filling out the job application, I stood up, crossed the room, and handed it to her. She scanned it, put it in a file folder and laid it on her desk.

"So," she said with a tinge of disgust. "You've gotten a job in a real estate office when you don't have a broker's license or even any experience."

It was then the intercom on her desk buzzed.

"How may I help you?" she asked in an accommodating tone of voice after she flipped it on.

"Why haven't you brought in my coffee and strudel?" Came a man's impatient voice.

"I'll get to it right away," she said.

"Don't take all day."

She flipped the intercom off and looked at me. "Something you might be qualified to do. Follow me," she added a bit sarcastically as she got up from her desk and headed down a hallway.

The way she was dressed made me feel dowdy. I would have to buy new clothes if I was going to work here. Not to mention new shoes and a visit to a beauty shop. She led me into a kitchen area equally as pristine as what I had seen so far.

"I'll show you how to brew Mr. Landon Fitzgerald's coffee. You must be precise with the measurements, or he will let you know about it in no uncertain terms. Once you have the coffee brewing, you'll go to the refrigerator and take out a package of cream cheese and raspberry strudel from the freezer. Take one of the strudels, place it on this exact plate, and put it in the microwave for exactly 22 seconds. He wants it barely warm when he gets it. You will also take a pack of wet wipes from this drawer and a cloth napkin from this other drawer and put it on a tray. When the coffee is almost finished perking, put the plate with the strudel on it in the microwave for the right amount of time. His coffee is to be served in this mug and no other. That's why there are four mugs exactly alike in the cabinet. Nothing else is to be put in the cabinets other than what is in it right now. Got it?"

"Yes," I told her and looked at the coffee maker to see how close it was to being finished.

"The coffee maker is fast. Put the strudel in right now."

I did as she said and hit 22 seconds on the timer. Once I did that, I took a mug from the cabinet and poured the coffee in it and set it on the tray along with the wet wipe and cloth napkin. The microwave dinged and I took the strudel out and placed it on the tray and picked it up.

"Where is his office?" I asked.

"Follow me," she said and hurried down the hallway in the opposite direction from her desk. "I'm assuming you know not to spill a drop of anything on the tray. Mr. Fitzgerald will not tolerate such carelessness. Also, you will need to balance the tray with one hand while you give three brief knocks on his door before you open it and enter. You'll then place the tray on his desk in front of his chair which he is usually sitting in. If he's not at his desk, place the tray there and leave. Give him exactly fifteen minutes before returning for the tray. Got it?"

"Yes, I believe so," I told her as I easily balanced the tray, gave the door three knocks, and opened the door.

Mr. Landon Fitzgerald was sitting at his desk. He glanced up at me as I entered.

"Well, well. If it isn't the hooter girl. I see that Suzanne has already railroaded you into taking over a part of her responsibilities. Didn't take her long to discover what you are qualified for. You can leave now," he added as if I was an unwelcome irritation.

I didn't respond as I turned and walked out the door shutting it silently behind me. I looked at my watch to make sure when exactly fifteen minutes would be up and retraced my steps back to the front desk where Suzann was sitting. She picked up a handful of envelopes from her desk and handed them to me.

"You can deliver this morning's mail to Mr. Samuel Fitzgerald. His office is directly across the hall from Mr. Landon Fitzgerald's."

I took the mail from her hand.

"Remember fifteen minutes exactly," she informed me. "Don't be late."

I retraced my steps down the long hall until I came door across from Mr. Landon Fitzgerald's office. I gave three knocks and waited. Nothing. I gave three more knocks. Still nothing. I cautiously opened the door. Samuel Fitzgerald was talking on his phone, or more correctly listening. I held up the mail for him to see. He pointed at a rack with INBOX printed on it. I put the mail in the rack, turned and left without a word from Samuel Fitzgerald.

I looked at my watch. I still had five minutes to get the tray from Landon Fitzgerald. I stood there not knowing what I should do. I didn't have time to go back to Suzann's desk and there was no other place I knew to go for five minutes. My best bet was to stand there waiting for the correct time and knock three times before I entered Mr. Landon Fitgerald's office.

I jumped when Samuel Fitzgerald opened the door.

"Why are you standing here?" he asked, a bit irritable.

"Waiting for fifteen minutes to be up so I can get Mr. Fitzgerald's tray."

"Go in and get it now."

"Can't. Susanne said to wait exactly fifteen minutes."

"She would," he said with a grin. "She's efficient to an irritating degree."

I didn't comment on that.

"I see she already has you doing her job," I noted he made the same comment his father had made. Like father like son, I thought.

I didn't know how to answer that, so I stayed silent.

"Do you know how to navigate this place yet."

"I know the direction from Suzanne's office to the kitchen and to these two offices."

He grinned slightly. "I mean do you know directions in navigating this town."

"No. I only arrived yesterday."

"Come into my office. I'll give you a map," he said as he opened his door.

I looked at my watch. "I need to get Mr. Fitzgerald's tray in thirty seconds."

He shook his head, crossed the hall, and opened his father's door.

"Good morning, Landon," he said. "Have you finished with your morning tray?"

"Why the duces are you asking me something like that?"

"I have something for Miss . . ." he hesitated and looked at me.

"Alona Anderson," I said.

"Miss Anderson to do."

"So?"

"Suzanne told her to get your tray in exactly fifteen minutes. She was waiting outside your door until the time was up."

"Time's up. She follows directions. I admire that." He nodded toward the tray.

I hurriedly crossed the room and picked up the tray from his desk.

"Good. Now, come into *my* office."

He held the door open for me to leave. He closed his father's door and opened his.

I followed him into his office, holding the tray with the mug balanced on it.

"Put the tray on my desk," he said as he opened a desk drawer and took out a map.

"Traversing this place is very easy once you driven it a time or two. I'll have you delivering a lot of things for me."

*

I had been working there one month and three days when I got enough determination to talk to Mr. Samuel Fitzgearld. He was right about having me deliver things for him. He and his father both had me running all over the place delivering and picking up everything from briefs, office supplies, as well as personal things such as food along with their laundry. And it wasn't just in the city. I was traveling as much as fifty or sixty miles away. I didn't mind the traveling, but I did mind having to use my own car without being compensated for so much as the gas it took.

When I mentioned it to Mr. Samuel Fitzgearld he said, "Alona, I realize you are young an unfamiliar how the work force operates. You need to realize traveling comes with the job of being a gopher. After you've been here six weeks, you'll get a ten cent per hour raise. After that, raises will be according to performance."

That was only eighty cents a day. A gallon of gas costs more than that amount. Deliveries took as much as two to three gallons a day if not more.

"Can you provide me with a company vehicle instead of me having to use my own car?"

"Only staff with seniority get such perks," he told me like I was being a naïve idiot.

"How about compensating me for gas? I've been paying for it out of pocket all month."

"The company isn't set up for such as that."

I had seen private gas tanks on the property with company cars filling up. "There's gas tanks . . ." I began.

"Only for the use of company cars," he told me as he handed a manilla envelope across the desk toward me. Give this to Susanne," he said as a dismissal of me.

I gritted my teeth, took the manilla envelope and left his office.

"What has you in a snit?" Susanne asked as I placed the envelope on her desk.

I told her about the cost of my deliveries and Mr. Samuel Fitzgerald refusing to compensate me for the gas.

"That's why we usually have only young people who live with their parents as gophers. Along with a few greedy people who think they can get their foot in the door which will lead to something better."

"Does it lead to something better?" I asked feeling like she had directly insulted me to my face.

"Seldom," she answered. "Gophers like yourself are too easily replaced."

At least she was honest with me.

I was getting paid every two weeks. When I got my paycheck, I was dumbfounded that half the amount went to pay for the gas I had used. The other half went to half of the small trailer. I was paying the other half out of my pocket. It didn't take a genius to figure out I wasn't getting ahead in this job.

There was no wonder the FitzGeralds were as rich as King Mitas. It was obvious they were taking advantage of those who could least afford it.

"Do I need to turn in a two-week resignation notice?" I asked her.

"Most gophers simply stop showing up. By law, I must mail them their last paycheck, which I wouldn't otherwise. I'm not fond of workers who walk out on their responsibility. Once they quit, they're not allowed to enter the gate again. I have a delivery that needs to go to Fort Myers," she said as she moved a packet toward me as though she expected me to deliver it without further complaint.

In other words, I was little more than a poorly compensated slave to the richest company in Naples.

"I need to use the restroom," I told her without picking up the packet.

I got halfway down the hall before a stronger surge of anger hit me. Instead of going through the bathroom door, I went out the exit door. I got in my car and drove through the gate, never to return.

I went to the trailer to allow my anger to settle down. I had just paid for my second month's rent. The trailer wasn't much, but I had it for another month. I had done very little while I was here other than work six days a week. I now had a chance to check out the place.

I liked walking on the beaches on Sunday, which was my day off. The bareness of the sand and water was entirely different than what I expected. So was the number of people on the beaches. There was no privacy. If I sat down in the sand, it was within inches of someone else. I wondered why people loved the beach so much. There was sand and a non-ending supply of Gulf of Mexico water that appeared to go on until it met with a distant sky. There was no vegetation anywhere except for a few sea oats growing a distance from the beach. As for animal life, it mainly consisted of squawking seagulls.

My anxiety of walking out on my job made me need to relax. A walk on the beach might help me relax since there weren't as many people on a workday as there were on Sundays. I decided Naples was a beautiful place to visit, but I wouldn't want to live here permanently. And yet I wasn't sure where I wanted to live. Going back home wasn't an option.

Sometimes I wondered about the things Jimbo had taught me, along with the money he put in a bank account for me. There was no doubt that it was crime money that would have supported more crime if Jimbo and I hadn't taken it. I would have preferred that it was money I had legally earned for myself. Perhaps I should be even more thankful for it and put it to good use other than keeping it my bank account. At least I did have the money from selling Mother's and my home. That was money I didn't want to use until I found a home I wanted to buy, but I was. I needed to find another job.

I left walking on the beach and went to The Clock for lunch. The place was packed. Every seat was taken, and the place was definitely in the weeds.

"There will be at least a thirty-minute wait," the tired-looking receptionist told me. "Get in the back of the line and wait."

It didn't take long watching the wait staff to realize the place needed more waitresses. I left the line and went back to the receptionist. "Are you short on waitstaff?"

"You could say that. One didn't show up for work, and two are in training, but their learning curve is slow," she said as she gave me an irritated look as though silently saying *what business is it of yours?*

"I'm an experienced waitress. I'll take the job if the place is hiring."

"We're definitely hiring," she said. "How much experience do you have?"

"Almost ten years."

She gave me a skeptical look. "Really?" she added with disbelief.

"Yes really. I started working in my mother's restaurant when I had to stand in a chair to wash dishes."

"Why aren't you still working there?"

"Mother died and my aunt got the restaurant. I decided it was time to make a life of my own."

"Okay. I'll give you a trial run to see how you work out. Go in the back and tell Hanna Lena said to show you the ropes."

Instead of eating as I had planned, I went in the back.

"Can I help you?" A woman asked a bit irritated at my presence in the kitchen.

"Are you Hanna?"

"I am."

"I was told by Lena that you would show me the ropes. I'm a new waitress."

She let out a huff. "What was Lena thinking? Sending a newbie at a time like this. I don't have time to show you the ropes or even set you up on the time clock."

"No problem," I assured her. "I'll work for free until the rush is over. If I do a good job, you can put me on the payroll, if not, then you haven't lost anything."

"Deal. Put your purse in an empty backroom locker and put on an apron. You'll find a pad and pen in the pocket."

Waitressing came natural for me. The other waitresses seemed relieved when I stepped onto the floor. I didn't wait for the dishwasher to bus tables. I picked up everything in my arms and took it to the kitchen where a hassled-looking, skinny young girl was doing her best to keep up with the dish washing. I instantly had sympathy for the young girl. There was no way she could keep up with busing the tables and washing dishes both. It was obvious she was far along in pregnancy. A glance at her face told me she was ready to burst into tears. My heart went out to her.

"I'll bus the tables," I assured her. It was easy to see the relief on her face. "I spent years washing dishes and bussing tables. I'm rather good at it," I added.

I returned to the dining room with a damp cloth having a dab of bleach on it to wipe off the table and placed two glasses on it. I took two menus and guided the next two people in line to their seats. The receptionist gave me a thankful look.

"Do you need a few minutes, or are you ready to order?" I asked them.

"We'll take the special along with sweet tea."

"It will be right out," I assured them as I took the picture of sweet tea and filled their glasses for them.

Daily specials were already prepared and ready to dish up. I went into the kitchen where the chef was just short of going into hysterics because of the rush of orders he had to prepare. I took it upon myself to dish up the daily special. He gave me a nod, and I took the two specials out front.

I had eight tables during the lunch rush, plus bused tables when I had a few minutes between rushing about to keep everyone served.

The rush continued for the next two hours before it finally slacked off. Everyone breathed a sigh of relief, including me.

"Thank you for helping out on such short notice," Lena, the receptionist told me. "We're always busy, but not like this. We had three tour buses arrive at the same time without being forewarned."

"You're welcome," I told her. "I know only too well what it's like to be deep in the weeds. It makes everyone unhappy including hungry customers."

She squinted her eyes and took a good look at me. "You look familiar. Weren't you in here a few weeks ago? Didn't you get hired by the Fitzgeralds?"

I was surprised at her remembering me. "You have a good memory."

"Only because the Fitzgeralds made the grand sacrifice of eating here. Did you take the job?" she repeated her question.

"I did, but the job wasn't what I expected."

"I've heard that happens to a lot of people who start working there. How long did you last?"

"Until this morning," I told her.

"How long do you think you will stick around this town if I hire you full time?"

"I don't have an answer to that. I've paid for this month's rent."

"That's longer than most restaurant workers last. How were your tips?"

"Good enough," I told her. The customers appreciated my quick response to their wants and need, along with a friendly, smiling face. I got more tips in two hours than I got working eight hours for the Fitzgeralds, and I didn't have to buy my own gas for deliveries.

"I suppose I can hire you on a part time basis. I don't expect either of the two new waitresses I've already hired to hang around long. And poor little Angie Bell, she's not capable of handling busing tables and washing dishes when there's a rush. I noticed you were helping her out." She lowered her voice to a whisper. "She's in such need that I don't have the heart to let her go. I don't think she'll be able to work after her baby is born. Her boyfriend or maybe husband... well, I don't like talking bad about people, but let's just say he's not much account."

Chapter 16

*

Working in a restaurant again was not what I had in mind, but part-time work would be okay for a while. It was something I could do with my time, plus it would be enough to pay for my expenses until I figured out where I belonged. The good part was that part-time work allowed me to have time to do as I pleased. I'd never actually had time for myself. Time to be a teenager. Time to experience the things girls I went to school experienced. Time to be selfish. Now that I had the time, I felt at a loss.

I went for an early morning walk on the beach. The white sand beach held a fascination for me, although I still found it deserted of wildlife and vegetation. The never-ending horizon of the ocean held my interest along with a kind of fear. I found it difficult to believe there was more water in the ocean than there was land even though I was taught such as that in school. Standing on the beach looking at the never-ending ocean was a far different experience than studying about it in books.

No one was out this early in the five o'clock morning coolness, which I liked. I had the entire beach, this entire morning walk, all to myself. The salty air was crisp and comfortable. I liked the sound the waves were making as they washed up on the sand. I even found myself liking the screeching of the sea gulls as they searched for morning food. All this gave me a peaceful feeling, and yet, I wasn't at peace. I knew without question this wasn't the place I wanted to make my home. It was like where I was supposed to be this moment in time, but not where I belonged.

Belong. That had become the magic word that I was seeking. A mythical place I sought, but I was beginning to believe that I would never find such a place. I had heard girls at school talk about finding themselves. That wasn't what I looked for. I had no need to find myself. I already knew who I was – who I had been. An only child whose mother was dying from cancer. A child whose father never wanted her to exist. A child whose father ran away from her beautiful mother because she was pregnant. A girl with an aunt who wanted her as slave labor. Yes, I knew all too well who I was. What I desperately needed was a place where I belonged. A place that would be home to me.

At five-thirty, I left the peaceful beach and headed to the restaurant to help with the morning prep work. I wasn't to start work until six o'clock. I came in early because I wanted to. The Clock Restaurant opened at six o'clock sharp. Lena Roark was the woman who owned the place, and the one who did most of the work. She wasn't in the least bit like Aunt Mary or Mother. She was firm and hard as a rock on the outside and inside. She knew exactly how she wanted things done and was willing to do the work to accomplish exactly that.

Oddly enough I liked her, and I think she might have liked me a little, but she made a point of not showing it, which was the same thing she did with everyone.

"Good morning," I said as I came in the back door. She kind of grunted, which was her usual response. "Need help in prepping?"

She grunted again and pointed at a fifty-pound sack of potatoes and then at a fifty-pound sack of apples that I was to peel and slice. At least the green beans came in one gallon ten cans instead of fresh. I wouldn't have to string and break them. Without saying a word, Lena walked over to the walk-in freezer and opened the door letting a blast of cold come into the hot kitchen. It felt good and yet it brought a shiver to me. There was half an angus steer hanging from the sealing of the cooler with portions of hog meat spread out on a table. Lena Roark believed in having an abundance of food stuff on hand. "Can't cook it if you don't have it," I had heard her say.

It was then the back door opened, and a man walked in. The first thing I noticed was his size. Not in height, although he was around five foot ten or eleven inches, but the broadness of his shoulders. The next thing I noticed was the color of his skin. It was a combination of tan and ruddiness. Then there was his hair, which was a lot too long with black roots while the longer parts were a blondish red as though some hair stylist had done a job of bleaching and highlighting, which didn't fit with the rugged looks of him.

"How many you want?" he asked Lena in a deep husky voice that reminded me a lot of the actor Sam Elliott's deep, husky voice.

"Three. Put 'em in the cooler next to the hog meat you brought yesterday."

He turned and walked out the door. He came back in with a long bulky chunk of white meat that I couldn't identify. On his third trip Lena stopped prepping carrots to follow him into the cooler to inspect what he had placed there. She came back out with him while nodding her head in approval. She closed the cooler door behind them.

"Same price?" she questioned.

"Yep," he answered.

She pulled a roll of bills from her pants pocket and counted out what she owed him. "Come back day after tomorrow," she said. "Bring two gator tails and some more hog meat. Make it tender meat this time instead of that tough boar meat."

"That's early," he told her.

"Had a rush. Expecting another rush," she said. "College kids. Summer vacationers."

"Pigs cost more than boars."

"I know that already."

He left without exchanging more words with Lena or even glancing at me.

"He took a fancy to you," Lena surprised me by saying once he was out the door.

"He what?" I questioned. He hadn't even looked in my direction. Not once.

"He was eying you."

"No, he wasn't."

"He's not obvious in what he does. He's Seminole."

"Seminole?" I questioned.

"Indian. You know, Osceola. Seminole winds," she said as she gave me a look and shook her head. "Don't know much about history or the place you've landed in, do you," she sounded accusing as though my lack of knowledge was offensive. "You eyed him too."

"I couldn't help it. I was looking at the way he was dressed along with his hair and complexion," I blurted out in self-defense, while feeling embarrassed because she had caught me eying him. He was good looking in a rough-cut kind of way that instantly got my attention. So far, a lot of the men I'd seen in this place were the clean-cut suit-wearing kind or more correctly the older people who had been the suit wearing kind before they retired.

"Sun bleached," Lena said as though she understood my thoughts. "Cuts his own hair with the same straight razor he shaves with. Not that full blooded Indians have much beard to shave. Real man, nevertheless. He don't squat to take a piss."

"Uh," I mumbled. "Okay. Uh, what kind of meat did he bring?" I wanted to change the subject, and at the same time I wanted to ask more questions about the man I'd been trying not to admit I had been staring at.

"Gator tail."

"Gator tail?" I questioned.

"Alligator. Tail tastes like chicken only better. Plus, you get a lot of meat and no chicken bones."

"There are no bones in their tails?" I asked as I imagined the tail of an alligator.

"There is but not like the bones in a chicken or fish. You get more meat for your money."

Never in my life had I thought of such, much less heard of eating alligator's tail. "People kill and eat alligators?" I questioned in astonishment as I thought of the gray, tough, scaled and pot-marked hide that was used in making boots and pocketbooks.

"Yep. He has a gator farm. Raises them by the hundreds. Brings in tourist money by showing off his gators, along with taking tourists on airboat rides through the swamps. He's kind of like a present-day Tarzan who doesn't swing on vines. Good man."

That was the most I had heard her say about anybody. "Present day Tarzan?" I questioned.

"Yep. Untamed. Hard to handle. If only I was young again," she sighed longingly.

I tried not to smile. I knew what she meant. He did give off that all-male vibe. Not to mention those powerful looking muscles that filled out his worn and faded clothes.

"Too bad Angie Bell didn't get one like him, but then she took up where she belongs, I reckon." she added with a shake of her head as she looked at the time clock. Angie was running late again. I would have to start washing up things as Lena prepped. "She definitely hooked up with trash. Beats her. Takes her money," Lena added. "Won't let her take time off regardless of her condition. Meets her at the door on payday. Ought to fire her, but he'd probably kill her if I did."

"He should be arrested," I said with defiance.

"Might be if she took out a warrant, but she won't."

"Why not?"

"Too afraid of him."

"Yes, but . . ." I didn't know what to add to that.

"What I just said is between you and me. Best not to mess in anyone else's business. Do-gooders don't do well sticking their noses where they don't belong."

I now knew she thought of me as being a do-gooder just because I tried to help Angie out when the dishes piled up. After all, she was in her last stages of pregnancy. "Where does Angie belong?" I dared ask.

"She's from the swamps with others like her kind," Lena said as a matter of fact instead of an insult.

"Is she Seminole?"

"Nope, don't think there's any Indian blood in her. If there was, she might have more spunk to get rid of that no-account so-called boyfriend-husband of hers. He's bad news for the girl. He's even been run out of the town of Immokalee. A man has to be a mighty disgusting human being to be run out of there."

"Immokalee?" I questioned.

"Yep. It's a little town North of here. Let's just say it's not known for being a place where the rich and elegant hang out."

"He's the father of her baby?"

"So it would seem, being she claims she is married to him, but who knows."

"Meaning?" I questioned.

"Meaning, Angie Bell is the kind of girl men take advantage of. No backbone in that girl. If you ask me, I'd say she jumped out of the frying pan into the fire when she took up with Hanson Bell."

"What about her parents?" I asked, thinking they should protect her.

Her mom disappeared years ago. Her dad hides out from the law in the swamps. Bootleg liquor is his trade. Makes some mighty powerful brew. Most folks around here buy it from him. I've bought a plenty. It's good for just about everything. High alcohol content makes a great disinfectant. Reminds me I've nearly run out."

I was about to ask more questions when two other waitresses came into the kitchen along with Johnathan, the chef, or cook as Lena called him. She glanced at the clock and her talking dried up with their entrance. She made a point of letting her employees know they were there to work, not gossip or set up a friends' club. Why she had told me what she did was not at all like her. Could it be that I wasn't put on the payroll until six o'clock, therefore we weren't wasting time when I should be paid for working.

Chapter 17

*

The alligator man returned to the restaurant for lunch. I wasn't sure if he made a point of sitting at my table or if it just happened that way. After I took his order, I decided it was unintentional. Never once did he look at me as he ordered the daily special along with coffee.

When I went into the kitchen Lena looked at me with a smug expression on her face as though she knew something no one else did.

"What?" I questioned as I intercepted her look.

"Get back to work and stop lollygagging," she told me firmly, but with that same smug look on her face.

"I'm not lollygagging," I told her.

"No sassing," she said firmly. "And wipe that grin off your face," she added in a hushed tone.

I wasn't sassing or grinning, but I said nothing else as I left the kitchen and picked up the fresh pot of coffee to fill the alligator man's cup.

"Creamer?" I asked as I poured his coffee.

"Black," he said, hardly acknowledging my presence.

"My name is Alona Anderson," I introduced myself for some reason, although I wore a name badge with Alona on it. For the first time, he turned his face away from the table and looked me in the eyes. A smile turned his face into friendliness. He had the whitest, most perfect teeth glowing in his tanned face along with full lips that could actually turn into a smile.

"Nokosi Micco," he introduced himself as his smile turned into a full-faced grin. "You can call me Mic if you want."

"Seminole name?" I questioned.

"Right. Nokosi means bear. Micco means chief."

"Are you a chief?" I ask.

"Right. With a tribe of one. Only ruling over myself."

"If you can do that, you do better than most people I know."

"Well put. I've not seen you in here before."

"I'm a newbie. Just started working here."

"You from up North?"

"Illinois."

"Chicago. You've got that Northern accent."

I didn't bother telling him that seventy-five percent of Illinois was farming land. People automatically thought of Chicago when I said Illinois. They seemed to have no idea Illinois grew thousands of acres of wheat, soybeans, and corn and not just a city.

"You have a . . ." I hesitated, not knowing what to attribute his accent to.

"A mixture of Seminole and Cracker," he answered for me as though he knew what I had started to say. "My mother was Seminole, and my dad was Cracker. Of course, there still remains a few of us who speak Hitchiti."

"Cracker?" I questioned. "Hitchiti?"

"Hitchiti is an Indian language. Seldom used these days. Cracker is the name used for the white man who was and is native to this area of Florida. You know, like the Georgia Crackers. What are the native Chicagoans called?"

"Chicagolanders, Chic-towners, Midwesterners, or even Windy City locals," I told him several of the names I'd heard the people who lived in Chicago called. I didn't add that I grew up in a small town that wasn't anywhere near the big city. "People from Illinois are referred to as Illinoisans," I added as an afterthought.

"What brought you here?" he asked in that deep voice of his. "Relatives moved here seeking their fortune no doubt?"

I wasn't sure how much I should talk about myself to someone I knew nothing about. Him knowing I was from Illinois was more information than I was comfortable giving out. I still thought of myself as hiding who I really was. I preferred to be the person Jimbo made me than being my real self. I'd have to think about that later on when I had a lot of free time.

"I wanted to stay warm all year long," I answered his question, although summers in Illinois got plenty hot.

"Always wanted to know what a snowstorm is like," he said.

"Have you ever heard of lake-effect snow? It's freezing cold," I told him as Lena dinged her pick-up bell twice that his food was ready.

She had that all-knowing look on her face as she looked at me through the serving window. I picked up his plate and said nothing to her.

"Don't neglect your other tables," she said, warning me not to slack up. Like I had ever been slack or neglected a customer. I just kind of shook my head at her and shrugged.

He ate hardily, and I refilled his coffee twice.

"Ever been on an airboat ride?" He asked as I poured that third cup of coffee.

"What's an airboat ride? I asked.

"It's a boat that takes you through the everglades. It's one of my ways of getting money for entertaining tourists."

"I see," I told him. Everyone wanted to get money from tourists, and every tourist was willing to pay to be entertained. "Would you like desert?"

"Does it come with the meal?"

"It costs extra."

"Then I'll pass," he said with a grin as his dark hazel eyes met mine in a knowing way.

"Hope you enjoyed your meal," I said politely as I placed his bill face down on the table. "Come again," I said.

"I probably will," he said seriously, although he didn't seem happy about it. I wasn't sure how I felt about him returning. I didn't even know how I was feeling about him, but I was definitely feeling something.

I hadn't thought about a boyfriend since Sensei York. I missed the excited feelings that falling in love brought more than I missed the intimacy. I admit there were times when I longed to have warm arms holding me along with the passion that went along with it. Most of all I wanted to belong to someone who belonged to me. *Belong*! It was obvious that was the key feeling I was longing for as I looked at him. It was a word that kept returning to my mind several times a day. I realized it wasn't just a place I was looking for, but also a person I was longing for.

*

I bussed a table of dishes and took them into the kitchen where Angie Bell had finally shown up and was washing dishes. She didn't look at me as I placed the dishes on the counter beside her. Straggly, unwashed hair was hanging from her head mostly concealing her face. Her hands were in the rinse water with the cuffs of her shirt getting wet because she hadn't pushed the sleeves up her arms. I started to ask if she was alright but didn't. It was obvious something was bad wrong with her. It was also obvious that she was trying to be invisible.

"Let me know if I can help," I told her. When she ignored me, I turned around and walked away. I got the idea she didn't want anyone to know what had happened to her. I looked at Lena as I picked up my next order. Her teeth were clinched as she gave me a slight shake of her head along with a roll of her eyes as if silently warning me not to butt my nose in other people's business.

I took food to a table. "Anything else I can get for you?" I asked the couple.

"A coffee refill," the man said as he pushed his cup to the edge of the table. Coffee came with the meal and people drank a lot of it.

"Angie . . ." I whispered to Dela, one of the other waitresses who was also getting a fresh pot of coffee.

"No big deal. She comes in looking like that often since she started working here. It's to be expected."

"She gets beat-up that often? She's pregnant," I said in disbelief that a pregnant girl would come in to work looking the way she does, and no one thought it a big deal.

"She's swamp trash living with swamp trash," she said as if that answered all the questions I might have.

"But . . ."

"You'll learn to mind your own business if you stick around this place long," she informed me none too friendly.

She picked up one of the pots of coffee and walked off without showing the least bit of concern for Angie Bell. I couldn't believe she, or anyone else, didn't care about the pregnant girl who was getting beat up. I cared, and I was a stranger who knew nothing at all about the girl. A town as pristine as Naples surely had some kind of protection for those being abused.

"How old is she?" I questioned Dela as we met again at the coffee maker.

"Who?"

"Angie Bell," I told her.

"Good grief. You've got her stuck in your craw. Forget about her. Mind your own business instead of trying to mind hers."

"If she needs help . . ."

"She doesn't," Dela interrupted what I was about to say. "Unlike you, she's satisfied with her life."

I was taken back by what she said. Angie Bell couldn't possibly be satisfied with her life. Even worse was that Dela knew I wasn't satisfied with my life. Was I that easy to read?

"How can a pregnant girl be satisfied with being beat on?" I demanded, as I pretended to ignore what she said about me.

"It's all she's ever known. It's normal life for her," she told me and walked away to refill cups of coffee and glasses of tea and water.

*

Nokosi Micco showed up at five-forty-five the next morning with the alligator tails and hog meat. I smiled at him and started to say good morning, but he turned his back and paid no attention to me. He didn't even look toward me or acknowledge my presence. I was taken back, not knowing what to do or say. I thought he had been friendly when I served him a few days ago, but he certainly wasn't being friendly now. He was downright rude. I was both relieved and disappointed when he left with Lena's money in his pocket.

"He's sure enough got the hots for you," Lena said without looking at me.

I let out a disbelieving snort of irritation. "He's rude. He acted like I didn't exist."

"Not to me, he didn't. It was all he could do not to reach out and touch you with those big, callused hands of his."

I let out a sound similar to a laugh, but I didn't think there was anything funny.

"You don't know him or his ways. I do, and I'm telling you he was fairly sizzling from being near you. I've never known him to take a shine to anyone the way he has you."

If ignoring me was sizzling, then I had learned nothing about reading people and their behavior. His action told me that he detested my presence so much he was unable to look at me or say a friendly hello. How could I have ever felt the least amount of attraction for such a man? He might be an Indian, but he was also from the South. Where was the renowned Southern hospitality or at least a trace of civility?

"This weekend is gonna be a rush," Lena said. "You can take off Monday instead of Sunday," Lena told me.

"Thought I was only hired to work part time." I pointed out.

"That's why you get off at three o'clock each day."

"That's nine hours a day," I pointed out.

"Nope. You get an hour and a half off for lunch and breaks. Makes it seven and a half hours a day. You can take off both Monday and Tuesday each week. That'll make you part time."

Like I actually got off an hour and a half. I seldom had time to eat or take a bathroom break. I understood how restaurants got in the weeds during lunchtime along with the small amount of profit they brought in. I also understood why there was so much employee turnover. Being a waitress was hard work with little pay. Every waitress sought those tips to help them make their own payments. Plus, breakfast and lunch tips were small, which were the times I worked. I had no doubt that burnout would hit me soon considering working at a restaurant was what I was running away from.

Although breakfast and lunch tips were small, I was a good waitress, which led me to get a fair amount of tips. I could tell the other two waitresses resented it. They had started telling Lena that all tips should be put in a jar and divided among the three waitresses and Angie. I had to grin at that. It would mean that poor little Angie would also get her fair share of tips. So far Lena had rightly refused. Such as that would punish the good waitresses and encourage the lazy waitresses to become even more lazy.

The waitresses were supposed to give the person who bussed tables and washed dishes ten percent of their tips, but they seldom did. It was obvious the other two waitresses were claiming they were getting less tips than they actually got. I was the only one who made a point of bussing tables along with giving Angie half of the tips I took in. Angie never said thank you or appeared to notice how generous I was being. The other waitresses noticed and disapproved of my generosity and of me.

"It's nice to be rich." "Throwing money away on trash." "Buying their drugs." Or "Trying to make us look bad." Were comments they made to my face and probably worse behind my back.

"The money Angie gets doesn't go to her," Lena pointed out. "Her so-called husband takes every cent she makes."

I knew that wasn't entirely true. I'd seen her slip a few dollars under the sole of her worn-out shoes after I gave her extra tip money. I was hoping she would be able to save up enough to get herself and her baby away from her husband once the baby was born if not before.

"If you need help, let me know," I told her every day and hoped she realized I wasn't only talking about bussing tables and washing dishes. Never once did she comment in any way. At least she would sometimes acknowledge my comment by nodding slightly.

Chapter 18

*

Although Monday was my day off, I chose to take my usual early morning beach walk instead of lying in bed. The mattress in the little trailer wasn't comfortable enough to snuggle up for extra sleep. I needed to start looking for a better place to rent, but I found the price of other rental places prohibitive.

I wore shorts and a tank top as I shuffled my bare feet in the sand, my flipflops in my hand as I thought about paying for another month's rent. I had already been there for almost two months and wondered if I wanted to make it three.

"Not many fire ants in beach sand. They don't like salt water."

I jumped, startled at the sound of a man's voice in what I thought was an empty beach. I turned quickly to see Nokosi Micco sitting on a protrusion of rocks that jutted up every so often through the sand. He blended in so perfectly I hadn't noticed him, not that I was paying much attention.

"What are you doing on the beach?" I said in surprise as though an Indian couldn't possibly be interested in an early morning beach sunrise.

"Waiting for you," he admitted.

A feeling of apprehension came over me. "Why?" I demanded.

"Because I like you. I thought you might like to pay a visit to my place."

"Your place?" I questioned, feeling even more uncomfortable.

"Didn't Lena tell you about my airboat rides along with my animals?"

"She mentioned it."

"Tourists enjoy it," he said.

"I'm not a tourist," I pointed out.

"If you were, I wouldn't be inviting you to be shown around for free."

I must have given him an odd look because he continued to talk.

"Don't worry. I'm not one of those perverts or anything like that. I simply like you enough to want to show my place of business in your return for your honest opinion if there's anything that needs improving."

"Why?"

"Why do I like you or why do I want to show my place to you?"

"Both," I told him.

"I'm proud of my place and want to brag a little, plus I find honest opinions helpful. I have no answer to why I like you. I just do."

I found his answers honest. "I bet you tell that to all the women," I couldn't resist saying.

"No," he said with sincerity. "You're the first."

Somehow, I doubted that, but it might be the truth considering how reserved he appeared. "Why didn't you invite me at the restaurant instead of stalking me at the beach? How did you know I'd be here," I added to my questions.

"Didn't want to give Lena more to gossip about. You know how she can talk."

I almost laughed at that. She was only a talker before six o'clock in the morning.

"Don't mean to speak out of place. It's just that . . . well like I just said, I kind of took a liking to you," he told me again.

I didn't know what to say. "Is Monday's your day off?" I questioned.

He shook his head. "I don't get time off. I'm working except for the time I sleep at night."

"But you took time off from work to eat at the restaurant and meet me here."

He downed his head, and his face flushed with embarrassment. "Lena told me you walked the beach around this time. She said . . . well you know how she talks. I was making deliveries to other places, and you came to mind. I had this great idea of giving you a personal invitation."

So, Lena was the one who put him up to stalking me here. Why was she pushing me and him together?"

"Is Lena related to you?"

"No. She comes by my place once in a while."

"Why?" I asked as I looked him in the eyes.

"I reckon that's between me and her."

The look I gave him made his face turn redder.

"It's strictly business. She hires my airboat once in a while."

I couldn't imagine Lena going for airboat rides or wasting a minute of her time on visiting a tourist trap. And then it hit me. "Do you take a lot of people for rides into the swamp?"

He looked surprised for a moment before his face became blank again.

"She said she was about out of disinfectant," I told him in a knowing sort of way.

Again, he looked surprised. "Lena's business is her business. Not mine."

So, my guess was right. Lena hired him to take her out into some dismal swamp land to buy her supply of illegal liquor.

"Does Angie Bell ride an airboat to get to work?" I asked.

His brows lifted and he shook his head as a puzzled look crossed his face. "She doesn't live with her folks."

Lena told me she was from the swamp. "Where does she live?"

"Her man's got a place. She stays there most of the time."

"Do you know her husband?" I asked him.

"Know of him. Seen him about a right smart. Why do you ask?"

"Lena doesn't like him."

"Nobody does."

"He beats on Angie."

His jaws clinched for a moment. "Not my place to stick my nose in other people's business. You ought not to either."

"Somebody should," I told him with conviction.

He nodded as though he was thinking what his next words would be. "Did you know that a gator can take the body of their prey down deep in the water and lodge the body under a bank or in a tangle of Cyprus tree roots until they're hungry or the body rots enough to satisfy the gator's taste buds?"

I cringed. His words sounded like a warning to me.

"I learned a long time ago that it's best not to mess in somebody else's business," he repeated. "Time's wasting. How about letting me show you around the best tourist trap in this section of Florida?"

What he had just told me about alligators made me leery of him. I wasn't comfortable going to an alligator farm with someone I knew so little about. "Can't. I need to catch up on a few things," I told him.

"Such as?" he gave me a questioning look.

"Laundry. Cleaning up a few loose ends. Washing my hair."

He looked disappointed. "In other words, you don't like me or trust my intentions."

"I don't know you," I was quick to respond without commenting further.

"I'm part Seminole, part white. I'm honorable and trustworthy. I don't drink liquor or do anything I consider to be wrong," he said with pride as he stood up from the rocks he had been sitting on and dusted the sand off his clothes. "I know less about you," he added as he turned his back on me and stalked away. It was obvious I had hurt his pride along with silently questioning his honor.

I made a point of leaving the beach and driving to the 7-Eleven where the talkative woman was working. I bought a Gatorade drink and a bar of dark chocolate candy.

"That time of month, huh," she said with a grin. "I stuff my face with dark chocolate every single month."

"I would eat dark chocolate every day of every month if it wasn't so fattening," I told her.

She looked me over and grinned. "You're not much bigger around than a pencil. Most men I know like girls with a little meat on 'em. You oughta buy two bars of chocolate."

"Thank you," I told her, ignoring the mean part of the comment, but I was five pounds overweight for my height. "Can I ask you a question?"

"Of course. You wouldn't believe all the questions I get asked," she said with a friendly chuckle. "I even get propositioned once in a while," she added with a grin and a shake of her head. "What do you want to know?"

"I heard about a place that raised alligators and had airboat rides. Know anything about the place?"

"Oh, sure. Every local knows about that place. It's a small tourist attraction."

"Is it safe to visit?"

"Perfectly safe. No one has ever been eaten by alligators or fell off the airboats."

"Is it locally owned?" I questioned, wanting to know more about Nokosi Micco without having to ask.

"It is. Used to be owned by two brothers, but one of them got killed in an airplane crash. The remaining brother runs it by himself now."

"Does his wife help him run it?" I hoped I didn't sound too inquisitive. "I wouldn't feel comfortable having children around alligators."

"No, Nokosi Micco has never been married to my knowledge. Not that a lot of single girls and women haven't gone after him. He is one of the best-looking men I've set my eyes on."

"Is he gay?" I couldn't resist asking.

"I doubt it, although around here you never know."

"Nokosi Micco?" I pronounced his name the way she did.

"Seminole Indian name. I've heard some locals call him Mic. I call him a hunk."

"So, this airboat, alligator farm place is safe to visit?"

"Perfectly safe. He certainly doesn't want a lawsuit on his hands. He's one of the nicest men you'll ever meet once you get to know him, which isn't easy to do. He likes to keep to himself, plus he's a man of few words."

When someone came to the cash register to pay for gas, I left the store with my chocolate bar, Gatorade, and a little more information. What she had told me about Nokosi Micco left me feeling guilty by having distrustful thoughts about him. Maybe I should show up at his place as a paying tourist. I had rather make friends than enemies.

*

An older, tired looking woman took my twenty-five-dollar entry fee at the gate and handed me a copy of a hand drawn map showing where all the exhibits were located. She sat under the shade of a roughly constructed three-sided shelter. Her face was tanned dark and deeply wrinkled beneath a crown of snowy-white hair. I wondered if she was related to Nokosi Micco, perhaps his mother, but I didn't want to impose enough to ask. Two visitors were in front of me, while three other visitors were entering behind me helping me feel safer by showing up at an alligator farm.

I followed the other visitors hoping I would blend in with them. Only a part of me longed to see Nokosi Micco, while the other part hoped he never knew I was here. The first attraction was the swamp buggy ride which was to start in fifteen minutes. The length of the ride was to be about thirty minutes. The swamp buggy arrived, and a dozen tourists climbed down the steps of the high off the ground buggy before the ones of us waiting could get on.

"Welcome aboard," the driver said with a touch of humor.

He had a scruff of beard and wore his hair slightly long. I had an idea he also had some Seminole ancestors.

"Hope you enjoy this ride. As you've already noticed, this swamp buggy is several feet off the ground. There's a reason for that. We will be coming in contact with wild animals such as snakes, wild hogs, alligators along with a slew of other wild vermin. The higher up you are, the safer you'll be."

Several of the tourists looked at each other with wide eyes. It didn't occur to them that the last group did not look the least bit frightened, and a few looked slightly bored. It didn't take long until we were under way rolling along a sandy trail through the woods. I was surprised at the thick cropping of trees growing along the sandy trail that was wet in a place referred to as a swamp. He stopped the Swamp Buggy underneath two trees.

"As you can see these are a rare type of nut tree that grows in the Florida everglades. The male and a female tree must grow side by side in order to have pollination for their fruit. The one on your left that is in full bloom is the male tree, while the one on the right has blooms that is so small you hardly notice them. It is the female tree. The male tree is the one that produces while the female tree stays barren. The female tree is only for pollination."

"Really?" One of the more intellectual women questioned his statement. "Isn't it usually the female that produces?"

"Oh, no," he was quick to answer. "It's only the males who have nuts."

There was a moment of silence before everyone burst into laughter.

He drove a little way further until he stopped again. He took a bag of marshmallows from a wooden box. He let out a sharp whistle and suddenly the swamp buggy was surrounded by raccoons. He pitched out the marshmallow as the riders watched them scramble for the sweet treats. When the bag was empty, he drove on. I wondered how he had them trained to only come when he whistled and asked him about it.

"Simple. If they show up before I whistle, they don't get marshmallows."

He drove about a fourth of a mile further explaining the flora and fauna along the way. Again, he stopped and called out sue-ee, sue-ee. A sow and a dozen spotted pigs came running out of the brush. "These are Florida wild hogs. They are extremely destructive animals along with being equally dangerous to humans and animals," he said as he opened his box and got out a bag of shelled corn and tossed out a few handfuls for them to eat. He went on to talk about wild hogs. I found it questionable. All the wild hogs I'd ever seen were dark colored with long noses, while the wild pigs looked like little stripped chipmunks. These pigs had short noses and were black and white spotted. The intellectual woman made no comment about such, and I didn't either. But the man didn't hesitate to make his point.

"Some of you may be wondering about the coloring of our wild hogs. As you may or may not know, a pure strand of wild hogs is beyond vicious. They will attack and kill for the fun of the attack. We chose to breed a gentler type of wild hog for security reasons. When we went with a traditional breed of wild hogs it became expensive to replace the tires on our swamp buggies, which occurred on almost every ride.

It didn't give the riders a warm and fuzzy feeling at the thought of being eaten while still alive.

"Our next stop will be into the thick swamp where there is a marsh and water area. This area is highly infested with alligators in one of their natural habitats. As we get closer, you will hear grunts and bellows. This time of year is their mating season. The males will often let out ear splitting roars, especially during the nighttime hours, in an effort to attract females. There can also be some mighty rough fights going on.

"Alligators in the wild can take from six to ten years to reach dependable egg production. They usually lay thirty eggs or a few more. However, most of the hatchlings don't survive preditors. Oddly enough, when wild alligators are brought in for gator farm reproduction, it is common for them to start laying eggs in their first year of captivity. However, their egg production, along with the hatchability of their eggs, are lower than their wild relatives. Therefore, alligator farmers have gone to great lengths to get better egg hatchability. Unlike chickens, alligator eggs must not be rolled, shaken, clumsily handled, or even disturbed during their viable delicate cycle, which makes it mighty tricky for the farmers who gather their eggs. Not to mention the danger of a protective mother alligator. Farmers must watch their captive alligators very closely to either very carefully gather their eggs at 7 days after laying or after they are 4 weeks old. The days in between are their most vulnerable time. Eggs hatch in approximately 65 days. If you've ever seen an angry mother alligator protecting her nest, you'll understand why the farmers age faster than average people do."

I could definitely understand why.

"How often do alligator farmers get killed?" asked the curious woman.

"Too often," was the driver's reply. "You will later be able to visit our own alligator farm and hatching facility. We also have young alligators you can hold if you wish. If you're the brave sort of showoff willing to sign a lengthy non-responsibility document for loss of limb or life, you can even try your hand at gathering eggs. Alligators are not particular as to what they eat. Some have been known to prefer human flesh as a delicacy. I have documents right here in my box. If you want one speak up and sign now before we reach the egg laying area of the swamp."

He got a document from his box and offered it and a pen to each person. No one volunteered to sign.

The wild alligators were very impressive in their natural habitat. Just looking at them made my skin crawl. Their grunts and bellows sent an extra chill running over my body. How wildlife and humans manage to survive such fierce prehistoric creatures was beyond me. I could see why there was a long, high fence enclosing the extensive swamp area. If not for the fence, I was sure there would be less hogs and fewer racoons. I tried to guess the cost of putting in the fencing. Probably much more than the amount of drug money Jimbo and I got from the motorcycle riding dealer.

By the time we had circled the area and disembarked the swamp buggy, an exact thirty minutes had passed.

"Next on your agenda is the Airboat ride," the driver announced as we climbed down the steps where new visitors waited to get on. By the end of the day, I was sure the racoons would be having a sugar coma, and the so-called wild hogs would be well fed.

The riders and I had walked a few feet away when a hand took hold of my arm. I jumped and turned to face Nokosi Micco. I shouldn't have been surprised to see his hand holding onto my arm, but I was.

"I'll go with you on the airboat ride," he told me. "Being you are not the trusting kind. It isn't as safe as the swamp buggy ride."

"It's not safe?" I said, feeling my eyes widen.

"Perfectly safe if you don't get seasick and tumble off the boat into the gator-filled water."

I thought I saw his eyes twinkle, but I wasn't sure. "Maybe I should skip the ride," I told him.

"No way. You should get your money's worth being you didn't accept my free invitation earlier today. Besides, you'll love it."

I was even less sure about loving it, along with the safety factor, as he led me to the airboat. We appeared to be the last passengers getting on. The airboat was basically flat with only a foot or so of fender around it.

"We chose to have a fender to keep passengers from falling off into the water when we get to going fast," he told me. "As you can see, the gators surround the boat with high hopes of an easy meal."

I cringed as I watched the alligators surrounded the airboat. I tried to remember what the woman at the 7-Eleven told me. No one died, because Nokosi Micco didn't want to be sued. I wondered what would happen if a lone person without a family fell off. When we paid our entrance fees, we had to sign a document stating there would be no responsibility on the attraction's part if there was any type of accident.

Nokosi Micco held my arm as he helped me step over the fender. "You see that alligator you stepped over? His name is Gimp. Lost his leg somehow. He's become my pet. Thinks he should be fed fish every time he sees a person."

That was some kind of eight-foot, opened mouthed, snaggled toothed pet. I thought but had too much pride to admit to my repulsion. Nokosi Micco guided me to a grouping of seats that held several other people. He seated me in one of the two seats which were the highest up near the airboat's pilot. I was greatly relieved when he reached around me and pulled out a seatbelt and fastened it around my stomach.

"Make sure your seatbelts are fastened," the pilot called out. "We'll be moving fast. Don't want anyone to be slung out of the boat. Nokosi Micco fastened his belt, but I glanced back to notice the pilot had not fastened his.

"He'll check everyone's seat belts before we start. Some people don't fasten them properly. Wind and water aren't to be taken lightly," he told me. "You can see why it is called an airboat by the huge fan sitting behind us. An airboat can go as fast as 130 miles per hour depending on the fan, size of engine, and quality of the boat. We have the very best airboats made."

"Will we be going that fast?" I questioned, thinking we could all be blown off the boat at that speed regardless of the seatbelts.

"No. Can't see much at that speed. Wind gets in your eyes and can take your breath away. It's mainly drug dealers running from the law that hit such speeds."

I instantly thought of him saying he had the best boats made. "Where will we be going?" I asked.

"We'll take a little, fast spin in open waters to give the tourists a feel of our potential power for speed. When we get into thick vegetation we'll slow down and cut the engines to their lowest power so as not to scare the birds and other wildlife whose habitats are in the marsh. Many of the birds are nesting."

"Don't the alligators eat them?" I questioned.

"Sure. Some of them fall prey to gators. Worse than that are the snakes. People have bought snakes at pet stores, gotten tired of them when they reach unsafe sizes and turned them loose in the everglades. There are boa constrictors, which grow huge and prolific with the abundant supply of free food. Along with rat snakes, hognose snakes, garter snakes, kingsnakes, or the ones we call blacksnakes. Those are the gentler ones. There are four deadly venomous snakes I rather not come into contact with. The pygmy rattlesnake, the diamondback rattlesnake, the eastern coral snake, and the Florida cottonmouth. I also had reports of there being an invasion of venomous black mamba and other deadly snakes invading our land as the result of pure human stupidity. People can be the most ignorant, destructive, and dangerous to the earth's ecosystem. We now have snake hunters hired to kill snakes."

I thought of the old child's song, *I don't like spiders and snakes.* And that *was* what it took to scare the living daylights out of me. I certainly didn't want to take any slow walks in the everglades by moonlight or even in the bright light of day. I now understood why the swamp buggies really were high off the ground. It appeared to me Florida could be one of the most dangerous places in existence, especially for those who were inexperienced or naïve about the dangers.

"And people are willingly live here?"

"Some of the toughest people in existence live and thrive in the swamps."

I was reminded of Angie Bell and her relatives but didn't comment.

"There is a lot of difference in the people who inhabited this area from necessity and those who have made these areas into a vacation paradise. My ancestors were chased into the swamp land in order to escape being murdered. They learned how to survive long before my time. I suppose you've heard John Anderson sing the haunting song *Seminole Winds*. It has a way of adequately describing our culture along with our past and future."

There was no more talking as the engine started and revved up. The noise from the engine and fan was nearly deafening. The pilot sitting behind me wore earplugs and grinned with pleasure as the high winds hit us in the face. Nokosi Micco leaned over until his lips touched my ear.

"This is the feel of freedom," he whispered. "I live for it."

I decided the wind would feel nice if it was a summer day once the temperature reached way over 100 degrees. I was chilled from the wind although the day was warm. Nokosi Micco saw the chill bumps on my arms and silently slipped his arms around my shoulders. I let him. His touch felt strong and warm. It made me feel less vulnerable.

I admit the airboat ride wasn't my favorite experience. Knowing there were alligators in the water and dangerous snakes lying in wait in the swampy marshland we eased through left a creepy feeling inside me. And, at the same time, I was fascinated with the birds that made the marshland their home as they perched in scrub trees ignoring us. Like the native people, they learned how to survive.

Relief washed over me as my feet left the movement of the boat and landed on solid ground. My legs felt kind of rubbery. I could understand the impulse to get down on my knees and kiss the ground. Nokosi Micco was grinning at me as though he understood what I was feeling and thought it amusing.

"It's getting late. I need to be getting back," I managed to tell him.

"Not yet," he told me gently. "The rest of the tour will be walking about designated areas to see the animal sanctuary. I'm proud of the improvements I've managed to make."

"You did all this on your own?" I questioned his ability and his ego.

"No, I can't take credit for what many of my people helped accomplish. I do take credit for improving the attraction until it has become a well-known tourist destination. That's one of the reasons I wanted to give you a tour. I value the reaction of people who know nothing about this place and what it has to offer. I call it shock factor analysis."

Okay, maybe I had been wrong. From Lena's comments, I had thought he might have been attracted enough to me to want to impress me. He took me by the elbow and led me down a walkway.

"This is my least favorite exhibit," he told me as he stopped at a deep concrete enclosure with the top closed off by closely woven mesh wire. "Admittedly, I have a snake phobia. I'll go into the gator enclosure and gather eggs, but I'll not get closer than this to the snake pit."

I was surprised by his confession as I looked down into the covered pit. There were a number of snakes crawling in and out of what I assumed was meant to be their natural habitat. There were also laminated photos on the pit wall of the different kinds of snakes with information about them. I could tell he was anxious to get away as he placed his callused hand on my back and hurried me away.

Next came the Alligator exhibit area.

"This is my favorite, if I don't include my pet cats," he told me.

The area was a small pond surrounded by concrete walkways with a natural area where a lot of vegetation that looked like palm fronds, swamp grass, limbs and perhaps hay were prevalent. There were probably two dozen large alligators lying about in the sun. This exhibit was surrounded by two chain length fences about six feet apart with curls of barbwire on the top of the inner fence. I assumed the walkway between the fences was for the worker's convenience. I also assumed the razor wire was to keep the alligators from climbing over. There were signs that read: **STAY SAFE. Do not lean, sit, climb, or touch the fences. If you fall, the animals could eat you, and that might make them sick.**

"I had to put in two fences with razor wire," he told me as he leaned his hands on the outer fence. "Tourists would hold their children over the wire so they could get a better look at the gators. They didn't realize what would happen if one of the children fell inside the enclosure."

I got the image.

"You wouldn't believe the precautions we have to take. Or the cost of insurance we carry."

One of the alligators let out a loud bellow as he moved out of the pond toward a group of other alligators.

"That's a male. Unlike in the swamp, I only keep one male in the breeding exhibit pond. Males tend to fight over breeding rights. Females aren't too docile either. Those large clumps of limbs and grasses are their nests. I gather the eggs on a regular basis and put them in the hatching chambers."

"You collect the eggs?" I questioned in surprise. I had assumed he hired workers to do it.

"It's too dangerous to have employees in there."

I lifted my brows at him. He was afraid of snakes and yet he robbed the alligator nests.

"I only go in while they are being fed. They are more interested in food than in what I'm doing. I'm too much of a coward to take a foolish risk."

He gave me a smile as he spoke, and his entire face lit up. I was struck again by how much his rugged appearance appealed to me. I felt drawn to him by his looks alone. I wasn't so sure about the person he was inside.

"Why have you never married?" I surprised myself by asking.

"How do you know I've never married?"

"Actually, I don't know that. I assumed you weren't since you're not wearing a wedding ring."

"Would you be willing to marry a man who lives the kind of life I live?"

How did I respond to that? I wouldn't like to live such a life, but I'm sure there were a lot of women who would. "When there is enough love between two people, the living conditions aren't important."

He let out a laugh at that before he became serious again. "You're wrong about that, Alona. Living conditions always matter to people as well as to animals. Look at the rich people who live in Naples. Take the Fitzgeralds, for example. They have the finest of everything, plus bank accounts that's nothing short of staggering. Yet, they have been married and divorced several times. They are so greedy they hardly pay their employees enough to live on. They've become wealthy on the backs of the poor. Obviously, it's the love of money they strive for instead of love between two people."

I related to what he was saying with first-hand experience.

"Take poor, little Angie Bell. She works every day of her life in hopes she will be able to better her living conditions. She even married Hanson Bell thinking life with him would be better than living in the swamp with her dad. She's still hopeful although she'll never be able to get ahead. Hanson takes every dime she earns. He believes women are to be used to make a man happy. He doesn't care a thing about her other than how she's a benefit to him," he said with derision. "Doesn't matter if she loves him beyond all reason, her living conditions do matter.

Obviously, he was more knowledgeable about Angie Bell as he pretended to be earlier. "She should leave him," I said with feelings.

"How?" he questioned.

"She's got a job. She should divorce him. She'd be better off living on her own," I told him with conviction.

"If she goes against him in any way, she'll end up gator food somewhere out in the everglades and she knows it."

"She has a father, siblings, and other relatives. Can't they protect her?"

He slowly shook his head. "They have the same attitude as Hanson Bell. A subservient woman is a handed-down tradition. One that is mighty convenient for men."

"What about law enforcement?" I asked. Surely the law would protect a pregnant woman who is being abused.

"Rich people's law doesn't apply to swamp dwellers."

"But . . ." I began.

"Some things can't be changed easily. Traditions are one of those things. Now, enough talk about the sad side of life. If you'll walk this way, I'll show my cats to you."

I followed him to a gate connected to the walkway that he unlocked and relocked after we entered. "I don't allow visitors in this area. My cats get upset when people are too close. That's why I have bamboo and palm fronds growing around the exhibit. It makes the cats feel protected. The believe they are stalking the people instead of the other way around."

As we stepped around a clump of bamboo, I saw what he was referring to. Two black Florida panthers were enclosed in large, separate cages. They were huge, shiny black in color and fiercely beautiful with glowing eyes.

"This one here is Helga. She's still half wild. She was shot in the front shoulder by some hunter. The wildlife authorities brought her to me rather than put her down. She lived, but as you can see, her injury is severe enough to keep her from living in the wild. She has an active hatred for people. She only slightly trusts me. I do all her feeding and care."

The panther was glaring at me through the bamboo and palm fronds. There was pure hatred in her eyes. I could imagine what that cat could do to a person.

"Now, this is Baby," he said as he went to the second enclosure where a sleeker, black panther paced. "I raised her on a bottle after the wildlife officers brought her to me. I had to get a special rehabilitation license to keep these two in captivity. A veterinarian must examine them, as well as the other animals, on a regular basis. You'll have to stay outside of the enclosure keeping the bamboo and palm fronds between you and the enclosure," he told me as he unlocked another gate and stepped through, closing the gate without locking it.

Much to my surprise, he unlocked the main gate to the younger panther's enclosure and walked in. The panther was on him in a moment's time. Her paws were on his shoulders with her mouth clamped on his arm. He mumbled soothing words to the cat, which brought a purring sound from her throat as she turned loose of his arm to rub her face against his.

"Good girl," he crooned. "That's my good girl."

I heard squeals about fifty feet from where I stood. I turned to see a group of women staring in terror.

"That man is in with that panther," she squealed. "Somebody get him out of there. He'll be killed."

"It's okay," I told her quickly. "She's his pet. He raised her on a bottle."

The women calmed down a little but not much. After my explanation the group of women settled down some.

Nokosi Micco heard her but pretended not to as he gave the cat a final rubbing. He left the enclosure, locking the gates behind him until he was with me again. The women walked on shaking their heads at the crazy man. In a way I agreed with them. A panther could severely hurt him without ever intending to do so.

"You never know how people will react to animals. That woman was right. A lot of people believe wild animals are nothing but gentle pets, but they are wrong. They have no idea what wild-animal instincts are capable of doing to recently domesticated animals."

"Do you have any idea?" I couldn't resist asking. He was the one going in with a panther.

"I do," he assured me. "Plus, you have to be able to judge their disposition. You never go in with them when they're restless.

He placed his hand on my back again. "Come on. I'll show you the baby gators and crocks. The one thing you don't want to do is get in with an animal that's angry or frightened. Even worse is when the animal is hungry. I make sure all the animals are well fed, including the snakes I'd rather not have, but visitors are fascinated with the creepy crawlers.

I have a few crocodiles here so people can see the difference between the two. The gators are as gentle as kittens compared to the crocks. Don't like them at all. They're dangerous."

Chapter 19

Angie Bell

"**M**ic took you on a private tour of his place?" Angie Bell gushed at me in surprise as she overheard me tell Lena about the black panthers. "He doesn't do that for anybody. Why did he do it with you?" Angie demanded.

"He said he wanted a stranger's input on his facilities."

"Bull shit," Angie said. "He gets more input than he knows what to do with."

"He likes her," Lena broke her silence to say.

"I can't believe it. Why would he like her?" Angie demanded as she turned toward Lena and then faced me. "You're . . . you don't belong here."

"He wanted the honest opinion of someone who wasn't a tourist or a native," I was quick to tell her.

"I guess you gave it to him, didn't you?" she added with a sneer before she added, "Like you're an expert on anything."

"I told him I was impressed with everything I saw, as well as the extreme care and maintenance of exhibits. It was obvious to me how much he cared about the animals along with the upkeep of his attraction."

"You're a regular goody-two-shoes, aren't you?" she accused me, but she also had an odd sort of expression on her face. "Mic is mighty particular in who he trusts. Certainly not a northern goody-two-shoes such as you are."

"I don't think it was a matter of trust," I told her, ignoring her attempted insult. "I think he was genuinely interested in a stranger's perspective."

"Humph," Angie gave a disbelieving grunt. "As if your opinion mattered."

I saw Lena's mouth twitch into a slight grin as she pretended to be fed up with us. "Get to work or get fired," Lena said in her way of addressing her employees when they were getting out of line.

I went out front into the dining area. I was surprised to see Nokosi Micco sitting at my section waiting for me to take his order.

"He insisted on being seated in your section," the receptionist whispered to me as she handed me a menu to give him. "It's a historical occurrence for him to show up here to eat, much less at breakfast time. That is if eating is what he has in mind," she added.

"We meet again," I used my friendliest tone of voice as I greeted him. "What can I get you this morning?"

"Big breakfast," he was quick to say. "Plus, dinner with me tonight," he added in the same tone of voice, but low enough for no one else to hear.

"A big breakfast coming right up," I told him ignoring the other part.

"And dinner?"

"I..." I began and hesitated as I searched for an excuse to refuse.

"Your hair is beautiful, and I can't see a thing you need to clean up."

I smiled at that.

"Actually," he continued, "I would like to share an original Seminole meal with you. My people have delicious restaurants along with other stores in their own tourist traps. They are also good at giving tourists a pleasant experience for their money."

"I haven't recovered from yesterday," I told him.

"Good. That means it was memorable. I'll pick you up after your shift is over."

"No, that's not workable. I get off at 3:00. I need time to rest after work."

"I know when you get off work. You'll have time to rest with me."

I gave him a puzzled look, not believing his insistence. "After working here, I need to go home, take a shower, and put on clean clothes. I don't find the lingering smells of a restaurant refreshing."

"Okay, then, I'll pick you up at the trailer park at 3:30."

"That's much too early for dinner," I insisted. Did he really think I could take a drive across town, take a shower, and be ready in thirty minutes?

It'll give you time to become acquainted with my people's culture before we eat."

I didn't want to be rude by telling him I was only slightly interested in his people's culture. I was a long way from being a history buff of any kind of heritage. Not only that, but I also wasn't sure I wanted to spend private time with him.

"I'm not the only Seminole who takes the opportunity tourists offer by wanting to empty their pockets in trade for their entertainment."

"I don't know about dinner," I told him hesitantly, although looking at him right now made me want to accept his invitation. His all-male appearance appealed to me. His masculinity reminded me of Sensi York. I missed what we shared together. Could this man be a replacement for what I had with my instructor? I missed having someone who meant more than friendship to me. I might as well admit to myself that I was lonely along with a dose of youthful, raging hormones. I longed to have someone special in my life. Maybe Nokosi Micco could be the answer I had been seeking, but I wasn't optimistic.

"Okay," I hesitantly said. "Dinner does sound good but pick me up at four-thirty. You want black coffee, right?"

"Right," he told me with a pleased expression on his face.

I cleared a table and carried the dishes into the kitchen. Angie glared at me when I sat the dishes down on the counter next to her.

"Leave him alone," she whispered low enough for no one other than me to hear her. "He's not your kind."

"What did you just say?" I questioned, although I had heard here very clearly.

"Go back where you belong," she added in an even lower whisper. "You'll only cause him trouble with his people."

I was surprised at the anger that was flashing in her eyes as she looked me in the face. What was it to her if I was friends with Nokosi Micco? Was he the man she wanted for herself, even though she was already married? Not that I could blame her considering the kind of husband she had. That was the only explanation I could think of for her verbal attack on me. My hackles raised, and I couldn't resist responding.

"What is Mic to you?" I used the name he had told me I could use. Her eyes widened; her lips drew back as though she was about to continue her verbal attack.

Reta, one of the other waitresses, came into the kitchen and Angie turned away from me as though she hadn't even acknowledged my presence much less been furious with me. I looked toward Lena to judge if she had heard what Angie Bell had said. She was ignoring both of us. What was wrong with me being friends with Nokosi Micco?

I picked up Nokosi Micco's order and took it to his table. He looked up at me with those dark, twinkling eyes and a warm smile. I hadn't expected the warm feeling his expression would give me. For the first time since I had arrived in this town, I didn't feel completely alone. Finally, I could have a friend who enjoyed my company if nothing more. I would be foolish to turn away from what he willingly offered.

"Anything else I can get you?" I asked him the same question I always ask customers. His dark eyes twinkled even more brightly with whatever thought entered his mind.

"Not at this moment," he answered.

I left his bill on the table and busied myself with other tables.

I was in the kitchen when Nokosi Micco paid his bill and left the restaurant. I bused his table finding a ten-dollar tip under his plate. I would make sure Angie got the full amount even though she had verbally attacked me. I now felt more than sorry for her. Not only was she married to an abusive man; she was having longings for someone else. I decided that her anger toward me was because it was Nokosi Micco she fantasized about. I sat the dishes on the counter beside her.

"Here," I said as I handed her the ten-dollar bill. "He left this for you. Save it for your baby."

She didn't so much as acknowledge my presence, but she didn't hesitate to grab the ten-dollar bill and quickly stick it down the neck of her old t-shirt into her bra.

Good for you, I thought. I hoped she had been able to squirrel enough money for her and her baby to disappear from the man who left all those bruises on her. Surely, she realized a man who abused his wife would also abuse his child.

"Divorce him," I whispered as I leaned close enough for her to hear what I said without others hearing me.

"I can't," she surprised me by whispering back devoid of her earlier burst of anger. "He'll kill me if I try."

"I'll help you disappear," I surprised myself by saying.

"How?" she whispered back.

Before I could think of an answer; Reta came into the kitchen with more dirty dishes. Lena decided it was the waitresses' job to bus their own tables instead of having the very pregnant Angie waddling through the dining room. In my opinion she would have gotten more tips than all the waitresses put together. Evidently Lena thought it wouldn't be a good look for the restaurant.

My thoughts were on Angie and Nokosi Micco for the rest of my shift at the restaurant. I could understand her attraction for Nokosi Micco, but I couldn't see him being attracted to her. She was bone thin with sandy colored, straggly hair. Her face might have been pretty enough if it wasn't for the angry expression she always wore making her thin lips turn downward into a frown. Worst of all were her eyes. They squinted at everything with pure hatred. Again, I wondered why Lena kept her at the restaurant considering her attitude. Lena knew all too well that the money she earned wasn't going to help her or the baby she carried. Hanson Bell was the one that benefited. Lena also knew I was slipping Angie my tip money in hopes she could hide it from her drug addicted husband.

"Your tip money won't do any good," Lena whispered to me when Angie went to the restroom, which she was doing more often with each day that passed. "She'll never leave him even if she had enough money to do so."

"She can't stay with him. He beats her, and he'll beat the baby."

"It's what she knows. She grew up with her parents beating each other and their children."

"She can change it."

"How?" Lena asked mostly to see what I would answer.

"She can move far away. Disappear by changing her name or even by marrying someone else."

"She doesn't have the means to move or try to get a divorce. Besides, she's too afraid of him to do either one."

"What about her siblings? Can't they help her?"

"They ran away to greener pastures long ago. Left the littlest one behind to fend for herself."

"She didn't run away like they did?"

"She thought running away consisted of marrying Hanson Bell."

"We could help her," I said.

Lena shook her head like I was being ridiculous. "You can't help someone who doesn't want your help. She'd rather take beatings than be without him. She sees him as belonging to her when she has precious little that belongs to her."

"What about her baby. It belongs to her. Doesn't she care about its safety?"

Angie returned before Lena could say anything more. I clocked out wondering how a mother could care more about a man than the safety of her baby.

I drove to the little trailer and went straight to the shower to wash the smell of the restaurant off my skin and hair. It occurred to me that I hadn't improved my life much by moving here. I was still working in a restaurant the same as I did with Aunt Mary. At least I was being paid a little for the work I did. The place I was now living in had only two rooms and a bathroom. The tiny living room and kitchen were together, with the bedroom so small there was only enough room to walk on one side of the bed. The tiny closet was at the foot of the bed and held only a dozen clothes hangers. I had to squeeze between the foot of the bed to get to the closet. It wasn't a pleasant trailer or a pleasant trailer park. The trailers were crammed together. There wasn't more than ten feet between each trailer where a car could be parked. Thankfully, there were mainly old people renting the trailers, so there wasn't a lot of noise during the day or night. I wasn't noisy or had any visitors. Therefore, neither the landlord nor other renters complained about me.

There was barely enough time for me to shower and dress. I longed for a few precious minutes to sit down, clear my mind while doing absolutely nothing. I didn't get those few minutes of rest. At four-thirty sharp Nokosi Micco stopped in front of the trailer. I rushed outside not wanting him to see the inside of the dinky trailer. He had gotten out of the car but didn't have time to reach the trailer. Instead, he turned around to open the passenger car door for me. I hurriedly got in and took a deep breath of something similar to relief at sitting down, although I wasn't looking forward to meeting any of his relatives or sharing a meal with him, which told me a lot about the friendship I was trying to establish.

"You seem sad," he said as he started the car and backed out of the narrow space. "Why is that?"

"I find this place depressing," I told him, not meaning just the trailer. I was finding everything about this town to be less than I had expected. I came here thinking this was a tropical paradise that I would be able to call home. I was becoming more delusional with each day that passed.

"Move," he said. "You don't have to rent this place."

"It's the cheapest rent I can find," I told him.

"Understood. Most places in this town cost a bundle to rent. If you travel several miles out of town, rent is more reasonable."

"Do you have a house near your airboat attraction?" I had seen buildings but nothing that looked like a lived-in home.

"No. I have a house in LaBell. I wanted a place where I could get away from my so-called work environment. As much as I love what I have accomplished, I still need the peace and quiet of solitude, plus I like playing a little golf now and then."

Somehow, him playing golf didn't fit my image of him. I saw more of a dark-skinned Indian wearing a loin cloth running through the jungle, or in his case, through the sawgrass of the everglades.

"LaBell is more of a normal man's paradise," he said with a grin. "Port Royal is the paradise of the ultra-rich."

"Port Royal?" I questioned.

"The elite of Naples. It was once five or even ten-acre estates. The land has become so valuable that it is being sub-divided. Which I think is a crying shame. Some things should be left alone for future generations to ogle at. Alas, cash money had become more important than nostalgia."

"I think it's called progress," I said.

"Progress," he repeated as though it was a dirty word. "Even my own people want progress. Only the elders remember a time that has long passed. But then, yesterday is for memories and tomorrow is for the future. Memory is to learn from, tomorrow is to live for."

Chapter 20

*

The first place Nokosi Micco took me was called Ah-Tah-Thi-Ki. When translated it means a place to learn. It is a reverent place where visitors can learn about the history and culture of the Seminole people. I was impressed with the place along with its 30,000-plus artifacts.

"This place has put on public display a lot of my people's history. Having a history is important for all people no matter who they are or where they come from," he told me as though he was making a point.

His words hit home. I hadn't realized it was so obvious I was in a town where I didn't belong. Was it obvious to everyone I met? But then I had brought the only culture I had known with me. I grew up working in a restaurant with no pay, and I was still working in a restaurant with very little pay. I had thought I was bettering myself, but I hadn't progressed very far.

"Are you ready to leave?" he asked. "We'll take a little walk so you can see more of what my people have accomplished."

I readily agreed. I had found that walking about was something I enjoyed doing be it early of a morning or late of the evening when the sun went down, and the temperature dropped. We hadn't gone far when he put his huge hand on my back in a comforting sort of way.

"You're still sad," he said, disrupting my introspective thoughts. "What's bothering you, little Alona?"

I couldn't make myself tell him what was really bothering me. If I did, I would sound self-centered and petty. Instead, I said: "I'm worried about Angie Bell. Every day she comes to work with more bruises."

"More bruises?" he questioned as though he didn't know what I was referring to.

"Her husband beats her." I told him what he already knew.

"That shouldn't come as a surprise. She knew what she was getting into before she married the likes of him. It's almost a tradition with some families. Beat and be beaten is more common than anyone realizes."

I didn't like even the thought of what he was saying. No one, and I mean no one should be beaten. It was cruel to both the body and soul. It destroyed what was deep inside a person that should be encouraged not destroyed. "Were you and her friends before she married?" What I really wanted to know was if they ever dated, but I didn't think it was my place to ask.

"Not really. I saw her out and about just like I saw Hanson Bell out and about. This is a small area where a lot of gossip abounds, although, the elite likes to believe they live in their own paradise, but there are local people with eyes that are always watching."

I believed that to be true. "Lena says he takes the money she earns and uses it for drugs."

"That's not good," he said, but didn't seem too concerned. "Unfortunately, it's a way of life for some people. I might add it happens not only to the likes of Angie, but for the ultra-rich as well. Women are, and always have been, the weaker sex who often get taken advantage of in more ways than one."

That might be so, but I wasn't seeing the results of it every day the way I was seeing it with Angie Bell. "He'll cause her to lose her baby," I added with anger and disgust.

"Baby?"

"The one she's not too far away from giving birth too."

"Humph," he grunted. "Didn't know she was expecting."

"You seem surprised."

"I am. She visited our healing woman to get herbs to keep her from conceiving. Our healing woman gave her herbs and also sent her to the free clinic for birth control pills. Seems I haven't paid too much attention to her lately."

I wondered how he knew she had gotten herbs. Evidently, they hadn't worked for her. He must have known what I was thinking for he answered my curiosity.

"Gossip spreads quickly among the women of my people as well as those who live in the swamps. Amazing what you can learn if you keep your mouth shut and your ears open."

If that was true, then why didn't he know she was expecting? I thought about asking him when he again answered my curiosity.

"Since I moved to LaBell I've not been privy to as much gossip. Some of my people consider me trying to get above my raising."

Yes, I knew what he meant. Aunt Mary thought the same of me, which really was true. I wanted to get above my raising. I didn't want to work for Aunt Mary for the rest of my life. I certainly didn't want to rely on being a thief to have enough money to survive. Yet, I would forever be grateful to Jimbo for what he did for my mother and for me. He had also given me a false identity along with money enough to live on for a while.

A false identity. Was that really what I wanted for myself?

How could I possibly find the place I belonged without being willing to use my real name? Nokosi Micco interrupted my thoughts when he spoke.

"There are those, both my people and others, who resent my success. Some of my relatives think I should share what I've worked hard to earn with them. When I refused, it didn't go over too well. You see, I believe the person who does the work should be the recipient of the benefits. There are also white people who believe Indians deserve little regardless of how many hours, days and years they work for what little success they manage to obtain."

I didn't tell him about Aunt Mary or my so-called father's brother. I was not ready to open up to someone who might become a friend but was still a stranger to me.

We walked through mostly tourist areas instead of visiting where his mother lived, which I thought we were going to do.

"Are we going to eat with your parents?" I questioned.

"No," he didn't hesitate to tell me. "My father is no longer a part of my life. My mother chose to return to her people after my brother and father were killed in a plane crash."

"I'm sorry to hear about the accident," I told him with genuine sympathy.

"Thank you. It was a life-changing experience for me as well as for my mother, but it's in the past. Both my mother and I have continued with our lives."

"What caused the plane crash?" I was bold enough to ask.

"A cause was never determined," he said. "Have you worked up an appetite yet?"

I got the feeling he wanted to avoid talking about the plane crash, which made me think there really might have been something drug related involved. The thought put chills up my backbone. It might not be safe to become involved with anyone who was involved in drugs.

"We'll walk to my car," he told me. "The best restaurant is a little too far for us to walk. It will be dark before we get through eating."

I had noticed how sudden things changed here. The sun would be blazing hot one minute and the next a rainstorm would hit that cooled things down before it became hot again. One minute the morning would be dark and the next minute the birds would be welcoming full daylight with their songs.

The same thing happened at night. There would be no slowness of long, dark shadows before darkness came.

I dreaded getting into his car. Although he parked it in the shade of a huge tree, it would be too hot for comfort before the air conditioner had time to cool the inside off. Again, I could only imagine what the temperature would be like during high noon in August.

Nokosi Micco unlocked the door and held it open for me. I got in and took a reluctant breath of the over-heated air as Nokosi Micco walked around the car and got behind the wheel. I was thankful his vehicle had cloth seats instead of leather. I had discovered leather seats got hot enough to burn flesh during Florida summers. He turned the key and started the engine at the same time I got a glimpse of someone darting from behind the trunk of the huge tree. The back door flew open, and someone jumped in and slammed the door close.

"Keep driving," said a woman's panicked voice.

"What the hell?" ejected Nokosi Micco as we both turned to see who was in the back seat.

"Hurry, keep driving. I need help," sobbed Angie Bell. Her entire voice along with her body was shaking until I wouldn't be surprised if her very bones might break.

"What's going on," demanded Nokosi Micco.

Angie's face was blooded. Her nose crooked, and her lips split. Her hair was tangled with leaves and twigs. Both her eyes were huge and showing recent bruising. It was obvious she was in a terrible state.

"Sorry, Mic. I need help bad and you're the only one who's ever been willing to help me. There's no one else I can trust."

"What happened?" he asked in a voice that sounded unusually calm considering the hysteria Angie was having.

"Hanson," she whimpered as she lifted her blood and dirt-stained hands to cradle her face.

"He beat the hell of you again," Nokosi Micco needlessly said.

"He wanted to kill my baby while it was in my belly. He was afraid I would stop working after it was born. I fought him," she whined as her shaking increased. "I – I killed him."

"You killed him?" his eyebrows raised in disbelief. "How could you do such as that?"

"I took a knife from the restaurant. I didn't want to be beat on any longer. Alona has been slipping me money. She said she would help me run away. That's why I hid the money," Angie blurted out as she cried harder.

"You did?" he glanced at me with disapproval as he drove away. "You gave her money and promised to help her run away?" he questioned like I had done something unforgivably stupid.

"I did," I admitted. "No one should be forced to endure what she has been going through. I was trying to help her."

"I see. I warned you about interfering in other people's lives, didn't I?"

"She wanted to help me," Angie said in a broken voice. "She's the only one who understood."

"You've should have come to me," he told her.

"I'm coming to you now," she said. "You have to help me. We've got to get rid of his body. You can take it out into the sawgrass swamp and let the gators eat him."

"Shit! Angie, I can't do that. I don't want to be part of a murder, much less be implicated in getting rid of a body."

"Me either," she moaned out. They'll put me in jail. Take my baby away from me. I'd rather both of us were dead than have that happen."

"You should have thought of that earlier," he told her.

"It's difficult to think when you're getting the life beat out of you," I told Nokosi Micco as I came to Angie's defense.

"Please help me," she begged both of us. "You know what he was like, Mic. I didn't want to hurt him or anyone else. It was self-defense. I'm desperate, Mic. You're my only hope in staying out of jail and keeping my baby." Not only was Angie shaking; tears were now streaming down her face washing lines in the dirt and blood of her face.

"Why can't you help her?" I asked him. "You told me the swamp was the best way to get rid of a body. If nothing else, you can dump him in with your own gators. It'll save on feeding them," I added as I thought of all the beatings Angie had taken.

He gave me a hateful look before he spoke. "Where's his body?" he asked Angie as he glanced at the pitiful condition of her crooked nose and beaten face.

On a side road off Alligator Alley."

"How did you get from there to my car?"

"I drove his car. It's not that far."

"It's several miles," he said. "Someone had to see you waiting on me."

"They didn't. I made sure I stayed hidden. I parked his car and snuck through the bushes until I saw your car. I didn't want anyone seeing me looking like this. They'd know something bad happened."

"Didn't you work tonight?" I questioned. She was at the restaurant when I left hours ago.

"Lena let me off early. That made Hanson mad. Plus, he found some of the money you gave me and knew I was holding out on him. He went crazier than ever before."

"How did you know where to find me?" Nokosi Micco continued to ask her questions.

"Lena overheard you talking to Alona. She told me what you'd said."

"No secrets in this town," he repeated.

"It'll be pitch dark soon. I'll take you where he is." Angie told us as though we had agreed to do her bidding.

"Leave his body where it's at," Nokosi Micco told her. "Let wild animals and insects demolish him."

"Someone will find him. There'll be buzzards circling," she whimpered. "They'll find him with my blood on him from where he beat me. You know they will."

"Not if the wildlife gets at him first."

I couldn't believe Nokosi Micco was being so insensitive when it was obvious what Angie Bell was going through as she burst into another round of almost incoherent desperate pleading.

"Shit," he said again. "You're making me and Alona an accomplice in murder by showing up, let along expecting us to help you."

She covered her face again with blood-stained hands. "It was self-defense, but who is willing to believe someone like me? I'm swamp trash. Nobody helps swamp trash. Lock 'em up and throw away the key is the best solution. Always has been, and you know it. Please, please help me, Mic."

My heart broke for the pregnant girl. "I'll help you if he won't," I bravely told her.

"You'll help even if I do," he informed me, still angry at the situation Angie put us in. "Can you find his body in the dark?" he asked Angie.

"Yes, it's where he always takes me when he is going to beat on me. Fear excites him, but I can't help panicking when he starts driving to alligator alley."

"Okay, okay," he finally said. "Once it's dark enough, I'll drive you back to his car and we'll follow you to his body. Until then, you'll clean yourself up and burn your clothes, while Alona and I clean the back seat of my car. There can't be one speck of your or his blood left in it or on either of us."

"And then what? You'll not turn me in, will you?" she asked, appearing apprehensive as to whether he planned on helping her or turning her in to the law.

"The three of us will wrap him in plastic and put him in his car. You'll drive to the hidden boat dock you're well familiar with. Then Alona and I will meet you there in the airboat."

Relief showed on Angie's swollen face, while Nokosi Micco's inner anger was still raging. I didn't blame him in the least. He hadn't asked for this, and neither had I. We both knew Angie might not get away with what she had done even if it was proven to be in self-defense. Worse was that she had already involved both of us. Our only solution was to turn her in or help her get rid of the body. There was no way we could pretend we knew nothing of the murder.

He dropped Angie off at Hanson's shack. "We'll be back in one hour," he told her. Make sure you're ready."

We then drove to Nokosi Micco's place in LaBell. He pushed a button on his remote and the garage door opened. He pulled in and closed the door. I'm going to get a vacuum cleaner and several bottles of hydrogen peroxide. You can vacuum while I make sure I've eliminated any possibly of a trace of blood."

"Do you think it's safe to leave his body this long?" I questioned when he returned as I took the vacuum from his hands.

"Nothing is safe. If his body is discovered before we get to him. We'll claim we know nothing about him or Angie."

I didn't think that would be fair to Angie, but I wasn't about to argue the point. Angie hadn't been fair in involving us in a murder, but who else could she turn to? Angie and I both had to trust Nokosi Micco to do what was best for everyone.

Once the car was cleaned to his satisfaction, he put a large amount of folded black plastic over the back seat and floor where Angie would be sitting. For some reason, I got the idea he had done something similar before. As soon as he was satisfied with the cleaning, along with the bag of supplies he put in the trunk, we got in and drove back where he had left Angie.

She came out of the shack scrubbed and looking slightly better than when we had left her. She had even tried to tape straight her broken nose. There was a thin trail of smoke coming from a stove pipe sticking out of the shack. I assumed it was where she had burned her clothes.

"Get in and don't touch anything," he told her as he opened the back door for her.

Angie didn't say one word as she carefully got into the back seat of the car. Not one of us talked as we drove back to the large grove of trees where she had left Hanson's car.

"Don't touch the door," he told her before he stopped. "I'll open the door for you. I don't want your fingerprints on anything."

Angie was like a robot making sure she did exactly as he instructed.

"Drive to where you left him, but don't turn off on the road if there is any traffic to be seen."

She nodded, got in the car, started it up and drove away. Nokosi Micco followed at a distance behind her that didn't indicate he was following her.

There was little chance another car would take the dirt path that cut through the undergrowth from Alligator Alley. The path turned and twisted at least a mile after we turned off the highway.

"There are more such dirt paths in this area of Florida than outsiders can imagine. Local people know how to stay away from places like this. They are filled with drug dealers and worse. We're taking our life in our hands by coming here regardless of the reason."

The way he said that made more chills creep over me – like I wasn't freaked out enough by what we were doing.

"If we're caught, we'll both claim Angie stopped us on the way home and insisted we follow her. We followed not knowing what was going on. Got it?"

"Got it," I told him, knowing such a claim would be only an attempt to cover ourselves while we threw Angie to the wolves.

When the path ended, Angie stopped and got out of the car. She was standing in one spot with her body twitching all over as we got out of the car and went to where she stood.

"Lead the way," he told her.

I was surprised to see rocks in front of her car that showed where fires were often built.

"He liked to bring me here," Angie managed to say as tears came to her eyes. "He called it his. . ." she didn't finish her sentence as she pointed a few feet from where we stood. "I dragged him into the weeds."

Nokosi Micco opened the trunk and took out three pairs of gloves and shoe covers. "Put these on," he told us as he took out three plastic coveralls and indicated for us to also put them on. "Don't spit or get scratched on anything. It's important we don't leave any DNA to be traced."

"Mine's already here," Angie said.

"Too late to do anything about that," he told her. "Hopefully, there will be several rains before anyone shows up here again if luck is on our side."

He parted the weeds to find where the body was laying. Angie sucked in her breath and closed her eyes. "I – I can't . . ."

"Get in his car," he told her. "Alona and I will put him in the trunk."

He made sure he wrapped Hanson's body in the plastic before he had me pick up his feet wrapped in plastic while he took his upper body. I had expected him to be stiff with rigor mortis, but his body had been dead long enough to become pliable. Nokosi Micco was extremely strong and was able to carry him without much help on my part. He easily stuffed him into the trunk of Hanson's car, making sure the body was wrapped in enough plastic to keep any trace of blood from seeping into the trunk.

"Don't take anything off," he told me and then turned to Angie. "Drive to your shack and pack his clothes and what valuables he has. Don't pack anything that belongs to you.

Then drive him to the dock without opening the trunk and wait on us," he told Angie.

She merely nodded, turned the key, and started the rough sounding engine of the old, rusty car and drove off.

"Now what?" I managed to ask.

"We'll stop before we reach my place and take these things off. I don't want my security to see us dressed like this. We'll put them back on once we're in the swamp."

I swallowed hard. I was scared stiff at being smack in the middle of something I never expected to be in. Thankfully, Nokosi Micco seemed to know what needed to be done.

*

I shouldn't have been surprised when security stopped us as we reached the gate to the Airboat attraction, but I was. I feared he would know what we had done just by looking at us.

"Hi George," Nokosi Micco said in his usual tone of voice. "How are things tonight?"

"Good," he answered. "What are you doing back here this time of night when everything is closed down?"

"I'm here because it is a beautiful night. I'm taking Alona for a private moonlight ride in an airboat. I want her to experience the beauty and alure of a romantic ride through the swamp once the moon has risen. I'll be taking the small boat out."

George nodded. "Enjoy," he said with a knowing grin. "Wish I could do the same thing with a beautiful woman. Regretfully such as that ended for me years ago."

"He thinks we'll . . ." I began once we had driven through the gate.

"Yeah," Nokosi Micco was quick to say. That's what we want him to think if anyone should ask why we were taking an airboat into the swamp late at night. We'll both claim we indulged in as much hot and heavy sex as the boat would allow. I'll even put a couple of hickeys on your neck as evidence before we return if it's all right with you – in order to leave evidence to be on the safe side," he added.

I wanted to object, but logic was best I didn't.

He took me to a shed where the airboats were stored. He took a light from a shelf and turned the beam on. I was thankful it wasn't the big airboat he took on tour. This boat he took me to was small and appeared to be built for speed and silence. He held out his hand and helped me get in. I tried not to look down in the dark water where I knew the alligators waited for their nighttime hunts. It would be all too easy to fall in or even be pushed into the foreboding blackness of endless water.

Once in the boat, he fastened a seatbelt around me. "Don't be afraid," he told me. "I won't let anything happen to you."

I didn't tell him something I never expected had already happened to both of us. I wasn't sure what was going to happen next. I was surprised at how smooth and quiet the airboat was once he started the engine. It was nothing like the tour boat we had ridden on earlier. The boat glided into the water with almost silent ease.

I thought of the drug runners who frequented the swamps. I had no doubt Nokosi Micco, along with his father and brother, had been well acquainted with what went on and most likely Nokosi Micco still did. Getting the Airboat rides set up had to take a great deal of cash, not to mention the continuous upkeep. It would also be a great way to launder drug money.

He left the boat lights turned on as long as George had a chance of seeing us. Once we were far enough in the swamp to be out of sight, he cut the lights and headed in a different direction. Neither of us talked as he guided the boat by only the light of the moon and his instincts.

It took what felt like forever for us to reach the dock where Angie was waiting. I was holding my breath when he fastened the boat to the dock and helped me get out. He handed me the plastic coveralls, gloves, and shoe covers from inside his shirt.

"Put these on," he said. "I'll need your help getting him out of the trunk and carrying him to the boat. I don't want to drop him over the side and have to fish him out."

Angie turned her back to us as we carried the body to the boat and eased him in without dropping him.

"Angie, drive his car to the levee in the deep swamp and wait there for Alona and me. It'll take us about two hours."

"Why?" Angie asked.

"I'll let you know when we get there. Make sure you do exactly as I tell you."

"Okay," Angie mumbled tearfully as she tried not to look at the boat.

"She loved him," I said once we had gotten a distance in the water.

"Yes, she did," he agreed. "Interesting how a person can love someone who is brutal to them. Hanson was always good at making people believe it was their fault he was doing what he did."

"I'm surprised she didn't kill him sooner," I told him.

"I'm not. She never had someone like you to give her encouragement that it was possible for her to escape, plus give her money. Not that she really wanted to escape from him. I have no doubt she never intended to kill him or leave him. As she said, she simply fought back because she didn't want her baby to be harmed. He was the one who ended up dead."

"Now what?" I asked.

"I'm still thinking. I know one thing for sure. If you and I are to still be safe, we can't allow Angie to remain here. She's sure to break down and confess what happened. That's one of the reasons why I didn't want either of us to get involved."

Made sense, but it was too late now to alter what we were doing.

"I'll have you take Angie and drive her far away from here. You'll need to find a place for her to settle in and have her baby. Once that happens, you're to pack up and leave her behind before she knows you're gone."

"Me?" I said with shock. "Why me?"

"Who else is there to do it?" he asked.

"You can do it," I told him. "She's your friend not mine."

He shook his head in bewilderment when I said that. "You're the one who butted into her business and even gave her money to encourage her to leave him," he told me with irritation. "Not only do I want her gone, I want you a long way from here and then from her. You can't stay with her no matter how she begs, and she will if she finds out you're leaving her. She's the kind who attaches herself to other people like a clinging vine. I'm going to give you enough money to get her settled in and to hold her for a while. Also, I'll give you enough money to find a place far away from Florida and Angie. I know you dislike Naples and want to leave it behind."

"Why would you do all that?" I wanted to know.

"Because I involved you. I was hoping things would work out for us. I took one look at you and had unrealistic expectations. I should have known from the beginning that you and I would never mesh. Angie just provided me with enough of a reason to send you away."

I didn't know what to say as he guided the boat into what looked like a field of tall grass. I'd had a few fantasies about him, but none of them were serious ones.

"I'm going to go farther in before I unwrap him and roll him into the water. The gators are trailing us. They will have him before he gets good and wet."

"Are you sure?" I questioned. What if they don't get him and he floated out of the sawgrass, and someone happened to see him? Like an airplane or fishing boat.

"I'm sure. Besides, most people in this area know how to mind their own business. It's the outsiders that cause problems."

I didn't agree with that, but I wasn't going to argue. "Why did you tell Angie to pack his clothes but not hers?"

"I wanted it to look like he was the one to leave instead of the other way around. Once we sink his car in the levee, it will appear he left town and Angie didn't."

"Won't there be a search for Angie if she goes missing?"

"You've got a point. Once we get to her place, you can help her pack her things. It will be better if it looks like they left together."

"Oh," I said, thinking this was getting more complicated as time passed. I never imagined wanting to help Angie would lead to all this. I recalled what Jimbo had once said. *"A good deed never goes unpunished."*

I wondered how Jimbo was being punished for the good deeds he did for me.

It was after midnight when Nokosi Micco docked the boat back at the airboat ride. I reached to release my seat belt.

"Not so fast," he told me. "Have you forgotten about those hickeys?"

I had forgotten. "Surely, you weren't serious."

"I was and am. I don't believe in leaving any loose ends. It won't take a minute. Besides, we might both enjoy it."

He reached for me and pulled me against. Instead of going for my neck, his mouth sought mine. The kiss was far more than functional. It held the fire and passion I suspected was holed up inside him. I found myself responding slightly before I could stop myself. It had been a long time since lips met mine. After a moment, his mouth lowered and latched onto my neck. The suction hurt slightly before he moved his mouth to the other side of my neck.

He sighed as he pulled away from me. "To be truthful, I would like to have my mouth all over you, but I'm afraid it will never happen. I can only dream of what might have been," he told me as he unsnapped my seatbelt and helped me out of the boat. He guided my shaky legs to his car and helped me get in.

George grinned as he opened the gate for us to leave.

"See that I'm not bothered for the rest of the night," Nokosi Micco told George.

"Will do. Hope the rest of your night is a good one," George said with a wide, knowing grin.

I wanted to go to the little trailer so my mind could settle enough for me to stop the trembling that had entered my body. How could I possibly have been foolish enough to get myself into such a situation?

"Take me to the trailer," I said.

"That's where we're headed. Once you get there, try to get some sleep. Pack your suitcase in the morning and leave the key with the landlord. Tell him you're leaving town. Go by The Clock and tell Lena you decided to go back home. She'll ask you if I had anything to do with your decision. Tell her maybe a little and that you're not ready to get serious with anyone. We need her to think you're leaving because of me. Think you can manage that?"

"Yes," I told him. "But I'm not sure that is the best thing for me to do."

"I'm sure. Don't even think about questioning me on this. Meet me at the beach after you tell Lena you're leaving. I'll give you enough money to get you gone and Angie settled in. I don't want Angie to see me give it to you when we arrive at her place. After that, go by the bank and take out what little money you have in your account. Then we'll meet Angie at the shack and tell her what's going to happen."

He stopped as close to the trailer door as he could get." I'll watch until you enter the door. Didn't want us to end like this," he told me before he leaned in and kissed me lightly on the lips. "See you in the morning," he said.

I didn't sleep much that night. What had occurred kept running through my mind in vivid color. Why did I have to be the one to be responsible Angie? I shouldn't be the one to find her a place to settle and have her baby. Even if I did all Nokosi Micco told me to do, what was there to stop Angie from returning to Naples and confessing what had gone on with Hanson Bell? What was there to stop her from claiming we were the ones who killed him instead of her?

My salvation could be that I had used a fake name while I was there. Once I left here, I could become my real self. That was what I wanted, wasn't it?"

Angie. She might be able to find out the difference if I took her with me. It was true I wanted to protect her from an abusive husband as well as from being convicted of murder, but I shouldn't be the one responsible for her. Shouldn't Nokosi Micco be the one to relocate Angie Bell? Why couldn't he take her somewhere and settle her in? She would trust him much more than he would trust me.

By the time morning came I had decided to do exactly what he had suggested – at least in the beginning. It would be the safest way to keep myself safe from being accused as an accessory to concealing a murder. As soon as I found a place for Angie, I would pull out without hesitation, while leaving her with the money Nokosi Micco had given her to get by on. I hoped she would be too afraid of facing a murder charge to return to Naples.

The landlord looked up from his desk as I entered. "Come to pay for next month's rent?" he questioned although I still had a few days before rent was due.

"No," I told him. "I'm going to move on."

"Why?" he demanded as though I had offended him. "You ought to have more sense than to move in with that half-breed. He's bad news."

I agreed with him on the bad news part. I would have been better off if I'd never met the man. "I'm not moving in with him or anyone else. I've decided to travel on. I can't find a decent paying job here."

"Happens," he said as he took the key I dropped on his desk.

I drove away from the place with a feeling of relief. I wouldn't miss the little trailer or the watching eyes of the landlord.

"You're late," Lena said as I came in the door. "It's six o'clock."

"Hope I'm not going leaving you in the lurch," I said apologetically. "I've decided it's time for me to move on."

"Move on as in how?"

"As in leaving town." I didn't mention going back home. I didn't want her to ask where my home was.

Her brows furrowed as she looked at my neck. "Does this have anything to do with Mic?"

"Maybe," I admitted. "A little anyway. I'm not ready to settle down." I used the excuse he had told me to use.

"And he is?"

"I think that's what he has in mind."

"Thought so. He's a good man. You could do worse."

"He needs one of his own people. I could never make him happy."

"I think you might. You're adaptable. Have you discussed your leaving with him."

I nodded.

"And he agreed?"

"He thought it was for the best."

"He wouldn't want a woman who didn't feel the same way he does. If you don't, then it's best you're moving on. It's not like you'll be pulling up your roots."

She was right about that. Nokosi Micco had too many roots for him to pull up for Angie Bell. I didn't.

"Take care of yourself," she said. "Oh, wait a minute. I owe you money."

I waited. I feared I'd need all the money I could get, even if it was only a few dollars.

She paid me in cash.

Nokosi Micco was waiting at the beach for me to arrive. I had driven through Naples a few times before I headed for the beach. I had no idea why I wanted to take a last look at the trees and flowers that were in bloom. I might even miss the feel of sand on my bare feet along with the sight of coconuts lying under palm trees, but I wouldn't miss the squawking of sea gulls.

"Let's go for a walk. It'll be another hour until the bank opens," he told me.

I was agreeable.

"I think this is for the best," he told me as if I needed further assurance. "If I were to leave long enough to move Angie, people would become suspicious and dig in where they don't belong. As it is, like I told you last night, I'm counting on people thinking Hanson packed Angie up and left town."

"What about me leaving town at the same time as Angie?"

"No offence intended, but I'm the only person who knows why you left or even care if you did leave."

"What about Lena?"

"She cares about her income, not her employees."

I wasn't sure that was true, but I wasn't going to argue with him. "She'll certainly miss Angie Bell. She'll be short a dishwasher and a waitress."

"Worse has happened before. She'll hire replacements before tomorrow morning if not by lunch time."

"Where should I take Angie?" I questioned.

"West," he answered. "Montana, California, North Dekota. Any place far away from here. She'll be afraid to return to this state. She doesn't want to go to jail."

"And me?" I dared question.

"My darling girl, you will be free to go any place you choose."

"But not back here?"

"I wish you could return, but I don't think you ever will after what we've done for Angie. If you do, I'll welcome you and do my best to keep us both safe."

I didn't have anything else to ask him or say to him, so we walked along the beach in silence before we turned around. Once we reached the parking lot, he took thick folders from the trunk of his car and placed them in the trunk of my car. "Don't let Angie know you have this. Keep it in your trunk and don't open it until you need it, or a long way from here."

"I ..." I started to say something but changed my mind. What was there for me to say? I didn't want his money, but there was no question Angie would need it. I certainly didn't want to use the money from Jimbo to re-establish Angie Bell.

"I'll follow you to the bank and park across the street. Don't want people to think we're together. From there we can drive to Hanson's shack to get Angie. She'll have to lie down in your back seat, so she won't be seen leaving town with you."

"Okay," I said. "Giving in to whatever he thought was best."

He parked down the street from the bank, but where he could watch my car. I took an empty briefcase into the bank with me. It would take it. along with my purse, to put my money in. The sale of my house money was hidden away in my car. Hopefully, I wouldn't wreck and cause the car to catch on fire. I would lose all my financial security if that happened.

The teller didn't look pleased when I told her I wanted to draw all my money out of the bank in cash. "Please go into Mr. Marsh's office while we gather enough cash. Would you consider taking it or at least part of it in a cashier's check?"

I considered it. "No," I told her. I would like to withdraw cash."

"Anything ten thousand dollars or over will require you to fill out a government form," she told me.

"No," I told her. "I'm familiar with that ruling. It won't go into effect until January the first."

She gave me an irritated look because I was right. I handed her my briefcase. "You can put the cash in there. You and I can both count it to make sure the amount is correct."

It took longer to get my money than I expected. I knew Nokosi Micco would be getting restless as well as wondering what was going on. I half expected him to come into the bank. I was sure he would have if he hadn't been making sure no one at the bank would see us in the bank at the same time.

Finally, the briefcase held the right amount. I closed it, thanked the irritated woman, and left the bank. I unlocked my car that was already heating up inside and drove out of the parking lot toward Angie's shack. I saw Nokosi Micco's car several cars behind me. He was making sure no one would think he was following me.

The traffic thinned the farther I got out of town until there was only the two of us driving on a deserted road. I stopped in front of the shack and Nokosi Micco stopped beside me.

"The car's not here," I pointed out.

"I know," he told me. "I took care of it last night. Let's get Angie so the two of you can be on your way."

I followed him into the house dreading the long trip to a faraway place Angie and I were about to take. I heard a sound that brought chills crawling up my backbone. It was the faintest sound of a groan. Nokosi Micco moved his hand and placed me behind him as though he was protecting me from what or who was causing such a pitiful sound. Could there be someone else in the shack with Angie? I had left the pistol in the car thinking it wouldn't be needed.

Nokosi Micco motioned for me to stay put as he eased into the second room of the two-room shack.

"Oh, hell. Alona, come quick," he called out.

I rushed into the narrow room and caught my breath at what I saw. Angie was lying on the bed with a gob of bloody substance protruding between her legs. I sucked in a breath as I stared at it. I had no idea what it was, but it looked ominous.

"She has given birth. The baby is still in the sack." His hands moved quickly as his fingers tore at the membrane covering the baby. "We've got to get the baby out of the sack while it's still alive. Check on Angie. I'm not sure she is breathing."

I went to Angie's head and patted her in the face. "Angie," I called out. "Angie, are you okay? Can you hear me?"

Her eyes slowly opened, and she glared at me in desperation. "I give my baby to you," she mumbled. "Take care of her. Raise her as your own," she managed to say with great effort as life left her body and she appeared to sink further into the worn-out mattress.

"Don't you dare die," I yelled at her as I grabbed her by the shoulders and shook her. Her eyes cracked open again, but they weren't seeing me – or anything else.

"She died," I screeched. "I think she died. Do something," I yelled at Nokosi Micco.

"There's nothing I can do for her now. By the looks of things, she's bled out." He was holding the tiny baby in the air by its ankles while the umbilical cord was still attached to Angie.

A gasp and a faint mewing sound came from the baby. "It's alive," I said in disbelief.

"It appears so. Tear a strip off from the sheet and tie off the cord while I clear the mucus from its mouth."

I ripped the dingy sheet, wondering at its cleanliness.

"Tie the cord close to its belly as tight as you can so it won't bleed. There's nothing we can do for Angie now."

I tied the cord as he instructed. I was at a loss as what to do next. I stood there watching him pat the baby on its bottom as liquid oozed from its mouth and nose. He wiped the ooze away with his hand. The baby drew in a deeper gasp and let out a louder cry.

"I think it's going to live," he said. "Looks like Angie has baby blankets and some clothes on top of that shelf. Bring me one of those blankets."

I did as he said and watched as he cleaned the blood and mucus off the baby's head, face, and body.

"This complicates things," he said. "She must have gone into labor during the night and was unable to get help. The beating Hanson gave her most likely put her into labor."

"Maybe she's only resting," I said hopefully as I looked from the baby to Angie and the blood-soaked bed. There was blood still dripping from the mattress making a pool underneath the bed.

"I'm afraid she's resting permanently. I shouldn't have left her alone. Now we'll have to take care of this too."

"We have nothing to do with this," I told him.

"I'm afraid we do. We can't leave the baby here until her body is discovered. It will surely die if we do. If we report it, there will be investigations of her death and the cause for it. They'll want to know why we showed up here. They'll also discover that Hanson is missing and try to find where he has gone. It's obvious Angie has been severely beaten. The fact that you and Angie worked together will also be investigated, as will you suddenly leaving town."

"Won't they think Hanson Bell beat her, she died, and Hanson Bell ran away?" I asked hopefully.

"Maybe, but we better not take a chance on it. His car is sunk in the levee. It would be easy for a diver to find it. If that should happen, it might not be good for us."

"They could think Angie drove it in there."

"They wouldn't stop investigating Hanson's absence or Angie's death. Plus, what about the baby? It's alive without its mother. It wouldn't be in our best interest to claim we just happened to stop by to check on her and found this situation, although that's close to what happened."

"What are we going to do?" I questioned in a near panic.

"We're going to do what she said for you to do. You're going to take her baby and leave town with it as we planned."

"I'm not taking her baby. I don't know what to do with a baby."

"You'll learn fast enough. We're in this too deep to take a chance when we don't have to."

"No," I insisted. "We're not going through with such an idea. Me taking her baby with me as I leave town is ridiculous."

"Listen to me, Alona. I'm going to stay here and take care of things. We're going to put on the gloves, shoe covers and coveralls that I keep in my car. After that you're going to search the place and find everything she had gathered for the baby and then you're going to leave here *with the baby*."

"No. There has to be another way," I insisted.

"Then tell me what other way there is. I'm definitely willing to listen. I don't want to be in this situation any more than you do."

"I'll tell the police I came to check on her after she didn't come in to work and found her dead. They'll find a place for her baby."

"Have you forgotten you left the restaurant before it was time for her to arrive? You'll need a better reason why you came here after drawing all of your money out of the bank. Not only that, but are you going to be able to stand up to all the interrogation law enforcements will put you through? They will want to know where you were last night and what suddenly made you want to leave town. It'll come out that we were together last night. How long will it take until they discover your and my testimonies have flaws in them even if we confer with each other on everything beforehand?"

He had a point, but I didn't want to admit it. "Can't we just leave here and pretend we know nothing about what happened?"

"Yes, we can as long as you do what I say."

"I don't want the baby," I repeated.

"Had you rather we get rid of the baby along with its father and mother?"

"Rid like in kill?" I asked with revulsion.

"I'm open for better suggestions," he said. "Get another blanket to wrap the little girl in. I don't want her to get cold. It was over ninety degrees inside her mother."

I considered telling him the Florida temperature was over ninety degrees outside also.

I looked at the tiny dark-haired baby as he wrapped it in the only other blanket. "Can't some of your people take it?"

"Along with what kind of explanation?"

"Tell them you found it beside the road."

He kind of laughed at that. "Listen to me, Alona. You'll put those protective clothes on, search this place for baby things, put them and this baby in your car and get out of town as fast as you can. Let me take care of everything else."

"How will you do it?" I asked.

"I'll get rid of all the evidence and give Angie a proper burial. You hold the baby while I get the things out of my car for us to put on. I don't want us to leave more of our DNA for me to get rid of."

I didn't want to take the baby or leave him behind to see things were *taken care of*, but he was leaving me little choice. He had pointed out that he didn't want me further implicated in what he had to *take care of*, and neither did I.

"Can't you get it through that hard head of yours that I'm trying to protect you? Once you are gone, no one will be able to find you, or even want to. Should there be a question about you leaving town, both your landlord and Lena as well as the bank can testify you were alone and seemed normal when you told them you were leaving."

"But. . ."

"No more buts," he said. "Do as I tell you unless you want both of us to be implicated in a murder."

I did as he said without further objections.

Once he was satisfied, I took off the protective plastic clothes he'd made me put on and handed them to him.

"You've found all the baby things. Put them and the baby in your car and leave right now," he told me without leaving any room for me to argue.

"And you?" I questioned again.

"I'll be better off without you here. Surely you can get it through that head of yours I don't want you here one minute longer – both for your sake and mine."

I knew he was right. It would be better for both of us if I left. As for the baby, he wasn't giving me a choice. I'd have to take it with me until I found an orphanage to leave it at. One thing was for sure, I couldn't leave it anywhere near Florida. I was sure the police had Hanson Bell's DNA on file. It would be easy to trace the baby's DNA back to him and perhaps even Angie.

I was thankful that Angie had a used car seat along with an unopened pacifier. Nokosi Micco fastened the baby seat in the passenger side of the front seat, strapped the baby in and put the pacifier in its little mouth. He then gave me a quick kiss on the lips.

"I don't regret meeting you, but for both our sakes, never come back here," he said as he turned away from me and went back into the shack.

I felt a twinge of regret for what might have been as I started the car engine and drove down the dirt-path of a road. I had no idea where I was going, but I didn't think it mattered as long as it was in the opposite direction from here.

Chapter 21

*

I had driven for hours when the baby woke up and started crying. I knew enough about babies to know it was probably hungry when the pacifier wasn't enough to silence it. I wasn't out of the state yet, but the baby didn't know that. I tried to ignore its crying, but it was driving me to distraction. I had no choice other than to pull off somewhere and see if I could feed it. Thankfully Angie had been smart enough to have a bottle and several cans of ready to use baby formula. Evidently, she had not planned on breast feeding.

I pulled into a Walmart parking lot, got a bottle from the back seat, opened a can of formula, and poured milk from it into the bottle. There was no way I could warm the milk, but it wasn't exactly cold. I stuck the bottle in the baby's mouth. The crying stopped and I heard little sucking sounds. I had no idea how much milk I should let it have. It took only a minute or so for the sucking to stop. I took the bottle away when milk drippled from the corner of its mouth.

I drove for another two hours before a smell reached my nose. It was obvious the baby needed a clean diaper. This would also be a new experience for me. Where were all the babies when I was growing up? I couldn't recall one person close to me that had a baby. All I knew about caring for babies came from watching television. Which amounted too little to nothing.

Again, I pulled into the parking lot of a mall. This time I had to take the baby out of the car seat. It felt so small, much like the doll I sometimes played with as a child. Nokosi

Micco had put a doll size undershirt and a diaper on the baby before he placed it in the car seat. He was evidently knowledgeable about babies where I was sorely lacking.

I was glad Angie had bought newborn disposable diapers although there wasn't much poop in the diaper. Still, there was a strong smell. I wondered if all baby poop smelled this bad. I really needed to find out more about babies. I had to keep it alive and well cared for until I found an orphanage to leave it in.

As soon as I had the diaper on, it started to cry again. I got the bottle and held the little thing in my arms as I put the bottle in its mouth. How could something so small and helpless be alive? I didn't think it weighed more than a five-pound bag of sugar. What if this little thing didn't make it? I would be responsible for not taking proper care of it.

Again, it only drunk a small amount of milk before it fell asleep again. I eased it back in the car seat to keep it safe while I drove. I still didn't know where I was going or even which interstate I was on. It didn't matter as long as I was leaving Florida and not heading toward Chicago.

I almost laughed at the irony as I looked through the windshield at the endless interstate stretching ahead of me. I was no longer traveling alone – but I wished I was.

The next time I pulled off the road to feed the baby, I took all my identification stating I was Alona Georgette Anderson and ripped it to shreds. From this moment on, I would be Millie James again. I had rather be faced with relatives than face being an accomplish to a murder coverup. Every few miles or so I tossed a bit of the torn identification out the window. I wanted to make sure it would be impossible to put Alona Anderson back together again.

*

The weather had cooled down drastically, and the sky had darkened when I realized how late it was. I had stopped twice to fill up with gas along with many times to feed and care for the baby. I had to go inside to pay for gas as I no longer had a credit card belonging to Alona Anderson. The good thing was that I couldn't be traced by using a debit card.

I saw an advertisement for a motel and decided it was time I stopped for the night. The adrenaline I had been running on was giving out leaving me both mentally and physically exhausted. Also, the baby was getting fussy again. It was in need of a diaper change and being fed again. It hadn't cried much at all. Only when it was hungry. I hoped it would be okay even though I didn't know a thing about caring for it. I certainly didn't want another body needing disposed of. Certainly not such a tiny little doll thing who was innocent of all that had happened.

I pulled into the motel and stopped my car directly in front of the office door before I got out, took my purse, and locked the car door before I went in.

"You can't park your car there," a grouchy man said as I came in the door.

"My baby is in the car. I don't want to wake her by bringing her in."

"Then pay for a room and move it," he informed me.

I paid in cash and received an old fashion key instead of a card. "You'll get two dollars back if you'll drop off the key in the office as you leave," he told me as though he was doing me a favor. "I hope that baby doesn't cry and keep up others who are trying to get some sleep."

He had no need to worry. He had given me a room as far away from other occupants as possible. I didn't mind at all. I wouldn't know what to do if the baby cried all night long other than feed and diaper it.

Fortunately, after I diapered and fed it, the baby went right back to sleep again. I saw there was a Wi-Fi hook-up for a computer. I left the baby on the bed as I went to the car and got my computer. I sat on the bed beside the sleeping baby and pulled up all kinds of information on how to take care of a newborn baby. I discovered it needed to be burped after each feeding. Something else I knew nothing about. I hoped I hadn't damaged it by not burping it. I picked it up and very gently laid it against my shoulder according to the picture on the google site. It didn't burp or wake up. Maybe it hadn't drunk enough milk or sucked in enough air to make a burp bubble. The site also said a baby should be bathed daily. This little thing hadn't been bathed at all. It had only gotten wiped off with a blanket. It also said the navel cord should have a few drops of iodine put on it to ward of infection. Tomorrow I would stop at a drug store and buy iodine and anything else the site said a newborn baby needed. Tonight I needed to sleep for a while.

Sometime during the night, I woke up with a startle. It took me a few moments to realize the baby was crying. I got up, felt its diaper to check if it needed to be change, and found the bottle of milk. There was plenty still in the bottle. It didn't drink more than half an ounce at a time.

The room had grown lighter before the baby cried again. I was still sleepy after I got up to feed it. It sucked even less before it fell back to sleep. I held it against my shoulder and patted its back for a while. Giving up on a burp, I placed it on the bed beside me again and we both fell asleep.

It was long past daylight before we woke up again. I was hungry and so was the baby. I got the bottle. It suddenly occurred to me to check the milk. Just as I feared, it had turned sour during the night. I poured the milk down the sink, made sure I thoroughly washed the bottle and poured a fresh can of formula in it. I fed the baby, washed its little body with warm water and a washcloth, and put a clean, tiny white under shirt and a diaper on the little thing. This time its little eyes opened and appeared to look at my face. It whimpered a little before its eyes closed and it fell back to sleep.

I instantly thought of Angie Bell. She had obviously loved and wanted this baby girl. They would still be together if Nokosi Micco and I hadn't left her alone in that isolated shack without a car and no way to get herself to the hospital.

We were guilty that this little baby no longer had a mother. I wondered if Nokosi Micco had given Angie a proper burial. I didn't want alligators to eat her flesh the way they had surely done to this baby's father, but I knew that was exactly what would happen. I also wondered how he had managed to clean up all the blood that had soaked the bed and the floor. I had no doubt the blood had seeped through the floorboards into the dirt beneath. Would he be able to clean up that blood without there being enough left to trace?

I had a sudden image of him setting the place on fire. It would surely burn to the ground before anyone noticed the smoke and reported it to the fire department, considering its location deep in the swamp. I was sure they would spray the coals with a fire retardant, which might wipe out any blood stains on the ground along with contaminate any DNA left behind. Most likely everyone would think Hanson had set the place on fire before he took off and that Angie had left with him if Nokosi Micco had done a good enough job of taking care of everything. I had an idea he knew only too well how to cover things up. Maybe Angie had more reasons than one to warn me away from him. After all she had entrusted her baby to my care with her dying breath.

I took my slow time in taking my own bath and getting dressed. I wanted to feed the baby again before I put it in the car. As for my own breakfast, I'd get something at a drive through and be on my way.

To where? I asked myself. I didn't so much as know where I was much less where I was going.

Once I had everything in the car, I stopped in front of the office door again. I locked the car door and went inside the office. "Here's the key," I said to a woman behind the counter as I waited for the two dollars. I feared the time would come when I needed every dollar I could get. I wasn't going to waste even two dollars if I could help it. Once I got the two dollars back, I left the office, unlocked the car door, and drove away.

I still didn't know where I was going, but I was on my way again with a newborn baby in a car seat. A baby I didn't want but had the responsibility of keeping alive and healthy until I found a proper place for it.

I drove into Bojangles and got a ham and egg biscuit along with a cup of coffee with extra cream. Unlike Nokosi Micco, I couldn't take black coffee. I longed to stop at a phone booth and make a call to him. I didn't because there were no longer phone booths at every service station. I considered getting a burner phone, but quickly decided it was for the best if we never got in touch with each other again. There was no reason for me to know what was going on with Nokosi Micco, and no reason for him to know what was going on with me and the baby regardless of curiosity.

Alona Anderson was dead as surely as Angie Bell was dead. That thought had me fighting back tears. I had the strongest need to seek what advice Jimbo would give to Millie James at a time like this.

Once I crossed the Georgia line, I realized what I was doing. I was retracing the road I had traveled to Florida on. One thing was for certain, as much as I wanted Jimbo, I couldn't go back to Illinois and the life I had once lived.

I took an exit and found a drug store. It was too hot to leave the baby in the car even for a short time. I snuggled the blanket around it and took it in my arms much like I did with one of my dolls when I was a child. I was hardly through the door when an elderly woman placed herself directly in front of me.

"Oh, you have a tiny baby. It's a girl, isn't it? It has a pink blanket."

"Yes," I said as I held it closer my body as though she would know what happened if she looked close enough.

"What's her name? I always like to know what mothers name their babies."

I considered telling her it was none of her business, but that would only cause her to remember me when I wanted to be invisible.

"Mitzie," I was quick to tell her. The baby really was mini in size. I had no idea how early it had been born, or how much it weighed.

"You should get a snuggly type of baby carrier to put her in. That way you can carry her while your hands are free. My granddaughter has one she raves about. They have them for sale in the baby aisle."

"I might do that," I told her as I hurried away from the snoopy woman and went to the baby aisle. I never realized there was so much stuff for babies. Not only did I need iodine; I saw a dozen other things the google site suggested a baby needed. I went back to the front of the store and got a buggy. I held the baby in one arm and pushed the buggy with my free hand. A snuggly was a good idea.

I left the drugstore with more items than I ever imagined buying. I'd gotten an entire case of baby formula including a can of powdered formula to go with the ready-to-use cans. I also bought several bottles so I could put a few ounces of formula in each bottle. Not only did I get a snuggly-type carrier, I bought several little pink outfits and more blankets and diapers. I had no idea how long it would be until I found a place for the baby, and I didn't want to run low on supplies.

Once I was at the counter, I saw a map of Georgia and added it to my supplies. I wasn't far enough away from Florida to feel comfortable, but I needed a place to settle long enough to make plans. I would be better off to take Nokosi Micco suggestion and go west to Montana or California, but both places were many miles away, while I was right here. I'd make do with a remote place in Georgia for a day or two.

Chapter 22

*

The next time I stopped to change and feed the baby, I took out the map and scanned it closely. At least I now knew where I was at. What I didn't know was where I was going, but I had to go somewhere. If anyone wanted to find me, where was the most likely place they would look?

There were two giveaways if someone wanted to find out information about me. First was the name Alona Georgette Anderson. I had used that name in two banks. One in Florida and one in Illinois. I had told several people that I was from the Chicago area. Such information could be traced. Having eliminated that identification was a good thing.

The second was my picture and fingerprints. Could and would anyone care enough about finding me to go after something such as that? Only Nokosi Micco knew I had been involved in a murder coverup along with what happened to Angie and her baby.

There was another concern that hit me. If there should be an investigation of Hanson and Angie Bell's disappearance, would Nokosi Micco be implicated. Was he really good enough to cover up all his tracks along with mine as well? What about the baby Angie was expecting? Angie did have relatives, and I assume that Hanson Bell did also. Another concern was Hanson Bell's car sunken in the levy. I remembered Nokosi Micco telling me that Hanson Bell was such a despicable man he was no longer allowed in the town of Immokalee. Hopefully, everyone would be glad he had left the area and taken Angie with him.

So much relied on Nokosi Micco's ability.

It also relied on my own ability to disappear.

The car Jimbo had bought for me came to mind. He told me he wanted me to have one of the most reliable cars that was ever made. I have to admit, I was a little disappointed it wasn't a new car, but it was known as a classic. I had never looked at the title to know whose name it was in as I hadn't needed a tag renewal. Was it Alona Georgette Anderson's name? If it was, then there would be a way of tracing me. I searched in the glove compartment until I found the envelope with the words *Car Title* handwritten on it. I opened the envelope and stared at its contents in shock. Not only was the title to the 1988 Mercedes Benz 420 SEL, but there was also a social security card, a driver's license, along with a birth certificate made out in my real name of Miliana Doris James.

I was stunned to say the least. How could Jimbo possibly know I would no longer be able to use the name of Alona Georgette Anderson? Of course, Jimbo was always thinking ahead as though he was able to see the future.

There was also another folded piece of paper in the envelope. I opened it. Again, I was stunned to say the least. It was my marriage certificate to Stanley York, along with a newspaper clipping stating his death.

The first thought to hit me was that Jimbo's real name was Stanley York. Then another realization hit me. This Stanley York was only twenty-eight years old. It was obvious that Jimbo had gotten one of his acquaintances to fake another scenario for me along with a marriage certificate, a gold wedding band, and death notification. He'd hidden it inside the envelope, along with the car title, in case I ever needed it. I didn't know if I should be thankful or angry. Neither did I know if I should use my real identification. Did I want to continue being someone else, or even if I wanted to be someone other than myself? At least my given name was Miliana, but Mother had always called me Millie.

A creepy feeling came over me. I made a thorough search of the glove compartment. There was the usual information about the Mercedes, but nothing else. There for a while I feared that Jimbo had someone watching me in order to know what was going on. I half expected to find a birth certificate stating that the baby belonged to me and Stanley York. It then occurred to me that Jimbo had known about my relationship with Sensei York and had tried to predict things in case I had left pregnant. There was nothing in reference to the baby, which would make it easier for me to find her a suitable home. For some reason, perhaps just because it came from Jimbo, I slipped the wedding band on the third finger of my left hand in case I needed to claim the baby was mine and I needed evidence of a husband to go with her.

I allowed myself to settle down while I diapered the baby and made an attempt to have it drink more milk. I then held the little thing against my shoulder as I tried to burp her. A tiny little burp escaped her rosebud of a mouth. I felt proud of us both as well as relieved that I wasn't allowing something harmful to happen to this tiny child.

I put her back into her car seat and studied the map again. Regardless of what name I used, I needed a place to stay that wasn't a motel room. Motel rooms and gas were expensive, plus I didn't want to keep traveling while having to stop every few hours to take care of a baby. I needed to find a place to rent until my mind settled enough for me to make plans. Ideally, a place that wasn't too expensive.

I could either hide out in a remote area or a heavily populated area. In a heavily populated area, more people would see me and remember that I had a baby, but fewer people would care. In a remote area there was a chance of people knowing every stranger who came to the area and would remember me and the baby ever more so.

The name of Ellijay caught my attention as did Tally Mountain.

I took out a penny from the little pocket on the dashboard. Heads would be Elijay and Tally Mountain. Tails would be for me traveling to a densely populated city and trying to hide in a crowd. I flipped the coin and watched as it landed on the floor of the passenger side.

It was heads.

I left the penny where it landed, started the engine, and headed out to find the roads that lead to Ellijay and Tally Mountain in hopes of it being a place where I could stay long enough to make plans for whatever was to come next.

The closer I got to my intended destination the cooler the weather got. I hadn't realized how hot and muggy the air in Florida was until I got far away from the ocean breeze. I got out of the car to pump gas and took in a breath of fresh air blowing down from the mountains.

I was surprised when a middle-aged man hurried out the door of a service station as I took the hose from the pump.

"I'll do that for you, little lady," he said in a slow drawl similar to the accent of the native crackers in Florida.

I had been pumping my own gas at every station since I left Illinois, but I allowed him to fill the tank.

"Where you heading?" he asked as he looked in the car at the sleeping baby. "How old?" he questioned.

"She's a month old," I fibbed. How could I explain traveling with a two-day old baby?

"You live around here?" he continued.

"I have family and friends in Ellijay," I told him as I opened my purse to pay him.

"What's their names? I know a right smart of folks up that away."

What was I supposed to say? I knew no names of people who lived in this area. "I married a York," I told him.

"Humm," he grunted. "Must not have been from around these parts. What's your relatives' names?"

"Wright," I said, remembering a sign I'd seen on a building I'd passed several miles back.

"Oh, yeah. I know a lot of Wrights. I'm not related to any of 'em I know of."

I quickly handed him the money for the gas. He reached in his pocket and handed me the change.

"Hang on and I'll wash your windshield for you."

"Thanks, but I'm in a hurry. I need to be on my way before my baby wakes up."

"Stop back by when you need more gas," he told me in his friendly voice.

The sun was going down when I decided I needed to find a motel room where I could get some rest from continuous traveling. I also wanted to get back on the computer to make sure the baby was doing okay. I had no idea if it was normal for a baby to sleep as much as she was sleeping. So far, she had been no trouble other than needing to stop for feeding and diaper changes. I also wondered where one of those baby-safe deposit boxes – or whatever they were called there might be. I had read about them sometime or other and now thought it could be the perfect answer for this baby. I would know that she would be safe and taken care of without showing myself.

I drove a while longer before I saw a sign that advertised a motel. I took the exit and found myself driving on a narrow two-lane road that was sparsely populated with businesses and residences. I had surely exited before I should have. I was looking for a wide place in the road where I could easily turn around and backtrack when I saw a motel up ahead.

I cringed when I came to the motel. It was out in the middle of nowhere, had about ten rooms. Four trucks that were worse for wear sat in the parking lot. I saw a man near one of the trucks. I stopped next to him and rolled down the car window.

"Uh," I said hesitantly as he turned from the back of the truck to look at me. "Are you staying at this motel?"

"Nope, can't you tell I'm a construction worker?" he grinned patting the tool belt hanging around his waist.

"Oh," I said hesitantly. It was obvious this young man was a typical construction worker with muscles along with the smell of fresh sawn lumber clinging to him.

"If you're looking for a place to stay, this is not it. It's closed for repairs. Won't be open for another two weeks or so. Hopefully, we'll be done in time for the summer vacation rush. Folk around here gotta make money when the opportunity presents itself."

"Do you know where a decent motel is?"

"There's plenty of 'em up in Ellijay."

"How far is Ellijay?"

"A good ways from here. I'm guessing about a three-hour drive. You look plum tuckered out and your baby is gettin' fussy. Why don't you check in at Granny Gleason's place? She takes in renters for a night or longer. It's where I'd stay if I was you. It's a right nice bed and breakfast place."

He was right I was *plum tuckered out*, and the baby had woken up when I stopped the car and was starting to cry. All the stress of running away was getting to me, and probably to the baby also. A three-hour drive was more than I wanted to consider.

"It's a safe place to stay?" I questioned.

He appeared a bit put-out by my question. "No safer place in existence. Granny Gleason is a fine, Christian woman. Never done anybody wrong and she don't intend to start now."

"Where is the place located?"

"Drive on this road for about five more minutes then take the first gravel road on the right. You'll run into Granny Gleason's place."

"Stop gabbin' to the pretty woman, Cliff. Get your hind end back up here. Daylight's a burnin'," a man hollered from the top of the building.

"Shut your pie-hole, Ben. I'm a comin'," the man I was talking to called back.

He nodded to me and walked away before I could properly thank him.

The baby didn't stop crying as I hoped she would when I started the car. I didn't want to linger in the parking lot to change her diaper and feed her with the workers looking on. I drove a few miles until I came to a wide spot in the road and pulled off. I got the bottle of milk, opened it, and sniffed. Like I had feared, it was starting to turn. I put it back in the diaper bag I had bought at the drug store, got a new bottle, and opened a fresh can of formula. I had wasted a lot of formula, and that stuff was unbelievable expensive. There was evidently a lot of money to be made from the birth of babies. I should have bought a cooler and ice, along with something to plug into the cigarette lighter to warm the milk. I was sure there were far more items available for babies than I had bought or could imagine.

I took the baby out of the carrier and gave her the bottle. She sucked hungrily for about two minutes before her little eyes closed, and she stopped sucking. I sat the bottle aside and moved her to the back seat to diaper her. I'd discovered she would drink a little more if I woke her up by changing her diaper and washing and powdering her tiny bottom.

Finally, I gave up on getting her to eat more than an ounce at a time. I burped her and put her back in her car seat. She went right back to sleep.

The word coddiwomple came to mind. I was traveling with a purpose but without a destination. A longing came over me stronger than I had ever had before. I was becoming desperate to find a place where I could do little other than rest. I had given up on finding a place where I belonged, at least for the time being. I needed a quiet place where there were few to no people, along with a soft bed and plenty of hot water for me to sink into a tub to ease my aching muscles that came from stress and continuous driving.

As for Angie's precious little baby, the one thing she needed was no longer available. She would never know the love of a biological mother. Never be able to feel a mother's heartbeat as she nursed at a warm breast while loving arms held her. It was a love that continued growing from the moment her mother realized she had been conceived. Exhaustion along with the thought of what this tiny baby had lost brought me to tears.

This little baby deserved the kind of love my mother had always given me.

Without intending to, I burst into a full-fledged crying bout. Tears ran from my eyes, down my cheeks, and dripped onto my shirt. None of this was what I had in mind when I had said goodbye to Jimbo along with everything I had grown up with. At least I still had my mother's ashes in an urn. This little baby didn't have so much as that. I pulled out a baby wipe from the pack I had bought at the drug store and wiped my face.

It took a while for me to get my crying spell under control in time to see the road Cliff had told me about. I rounded a curve expecting to see Granny Gleason's bed and breakfast, but all I saw was a narrow gravel road with tall trees growing on each side.

I had driven several miles on the narrow road when I decided I had surely taken a wrong turn. I would turn around when I found a wide enough place. I was about to give up hope on finding a turnaround when I drove around a sharp curve and saw a wooden structure up ahead. There was a neat hand-painted sign that read Welcome to Granny Gleason's Bed and Breakfast. There wasn't a single car in the small parking lot.

A feeling of trepidation came over me as I stopped in the parking lot near the front porch. The house was void of any paint and yet there had been an attempt to make everything neat and appealing in an old-timey way. There were two clay pots of red-blooming Geraniums growing on the porch on each side of three wooden steps. A four-foot stand with a large fern was beside the front door.

A little granny-looking woman rushed out the front door and down the three steps with agility I hadn't expected from a heavy-set woman. She had on a ruffled, bibbed apron with a dusting of flour on it. Her salt and pepper hair was in a twist at the nap of her neck.

"Oh, goodness," she called out when I rolled down the window. "I hadn't expected visitors this early in the season, but you are mighty welcome. I do my best to keep things up-to-snuff even when I don't have a single guest. I'm Granny Gleason," she said as she hurried up to my open window and looked in.

"You're not one of my regulars, but that's okay. Oh, my. You've got a tiny baby. Where's your husband?"

I was taken back by her straightforward question. "I lost him before my baby was born," I found myself telling her what Jimbo had provided for me about having a husband.

"Oh, my goodness. I'm sorry to hear that. The only thing worse than having a husband die is having him run off with another woman."

I didn't know how to react to a statement such as that, so I said: "A man named Cliff suggested I could rent a room here."

"Ah, yes. I rent rooms for the night, week or even by the month. How long do you want to stay?"

"I'm not sure," I told her truthfully. "I'm . . . I think I'm running away from memories." What I told her had way too much truth to it.

She gave me an understanding look. "Folks need to do such as that every now and again. Get out, bring your baby inside and see if this place is suitable for you. I don't have nothing fancy like some city places do, but I take pride that every person who stays here feels welcome. I make sure things are always clean and comfortable. Not to mention I'm the best cook in the county if not the country."

I opened the door and got out. My head felt a little funny like I was still driving on an unending highway. It was time

I stopped to rest. I drew in a steadying breath of the cool air and walked around the car and draped the diaper bag over my shoulder before I took the baby out of the car seat. I suspected she would need a dry diaper.

"Oh, my. That precious baby is even younger than I thought. It can't be more'n a couple weeks old. No wonder you're looking peaked."

"She's almost a month old," I told her. "She came a little early."

"A precious little girl. What's her name?"

"Mitzie." I told her the same name I'd told the woman at the drug store.

"I'd say you've been pushing yourself right hard. Come on inside and we'll take care of the paperwork. Then I'll get you something to drink. You and your baby can rest for a spell while supper finishes cooking. It won't be no more'n fifteen or twenty minutes. I just put the biscuits in the oven. I don't have any guests here right now, but my grandson always eats supper with me. Don't like cookin' just for myself, and he doesn't either. I always cook too much, and then I eat too much when I'm alone," she said with a little chuckle as she patted her round stomach.

In a way it felt good to let someone take over and guide me as what to do next. She was correct on one thing. I had been pushing myself hard. Taking care of the baby had been stressful and different from anything I had ever done. Trying to decide how to find her a good home was more than I knew how to accomplish. I took the tiny bundle out of the car seat and held her against my chest. She wiggled and her little mouth yawned like a real person would do. I suddenly realized this was a real little person instead of a doll that needed fed and diapered. She needed the love and care of someone who wanted her more than anything else in their world. Someone who could become a real mother to this tiny baby.

"She sleeps a lot," I found myself saying.

"Oh, yes. All babies do, especially when riding in a car. The motion seems to sooth them. I'll carry your diaper bag in for you. Do you have a lot of luggage?"

"No. I have only one bag and baby things."

"That's good. A new mother doesn't need to be carrying anything heavy. Back in my day mothers had to stay in bed for nine days after giving birth. Nowadays doctors have the mothers up and going the same day they give birth. Don't agree with that myself."

I followed her up the three steps to the porch and inside the house. I was pleased to see how welcoming the front room appeared. It was like a room in the home I had always imagined. One where a real grandmother would welcome her children and grandchildren. Everything about the room made me want to sit down, sink into the couch, and rest a spell.

"I'm sorry I don't have a downstairs bedroom for you. Mine is the only one down here. I hope you are able to walk upstairs without pain. Then, after a month, you should be far along in the healing process if I remember correctly."

"I'm good. I won't have any trouble walking upstairs," I told her. I knew nothing at all about having babies including the healing process. I would pull up information on the computer to be a little more acknowledgeable about the process. "You do have WI-FI, don't you?" I asked.

"Certainly. It's a necessity this day and time. I couldn't get visitors without it. And let me tell you, it wasn't easy to get service run this far up in the mountain. People just don't appreciate the value of communing with nature anymore."

Communing with nature. The closest I'd come to something such as that was walking on the beach and riding in the airboat. And, perhaps, the little park where I once met with Jimbo. I had been gone from my childhood home for only short time and it already felt like a lifetime ago.

Granny Gleason told me the price for a night, a week, and a month. I chose a week. I didn't think one night would be enough time for me to rest until my brain started working.

Right now, my mind was in turmoil. As much as I tried not to acknowledge it, I kept seeing Angie Bell face as she lay on the blood covered bed dying. *"I give my baby to you,"* she mumbled. *"Take care of her. Raise her as your own."* If I had done as everyone said and minded my own business, Angie Bell might still be alive to take care of her baby.

Chapter 23

*

I took the tiny baby from her car seat and placed her on the bed where she could stretch her little body out. Never had I seen a real live human baby that was this cute. There was no question in my mind that Angie Bell would have been head-over-heels in love with this baby girl. As I watched this perfect little person, I racked my mind as I wondered to what extent Nokosi Micco and I actually had in her mother's death. We had left her alone without transportation, but she hadn't asked us to do otherwise.

It had been Angie who had sought help from Nokosi Micco in covering up that she had murdered her husband. She most likely was too traumatized to realize the extent of the horrible beating Hanson Bell had put her through. Not to mention the mental trauma. Such treatment had most likely caused her to go into labor. There was no way of knowing what kind of injuries he had done to her internally without any of us realizing it. She did say he was trying to kill the baby she carried. I tried to stop imagining what Angie went through. It didn't help Angie, the baby, or me.

I diapered and made sure she was not hungry before I lay down beside her. It was the most comfortable bed I had ever come into contact with. It was nothing at all like the lumpy mattress in the little rental trailer or in a motel room. This mattress was better than Mother was ever able to provide for us. It was obvious Granny Gleason had her guests' comfort in mind in an old-fashioned way that made a person feel well cared for.

I got the feeling I was stepping back into a time when Granny Gleason was a young girl. A time without modern conveniences, but then there was Wi-Fi. It wouldn't be long until vacationers would be arriving who obviously wanted to relive the feeling that they were living in the past.

Regardless of the circumstances I found myself in, I knew it was best for me not to stay here long, although the chances of someone recognizing me in this remote place would be slim. A week of complete rest and silence might be what was needed to settle my troubled mind and ease the panic that had its hold on me.

But where could I go if I left here? And most important, where could I find a good home with someone who would be a great mother for Angie's helpless baby girl? I owed Angie and the baby that much. I wanted this baby to have a mother who could provide the love and security every child deserved, a mother who would be able to grow old, healthy, and happy. Definitely not a child who had to rely on stealing to pay her mother's bills.

I fell asleep with these troubled thoughts disturbing my mind. I woke up with Granny Gleason tapping on the bedroom door.

"Are you awake?" she called out loud enough to wake me up if her knocking hadn't already done the job.

"I'm awake," I answered without adding *now*. I felt a bit irritated from being woken up from peaceful, much needed, sleep. I was having the most peaceful rest I had received in a very long time.

"Supper is ready. My grandson has already arrived, and he's starved as usual. Come on downstairs before he starts without you. As hungry as he is, there might not be much left."

"Okay," I said as I forced myself to come fully awake. I much preferred to continue getting some much-needed sleep than eat a meal.

"Hurry up, honey. Don't dawdle. Supper is getting cold." she added before I heard her footsteps move down the hall.

I looked beside me at the baby. She was still sleeping soundly. I didn't want to wake her up. At the same time, I hesitated to leave her alone in the bedroom. She hadn't been out of my sight since the moment she was born. I rolled the bedclothes into a tight roll and circled the baby with it until I was sure she wouldn't fall off the bed, not that she was old enough to roll. Mother often told me there was nothing that could replace caution. A few minutes of extra care could save a lifetime of regret. I would eat fast and then return to the room. I didn't want her to wake up by taking her downstairs with me.

I yawned as I made my way along the hall and down the stairs. All I wanted was a week's worth of restful sleep without being afraid someone would be able to find out what had happened. I hadn't seen any sign of being followed, but then I wasn't knowledgeable enough about such things to judge. The things I found in my glove compartment had caused a creepy feeling to enter my chest – not to mention my mind. What the dickens was going on with Jimbo – or was it with my father's relatives? Perhaps even Aunt Mary. I longed to drop any suspicion about Aunt Mary, but I couldn't make myself do it. She didn't have the money to chase me down. But then, I couldn't rule out the fact that she could agree to split the money I had gotten from the sale of Mother's house with someone.

Both Granny Gleason and her grandson were already seated at the table. I almost mis-stepped when I realized it was Cliff – the construction worker I had met earlier. It had been a given he would recommend I stay at his Grandmother's place.

"Finally," he said as though I had been doing something wrong. "You've taken enough time getting downstairs. At least you were smart enough to take my advice to stay here."

"Cliff," Granny Gleason admonished him fondly. "You must learn patience. I'm sure the little mother is exhausted and not nearly as hungry as you are."

"Obviously," he said as he looked me up and down in a way that would surely discourage any paying visitor.

What I was wearing was baggy, wrinkled and comfortable. What he was wearing was sweaty and covered in saw dust and some kind of dirt. He had no room to give me a critical look of any kind. Certainly not for being disheveled, sleep laden, or tardy.

"Take a seat so Granny can say grace over the food. She won't allow eating until after grace is said. A man could perish from hunger around here."

I took a seat at the long table where one of three place setting had been put. It was directly across the table from Granny Gleason. Cliff was seated at the head of the table like he was the man of the house.

Granny Gleason downed her head and said a prayer that was so long even I was getting restless. She also made a point of thanking God for my and my baby's safe arrival. I thanked God for the same thing. I also added I hoped the baby and I continued to be safe regardless of where we were.

Cliff was grabbing dishes as soon as Granny Gleason said her Amen as though he was truly starving. He rounded his plate up with food and started shoving it into his mouth. Granny Gleason rolled her eyes at me and grinned.

"That boy eats his weight in food every day. If he didn't work so hard, he would be as fat as a lard hog. Hope you don't mind serving yourself to each dish of food," she told me. "I'm not much at waiting on the table."

Hog was right, I thought. He didn't have the table manners of some of the rudest people who ate at my mother's restaurant.

"I wouldn't eat as much if you were a lousy cook," he told her. "A man can't get enough of food like this."

She smiled with pleasure at his offhanded compliment. It was obvious she adored her grandson. I hadn't decided yet what he adored – other than food.

There was a variety of dishes having enough food for a dozen people. I did as she said and reached for a biscuit and then mashed potatoes. I added baked apples and green beans to my plate before I started eating. My first bite was amazing. Cliff was right about his grandmother's cooking. It was without question the best food I had ever eaten. She should be running a restaurant or at least cooking in one.

"This is delicious," I told Granny Gleason.

"I told you, didn't I?" Cliff said as he moved the tall glass of iced tea from his mouth and refilled it from the pitcher on the corner of the table.

"Yes, you did."

"Didn't you believe me?" he quipped.

"Yes, I believed you, but there's nothing like tasting it for myself," I said as sweetly as I could possibly manage.

"Enough compliments about my cooking. I suggest you eat plenty. You need to put some meat on your bones. I'm surprised at how skinny you are after just giving birth to a baby. I gained forty pounds before my baby was born. Never have lost it."

I cringed at her observation. I didn't want her to know the baby wasn't mine. "I lost weight during pregnancy," I told her. "The smell of food made me sick." The last statement wasn't far from the truth. The continuous smell of restaurant food cooking made me not want to eat it.

"I don't doubt it considering what you went through. How far along were you when your husband died?"

"Not far," I told her, hoping it was obvious I didn't want to talk about it.

"What did she go through?" Cliff took time to ask between forking food from his plate to his mouth.

"She became a widow," Granny Gleason said with sympathy. "It's one thing to go through the loss of a husband when you and your man are old while entirely another thing when you're young. The good Lord knows I still miss my Homer after all this time. A body never gets over the death of a loved one, nor should they. Mourning over their loss is equal to how much you loved them."

"That's why I never plan on marrying," Cliff announced. "Don't need to, considering what good care Granny is at taking of me. There is nothing like being young and free. A wife only ties you down to a life of grungy work and debt - not to mention a house full of snotty nosed kids and a bitchy woman."

I didn't comment on his statement. I would also like to fill young and free, but I wondered how long it would be until I accomplished such a feat.

As good as the food was, it didn't take long until I had eaten my fill. Working all these years in a restaurant kept me from wanting to eat a lot. It was much like working in a pie factory. After a while, the thought of eating pie turned the stomach sour. Plus, I did not find being in the presence of Granny Gleason and her grandson pleasant. Perhaps it was simply sitting at a strange table that was meant to hold a dozen or so people. It was then I heard the baby cry. It didn't take me a moment to jump up. "She's awake," I said in concern. "Please excuse me."

"Of course," Granny Gleason said with a slight chuckle. "Welcome to motherhood."

I had made my way halfway up the stairs when the baby stopped crying. I hesitated in my rush to get to her. Granny Gleason's voice carried well enough for me to hear her say, "That's one lonely girl. I feel sorry for her and that little baby. Ask me, she's all alone in this world without anybody to look after her. You need to be nice to her, Cliff. She drives a Mercedes and can afford to travel. She just might turn out to be the kind of wife you ought to go after. I'm thinking her dead husband left a pile of insurance money behind. She could set you up right good with your own construction company."

"No match making, Granny. I just told you why I never want to get married, besides she's a Yankee. You can tell by the way she talks. You know what kind of folks those Yankees are."

I stood there for a few moments longer, listening. I had no prejudice against them; therefore, I didn't see why they should have prejudice against me just because I wasn't from around there. They didn't know what kind of person I was any more than I knew what kind of people they were. I did know I wanted nothing to do with Cliff.

"Now Cliff, I don't want to hear you talking like that. You've been listening to the wrong kind of talk from some of the men you work with. I thought you were able to think on your own instead of taking on the opinion of men like Ben Klinesmith. Besides, I didn't say you should marry her and take on raising her child, I said she might be the kind of wife you ought to be looking for."

He chuckled like he found it was humorous how quickly his grandmother had changed her tune. "There's nothing wrong with Ben," Cliff said in his buddy's defense.

"I didn't say there was anything wrong with him. I'm saying I don't always agree with the way he thinks, and neither should you. Now eat your desert before I do the dishes."

I was glad I continued listening. This wasn't the people or the kind of place I wanted to settle down in. It certainly wasn't where I wanted a baby to be raised.

"By the way, Ben's ole woman will be gone for two days next week. I invited him to eat supper with us while she's gone. I told him you wouldn't mind since you enjoyed feeding people."

"Fine, but don't make it a habit of inviting him. Don't want him showing up every meal, which he just might do. I've heard what a sorry cook his wife is."

*

Not only did the man named Ben show up again, but he also brought an older man with him. The man had to be sixty years old or nearing it. He was lean as a rail with tanned, leathery skin on his face, arms, and exposed area of his upper chest where his shirt was unbuttoned. It was obvious Granny Gleason disapproved of his arrival.

"Old Jack here showed up today and asked for a job. Ben hired him right off," Cliff explained to his grandmother. "He's got himself a right nice van and is camping out in the woods near the worksite so he can save up some cash. You always have so much leftover food, I knew you wouldn't mind him coming along," Cliff continued explaining. "You always say you can't stand to see a man go hungry."

Granny Gleason was being extra polite, but it was easy to see her disapproval of the new arrival as well as Ben. "Welcome to my table for this evening meal, but I'm afraid it will be a one-time thing. I won't be able to accommodate either Ben or you after today. I got notification that a family of five will be arriving tomorrow. Cliff and I will be eating our meals of leftovers in the kitchen after they have finished dining. You know how guests like their privacy."

"Ah, shit," Cliff said. "You know how I hate to be run off from our own table; besides, we're eating at the table with Milianna, and she's a paying guest. Don't see why we have to change things for just five other people."

"I've explained the procedure to you before. Guests expect to be catered to. It's good business sense, Cliff. I chose to welcome Milianna as though she is part of our family instead of setting her aside as a guest of one. Now, let's down our heads and say thanks to the Good Lord for this food we're about to partake of."

We downed our heads and closed our eyes while Granny Gleason said her usual grace, plus, she added a few extra words for me, Ben, and Jack to get nutritious benefit from the food God provided.

I didn't like being talked about as though I wasn't there, but I stayed silent as did the two other men. I got the feeling that Jack was looking me over even when he had only glanced at me and nodded his greeting instead of speaking directly to me.

"I appreciate the meal, Ma'am. A good homecooked meal is a treat for me. I do my own cookin' on a Coleman stove. Like Cliff done told you, I have a right nice van I stay in. Saves me money when on a job. You might call me a migrant worker being I travel about where jobs are available," Jack told her politely "It was a kindness for your grandson to invite me, but I realize it's a one-time invitation. I'm not a man to impose, and again, I thank you for your kindness."

"Do you have a family?" Granny Gleason asked.

"No, Ma'am. I never got around to taking a wife. Never considered myself as good enough husband material. I'm one of those incurable wanderers, a nomad you might call me."

"That's a pity. Family is the most important thing a man can have."

"Can't argue with that," he told her as he started eating hungrily.

"Jack is one hell of a worker," Ben said through a mouthful of food. "Lucky for us he showed up. Good workers such as him aren't easy to find, much less show up when he's needed. We're pushed to get the motel job finished in time for the season's rush. It's starting to get damned hot down south early this year. The heat is driving people north."

"That good, but Ben, in case Cliff hasn't informed you, I don't allow curse words at my table."

"Sorry," Ben said with a grin, obviously unaffected by her reprimand.

I detected a slight Midwest accent in Jack's voice, although it wasn't as pronounced as my own accent. It reminded me a lot of the way Jimbo pronounced his words. Thoughts of Jimbo put a sharp pain inside of me. I missed him almost as much as I missed my Mother. In a way, I even missed Aunt Mary, but not enough to want to go back to my earlier life – or even pay her a visit. That could change after I'd been gone years instead of months. As Granny Gleason had said, a family was the most important thing a man, or a woman, could have.

"Cliff is always a loyal friend to have. He cares about everyone he comes into contact with," Granny Gleason said with pride.

*

The family of five arrived the next day, a father, mother and three rowdy boys with loud voices and eyes full of mischief. It sounded like a herd of horses had arrived as they went upstairs to the two rooms they had rented. Thankfully, there were two bathrooms, one at each end of the hall for the guests to use. I considered it an inconvenience not to have a bathroom in my own room like there were in motels. Hopefully, the family would use one bathroom, and I could use the other. That hope faded as soon as they arrived. It appeared they considered the entire upstairs for their own personal use.

I managed to tolerate them the first day of their arrival, but they were getting to me on the second day. I told myself it was because I was an only child who was raised by adults. Surely, I could tolerate them for a few days longer. At least Granny Gleason let me to take meals in my room.

"Lord have mercy," she said to me one evening. "Those boys are rowdier and more destructive than they have been in the last three years. I would ask them to leave if I didn't need the income so badly. I hope you can ignore them for a while."

I stayed silent instead of telling her I wasn't in an ignoring mood, and neither was the baby.

The boys made so much noise they were continuously waking the baby. They chased each other up and down the stairs and along the hall shouting and shoving each other against the walls while yelling insults at each other. Much to my amazement, their parents paid little to no attention to the boys who appeared to be ten, eleven and twelve years old. Where was their parental guidance along with their respect for others? Instead, both parents appeared to be overjoyed to get a break from disciplining the boys as they totally ignored their antics. I could tell the rowdy boys were getting more on Granny Gleason's nerves with each day that passed. Still, she remained a very gracious hostess.

"They've paid for two weeks," Granny Gleason whispered to me, at least they're willing to pay my higher rates for people with children. I do need the income, or I would ask them to leave," she confessed again. "If I ask them to leave, I'll have to refund their money. If they leave on their own, I don't give a refund."

I knew she was telling me she would not give me a refund if I chose to leave.

The parents paid no attention to me – acting as though my baby and I didn't exist or deserve any kind of consideration from them or their boys. Granny Gleason never complained at me taking meals in my room instead of eating at the table with her five guests. It only took one day and night of their presence for me to start thinking it was time for me to move on although I still had paid days left. My patience came to an end when I went downstairs to get a bottle of milk out of the refrigerator to find all the bottles were missing. I had mixed three bottles of milk to do through the day and night. I looked out the kitchen window to see the three boys – each with a bottle of milk. They were squeezing the bottles using them like a squirt gun as they squirted milk on each other.

I immediately went upstairs and packed my few belongings and carried my suitcase and baby things to the car.

"Oh, my," Granny Gleason said as she met me opening the front door with a suitcase and car seat. "What are you doing?"

"Leaving," I told her.

"Why would you do such as that?" she questioned as though she didn't already know the reason.

"Need you ask?"

"Oh, my," she said again. "I don't know what to say other than boys will be boys. Besides, five paying customers is more important than one," she had the gall to admit.

"It's time for me to move on," I told her. "My baby can't get any rest, and I can't either. Destroying my baby's formula is the last straw I'm willing to tolerate."

"I don't refund money when you leave on you own," she told me. "But I'd be willing to refund half."

"I don't want a refund," I told her. "I simply want my baby to be able to sleep. Not to mention having her bottles and formula used as toys."

"What?" she asked in puzzlement.

"Never mind," I told her as I went out the door to place my things in the car. I was in a hurry to get my baby out of the room.

"Oh, my," she said again when she saw what the boys were doing. "This is unacceptable."

"Right," I told her as I unlocked my car door, put the suitcases inside the trunk, fastened the car seat inside, and relocked the car. I didn't trust the boys from not raiding the car's contents. I rushed upstairs and got my baby. Thankfully, Granny Gleasons didn't follow me as I carried my baby out to the car, fastened her in her seat and drove away.

Much to my surprise, when I reached the end of the driveway Jack was standing in the driveway in front of my car. I hit the brakes to keep from running into him. Anger had me driving a bit faster than usual. I rolled down the window.

"What are you doing? I nearly ran over you," I yelled at him when he didn't move out of my way.

"I need to talk to you," he said in a calm voice. "Can I get in the car and get you to drive me back to my van? It's just around the curve."

"No," I told him, still mad enough not to be civil to anyone.

"It's important. I have instructions from James Boden."

I was shocked speechless, to say the least. I didn't object as he moved from in front of my car, got into back seat, and closed the door.

"How do you know Jimbo?" I demanded.

"You might say we were comrades who keep in touch. Drive on," he said. "To make a long story short, I owe him my life. He called in my debt."

"Explain yourself. I'm not in a tolerant mood right now."

"I understand. Cliff told me this morning you were reaching the end of your patience with the three wild kids. He said you were likely to leave any minute. That's why I was coming to see you right now. My van's over there. Stop at it."

I was hesitant to do as he asked. I didn't like the idea of stopping at a van. I didn't like the idea of *him*.

"I have a packet in the van James wanted me to give you. He told me it was time you received it."

"How did you know where to find me?" I demanded of him.

"Surely you knew Jim Boden well enough to realize he would go to the ends of the earth to protect the little girl he loved. The girl he considered a granddaughter. Have to admit his attachment to you surprised the shit right outta me. He never was the paternal kind, to put it mildly."

"That's not answering my question," I snapped.

"He put a tracking device under your car."

"What?"

"He said to tell you he only wanted to make sure you were safe. He wasn't trying to intrude or clip his little bird's wings. He simply wasn't ready to allow you to disappear without him knowing where you were and how you were doing. He said you were too trusting of others."

"I don't believe this," I said, although I wasn't exactly surprised at Jimbo doing such a thing as bugging my car in order to keep track of me.

"Pull over. Don't worry, I'm safe. I'll give you what James left for you, and then I'll be on my way never to encounter you again. I'm good at construction, but Ben expects too much outta a man my age."

"Why didn't you give it to me before now?" I demanded.

"Wanted to give it to you at supper, but James said I should make sure I find you alone. You know, everything has to be a secret as far as James Boden is concerned. From what I can tell, you haven't left the house since I arrived. Didn't want to drag a ladder to your bedroom window. Figured I'd get shot. James said he gave you a pistol and taught you how to shoot it."

"Where is Jimbo?" I asked. "Why didn't he deliver the package himself?" I still wasn't trusting this man as far as I could throw his van.

"He died the day he gave me the packet and instructed me where to find you. He'd done a search on this place and put me on a rush job in case you left. He died of natural causes; I might add."

His words hit me hard. "He's dead?"

"He'd been sick for a long time. He told me he wanted to see you settled and happy before he gave in to the grim reaper. That's why he called in the favor I owed him and told me where to find you. He said to keep it all a secret – like I wouldn't without him having to tell me. Everything we said and did together was kept a secret if you know what I mean."

"Jimbo trusted you?"

"Men like us know how to keep out mouths shut. It's how we manage to stay alive and out of jail. Besides, I couldn't say no to a man who was on his death bed when I owed him my life as well as my freedom, now could I?"

"What do you mean by you owed him your life as well as your freedom?"

"Little lady, I've done told you more than I should. I'll just say James Boden and I had a past."

Thinking of Jimbo being dead left an icy knot from the top of my head to the bottom of my feet. The hurt was so deep I felt numb all over. I pulled in beside the van and stopped. He got out, opened the driver's door of his van, reached under the front seat, and pulled out a thick packet the size of a manila envelope.

"Here," he said as he returned to my car and held the envelope to the closed driver's window. I had locked the doors when he got out.

I rolled down the window and took the packet.

"I've delivered what James had me deliver. I owe him nothing now," he said as he turned his back to me. "Oh," he turned back around. "I'd get rid of that tracking device if I was you. Go through a powerful underbody car wash. The water might short it out. Then get a good, trustworthy mechanic to put your car on a lift to find it." He hesitated a moment. "Whose baby?"

"None of your business," I told him.

"Going to tell Lee York?"

"No!" I said, trying not to sound panicked.

"I won't either."

With those words he strode to his van, got in, started it up, and drove away. Leaving me sitting there, stunned – with the packet in my hand.

Things had happened so fast and unexpectedly that I just sat there staring at the back of the old, slightly rusted van with an Illinois license plate as it drove out of sight down the narrow road. I had no doubt that Jimbo had sent him to find me.

The sound of the baby fussing brought me back to life. I drove on. The movement of the car brought contentment to the baby, and she settled down to sleep. Poor little thing hadn't had an undisturbed sleep since the noisy boys had arrived. I hadn't either.

I stopped at the first carwash I came to. I went through the underbody wash three times. I surely had the cleanest car in existence. I drove away and stopped at the first full-service garage I came to. I parked in front of the office door, locked the car without waking the baby, and went inside.

"How can I help you?" the lady behind the window asked.

"I just discovered that my ex-husband put a tracking device under my car. Can someone please put it on a rack and remove it?"

The woman blinked at me several times at what I had just said.

"I got a restraining order on him, but. . ." I said no more.

"Are you running away from him?"

"I'm trying to."

"Should I call the police? You could be in danger."

"I've left town, and I don't want him to know where I'm going."

"How do you know he planted a tracking device?"

I didn't feel that I owed an explanation to the snoopy woman, but I answered anyway."

"A friend of his told his girlfriend. She called to tell me."

"Okay," she finally said. "I'll see if one of the men can put it up on the lift and check. You do know a cell phone can be traced?"

"I tossed my phone in the river and bought a burner phone."

"Good."

While waiting on my car to come off the lift, I was holding the fussy baby in my arms as I walked about the warm parking lot to get her back to sleep. Finally, the mechanic drove my car into the parking lot, got out, and came to me.

"You're right. I found one." He held his hand out and showed me the device.

"Only one?" I asked.

"Only one. I went over it inside and out."

"You're sure you got them all?"

"Pretty much. You must have gone through a carwash. It might have shorted it out, but I wouldn't count on it. What do you want me to do with it?"

I took it out of his hand. "I'll take care of it. How much do I owe you?"

"Ask Midge at the front desk. She handles that part of the business."

I was charged eighty dollars and was glad to pay it. I put the baby back in the car seat and drove away. I stopped in the first Walmart parking lot, rolled down the window and tossed the device into the back of the oldest truck I could spot and drove away. I wanted to put as much distance between Granny Gleason's and the man named Jack, which I didn't believe was his real name. I really did believe Jimbo had sent the man and the envelope to me, but I didn't want to take time to open it until I traveled as safe distance away. I cringed at the thought of anyone, even Jimbo, being able to track my car to Angie Bell's shack before I left town. The tracking device had to be working if Jimbo told the man where to find me. Jimbo could have suspected the secret I hoped to keep hidden. I should have asked the mechanic if the tracking device also had a listening device.

At least the man who called himself Jack, had said Jimbo had been the one who told him where to find me. Did that mean the man hadn't been able to track me? If that was true, perhaps I was still safe.

I drove in one direction until I ran low on gas, stopped, and filled up the tank and then drove in a different direction. Every time I stopped to feed the baby I filled up with gas. I didn't intend to stop at a motel. I was going to drive all night and the next day, or at least as long as my adrenalin lasted – and my eyes stayed open. I felt the same kind of panic I felt when I was driving away from Florida with Angie's baby. I wasn't even sure I no longer had a tracking device hidden somewhere.

I considered trading in my car for a new one but didn't want to take the time or even know how to go about it.

The sun was going down the next day when my fear settled down enough for me to pull into a roadside rest area and stop. I had driven through the night and now needed to change and feed the baby. I had taken the baby with me into a service station restroom twice to relieve myself – pulled off beside the highway and used a paper cup once. I had chosen a rest stop this time as I planned on resting for a bit and knew a gas station parking lot wasn't suitable to linger in. It was also time I opened the manila envelope to find out what Jimbo had sent me.

After taking the baby into the rest room, taking her into the stall with me, and then placing her on the counter as I washed my hands and face, I returned to the car to diaper and feed her. I then put her in her car seat and got the packet from under the seat. I hesitated a moment before I squeezed the clip together and broke the seal that closed the envelope. It didn't appear it had been opened before. Hopefully, Jack hadn't read its content.

There was a thick envelope inside along with what appeared to be several documents. There was also an envelope with my name written on it in what appeared to be Jimbo's handwriting, although slightly shaky. I opened the envelope.

My beloved Granddaughter,

Please forgive me for the tracking device.

Understand that I had to make sure of your safety as well as your location. Not for your need, but for my own peace of mind. No one else knows where you are except the man I will send this packet by. He is trustworthy and knows nothing about where you have been or the contents of this packet. I trust him and so can you. I did tell him about the tracking device, although I'm the only one with a receiver, which I will now destroy.

I have no one left who cares about me – unless it is you. Therefore, I want you to have what little I've left behind before I became who I am today. As you already know, I have not used my real name in so long I hardly remember it, and that's okay. The deed you'll find inside was transferred to you several years ago, but I held it back until Milianna James came of age. It is a legal document and has not come from one of my comrades. I had not planned on giving it to you for several years yet, but my time has come to an end sooner than I expected – which is a blessing to me. Being in unrelenting pain is no way to live one's last years.

The doctors told me to settle my affairs – and that is what I'm doing. My regret is that I will not be able to see you settled, but I trust you to do that very thing.

In case you haven't looked under the passenger seat, I put different license tags in case you ever needed such. Also, look in the glove compartment. I've discovered different identities can come in handy. Hopefully, my little one, you'll now be able to become yourself – my granddaughter I made you into - instead of the sad little girl I first me. You've also noticed I took the liberty of giving you a dead husband in case you should need one considering the time you spent in self-defense. That choice is up to you.

I hope you will take what I have bestowed upon you and make it your own.

Live happily my dear granddaughter.

With all my love,
Your Robin Hood

Chapter 24

*

I read and reread the letter. Could Jimbo really be dead? How could I know for certain? Jimbo wasn't exactly a perfect man. To be honest, he was a bigtime scammer and a thief. He had made me into a thief – a Robin Hood kind of thief, which wasn't altogether the worst kind to be – if I stretched the truth a bit. Still, he was always there when I was in need. I didn't want to think how things would have gone for my beloved mother if not for him.

I took a chance because I couldn't stop myself. I thought it was time for Karate class to start soon. I called the parks and recreation office on my disposable phone although I didn't want to come into contact with anyone from where I was from. Jimbo meant more to me than anyone in the whole wide world. I had to know for certain if he was forever lost to me.

The secretary answered the phone.

"Would Lee York be there by chance?" I asked.

"He's getting ready to start teaching class. May I take a message for him."

"I only need to speak with him for a moment."

"He doesn't like to be interrupted. He can call you back after class is over."

"I know that, but I wouldn't be calling if it wasn't extremely important," I persisted.

She hesitated for a few moments. "I'll check with him. Who shall I tell him is calling?" she asked with impatience.

"Alona," I dared to say.

It took less than a minute before I heard his voice. "Alona? Where are you?"

"In my car. Did my grandfather really die? Please tell me he didn't."

"I'm so very sorry, honey. He did pass away."

"What did he die from," I demanded as my heart twisted with pain.

"I don't know for sure. I think he'd been sick for a long time and my understanding was that his heart finally gave out on him."

"I don't believe it," I managed to say. "He can't be dead."

"I know, but it happens. Where are you? Are you alright?"

"I'm fine. Thank you for telling me. Take care of yourself," I was quick to say a moment before I cut the connection. Hearing his voice brought back too many of the old pains I'd gone through growing up.

I gritted my teeth and acknowledged the fact that the man who had meant so much to me would never be sitting on the bench in the little park again. Somehow, in the far reaches of my mind, I had thought he would always be there – waiting – in case I ever returned. I knew he was looking worse every time I saw him, but dead? Never dead. Not Jimbo. Not my Robin Hood.

I don't know how long I sat there staring straight ahead at nothing before I placed the letter on the dashboard and looked at another document. It was a deed made out in my name – my real name, Milianna James, along with a notarized copy of my birth certificate. I read the legal description with disbelief. It was for three hundred and thirty-one acres of land along with a house and outbuildings. I couldn't believe what I read, so I read it again – and again. No way could Jimbo give such a large amount of land to me. How could he possibly own such a large track of land plus a house and outbuildings? It had to be some kind of forgery that had been transferred to me from the life estate of Freda L. Whitley by her son, E.J. Whitley.

How could I find out its legitimacy or the lack of? Furthermore, did I want to? Did I dare?

I must have sat there for over an hour staring at the deed before I reached for the thick, white envelope. I wasn't the least surprised to find it filled with hundred-dollar bills. I counted them one bill at a time. There were twenty- eight of them. I knew right away that two thousand eight hundred dollars was Jimbo's life savings – and he had given it to me.

"Now what?" I whispered the two words out loud. Did I trust what I held in my lap, or did I take it as a forgery and keep running away in whatever direction my car happened to be pointed in?

I didn't trust the man called Jack – but I did trust the man I knew as Jimbo. I reread the deed again. The deed said that the land was located in Ashe County, North Carolina. Made sense now that Jimbo had left a North Carolina license plate in the glove compartment along with giving Milianna J. York a North Carolina address. I was most likely an idiot for doing what I did instead of heading as far West as I could travel. I got the map and opened it up. I found North Carolina and Ashe County, searched for the roads and road numbers to travel, started the engine, left the rest area, and pointed my car toward North Carolina.

By the time I was nearing the South Carolina and North Carolina line my eyes were so tired I could barely keep them open. I was so deadheaded I didn't trust myself to drive one more mile in the deepening shadows of the evening's twilight. I had already left the biggest towns behind and feared I would have to backtrack to find a place to stay for the night when I saw a small motel ahead on the right side of the road. The Sun and Sand was the motel's name. I counted ten doors along with an office on the ground floor. No upper floor which would keep down noise. It wasn't the fanciest place I'd ever seen, but it wasn't the worst. I counted five cars parked in front of doors. There was a Dodge, a Chevrolet and three Ford vehicles. I took that to mean it was a place to stop and rest for a night instead of a place to linger for a vacation. A place to rest for a night would suit me just fine. I pulled off on a frontage road and parked near the door marked office.

I made sure I took the baby out of her car seat, locked the car, and went inside.

"You look like you could use a room," were the first words the little old lady said to me. "You're red eyed and dragging. At least your baby is still asleep instead of squalling its head off."

"I know," I said without commenting on how well the baby slept while driving. Unfortunately, I couldn't do the same. I had still had no idea how much a newborn baby should sleep, but she appeared to be healthy according to the information I googled. "Can I get a room as far away from others in case my baby wakes up during the night?"

"You sure can, Honey. I'll put you on the very far end and put any other visitors together on the near end. How long are you staying?"

"Just until morning."

"We have a drink machine and snack machines, but if you want food, you'll have to drive into town. Nanny's Grill has right good food."

I thought about asking if there was a pizza delivery but was too tired to ask. She quoted a price which I gladly paid in cash, left the office, drove a few dozen feet, and parked in front of the door at the far end of the building. I unlocked the door and carried the baby inside with me. I flipped on the light. It certainly wasn't fancy, but it looked clean. I thought of what Mother always said, "Just because something looks clean doesn't mean it is. Right then, I was too tired to care.

I laid the baby on the bed and went to the car to bring in only what I'd need for the night. Thank goodness I still had a half-liter bottle of Mountain Dew and a Mounds candy bar that that was only slightly melted. I also had several unopened bottles of formula along with new baby bottles that had never been used as squirt guns.

I wasn't going to miss Granny Gleason's even though it was a peaceful place before five guests arrived.

The baby woke me up twice to be changed and fed. Once during the darkest part of the night and once around two o'clock in the morning. She went right back to sleep and so did I. It was almost five o'clock in the morning when she and I both woke up again. I washed the baby, changed her into fresh clothes and fed her a bottle. I took a quick shower in lukewarm water and put on my best dress. I didn't want to change before I searched out the attorney who had made the deed to me. To put it mildly, I didn't trust my good luck for it to be legit.

The sun was rising with golden and red lighting the sky by the time I saw the dark green of the Appalachian mountains looming in shades of blue in front of me. I recalled what my mother always said. Red clouds in the morning, shepherds take warning. Red clouds at night, shepherds delight. I hoped the red clouds weren't a sign of coming bad weather.

There were also small clouds of white early morning fog clinging to the valleys. I drove on watching the misty fog slowly dissipating as it raised its misty fingers toward the heavens. There was a quite restfulness lingering in those mountains that touched something deep inside me. I felt the urge to pull off beside the road and take in every drop of what I was seeing and feeling. Soon the sun would be fully up, the sky a Carolina blue, and the mist burned off while a day I both dreaded and anticipated would be in full swing. I should soon know if I had been scammed or if the deed was legal and authentic.

At least there was twenty-eight hundred dollars to go with the rest of the money Jimbo had seen that I had. That along with the sale of Mother's house was a rather good nest egg if I made sure I wasn't scammed out of it. A person never knew for sure when someone was trying to take advantage of them. I suppose knowing Aunt Mary and my father's twin brother had taught me to be wary.

There was no question that I was young and inexperienced in the ways of the world. Jimbo had shown me there were bad people out there waiting to take advantage of the innocent. What had happened with Angie Bell was another lesson to learn from.

I reminded myself that I also had the money Nokosi Micco had given me to relocate Angie Bell. I hadn't checked to see what the amount was, but I would save it for the new parents of the baby. I didn't expect it to be much since it came from a hard-working man whose income was from running a tourist trap. I wasn't sure how I would go about giving the money to whoever the new parents might be, but I would find a way. Maybe I could open a trust fund for the baby when she turned eighteen and needed college money. This reminded me that I needed to find the little thing a home soon before I became more attached to her than I already was. The baby deserved more than I could ever give her. I had never considered myself mother material.

I wanted her to have a loving home with both a mother and father along with grandparents, siblings, and cousins to ensure a life of happiness. It was such a lonely thing to be an only child. I knew that from experience.

Four hours later I arrived in the little town of Jefferson. North Carolina. It was a quaint town with sparce businesses scattered about. I found where the Ashe County courthouse was and carried the baby along with the deed inside. I found the Register of Deed's office and went inside.

"May I help you?" a friendly young woman asked.

"I have a deed, or perhaps a registered copy of one, and I want to know if it is on file."

"May I see what you have?"

I showed her. It only took her minutes to pull up the information on her computer. "Here it is. It has been on record for three years. What you have is a notarized copy."

"I actually own a house and all the land?" I asked in amazement.

"According to our records you do. It also shows that the taxes have been paid on time."

I was speechless for a moment. "Where is the office of Watson and Sons, law offices located?" I wouldn't bring myself to believe what the woman was telling me until I consulted with the attorney who had prepared the deed."

"It's only a little way from here. Take a right onto the highway and go down the road about half a mile. You'll see the building on the right across from Hardees."

"Thank you," I told her. "What do I owe you."

"Not a thing. I'm a public servant," she said with a smile.

I settled the baby back in her car seat and headed out to find Watson and Sons attorneys at law. I found the building easy enough, parked the car near the door, got the baby out of her seat again and went inside.

"How may I help you?" this lady also asked in a friendly tone of voice.

"I was wondering if I might be able to see Mr. Watson?"

"In reference to what, may I ask?"

"In reference to a house and property I have a deed for."

"May I ask what type of problem you are having with it?"

"I want to make sure I am the legal owner of it."

"And your name is?"

"Milianna James."

"Please be seated while I check to see if Mr. Watson Sr. has left the building yet."

She stood up and disappeared down the hall. I hadn't seen another car parked out front so I thought I might have a chance of seeing him. I sat down in a leather chair and settled the sleeping baby in my lap. I had left her car seat in the car.

It was too irritating to take it out then strap it back in every time I stopped to go in somewhere.

Minutes later she returned to open the door that led to a different inside hallway. "Follow me please to his conference room. Mr. Watson will see you shortly."

I sat at a long, polished table surrounded by eight leather chairs as I gently jiggled the baby to assure she stayed sleeping. I sat there waiting fifteen minutes for him to enter the room. What could be taking him so long? He could surely answer my question in a minute or two. I was ready to get up and go back inside the other room to ask his receptionist if I had been forgotten, when another door opened, and he entered the room. I assumed he had taken time to pull my file and review my deed before he met with me. As I expected, he was a short, older man with thinning gray hair and glasses. His face was lined with time-wrinkles, but his eyes were bright with a slightly surprised look to them – as though he hadn't expected to see me.

"I'm Ronald Watson Sr.," he said as he held out a hand for me to shake. "I take it you're Milianna James."

"Milianna James York," I added, thinking it might be best to claim I was married. Jimbo might have made me married for a reason. I took my right hand away from the baby long enough to shake his hand. I was surprised to find the older man had a firm handshake. Don't know why I thought his hand would be weak and flabby.

"So. It seems you have come of age and shown up to claim your property," he said in what sounded like a disapproving tone of voice as he sat down. "Is your husband with you?"

I took a deep breath and continued with the lie. "My husband died a while back," I said as I looked down at the baby for a few moments. "Actually, I just received a copy of the deed a few days ago. I've come to you to make sure everything is a legal and not some kind of scam."

He looked me over and nodded slowly. "It is not a scam, and it is legal," he told me. "The property has been in your name for some time now. However, it would not be transferred to you until you turned eighteen in accordance with E.J. Whitley's directive. It appears you have gotten married and had a baby since he deeded the land to you. Is that correct."

"Yes," I answered.

"I'm sorry to hear about your husband, but it doesn't change anything about your inheritance."

I wanted to ask if E.J. Whitley was Jimbo's real name? But then I doubt if this attorney would know one way or the other. "You're telling me I actually own a house and three hundred and thirty-one acres of land free and clear?" I asked.

"You do if you have proper identification such as a birth certificate and photo ID such as a driver's license or passport."

I took my purse from the floor and took out my billfold. It felt both odd and a relief that I was finally becoming my real self. I showed him my driver's license and then my birth certificate that Jimbo had provided for me, and that I had taken from the glove compartment and put in my purse before I went inside. Jimbo knew I would need them to show my true identity when I claimed what he had left me.

"I'll have my secretary make a copy of these to put in your file, if that is alright with you," he added as he stood up with my identification in his hand.

I watched him leave the room with an eerie feeling deep inside. I wasn't sure all was well. Was there a chance he would be able to figure out I had once claimed to be Alona Anderson, granddaughter of the alias George Anderson?

A short time later he returned with my identification. "Okay, Miss James, or should I say Mrs. York?" he asked as he looked at the baby I was holding.

"Millie is what I go by. You can call me Millie," I told him dodging his question. "How old?" he questioned as he looked at the baby.

I smiled down at the baby and snuggled her closer to my body. "She was a preemie and still sleeps a lot," I said lightly. "Is the house in fit condition for me to move into or will it require a lot of work?" I ask, still trying to avoid answering his question about the baby.

"It is, but both Mrs. Freda Whitley and her son, Mr. E. J. Whitley, have had a gentleman caretaker living there to look after the estate for several years."

"Someone is living there right now?" I asked with disappointment.

"To my understanding he's not living in the house itself. He is staying in the caretaker's house free of charge in return for looking after the place and seeing to Freda's needs before her demise. It is my understanding he also gets the funds from running the farm. He is full owner of the animals and whatever crops he has on it, whatever they might be."

"Does that mean I can't move into the house?" I didn't want all the effort it took to find a place to rent or a reasonable priced motel even for one more night. I was so tired even my bones ached.

"No, it doesn't. You are the owner. You have the right to move into the house at your discretion. You also have the right to terminate the caretaker's occupancy when his lease contract runs out if you so choose," he added a bit relunctly.

"So, he has to leave?"

"Only if you ask him to do so, but I think he has another year on his lease contract. You can also choose for him to stay longer on your own terms if he's willing to negotiate a new contract."

"Does he have a family?"

"He is not married. He does have a relative living with him, although there's nothing in his contract stating it is or is not permitted."

"A relative?" I questioned.

He seemed to grin as he said, "An elderly grandfather."

"Does he not have parents? I questioned.

"Both deceased."

"Can you give me directions to the place?" I said, starting to feel the effects of the last few days. It would be such a relief to have a place of my own where I could rest and get my mind and body together again.

"I'll give you an address along with a map. I also have an extra set of keys to the house and outbuildings in the file folder for you in case you showed up at my office, which I assumed you would do eventually."

"Thank you," I said. "How much do I own you?"

"Mr. Whitley made sure I was paid an adequate retainer in case you should need me. You have ten more hours of my service that has been prepaid."

"Did you know him personally?" I questioned, wanting to know more about Jimbo.

"Our correspondences were by phone." He placed the keys on the table in front of me as he stood up to open the door indicating it was time for me to leave. "By the way, I'm sure you've heard there is a storm brewing. I don't expect it to affect the mountains much, but rain can make the road to your place muddy and difficult to travel on."

I hadn't been listening to any weather reports, but I wasn't concerned about a storm. The weather outside was sunny and warm. I put the map, keys, and my identification in my purse, gathered the baby in my arms and left his office feeling both stunned and overwhelmed that I was actually the owner of a house and land. What I needed to do next was inspect the house and see if it was a place I could move into right away or if I'd have to make repairs.

I put the baby in the car seat, got behind the wheel and studied the map Mr. Watson had given me. Fifteen miles from his office to the house that belonged to me. Fifteen miles didn't seem too far from town. I wouldn't be stranded in no-man's land as I had feared. I hoped the house would be rather grand considering there was a caretaker's house along with an unbelievable amount of land to go with it. There had to be a great deal of wealth for someone to own that amount of real estate. I couldn't imagine anyone deeding it to me free and clear- even when that someone was Jimbo.

Some things are just too good to be trusted. Jimbo had proven that to me, and yet I had trusted him for years.

The farther from town I got, the narrower and more crooked the highway became. It got to the point where I was holding my breath with each blind curve I drove around. I questioned if there would be room for two cars going in opposite directions. Not only that but the sides of the road became steep and rocky. Some rocks stuck out like fists waiting to scrape the side of cars if they got too close to a non-existent ditch line. Fortunately, I met no cars on the tight curves and only a few cars going in my direction the entire eight miles of highway.

I got even more apprehensive when I came to the right-hand turnoff shown on the map. I drove over a narrow one-lane bridge that had seen better days. The bridge was superior to the road at the bridge's end. The road turned into one lane that was dotted with sparce gravel and an abundance of potholes. The first pothole my tires hit jarred my teeth. The second one slowed me down to a crawl. I certainly didn't need to pop a tire. I had never changed a flat tire before and didn't want to start now. To make matters worse, the sky suddenly turned from Carolina blue to gunmetal gray. Within minutes a sudden fury of winds hit strong enough to blow leaves off the trees and bend limbs until they broke off. On the heels of the winds came a deluge of unexpected hail and rain. I turned on my windshield wipers and slowed down to a crawl. Still yet I could barely see the road in front of me. I considered stopping the car right where it sat but I feared if I stopped, I would be run into by another driver blinded by the sudden storm.

I best keep going, I assured myself as the road became more like a narrow river of water. It was impossible to tell where the potholes were. I feared I would land in one deep enough to stall out the car.

This storm will surely pass quickly considering how suddenly it hit. I kept reassuring myself as I continued on at a snail's pace.

It didn't pass quickly. I continued climbing the seven miles of muddy road with tires slipping and spinning. I said prayers one after another that I was near my destination. The muddy road turned into an even narrower, muddy excuse of a path. I crept forward fearing the possibility I had missed the turn that led me to the house Jimbo had deeded to me. Considering the desolate area I faintly detected through the storm, a part of me hoped I had taken a wrong turn, and this was not where I was supposed to be.

Finally, I detected the blurred image of a white farmhouse through the rain-splattered windshield. The excuse of a path ended. I stopped the car because I could drive no further. One thing was for sure, I wasn't about to get out of the car in a storm such as this even if I had to sit here until tomorrow. I tilted the seat back and closed my eyes as I listened to the sound of rain and hail pounding down on the roof. Without the windshield wipers going, I could see nothing other than the water beating on the windows. It reminded me of going through a carwash. The only good thing I could think of was perhaps some of the mud would be washed off the car.

I was evidently more exhausted than I thought. I hadn't intended to fall asleep, but I obviously did. I awoke with a start as the door to the driver's side of the car jerked opened letting the cold air hit me in the face. At least the rain had stopped.

"What the hell you doin' here?" a man who resembled methuselah caked from head to toe in mud asked in a course, gravelly voice. His timeworn, leather face was crisscrossed with deep wrinkles along with tobacco stained, gray whiskers all over his chin, jaws, and upper lip. His offensive smell hit me in the face like a slap. His words along with his appearance caused my breath to catch in fear. I had seen pictures of reprehensible mountain men, and one was now holding my car door open. A horror even worse than those pictures brought had come to life inside me. I had woken up to a worse scenario than the book *Deliverance* portrayed.

"Who are you?" I managed to ask as I looked in the seat for some sort of weapon. My hand grabbed an empty baby bottle lying on the console.

"You're trespassing. You best explain what you're doing here since you won't be leaving any time soon."

I wouldn't be leaving anytime soon, put a new kind of fear in me. Still, I managed to get words out of my mouth. "Is uh, uh, is this the Freda Whitley place?" I managed to ask.

"Hain't none of your damned business," he shouted at me.

"Are you the caretaker?" I asked, trying to keep my voice from shaking.

"Hain't none of your damned business who I am. You best be telling me who you are and why you're trespassing on private property," he continued to shout.

"If this is the Freda Whitley place, I'm the new owner," I managed to say as I tried to mask the unbelievable fear I was feeling.

"The hell you say," he shouted out in an angry voice. "Ain't no fancy, smancy, snotty-nosed broad ownin' this place. You ain't the first fool that's shown up here to see what she can get away with. You've done got your lying ass in a right smart of a fix."

I instantly wished the baby bottle was a tube of pepper spray. He'd have a snoot full of pure burning fire.

"Gramps, what's going on?" said a dripping wet, mud-covered, stinking younger version of the neanderthal.

"This ten-year-old idiot is claiming she owns this place. Can you believe such nonsense? Let's go ahead and drown her in one of the potholes this storm washed out."

"Does she now?" The younger man said as he bent down to look me in the face. "She's obviously too young to own a driver's license much less this place."

"Easy enough for her to drive off a cliff in weather like this. Car might burn but it's too wet to catch the mountain on fire," the old man said in a tone of voice that brought renewed chills up my spine. Was he threatening to run the car over the cliff with the baby and me in it? Perhaps even setting it on fire?

A shot of bravado mixed with horrible fear hit me. I had traveled too long and too far to be threatened by the likes of these two. I picked up my burner phone and dialed 911 and pressed the button for speaker phone.

"911, what is your emergency?" said a woman's voice.

"This is Millie James York," I thought it might be best to add the last name of my supposed husband. "Two men are threatening me. I've just arrived at the house Attorney Ronald Watson confirmed that I owned, and I'm being threatened by two men."

"How are they threatening you?" she questioned.

"They have me and my baby trapped in my car. They're threatening to get rid of me by driving my car over a cliff and setting it on fire. Send the police right away."

"What is your address?"

I gave her the address Mr. Watson had given me.

"That's the old Whitley place, isn't it?"

"It is."

"I'd say you have come face to face with Wilburn and Morton McCray. They are both scary as the devil himself but they're both harmless."

"Harmless?" I shouted. "You're not the one being threatened. I need an officer of the law." I didn't intend to be run off by these two regardless of the fear I was feeling – or ignored by some woman who should already have law enforcement on the way.

"Did you say Ronald Watson?"

"Yes, I just came from his office. He gave me this address and the keys to the house. He assured me that I own both the house and land free and clear."

"Well, shit," she said. "If that don't beat all. Give Morton the phone so I can speak with him."

The younger man stuck out his hand, but I held onto the phone. This phone was my only connection to a somewhat sane person, and I wasn't about to hand it over. "He's hearing every word you're saying. Why aren't you sending the police?"

"Morton, are you and Wilburn harassing this woman?" she asked, instead of responding to me.

"Just trying to find out who she is and why she's here at a time like this. The flash flood just done us a whole shitload of damage, and I predict there is more rain on the way. You know what kind of trouble we've been having lately with trespassers," he said overloud toward the phone I still held as though he feared he couldn't be heard unless he shouted.

"Then let her tell you who she is and why she showed up. You can call Ronald Watson to find out if she's lying or not. If she calls this number again, I *will* send out Ralph and Pete to settle Wilburn's old rearend down along with yours. Got that?"

"Got it," he shouted toward the phone.

This beat all I had ever come across. Since when would a 911 operator refuse to send help to a defenseless woman, much less ask to speak to the aggressor? To my amazement the woman disconnected.

"I don't believe this," I said as I remembered the pistol I had hidden under the car seat. It appeared I would need it.

"Ah, hell . . ." the old man began.

"Hush, Gramps. You heard what Sussie May said. She's not joking about sending Ralph and Pete here. We'll let this girl tell us what's going on and then get rid of her." He turned to me as though he was giving me my last rights.

"As I just told you earlier, I own this place free and clear according to Attorney Ronald Watson. Freda Whitley owned it. After her death, the property reverted back to her only son, E. J. Whitley, whom I got the three hundred thirty-one acres plus the house and outbuildings from."

"My boy here has owned this place for the past ten years," the old man shouted at me. "You think we'll fall for that nonsense coming from the likes of you?"

"Gramps," the young man warned. "Calm it down. I've never owned this place, and you know it."

"You can damned well claim adverse possession."

"Not according to Attorney Watson. You are only the caretaker, and I have the right to evict you, which I'm doing right now," I blurted out regardless of the contract for another year. "Get off my property right now or I'll call 911 again," I threatened as I reached underneath the seat and pulled out the pistol to point it at the younger man.

"Whoa-ah here, young lady. There's no need for that," the old man said. His eyes had gotten bigger in his muddy, tobacco-streaked, beardy face.

"Put that thing down. There's no need for such as that. Somebody might accidentally get hurt. I suggest we all three calm down and talk reason about this situation," the younger man said in what he hoped was a reasonable tone of voice.

"I was willing to do that in the beginning, but I no longer feel the desire to do so," I informed them.

"Ma'am, I'm truly sorry about the reception you got. Try to understand that we've had one heck of a job trying to keep some of the younger animals from drowning in this unexpected downpour. We hadn't prepared for all the water that came flooding down this mountain. Surely when you, a total stranger we know nothing about, showed up claiming to own the place, Gramps' patience snapped. We've had problems with trespassers ever since Freda Whitley passed."

"You both threatened me," I said through clenched teeth to keep my chin from quivering from the fear I was still feeling.

"It is beyond imagination that such a young woman could be the owner of the Whitley place. It has been in the Whitley family for many generations. To my knowledge, the son never had children or if he ever married. The last time I heard he was still alive. I do know he sent money to his mother ever month until her death. Once the money arrived, she would have me drive her to town to buy supplies to last until the next month's money arrived." He let out a long-drawn-out breath. "If it meets with your approval, Gramps and I will go back to the caretakers' house and get dried off before we start on cleaning up from this flood. Hopefully, the storm is over, but I doubt it. We'll leave you to check out what has obviously become your property. We can discuss things later on if it's suitable with you."

I didn't trust them in the least. I wasn't about to fall for his attempt at fooling me about their intentions. I'd heard too many stories about drunk-crazed hillbillies such as I was looking at. I had even slipped and read the entire hair-raising book "Deliverance" without Mother knowing it. I pressed 911 again.

"Now what?" the same voice I spoke with earlier asked. She evidently had expected that I'd call back.

"She's as crazy as a loon," the old man shouted toward the phone before I could say anything. "She's got a pistol pointed at us."

"No shit!" the woman said. "Millie James, don't you dare shoot either one of them. I've talked to Ronald Watson and already sent Ralph and Pete to check things out. They were just up the river from there. Put the pistol down. They'll be there any minute."

"Hope they hurry," the older man shouted again. "She don't have the sense of a blind bat. She's liable to kill us both. You know how crazy Yankees are."

"Then you both better do as she says. Ronald said she does indeed own the place. Plus, she appeared to be an easy-going young mother of a tiny baby. I can see how you'd scare the common sense outta her. All three of you need to calm down. Ralph and Pete should be there any minute. They should be there any minute now. The storm along with the muddy road has slowing them down. Wilburn, you should have let the state put some gravel on that road instead of running them off the way you did."

"We don't need no government gravel," the old man shouted. "Don't want strangers crawling all over this mountain stealing and killing things. Gravel would let them get here easier."

"Shut up that yelling, Wilburn. I don't want to hear another peep outta you. Millie James, I repeat what I told you earlier. They are both harmless. Wilburn has a loud bark and no bite whatsoever. You need to put your pistol away. Those things have been known to go off and hurt somebody. You don't want to be thrown in jail for murdering one or both of these men."

The reminder of murder put another fear in me. I didn't want any reason to have a background check done on me, but I did want to stay alive and unharmed.

It was then I heard the engine of a vehicle roaring up the road. A mud-splattered Jeep came barreling around a large maple tree growing beside the driveway and slid to a stop behind my car a foot from my bumper. Two uniformed men nearly the size of the Jeep got out.

"What's going on here?" the smaller of the two men demanded as he strutted toward the two men. "Wilburn, have you been bullying this little lady?" he asked in a deep, cigarette roughened voice.

He even gave off a cigarette odor. As soon as they arrived, I quickly put my pistol back under the seat.

"You got things under control, Pete?" the 911 operator asked.

"Don's see no problem here," the man said as he glared at me and then at the two men. "Is there, Wilburn?"

"Nope. Nary a problem one."

"I'll hang up them. Considering the flooding rain we just got, there could be a real emergency call come in. By the way, more rain warnings are flashing on the emergency news channel. Ralph, you, and Pete best get off that mountain as soon as you can."

After she disconnected, the man who had to be Ralph said, "Suppose you tell me what's going on, little lady?"

I was more than willing to tell him. "I arrived here to inspect my property when these two men accosted me and then threatened to toss my car with me and my baby in it over a cliff."

"Morton?" Ralph questioned as though asking for his comment on what I'd just said.

"Not exactly," Morton said hesitantly. "You know how Gramps is. His mouth gets ahead of his brain. He was referring to the mud and her car sliding off the road – not tossing her and her car over a cliff."

"So, he did threaten her?" Pete asked.

"No. Like I just told you, Gramp's comment was in reference to the slick, muddy road. You now know firsthand what it's like driving on this road after a storm. She could have easily slid off the road. Gramps was only pointing it out."

"So, you're saying that the young lady misunderstood Wilburn's words of warning as a threat?"

"So it would seem," Morton said as he looked me in the eyes.

"Sussie Mae said something about her having a pistol."

Morton was quick to shake his head. "She had a baby bottle in her hand. She was shaking so badly Gramps mistook it for a pistol. You know how bad his eyesight is failing."

"I see," Pete said in a slow drawl. "You're stating that this little lady was trying to defend herself against the two of you with a baby bottle?"

"That's how it appeared to me."

Pete chuckled, and Ralph all but rolled his eyes. "Do you think you can keep Wilburn under control if we leave the three of you alone, or do we need to drag all three of your asses to jail for the night?"

"We're good," Morton said. "As you can see, we've got a mighty lot of work to clean up before nightfall after that cloudburst hit us. We can't leave the animals to fend for themselves in this mess."

I started to say that I wanted them evicted at once from what was now my property, but then I considered the pistol I had held on them. Neither of them had admitted I had it. If these two officers knew about it, they might take it away from me – or even charge me with some sort of crime. I didn't want to lose the pistol Jimbo had given me – or worse.

"Then I take it this misunderstanding is settled?" Ralph said to the younger man.

"It's settled. There shouldn't be any more misunderstandings. Right?" he directed the question at me.

"I certainly hope not," I said, still not at all that certain I would be safe if I was left with these two men.

Ralph must have seen my continued fear. "I can assure you these two men are harmless if you don't take into account their appearance and smell. I'd say they've got more cow and hog manure on them right now than the animals have on them. They'll clean up right nice, but they can't wash their ugly faces away," he added with intentional insult.

"You're just one laugh after another – considering your ugly mug favors a turkey's ass," Gramps said with derision, which didn't seem to affect Ralph in the least.

Pete shook his head as though he was ready for this encounter to come to an end. "You two cut it out. It's obvious this young lady isn't used to such goings on," he said as he turned to me. "Don't pay any attention to them. They're secretly fond of each other. Ma'am, would you like me and Ralph to help you carry your things in the house? You'll have your arms full with the baby. I think all this commotion is waking it up. Damned, if it ain't a cute little thing? It's a girl considering all the pink?"

"She is," I told him as I hesitated to respond to their offer. I still wasn't sure if it was safe for me to be here after these officers left. Pete seemed to realize what I was thinking.

"I can assure you again that these two men really are harmless. I've known 'em for years. Besides, Wilburn had a good point. The storm has made this road slick as glass. There are several cliffs without proper ditch lines to keep a vehicle from sliding over them. It raised my body hair trying to get here after that cloud burst and we were driving our 4-wheel drive jeep. Don't recommend driving your car outta here until this mud dries up some. It's clear all this was nothing more than a misunderstanding. Not to discount that Wilburn can scare the shit outta a person who don't know him – along with some that do. Morton has to be a saint to take him in and put up with his antics," Ralph said as he gave Wilburn and Morton both a *'you'd better be listening to me look.'*

"Okay," I mumbled, without being assured of their harmlessness.

"Morton, take Wilburn back to the house or barn. You both look scary as hell. I can see how your looks alone could scare this little lady nearly to death," Pete said.

"Good advice. Come on Gramps. We'll check on the animals again before we clean this crap off us. He's right, we've got enough cow shit on us to spread on the corn field."

"And Morton, both you and Wilburn stay far away from the little lady and this house. I don't want to make another trip up this road now or in the future. Got it."

"Got it."

Morton gave the old man a nod and they both stalked off leaving me with the two officers.

"Are you sure my baby and I will be safe?" I questioned once those two scary men were out of hearing.

"If we weren't sure of that, we wouldn't be leaving you here," he said with total assurance. "Once they know you're not an intruder, they'll take care of you like you're one of their animals. People would have taken advantage of old Freda if it hadn't been for Morton being here. He even scared the hell out of Preacher Tate when he showed up."

Great. Just what I wanted to hear. Like I wanted to be considered someone's animal, but I still had my reservations about being stuck in the house with a dangerous road of escape, while two crazy men were nearby.

"If you're still scared of them, or of staying here, we can cram you and your baby in the Jeep with us and take you back to town. You can stay in the hotel until you make other arrangements. Once the road dries off, we can bring you back to get your car. I've not got enough grit to try driving your car outta here. Do you Ralph?"

"Hell no."

I didn't want to be run off from what now belonged to me. I had a pistol that I was a crack-shot with. Plus, I had years of self-defense training. I wasn't a coward or a helpless *little lady*. Perhaps I was now madder at the two men than I was fearful of them. Besides, I was both emotionally and physically exhausted. Not to mention the overwhelming disappointment I was feeling. From what I'd seen of the house so far, it was a great letdown in need of maintenance. As for the land, I had never seen anything like it. I was a city girl used city streets and traffic congestion. I didn't know how to describe this wet and oozing mudhole of a place. My consolation at the moment was that Jimbo wanted me to have it. Something he would not have done if he thought I would not be safe here – I hoped.

"Are there rats and snakes in the house?" I found myself asking something that had not occurred to me before. As long as it had been empty, it might not be fit for habitation.

"Doubt it," Ralph said. "Morton called war on rats the day he took over as caretaker. Folks don't like the destruction rats cause, especially farmers. They can eat you out of house and home along with crapping on everything. Nasty things."

"And snakes?" I questioned.

"Snakes eat rats. No rats, no snakes," Pete added as though he was telling a fact.

"House will probably need a good scrubbing, but it should be in fine living condition. Morton is a man who takes his job seriously. He keeps it in better shape than most places hereabouts," Ralph assured me. "Freda was a particular one when it came to her things. Morton kept things up in lieu of rent. He's a hard worker. You're lucky he's the caretaker. Ask me, you ought to keep him on if he's willing."

I didn't like the idea of keeping him and his crazy Gramps on, but I could take care of that with Ronald Watson help. "What about her son?" I wanted to know more about Jimbo.

"He left out from here before I born. Never set eyes on him. Never returned home even for a visit with his momma to my knowledge. Freda talked fondly of her beloved son every time someone came into contact with her. According to her, she talked with him on the phone most all the time."

"Were those two crazy caretakers here when she was alive?" I asked, although Morton had commented on taking her into town.

"Morton has been here since he was a young boy. He became almost a replacement for her wayward son. Wilburn moved here sometime after Freda's death," he chuckled lightly at what he was obviously thinking. "Freda might have lived to be two hundred if she'd had Wilburn here to fight with. Those two were alike in more ways than one. Hard to figure out if they were crazy as loons or as intelligent as Einstein."

"Ask me, there's nothing wrong with Wilburn other than contrariness. He likes being hard to get along with. Don't know how Morton puts up with him," Pete added to the conversation. "Got stuff in the trunk for me to carry in?" he asked impatiently as though he was in a hurry to leave the storm-flooded, mud-ridden place.

"I'll get things out of the trunk later. You can take inside what is in the seats if you like," I told them as I got out of the car and cradled the fussy baby in my arms. "Best take her car seat in." I feared it would be the only place clean enough to put the baby. No telling what kind of germs were inside a vacant house.

"How long has Freda Whitley been dead?" I asked.

"It's been a few years. She was well over ninety when she passed on," Ralph told me. "She was dead-old the first time I ever set eyes on her, and I was only a boy at the time."

Then it had been after her death that Jimbo deeded me her house and land.

The grass in the yard had been mown recently and was sopping wet instead of being muddy as I had expected. Rain was still dripping off the roof while I chose the key that had the word *house* taped on it. The door opened without so much as a squeak. I walked into the front room to be surprised that the place looked cleaner than I expected. The room definitely appeared as though an elderly lady had lived there. The furniture was from at least sixty or more years in the past from what I could see. Much of it was covered with dusty tented sheets.

"Morton promised Freda he'd look after the place until her son returned. Looks like he's been keeping his promise," Ralph said as he walked past me and put the cooler containing milk supplies for the baby in the middle of the room. "She expected her son to return anytime and wanted things to be ready for him."

"She was as old as these mountains when she passed," Pete said. "Wouldn't surprise me one bit if her spirit is still roaming these old mountains along with this house. Did you buy the place from her son?"

"Yes," I told him – not that it was any of his business.

"Bet your husband paid a pretty penny for it considering how large a tract of land it is. Not many privately owned tracts left unless they belong to the government. Nowadays most land have been divided up and sold off. Why didn't he come with you? Don't seem right that a man would let his wife show up alone with a tiny baby."

"I'm capable of taking care of things without him," I said a bit sharper than I intended. "Thank you for helping me, and most of all, thank you for showing up when those idiots were threatening me. I was scared for myself and my baby's life."

"Doin' our job, Ma'am. Just doin' our job," Ralph said. "We best be on our way considering it's starting to rain again. This road isn't safe when it's raining."

*

Part of me wanted the officers gone while another part of me didn't want to be left alone in this place especially when those two men were somewhere near. The officers had repeatedly assured me that I would be safe, but considering my reception, it was difficult for me to put much faith in what they said. No doubt the old man really was as crazy as a loon. The younger man couldn't be much better.

I took the sheet off an old-fashioned oak table that appeared to be well worn and placed the car seat on it and put the baby in it while I prepared a bottle. It suddenly hit me that at least half a dozen people in this area thought I was the baby's mother. I tried to remember if I had told anyone I was her mother, but I had surely shown it by avoidance. I wasn't sure what kind of impression I had made. How was I going to explain giving the baby up for adoption? Oh well, I would take care of explanations when the time came. Right now, I had other problems to sort through. Like being stuck in this house with two crazies outside somewhere. At least I had cell phone coverage and a pistol. I needed to get the pistol right away.

I made sure the baby was safe on the table before I made a run for my car trying to ignore the rain. I unlocked the passenger door and grabbed my pistol and an extra clip along with the holster that fit on my leg. I made sure I locked the car before I ran across the soggy lawn and into the house. I breathed slightly easier with the pistol in my hand. I locked the door behind me and didn't hesitate to fasten the holster to my leg along with placing the pistol in it. It paid to be prepared. Again, I tried to reassure myself Jimbo wouldn't give me this place if it put me in danger. But then, he hadn't been here for many years. He might not have known about the caretaker and his grandfather otherwise he would have mentioned them.

After I had fed and changed the baby, I started checking out the place. It was a plain farmhouse type of home. Nothing fancy, but comfortable in its own way. There were four rooms downstairs – a kitchen, dining room, living room, and a bedroom – and three bedrooms upstairs. I was surprised to discover that both the upstairs plus the downstairs had a bathroom. I had heard of outhouses located in the garden but had never encountered such. After seeing the house, I feared that was exactly what I would find. I wondered if Freda Whitley had bought all the sheets protecting the furniture or if Morton McCray had purchased them after her death.

I considered using the downstairs bedroom but thought it would be safer if the baby and I slept upstairs on the chance I could hear someone climbing the stairs. I picked the largest upstairs bedroom and removed the sheets covering the bed, the dresser, and the wardrobe, putting the dusty sheets out in the hall. I figured an upstairs bedroom would allow me to hear someone coming up the squeaky stairs.

The furniture was made of Mahogony wood and appeared to have been well cared for with a slightly lingering bees wax smell. Beautiful curves and fruit carvings matched the bedroom furniture together. I didn't know if the furniture was valuable, but it was pretty in an old-fashioned way. There was a blue and white tufted bedspread that appeared to be clean enough considering the owner had been dead for years. I tossed the cover back to check on the cleanness of the bed linens. They were cotton with only a slight musty odor. I then tossed the spread and top sheet all the way to the foot of the bed and opened the window to let the bedclothes along with the room air out since I hadn't thought to buy clean sheets or any other kind of linens. Most likely the baby and I would be sleeping in this bed tonight.

I pulled the top dresser drawer open to discover several pairs of the old woman's panties folded nicely. They were all made of white cotton and well worn. I continued to open the drawers. The second drawer held cotton petticoats as plain and worn as the panties. In the bottom drawer were wool socks with matching pairs folded together. It was easy to tell every article belonged to an elderly woman.

I opened the closet door to find several long, cotton dresses hanging on wire hangers. Below them were two pairs of shoes, one black pair only slightly worn and the other brown pair showing use. I took them to be her Sunday and everyday shoes. There was also a high-topped pair of work boots that were badly scuffed with the soles worn down. All three pairs had a thick coating of wax and were buffed to as much of a shine as was possible.

A twinge of emotion came to me at the obvious care that had been taken with everything the old woman owned. I thought of Granny Gleason and the grandmother that I never had and still longed to have. For a moment, I even allowed myself to miss Aunt Mary. At least Mother had a sister while I had no one left who cared about me. Aunt Mary and I were always there for my mother.

I looked at the baby that was still sitting in her carrier where I had placed it on the bed. This little helpless thing had no one, and it was directly and indirectly my fault that she no longer had parents. I should never have given her encouragement to leave Hanson. Much less part of my tips. Yet, this baby still had a chance there might be parents and grandparents somewhere who would give her all the things I longed for as a child. I suddenly had the strongest urge to call Nokosi Micco and ask him a most important question. Did this baby have grandparents who would give her a loving home? If so, how would I go about getting her to them? The next big question I had was would I ever feel secure enough to make a call to him?

I put my emotions aside and tried to think with reason. This baby's grandparents raised both Angie and Hanson Bell. Considering how they both had turned out; I wouldn't want them raising this baby. She deserved a better life than either of her parents had. That realization ended that scenario along with my desire to call Nokosi Micco. It was entirely up to me to find the perfect parents for her.

Chapter 25

*

I slept fitfully from having fearful dreams about the two horrible men who were lurking nearby. Many times, I regretted not leaving this place with the two officers as I listened to the sound of rain beating on the tin roof. If not for the rain, I feared the two men would be outside my locked doors searching for a way to get inside. It didn't help soothe my anxiety when I realized they didn't need to find a way to get inside. Caretakers would have keys to everything including this house. They could come inside at will. Why hadn't I asked for their keys while the officers were here? Fear has a way of keeping common sense at bay.

I would have to do a lot of thinking about the situation I found myself in.

By the time I had gotten up to feed the baby the second time during the night, I had decided if we survived until morning, I would go straight to town and put this house and land up for sale. I had no intention of living where I was afraid all the time. I held the little, soft body against my left shoulder and patted her on the back until she burped. I laid back down snuggling the baby against my body to make sure she was safe and warm.

When I woke up again, the rain had stopped, and morning light was shining through the windows brightening the bedroom. I could hear sounds of what I took to be cattle lowing and a rooster crowing. It was more of a contented sound than coming from desperation. When I pulled the dusty curtain back from the rear window, I didn't see any animals. I could see a pale rosy color touching the top of the high mountain behind a barn. A feeling came to me that I didn't know how to describe. It certainly wasn't peacefulness or even a sense of security, It was a kind of reverence as though I was being transformed back in time.

Nothing bad had happened during the night or in the early morning hours. I looked out the front bedroom window just to make sure my car was still parked out front. It was. It looked clean where the hard downpour of rain had washed the mud off. I felt a touch of relief from my fears – but only a touch because there was standing water everywhere.

I left the baby in bed asleep as I put my shoes on and tiptoed out of the bedroom not knowing what I would find beyond the bedroom door. I had been so leery that I had chosen to sleep in my clothes with both the gun and knife strapped to my legs. I had my hand in my bottomless pocket with my hand on the gun as I eased along the hall and down the stairs listening for sound.

Once I reached the kitchen, I was surprised to find there was no gas or electric stove. Never had I been in a place without working stoves. Instead, there was an enamel and chrome antique type of stove sitting several feet from a wall. I had seen pictures of an old timey wood burning cookstove and here one sat along with a stove pipe and rock chimney. The top was a large flat surface with a hinged door on the left side and some sort of tank on the right side. I had no idea how to use such a stove. I had no idea how I was supposed to cook breakfast on such a thing? It was then it occurred to me that I hadn't bought any groceries before I arrived. I had become accustomed to eating at Mother's and Lena's restaurant or picking up fast food. Considering the seven miles of muddy road, and my lack of a 4-wheel drive, I wouldn't be leaving here any time soon. I ran through my mind what little junk food I had left in the car. I needed to get it because I was hungry. Thankfully, I had an extra supply of baby milk. At least she wouldn't be the one going hungry.

I looked out the kitchen window to see an early morning that brought a promise of a clear, sunny day ahead. Hopefully, the mud and water would dry up before I starved to death. At least things didn't seem as sinister as they did yesterday and last night. It appeared to be true that the morning's light shown a different view on a situation, but that didn't mean the situation had changed. The light of day didn't take away the fact that two crazed mountain men were somewhere out there.

Were they planning to get rid of me in some sort of accident? The two officers didn't appear to think the baby and I were in danger. It was their assurance that allowed me to be brave enough to open the kitchen door to make a run for the car and junk food. I almost stumbled over what was on the little porch in front of the door. There was a basket of eggs, butter, an unopened five-pound sack of flour, salt, a pint of canned sausage, which was something I'd never seen before, along with a half-gallon jar of milk sitting in a cardboard box. There was also a small pile of wood shavings along with a larger pile of bigger split wood. A box of matches sat beside the wood.

I didn't know if I should take the things inside or kick them off the porch. Reason told me the eggs couldn't have been tampered with and perhaps the sack of flour. I wasn't sure about the milk, sausage, and butter. Hunger made me take the box inside and sit it on the table. I noticed a slightly damp piece of paper stuck in the box. I pulled it out and read: *Sorry we scared you yesterday. Please, take this as a peace offering and welcome gift. Didn't know if you thought to bring groceries. There is plenty more where this came from if you want. Morton.*

What was I to think about this? Did I take it as a genuine peace offering? How I decided to take it didn't alter the fact I could certainly use some fried eggs for breakfast if not sausage and biscuits– which meant I had to get a fire started in the wood cook stove. What could be so difficult about that? I had dry wood, shavings, and matches. I opened the door again and brought the wood and matches inside. It took me a while to examine the stove and figure out where the fire should be built. I wasn't sure the wood shavings alone would be enough to get a flame going, so I ripped up a part of the box and put it in the stove. I then arranged the wood shavings and larger wood on top. I struck a match to the ripped pieces of cardboard and was satisfied when it flamed up to catch the shavings on fire.

I congratulated myself on my success at my first attempt to build a fire as smoke rose upward. I closed the lid on the fire hole, but the smoke wasn't going up the chimney like it was supposed to do. I grabbed hold of the stove lid and burned my fingers. I was amazed at how fast the smoke started filling the small kitchen. My eyes were burning, and I started coughing. There was no exhaust fan like we had in the restaurant. My only choice was to open the door and window. I grabbed one of the sheets I had folded yesterday and started fanning at the smoke in hopes to hurry it out the door, but more smoke was coming from the stove than was going out the door. Finally, the billowing smoke got the best of me, and I staggered outside with a fit of coughing and watering eyes.

"Are you all right?" a man's voice said. "Have you caught the place on fire? Oh, I see," he said as he rushed inside. "You didn't know to open the damper."

He did something to the stove and the smoke stopped bellowing into the room. He came outside with only a slight cough along with an obvious attempt not to grin.

"Never used a wood stove before, have you?" he questioned with a touch of understanding.

I shook my head and wiped my eyes.

"Never thought to tell you about opening the damper so the smoke can go up the chimney instead of into the room. The pots and pan are in the cabinet, but you probably know where to find such as that."

I nodded. Where else would pots and pans be? As for the damper, I didn't even know there was such a thing.

"You best stay outside for a few more minutes until the smoke clears out. Where is the baby? A baby doesn't need to breathe smoke."

"Upstairs asleep. I left the bedroom door closed." Hopefully, the smoke hadn't reached her.

"She should be okay. Don't think the smoke had time to fill the house. Do you know how to cook?" he asked.

"Of course, I know how to cook," I informed him without going into any personal details. "It's that I've never used a wood cookstove before." I allowed my gaze to look him over just to make sure he was the same horrible man I'd met yesterday. He certainly appeared different than the mud-covered, stinking, frightful man of yesterday. He was about five feet ten inches tall, with a full head of brown hair that gave off a smell of being recently shampooed. His cheeks were now smooth showing he had saved his beard that morning. He wore a checked shirt and a pair of blue jeans. However, his boots were still covered in mud. He was younger than I originally thought. I hadn't expected to think he was good looking in a rough lumberjack sort of way, but that's what crossed my mind.

"Good," he responded with a twinkle in his eyes. "I don't need to offer to cook your breakfast then."

"No, you don't. And thank you for the food. You're right. I forgot to buy groceries. I hadn't expected to get stranded here."

"This flood was unexpected. I heard it's washed out more than one road and even a few bridges. It'll be several days before Gramps gets it drivable. Thankfully, all the animals are safe." He looked me over much like I was looking at him. "Your showing up here unexpectedly came at the worst time possible. The cloud burst, along with your arrival, came as a surprise to us. We had no idea the place had sold and hadn't expected anyone with good intentions showing up during a flash flood that was threatening to drown some of our animals. Gramps can get overwrought at times when he thinks we have trespassers. He's become overprotective of this place – and for a good reason, I might add."

"Really?" I said with a bit of satire as my hand touched my pistol. I still didn't trust him or his grandpa.

"Since Freda died, we've had all kinds of people showing up claiming they owned this place or with some other kind of nonsense. Most of the furniture is antique and has significate value as does the farm equipment. As for the land, it's the last large mountain track of land in the area. We've had all kinds of wheeler-dealers trying to get their hands on it. Not to mention hunters running all over the mountain shooting at anything and everything. Gramps started doing a right good job of scaring them off since he moved in with me. As you already know, we're just the caretakers instead of the owners. Therefore, our actions have to be a bit unorthodox at times. I suppose you're out to sell this place, aren't you?"

"No," I told him, but he didn't appear to believe me.

"How did you get your hands on this place?" he continued questioning. "I tried to contact Freda's son many times about buying it, but he never responded. Freda only had a life estate to the place so I couldn't buy it from her."

"I was friends with her son," I told him, but I could tell he wasn't believing me.

"Really? He was slightly older than you, wasn't he?"

"Slightly," I said as I gave him a knowing look. "At least fifty some years or more. He never told me his age and I never asked. I met him when I was twelve years old. He became a kind of grandfather to me," I said and then regretted it when I realized I was giving him way too much information.

"Where did you meet him at?" he persisted.

"On a park bench. Thank you for opening the damper along with all the food and wood. Hopefully, the road will dry up until I can leave here soon."

"Wouldn't count on it. Worst flood we've had during my lifetime. Gramps said it was as bad as the forty-food. It'll take another week or so to get the road fit for a car to travel. Gramps and I can only do so much with the tractor. We'll have to wait until the county gets around to it. We've always been the last road on their list."

I was stunned at his comment. If what he said was true, I was stranded here.

"May I be just a bit forward with you considering how we met?"

I lifted my brows at that remark.

"If you decide to sell the place, will you consider giving me a first option to buy it? Gramps and I have become fond of the place. It's like ... well, like home to us."

Sell what Jimbo wanted me to have? Hadn't I decided during the early hours of morning that I would sell this place? At this moment, the idea didn't seem as appealing as it did last night.

"I don't plan on selling it," I surprised myself by telling him.

"Don't blame you, but would you let me buy a first option just in case you change your mind?"

"What's a first option?"

"I will pay you a certain amount of money for an agreement that states I'll pay you whatever price someone else is willing to pay if you decide to sell."

"I'll have to talk to my attorney," I told him.

"Let me know what you decide, and if you need anything, I'm here," he said and walked away.

I watched him go.

*

Instead of frying the eggs in the butter, I decided it would be safer to boil them. Morton McCray appeared more like a normal human being this morning, but I wasn't about to trust him or his grandfather with the food I ate or anything else.

By the time I had finished eating the two boiled eggs, the baby was awake and crying. I rushed upstairs to get her. It never ceased to amaze me this tiny thing could be a real, living, breathing human being instead of a doll. She wasn't any bigger than the doll I had as a young child. The main difference was that I didn't have to feed, bathe, and diaper the doll. I was finding that having a real baby came with a lot of work to make sure she was safe and well cared for. When I finally thought I was going to get my freedom from responsibility until I could do exactly as I pleased, I found myself with land, a house, and a baby. I wasn't altogether sure I wanted any of the three.

When I picked the baby up, she stopped crying, and her little fist went into her mouth.

"You're hungry aren't you little one," I cooed as I took one of the pre-prepared bottles out of her diaper bag. I found it much easier to buy the ready to use formula in a bottle than to wash bottles and mix water and constituted formula together while I traveled. The only drawback was the price I paid for convenience.

She latched onto the nipple and sucked hungrily. I studied her little face and tried to find any resemblance to Angie Bell. I saw none. As for Hanson Bell, I had never seen him closeup enough to see any facial features. What I hoped for was that her genetics didn't prove to run true. I suddenly thought of my own father. A daughter didn't have to take back after her father. I certainly hadn't. I wasn't sure I had taken back after my gentle mother. I couldn't see her doing all the illegal things I had done with Jimbo. Perhaps I was more like Aunt Mary – self-centered and greedy. I didn't want to be any of the things I considered bad. I wanted to be secure and happy – not to mention having a home where I belonged. I pushed the fear away that what I wanted were things I could never find. I quickly turned my thoughts back to Angie Bell.

From what I had seen of Angie Bell, she wasn't a bad person, although perhaps a selfish one. The thought of having two genetically bad parents concerned me. There was no question that heredity and environment affected a person. I had nothing to do with her heredity, but I could certainly determine the environment she would be raised in by choosing who adopted her. It was my responsibility to make sure she had the kind of parents a baby deserved.

The baby had just fallen asleep when I heard a horrible roaring noise near the house. I rushed to the bedroom window and looked out. That crazy old man was on some sort of contraption with chains on the tires and a huge scrape blade on the back. He was scraping the deep, muddy ruts in the road making it somewhat level. I suppose he was trying to make the road drivable until I would be able to leave. Both he and his grandson had made it clear they didn't want me here – didn't want me owning Jimbo's land, but I did own it, and I didn't think he would want me to sell what he had given to me.

I stayed inside as the day wore on. I didn't go outside in case I encountered one of the two men, although the sun was shining warm. Hopefully, the road the old man had scraped would dry out enough for me to drive on, but I suspected Morton was right, it would take longer than a day or two. At least the old man hadn't tried to harass me further. He had driven the machine back toward the barn. I think he put it in one of the sheds.

I ate more junk food when lunch time arrived while I debated on the safety of the other food stuff Morton McCray had left on my doorstep. I had put the milk, butter, and eggs in the old Frigidaire. It was cold and still running perfectly.

I nearly jumped out of my skin when a knock came on the kitchen door. I looked out the window to see the two McCray men. I hardly recognized the older man as he was now standing there in clean clothes, washed beard, a black hat, and downed head.

My hand went in my pocket touching my pistol. "What do you want?" I called out in my most demanding tone of voice.

"Gramps has come to apologize," Morton said. "He's sorry he scared you and I am too."

I saw Morton elbow his grandpa in the ribs.

"I'm mighty sorry, ma'am. I thought you were a trespasser. I wasn't in a mood to tolerate such as that after what we'd just gone through trying to save the animals and such."

Morton poked him in the ribs again.

"I've scraped the road for you, but it'll take a while for the mud to dry up. In the meantime, if there's airy thing we can do for you just let us know. We'll oblige you in any way we can."

"Good. Now you can leave me alone," I said none too charitably.

"I'm going to bring you some canned goods for your supper since you didn't bring groceries with you. I'll leave them on your doorstep along with more firewood. Remember to make sure the damper is open," Morton said, and they both walked away.

I didn't know what to think of their apologies, but I had a feeling they were trying to get on the good side of me. I had no doubt they had gotten in contact with Ronald Watson to confirm that I did own this place free and clear. I'm sure they didn't want to be run off as soon as their contract expired, which I certainly intended to do. I didn't want anyone around who caused me concern for my and the baby's safety.

Thinking about a phone had me search the kitchen and living room without finding one. Didn't someone say Freda talked to her son often? If so, she had a phone, but that was before her death. Why would Morton still be willing to pay a phone bill when no one used it? Still, I went into the downstairs bedroom to check. Sure enough, there was an old timey dial phone beside the bed. I picked it up and put it to my ear to hear the dial tone. I had the strongest urge to find her son's phone number and dial it just in case Jimbo might answer. I opened the drawer to the nightstand in hopes of finding his number. Instead, I found a thick leatherbound well-worn book that had DIARY embossed on the front. I picked it up to find that it had a tiny lock on it. I didn't want to invade the old woman's privacy, but I did want to find out Jimbo's phone number along with hoping the diary might have more about him. I searched through the drawer, moving aside bottles of pills and embroidered handkerchiefs to finally spot a tiny key. I stuck the key in the lock and opened the book with a grin. The little tabs holding the diary together would have easily pulled a part. The lock and key were only for show – and perhaps a fake feeling of privacy. There on the first page was a phone number. I hurriedly dialed the number to get a message that the number was no longer in service. I wasn't surprised, but I was disappointed. Sensi York had confirmed that Jimbo had died. I still didn't want to believe it.

I took the diary and key into the kitchen where the sunlight was shining in the window, sat down in a chair, and started reading Freda's diary. I was disappointed to find that it read more like a calendar than a diary. I flipped through several pages before I came to anything of interest.

"Jimmy got killed," it read. *"I told him not to buy that tractor, but he didn't listen. He flipped it going around the side of the hill. Little James saw it happen and came screaming to me for help. I couldn't help Jimmy, nor could I wipe the trauma from little James' eyes."*

"Funeral home took most of our cash money for burying Jimmy. I wanted him to have a good funeral. I'll have to work my fingers to the bone just to keep our body and soul together."

"Two weeks have passed since Jimmy was buried. The look in little James' eyes stay the same."

"Time is passing, and I miss my Jimmy something fierce, but I know it's nothing to the way James misses his daddy. They were as close as the fingers on one hand. Death is one thing, but seeing your daddy mashed to death under a tractor had lingering effects on a boy."

I could only imagine what a little boy went through after seeing his father killed. It would haunt him every moment of the day. Not to mention the nightmares he was surely having.

I continued to read about everyday happenings and how hard it was to survive until I came to a part that surprised me.

"I didn't know Jimmy had borrowed money on our house and land to buy the tractor that killed him until the banker man show up. He was repossessing everything we owned and tossed us out onto the big road. I had no place to go. The banker man sent someone to drop us off in a strange town with only the clothes on our backs."

It was then that I remembered what Jimbo had told me about his mother and the prostitutes. He'd said:

"I was a lot of things back then that I've never admitted to. Had to live by my wits. My own mother was thrown in jail for drug trafficking when I was eight years old. The police and social workers came after me, but I climbed out the top floor window of a whore house where my mother worked and hid on the roof until they were gone. Didn't like what those social workers or mother's pimp had in mind for me, so I hid out in the streets.

"I wasn't in the same fix you find yourself in. I had only myself to look after. I figured out how to do right well for myself even back then. Instead of staying the little beggar that I was, I figured out how to convince everyone I was one of the rich kids," he chuckled a little without any real humor. "I started sleeping in crawl spaces of rich people's houses. It got to the point where I learned how to slip into their houses and take whatever I needed.

"I was an intelligent little fart if I do say so myself. I went through a rich man's files and found information on his son who had – conveniently for me – died the year before from childhood leukemia. I stole his name, his birth certificate, some of his clothes along with the money from his piggy bank. His parents hadn't touched a thing in his room since his death.

"I convinced one of my mother's street walker friends to dress rather proper and take me to one of the schools nearby. She used the dead boy's name but changed the address when she put me in school. Whenever I needed a parent's signature for something, I had her sign for me. I learned a few things right off. First thing was that you need a thinking brain that's capable of outsmarting everybody else. The key to that was the ability to get a mighty fine education, and that included a formal education to go along with street smarts. Another thing was to learn how to find, or fake, documents as needed. I lived in crawl spaces for years, stealing the things required to stay alive."

I could hear him telling me those words as clearly as though he was sitting beside me, but he never told me anything else about his mother that I could remember. So, how did she end up with a large track of land and a house? I continued turning the pages as I read.

"I don't like to write about the next part of my life. To be honest, I didn't get to see my son again for years. In desperation, I took up with the wrong kind of people. It's mighty easy to get taken in when you and your son are starving and have nothing including hope. I did what I could, and it proved to be the wrong thing for me and my beloved son."

"I'm not going to write anything about that part of my life. It hurts too much to remember. Not that I remember much – which was and is a blessing."

"What I'm going to write about is that my son managed to buy back the house and farm that was taken away from us

after his daddy was killed. Much to my regret, he never moved back into the house with me. I suppose the memories were just too much hurt for him."

I had an idea it wasn't only the hurt of his memory about his father death that kept Jimbo from returning home. I was certain he was getting money by perfecting the tricks he introduced me to.

"Odd, how after years passed, the banker who took everything we had ended up losing everything he owned, including his wife. A short time later, he even lost his own life. Rumors were that he killed himself, but I don't know about such as that. He was the kind of man who loved himself."

I didn't realize how much time had passed until the baby cried. I folded the corner of the page over to keep my place, put the diary on the table, and prepared a bottle for the baby. The ready to use formula was a blessing, but I would run out soon. At least I had cans of condensed milk to be mixed with water along with two larger cans of powdered formula. I wanted to make sure I didn't run out of anything that the baby might need. I was taking responsibility of her seriously.

Once I had cared for the baby, I put her in her car seat and took her downstairs to the kitchen. I felt guilty about leaving her in the bedroom all this time, but she fell right back to sleep. I didn't hesitate to open the diary again.

"My boy makes a point of sending me enough money to pay bills and live on, but he refuses to come home even though I beg him. I would like to know if my boy grew up looking like his daddy or me. He claims he is too busy working to even pay me a visit. I should be thankful that he is able to work and send me enough money to get by on, but I miss him, which is odd. I haven't seen him since he was a little boy, but he is the only person I have left. I want a chance to make up to him for what happened to us both, but he only chuckled when I told him such. He tells me he is living the good life, but I want to make sure he is telling the truth. He

even suggested that I get a caretaker for the farm. It didn't seem right that all the land was growing up in weeds and brambles when it could be producing food. I took that idea seriously. At least I wouldn't be as lonely if someone else lived up this rugged old road."

"I rejected the idea of a caretaker for years. I didn't trust people for a reason. I finally gave in and was lucky to find a young man who was willing to work hard and wasn't offensive to me. Several people recommend him as being a fine young man. Don't know why he would be willing to work the farm for whatever profit he could make from it. He isn't nearly half my boy's age, but that is okay with me as well as with my boy. My boy! Oh, how I love those words almost as much as I love my boy. How I wish I could change things that happened long ago. If only my Jimmy hadn't taken out a loan for that tractor, life would have been different."

"Time flies by even when I feel like each day is creeping along. It has been a long time since I've written a word in this book. I feel rather silly writing my innermost thoughts down on a piece of paper, but I still do on occasion. It's kind of like talking to someone who doesn't judge me for all my failures. I have made many mistakes that I wish I could go back and correct, but that isn't possible. So, I must live with my past.

"I haven't words to explain how I feel every time I look in the mirror. I'm shocked at what I see. There is a dried-up old woman looking back at me. One I no longer recognize – and don't want to admit what life had done to me. When I walk outside, I see fields under cultivation and can't stop myself from thinking my Jimmy will come striding into the yard hungry for a good meal. He never comes. I'm forced to realize he never will. It is a stranger I see working the land. A young man I'm allowing to live in the little house. He's done a right smart of work on the little house in lieu of rent, plus he drives me into the store when I ask him to do so. He's kind to me and he doesn't drink or steal things. I'm angry *because he is here instead of my son. How I long to see my little boy one more time before my life comes to an end."*

I had compassion for the lonely woman who wanted the little boy she had been taken away from. At the same time, it was her fault by allowing herself to be drawn into drugs and prostitution. Surely, she could have found a different way to survive. Her little son had found a way. And then it hit me. Her son had also turned to crime in order to survive. Even I had done the same thing. I had no doubt that Jimbo had relied on crime in order to buy back his parent's farm for his mother. The same as I had. We had more in common than I ever imagined. Perhaps that was why he left this place to me.

I too had become a thief in order for my mother to survive. Not to mention I was still surviving on what Jimbo had provided for me. Was I willing to give the money, house, land, and car up because they could have come from ill-gotten gains? It wasn't like the money came from deserving people, or that it would be possible for me to give it back to those who were victims. All of what Jimbo provided came from crime worse than he and I had ever committed. Nothing about life was cut and dried. There was, and always will be, a fine line between right and wrong.

Chapter 26

*

It was the fourth day I'd been stranded inside the house when I looked out the kitchen window and much to my surprise, I saw the old man planting flowers in beds. I certainly hadn't expected such as that from the crude old man. He was handling the plants as though they were precious things. Most of the plants were in bloom, and I wondered where they came from if the road was not drivable. At least the sun was shining warm, and two butterflies were already checking out the blossoms. I had the strongest urge to go outside, but I didn't want to come into contact with the old man. I didn't trust him in the least. The old man made no bones about not wanting me to be there, but Morton pretended he wanted to help me. Each morning, I would find some kind of food at the kitchen door. Eggs, milk, along with mason jars of canned vegetables he had obviously put up himself.

I hadn't expected the surge of anger that hit. Why was I the one to be hiding in the house in fear? I owned this place, not them. Hiding inside the house was only giving them more power over me. It was time I girdled my loins and made a stand.

I didn't give myself time to change my mind as I yanked open the door and marched across the wet yard, across the poor excuse of a driveway to the rock flower beds.

"Mornin' Missie," he said. "It's good to see you're out and about," he said in a welcoming tone of voice that I hadn't expected. His countenance even appeared to be different.

I was stunned at his friendliness, but I was still mad. I opened my mouth and said, "I own this place."

"You're right about that, Missie. Thought you were a trespasser when you first arrived. Hope you understand that I was protecting what's yours. The way my grandboy did for Fredia since he took over the job as caretaker."

Instead of raking him over the coals the way I longed to do, I surprised myself by saying, "Where did you get the flowers?"

"From the greenhouse. The ones I'd planted earlier got washed out by the storm. Good thing I had extra."

"Greenhouse?" I questioned.

"Cheaper to grow 'em than buy 'em. I put it in when I came to stay with my grandboy."

I looked about and didn't see a greenhouse. He saw my look and answered my unspoken question.

"It's out behind the barn. Handy having it out there where the compost pile is. Nothin' like rotted manure to grow plants. Gotta add a lot of good dirt and lime to it. Too much manure can burn plants, especially if hasn't composted enough. You like flowers?"

I thought of the tiny bouquet of flowers we had put on the restaurant tables. They brightened the place up and seemed to soothe diners. Most of all I remembered all the roses Mother wanted to plant so she would leave something of beauty behind.

"Yes," I said. "I do like flowers. My Mother loved them."

"What's your favorite?" he asked.

"Roses," I told him. "Red roses."

"Right. That's most women's favorite. My favorite is Dallies."

Dallies? I was puzzled for a moment before I realized he meant dahlias.

"They have roots. They grow big and strong while still being beautiful. They make me think of my dear departed wife."

I was surprised to see a flicker of longing come to his face before his gruff expression returned.

"You and your little baby settling-in okay? Things gotta seem mighty strange to you after what you've been used to."

"What's makes you think that?" I asked. To me, he and his grandson were the ones who were strange, not to mention they were the reason I was afraid to settle-in.

"Considering you were able to afford to buy a place such as this is a right good sign you're well-off. Not to mention you're driving the best kind of car that was ever made."

I felt a stab of anger that he was judging me by the appearance of having money.

"My wife, Mattie, had one like it before she passed on. Sold it. Couldn't stand to look at it after she passed. Reminded me too much of her. Reckon I've got over it somewhat. Lookin' at yours don't bother me none. Mud ought to have dried up enough for me to scrape the road again as soon as I get done planting. Might be able to drive on it by the time I'm finished."

I was surprised such a gruff, old man had vocalized his pain of losing his wife. I was also surprised that such a shabbily dressed, beardy hillbilly type of man had a wife who drove a Mercedes. I thought a rusted, rundown piece of junk was more suitable for him and anyone connected to him.

He must have seen my surprise for he said, "I was president of Northwestern Bank back then. A full-fledged member of the rat race. After Mattie died, I came to my senses and moved here. I traded money for wildflowers and butterflies. Don't regret it none."

I stood there staring at him in disbelief.

"I'm gonna scrape the road now, Missie. I've run my mouth long enough."

He took his trowel and empty pots, turned his back to me and walked away. I stood there for a few minutes watching the two butterflies as they landed on the blossoms of the freshly planted flowers. I didn't know what to think about this old man. Part of me wondered if he just might be the biggest liar to ever exist.

*

Wilburn and his tractor did what he said he was going to do. He smoothed out the deep gullies in the road until it was smooth enough for me to drive on. Once he had finished, I wasted no time locking the door behind me, putting the baby in the car and driving down the narrow road. The road wasn't perfect, but it was drivable along with no longer having as many potholes.

The first place I went was the lawyer's office. The reception looked at me with slight surprise.

"Mr. Watson isn't in today," she told me. "Is there something I can help you with?"

"Wilburn and Morton McCray scare me. I want to know what I can do to get rid of them?" I blurted out what had been torturing me for the last four days.

Much to my surprise, she burst out laughing. If I didn't have the baby in my arms, I might have picked up something to throw at her.

"Forgive me for laughing," she finally said as she tried to regain her composure. "Believe me they're harmless – almost," she added.

"Almost?" I questioned.

"Neither of them will tolerate intruders. Morton protected Freda and her belongings since he was a boy. Believe me, he is trustworthy and reliable. As for Wilburn, folks either hate him or love him. It still pays not to get on his bad side. He was once a powerful man in the banking industry. He ruled his empire with an iron fist, so to speak. The death of his wife and then their only child was just about more than he could take. He resigned from his high-powered job and moved in with his grandson. He did everything in his power to buy Freda's place, but her son refused to sell. I'm amazed that you were able to get it. How did you manage that?"

"We were close." I wasn't about to divulge any more information about Jimbo.

"Were you related? As far as I know, Freda never mentioned you."

"Her son was a private person. Perhaps she was too," I was quick to tell her.

"I see," she said,

I was sure she already knew I had inherited the land instead of buying it.

"I suppose it had to go to somebody. Everyone thought it would be Morton. We were all surprised it went to such a young woman."

I'm sure she wasn't as surprised as I was.

"As you already know, Morton McCray has one more year on his caretaker's lease. You can talk with Ronald, but I doubt you can break the lease contract."

"Mrs. Whitley has been dead a long time. Surely the lease is no longer valid."

"It's my understanding her son was the one who renewed the lease contract. But you'll have to talk to Ronald about such as that. Now is there anything else I can do for you?"

"I want to make sure it's safe to live there."

"As I just got through telling you, as far as the McCray's are concerned, you're perfectly safe. Hope you have a good day."

"You too." I left the office not feeling any more relieved than when I arrived.

*

From there, I found an Ingles grocery store. I had no intention of being stuck any longer with junk food and the handouts Morton left on my doorstep. I also wanted to get a large supply of everything the baby might need. I was uneasy about her running out of things she might need. I hadn't expected how protective of this little baby I had become. I realized I was the only person in the world this baby had.

"Oh, how cute," gushed one of the shoppers, stopping in front of the shopping cart as she looked down on the baby sleeping in her car seat. "I dearly love babies. I was only able to have one baby. Unfortunately, my sweet Rachel inherited my condition. We both suffer from endometriosis. Doctor said it was a miracle sent straight from God that I had one baby. My Rachel is unable to have children. I have no doubt she would give up her own life if she could have a baby."

"Why doesn't she adopt?" I asked.

"She looked into it, but she doesn't have the money it takes. Doesn't seem right to me. Don't matter what kind of good home a person can provide, if they don't have a lot of money they're turned down.'

"She could be a foster parent," I suggested as I wondered if she and her husband would be a fit parents for little Mitzie.

"She checked on that too. She made the mistake of saying what she thought of parents who didn't take care of their own children. She also said once she was given a child to care for neither heaven nor hell would be able to take it away from her."

"I can understand that" I told her. "What is her name?"

"Rachel Craig. I'm Dottie Snyder, and you are?"

"I'm Millie James."

Her brows furrowed. "You're not from around here, are you?"

"No, I'm not."

"Is your husband from around here?"

"I'm a widow."

"Oh, my. I'm so sorry to hear that. What happened to him?"

"I don't like talking about it. Hurts too much," I made a point of telling her as I moved the shopping cart, but she still stood there blocking me.

"You here visiting friends or relatives?" she continued with her curiosity.

I was getting aggravated by her questions. I tried to ease my irritation by assuring myself she was trying to be friendly instead of snoopy – although I doubted it.

"Neither. I'm the new owner of Freda Whitley's place."

"Do tell," she said as her eyes widened in surprise. "Heard someone was moving into that place. Never thought it would be a pretty, young woman. Bet Morton and Wilburn can't get their eyes full."

"Hardly," I said a bit sharply at her comment. Yet, I tried to still be polite. If I was to live here, I didn't want to offend anyone. "They're not pleased with me being there," I made a point of telling her.

"Oh, honey, that is understandable. Morton has been there forever. He was more like a son to her than the son she always talked about. Don't know why she didn't leave the place to him. As for old Wilburn, he uses grouchiness in an attempt to cover up his tender heart. After his wife's death, all sorts of women chased him, but he wouldn't have anything to do with another woman. Poor man, he might as well of been buried in the grave with her considering the way he grieved."

I was now listening to her. Any information about those two men was welcome.

"I've got an idea him moving in with Morton was what kept him from taking his own life, especially after his son died."

"What happened to his son?" She was the second person today that said almost the same thing.

"His son and his wife were killed in a plane crash. They were going to a party along the coast when a deep fog set in. Found the plane in the water with them inside. It was Wilburn's plane."

Somehow Wilburn didn't seem like the type to own a plane, much less being president of a bank. "A plane? He seems ..." I hesitated, not knowing how to convey my impression of him being a poverty-stricken hillbilly.

"I know what you're thinking, but believe me, he can clean up mighty good when he wants to. Which doesn't happen often."

I surprised myself by wanting to ask questions about Morton, but I wasn't about to do so.

"Ask me, Morton takes back after his grandpa in looks. He's plain knock-out gorgeous, but I don't have to tell you something like that, do I? You've got eyes. Don't know why he's never got married. Folks who know him say he likes women well enough. Lord knows they like him. Ask me, he's one of them loners who likes his own company without any hassle."

Did this woman really think both of those men were handsome or was she just rattling on to see how I would react. I certainly didn't think they were in the least bit handsome. In my opinion they were both rude and crude. Nokosi Micco had far more appeal to me than Morton McCray did.

"Oh, my. Just listen to me going on like I'm doing. You're going to think I'm nothing but a gossiping old woman. I had no intention of bending your ear the way I'm doing.

I did think she was a gossiping old woman, but I was all ears where those McCrays were concerned. The more I knew about them the better.

"My goodness, would you look at the time. I've got to rush, or I'll be really late. It was so nice meeting you. Hope we run into each other again."

I was prepared to politely return her comment, but she twirled around and was gone in a rush. Everyone I'd met today had made a point of telling me the McCrays were fine people, therefore they shouldn't be a threat to me, so why was I still concerned?

I bought as many groceries as I could fit into the cart without taking the car seat out. The bottom of the cart was also packed high. It was enough to do me several days, and the baby several weeks. Thankfully, the check-out person was a young man who wasn't interested in me.

My mind was working overtime as I drove the seven miles of rough road back to the house. Was the worry and hassle I was experiencing worth trying to continue living at the place Jimbo had given me? Perhaps I should go ahead and sell the place. A man who owned his own airplane and was president of a bank should have enough money to pay for the place. I doubted Morton did. A farmer/caretaker wasn't exactly at the top of the income list.

If I sold the place, I would have enough money to find somewhere that would feel more like home. It would be mine all mine without the hassle of a caretaker. Suddenly, it occurred to me that I probably had enough money to buy my own place without having to sell what I inherited from Jimbo. I had money from selling Mother's house. Money that Nokosi Micco provided for the baby, along with the money Jimbo had provided for me throughout the years. I had been using the cash he had left me for gas and provisions for me and the baby.

I pulled to the end of the driveway and stopped. As I got out of the car, Morton showed up. He was clean-shaven and wearing clean clothes. He looked like he had recently bathed. He even had the slight aroma of aftershave. I looked from his boot-clad feet to the top of his sun-kissed hair. I thought about what the woman at the grocery store said about him being handsome. I suppose he was in that rough and rugged sort of way mountain men were noted for. He certainly had a powerful build with plenty of muscles throughout his chest, arms, and legs. He grinned slightly at my observation of him.

"You came back home," he said as though he hadn't expected me to do so.

Yes, I thought. I had come back home. This was the life Jimbo intended for me to have. Not the place he wanted Morton McCray to have.

"Did you make money off this land?" I demanded to know.

His brows lifted slightly. "I made a living, which I might not have been able to do if I'd paid rent for the house and use of the land."

"If your gramps was president of a bank, why did he end up here?"

He grinned. "I see you've been talking to people."

"Answer my question."

"He learned that money wasn't what made a person happy. Sharing life with someone you love did."

"Did you love Freda Whitley?"

He looked surprised at my question, but he answered anyway.

"Depends on what you refer to as love. If you're referring to the romantic kind, that would be far from anyone's ability to imagine. I didn't even love her as a mother figure. I think respect would be a better word for describing my feelings for her."

"You started working here because you respected her?"

"No," he didn't hesitate to answer. "I started working here because she was getting old. I hoped I could win her trust enough for her to sell me her land. Don't know why, but something inside me longed for this mountain. I felt like I belonged to it, and it should belong to me. Therefore, I wanted to make it mine - legally. I was certain Gramps would loan me enough money to buy it, but Freda refused to sell. I later found out the land belonged to her son instead of her. I tried to find her son but was unable to track him down. It was as if he'd disappeared off the face of the earth. If he hadn't been sending her money every month, I would have thought he was only a figment of her imagination. I finally eased my sorrow at my failure by realizing there was truth in the old saying, the garden belongs to the gardener. I became more of the owner of this land than Freda or her son ever would be."

I looked him in the eyes and knew he was telling me the truth. "You still want it," I said.

"I still want it. That's why I asked you for a first refusal."

"Do you want it bad enough to marry me?"

"Hell no," he blurted out the truth before he considered that I might take his answer as an insult. Which I didn't. I had much higher expectations than this hillbilly farmer. He was a clodhopper, a dirt-monkey, a mountain hick who would never amount to anything. As for his grandfather, he was nothing but a bully who would take advantage of me if I let him.

"Good. While you and your grandpa are on my land, if either of you make any kind of attempt to take advantage of me in any way, I'll take that *baby bottle* I was trying to defend myself with and shoot both of you dead center of your eyes."

He gave me a surprised look. "What the hell brought that on?"

"Truth," I told him. "I can't run you off before a year's time because you have an enforceable contract. But you can leave on your own taking your grandpa with you. That's what you're going to do the day your contract is up."

Once I'd said that, I turned my back on him and carried my little baby inside the house, but not before I heard him mumble, "Crazy woman. Don't have a lick of sense."

Chapter 27

*

There was no more milk, eggs or vegetables left on my doorstep. The lack of which didn't bother me. What bothered me was the lack of firewood for the cook stove. How was I supposed to cook my food? I knew nothing at all about gathering firewood.

I would buy an electric stove. I drove into town and shopped until I found one I liked. I would need to have the stove delivered along with having the correct wiring done, but it would take several days. My solution was to buy a small two-eye electric hotplate.

I plugged the hotplate in and stood in the kitchen looking at the drab, somewhat dilapidated room. I had the strongest urge to transform everything until I made this house mine. I could do nothing with the land for one year, but I could certainly update the house- starting with the kitchen.

I went into town I sought local construction companies to evaluate their timeline and price. I cringed at the price the construction companies quoted me to remodel everything in the kitchen that I wanted done. I even wondered if I would be able to do some of the remodeling myself.

"Ma'am," one of the workers that I had considered hiring said. "I've found that most folks who want to do some of their own work end up paying more than those who let professionals do all the work. Work ends up getting done faster and looks much better."

I considered what he said and decided he was right. I had never been exposed to any kind of carpentry work. How I wished I had Jimbo to ask for advice. I thought of the McCrays but quickly rejected them. I might as well face the fact that I was completely alone in my decision making. I was the one who would handle whatever I did or didn't do. Considering I had no source of income, I was hesitant to spend money on anything that wasn't necessary.

It was true that money had a way of going out faster than it came in.

*

I found the baby was taking more of my time than I expected. As for finding her a good home, I was beginning to wonder how I could accomplish such an important decision. Most everyone I had met believed she belonged to me, which would make it even more difficult for me to find her the wonderful parents I wanted for this baby. She deserved a mother and a father who loved her, along with grandparents to shower their love and spoiling on her. I could care for her and give her my love, but I couldn't give her a father and grandparents. I wanted her to have a better life than the one I had. I never wanted her to rely on stealing to keep someone she loved alive.

A feeling of guilt hit me. How could I possibly keep the land and house? How could I even think about keeping this baby when I was such a bad person?

What was I going to do about it? What should I do about it? Did I let Morton have the land he loved, get in the car Jimbo most likely bought with ill-gotten money and start driving west? I could probably find one of those places to leave the baby if I chose to leave.

Guilt and indecision started wearing on my mind. Much to my own surprise, I put the baby in the car seat and started driving. I kept going for several hours until I was sure I was far enough away until no one would know who I was. I finally came across what I was looking for. A church that should have a minister inside.

I parked, got out of the car, and gathered the baby in my arms and with determination went inside. I found a door with an office sign on it and went inside. A woman I took to be a secretary was sitting behind a desk that was covered in papers. It appeared she was writing checks to pay bills.

"Can I help you?" she asked with slight surprise at seeing me.

I came straight to the point. "I would like to talk to the minister."

"Just a moment," she said as she pushed a button on the phone. "There's a lady here who would like to speak with you."

"Send her in," said a man's voice.

"Go down this hall and take the first door on the left."

I did as she said. The door on the left was wide open. A man with a full head of bushy white hair sat behind a well-worn desk.

"Come in," he said in a friendly voice. "Have a seat. How old is your baby?"

I fibbed about her age again and instantly felt guilty for lying in a house of God.

"What can I do for you?" he asked in a soothing tone of voice.

I had no idea how to begin, or how much to tell him. "I've sinned," I blurted out. "I'm afraid I'll never be forgiven for the things I've done."

He nodded solemnly. "We've all sinned. No human being is an exception – unless it is the babies. I believe babies come into the world sinless. What are your sins that you're concerned about?"

I didn't want to answer, but I did in a way I hoped wouldn't tell him too much. "I've taken things that I didn't rightfully earn."

"What sort of things?" he asked with curiosity I didn't intend to answer. Yet, I did.

"Money . . . sex," I said with embarrassed hesitation. "I want to find this baby a good home where she can have both parents and grandparents."

"You fear you can't be a good mother?"

I nodded as I looked at the baby I was cuddling in my arms.

"Do you love this child?"

"Who wouldn't," I blurted out. "She's perfect."

"And you don't think you're perfect?"

"I know I'm not."

"My dear, in God's eyes you are perfect."

I started to argue but stopped myself. I didn't know why he said such a thing when we both knew better.

"The fact that you admit you have sinned and you're seeking God's forgiveness is what matters at this time. In my personal opinion, if you give up your baby because you feel unfit, it will be the greatest sin you'll ever commit. God wouldn't have granted you this precious baby if he didn't believe you can be a fit mother for her."

"I'm not married."

"I understand. You do realize that Mary, the mother of Jesus, was married, but her husband wasn't the father of her baby?"

"I know that."

"Someday you will most likely find a man who can become a good husband along with a good father to your child."

"But I'm a sinner. I want a better mother for her than I can ever become."

"Then it's up to you to become the mother you consider good enough to raise this child. Just because you have sinned in the past, doesn't mean you have to suffer from it forever. Ask God to forgive you and never sin again."

"I don't want to give up what little ill-gotten money I still have."

"If I may ask, where did the money come from."

"From people whose sins were far greater than mine," I said in my own defense.

"Did taking the money stop their sinning?"

"Probably not, but I believe it slowed them down some."

"Did you use the money to continue your sinning?"

"No," I told him firmly.

"What did you do with these ill-gotten gains?"

"Paid off doctor bills and other debts that belonged to someone else. I also ended up saving a little of it in case of emergencies."

"Are you still getting money from your sins?"

"No."

"Are you planning on receiving money in the same way as before?"

"No, definitely not."

"That's good. My advice to you is to forgive yourself for past sins and make sure you don't commit them ever again. Where your baby is concerned, it is obvious how much you love her and want the best for her. You should give her the kind of care and love you want for her. As for a father and grandparents, a mother's love is far more important. If you give her up, you'll blame yourself forever. She will someday find out her own mother gave her away. She can come to feel unworthy of a mother's love."

I nodded.

"You could also give the money to a church," he added. "My church is always in need of funds."

Those words hit me hard with sudden realization. If it was okay for a church to receive money from ill-gotten gains, it should be okay for an individual to do the same. "Thank you," I said as I stood up to leave. "You've given me the answers I sought."

*

"Why are you standing in the yard staring at the house with that sad look on your face? Is something wrong?"

Wilburn McCrays gravelly-deep voice made me jump. I hadn't expected him to deliberately seek me out. I bristled at his presence but tried to hide it.

"I'm thinking of remodeling it," I told him.

"Probably ought to. It's old and gets mighty cold in the wintertime. Folks didn't do much insulation back when it was built. Don't know how the old woman stayed warm. But then, most of the old folks weren't used to much comfort. Their main goal was to stay alive."

I was surprised he seemed friendly instead of being mad at me for what I'd said to Morton. Had Morton not told him?

"It will be expensive," I said.

"Yeah, but it'll pay for itself in the long run. Besides, you'll want that little baby to stay warm when the freezing winter temperatures hits. It gets mighty cold here on this mountain. Is the baby asleep?"

"She sleeps a lot."

"My boy did when he was a baby. So did Morton, but he doesn't sleep much anymore. He's as restless as a cat having kittens. I can hear him pacing about in the middle of the night."

I didn't comment on that. Didn't know how to. More to the point, I didn't care a fig about Morton McCray.

"His restlessness reminds me of back when he was a young fellow. Took him a mighty long time before he ever got a good night's sleep," he continued talking as if I would be interested in what he had to say. "He fell in love once back when he was hardly out of short britches. He was around eighteen with his hormones running as hot as spring sap. Got a girl pregnant. Wanted to marry her. Her parents got rid of her pregnancy and moved away with her before Morton knew what was happening. He never heard hide nor hair of her again – at least not to my knowledge."

I didn't comment. I wondered why he was telling me such. It wasn't like I cared.

"Don't think he will ever marry. Don't think he wants to. Hate that. Have to say I look forward to seeing your little one grow up on this ole farm– if I'm lucky enough to live that long."

"Why are you telling me all this?" I demanded with a touch of irritation. My baby certainly wouldn't be running around on the farm in a year's time. After that, he would be gone.

"Well, Missie. Reckon it's one of my ways of apologizing for the welcome I gave you when you first showed up. I know you've not got over it yet. Can't say as I blame you."

It would take me a long time to get over it, if ever. What he and Morton did was right up there with Aunt Mary and my father's brother. Just thinking about such made a chill pass over me. I felt like Jimbo was the only good thing that had happened to me. The only person who cared about me – and he was what society would label as a bad man – a criminal.

I thought again of what the minister had told me. Not one cent of the money Jimbo saw that I got had been, or was, being used for evil. Neither this house nor this land was being used for anything evil. But, in my opinion, what happened to Freda Whitley and her small son was evil. The bank took their home away because she didn't have enough money to pay off the remains of her husband's tractor loan. Only the tractor should have been taken.

I turned toward Wilburn McCray. "Were you the banker who foreclosed on this place?" I demanded.

"No, I was near her son's age back then, but I knew the banker who did," he answered as though he wasn't surprised at my question.

"Was it legit, or was she screwed out of her home?"

"It was legal as her husband used the farm as collateral for the loan, but everyone thought he was taken advantage of. Still do," he added.

"And now you and your grandson are living on her land and wanting to make it your own."

"Right," he said. "My darling wife was James Whitley's cousin. She couldn't stop talking about how Freda and her boy had their home taken away from them for what few dollars was still owed on a tractor. She wasn't exactly pleased when I started working at the bank. She made sure I never took advantage of anybody. My Mattie had nothing but praise for their son because he somehow managed to get it all back for his mother – except for her beloved husband. No one could take his place. Morton listened to Mattie's stories and took them to heart."

"Your grandson has one year left on his lease, what will you do when you leave here?"

"Both of us have sufficient means to relocate. It's not like either one of us is destitute or need to rely on this place for our survival. My grandboy and I both cherish the isolation this mountain offers. There are no near neighbors, plus this mountain backs up to government land, which means no houses or roads will be built. This place is a small treasure for people who long for the peace of near isolation, along with a degree of self-sufficiency."

And this place was mine. Given to me by Jimbo. I again assured myself if it was okay for a church to receive ill-gotten gains in order to do good with it, it was okay for me to do the same.

What Wilburn had told me about himself, and his grandson, was something for me to think about. It only stood to reason that the president of a bank would have the financial means to buy himself a house and land even if Morton didn't.

"Come with me if you've got a few minutes before your baby girl needs you. I want to show you about a little."

"Okay," I said hesitantly.

"First off, I want to take you to the garden and greenhouse. As you should have already gathered, I love flowers. I have this desire to add beauty to whatever space I occupy. I hope you'll allow some of it to remain after I'm no longer here."

I didn't comment as he led me around the back of the barn where the greenhouse was.

"Out behind the barn was an overgrown jungle when I came here. Like a lot of old barns, people who had no access to a garbage dump, had a trash pile behind their barn. It took me most of a month to pick up and shovel up all the trash."

"Morton hadn't cleaned it up?" I questioned.

"I hate to admit he hadn't. I understood that he needed to spend his time preparing the land for cultivation and caring for Freda and the animals. To his defense, he had put the old barn in good repair and had full intention of cleaning up the garbage pile once he had a month of free time. He worked every hour he wasn't sleeping, but he never got a month of free time. Once I came to live here, I could do some of the things Morton longed to get done. The first thing he asked me to do was get rid of that trash pile. I did, and then I put in the greenhouse on the spot."

He turned the corner of the barn to where a white picket fence protected at least an acre of ground. There were rows and rows of vegetation, some in early spring bloom and some in the early stages of growth.

"These are lupins," he said. "Over here are tulip beds."

I looked at all the blossoms in amazement. I hadn't known there were that many different kinds of tulip blooms in existence. Some of them looked almost like roses.

"And this bed is hyacinths. My Mattie loved their fragrance. And of course, you'll see beds of daffodils scattered about."

Again, I was astonished. I had never seen such different blooms and colors in daffodils. All I was familiar with was the standard yellow.

"Over the years I've planted a variety of cold hardy plants that come up every year. Trouble with those is that they only have a short blooming period like the spring blooming azaleas. I plant annuals among them to keep blooms from late April until it frosts in the fall of the year. At the far end of this patch of land is what I call the wildflower garden. Butterflies like it along with some of the songbirds. I've planted sunflowers at the far fence for cardinals to eat in the fall and winter. Their bloom is as big as a dinner plate and are filled with seeds."

Never in my life would I have placed this crusty, cranky old man as even looking at flowers much less growing them. He had made a first impression on me that would take a long time to change, if ever. I never would have placed him as the president of a bank either.

"I'll give you a quick look inside the greenhouse. You can inspect it better later at your own leisure. I don't want to keep you away from your baby for long. Never liked to leave a little one for long. Wished Mattie and I could have had more than one baby, but she had problems when our son was born. As you might guess, we both doted on our son and then Morton. Might have even spoiled both of them a little," he said with a grin.

The greenhouse was something to behold. Every inch of it was filled with some type of plant. It was like stepping into a tropical haven of beauty. He even had orchids growing in one section. I shuttered at the sight. The orchids made me think of Naples where such orchids grew wild in the trees. Again, I found myself wondering what was happening with Nokosi Micco. I hadn't had the nerve to call him, and I had no intention of doing so. Alona Anderson no longer existed, and I wanted to make sure she stayed that way.

"Beautiful," I mumbled.

"I was hoping you'd say that. Growing things have a way of soothing the soul. Morton grows vegetables and animals while I grow flowers along with many of his vegetable plants.

I can't call what I do as profitable, but I certainly call it rewarding."

I could see Morton being a farmer but there was no way I would have ever place Wilburn in a greenhouse filled with flowers. He would look more natural sitting on a dilapidated porch with a dog, gun, and jug of home distilled liquor. "Do you sell the plants and flowers?" I questioned.

"Nope. When I left the bank, I never wanted to deal with people ever again."

The greenhouse door opened, and Morton stepped inside. His eyes widened in surprise when he saw me. He kind of nodded his head at me in greeting before he turned to Wilburn.

"I need your help right away, Gramps. Betsy is having trouble calving. We'll have to pull it. Hope I haven't waited too long to help her with the calf."

"Lead the way," Wilburn said as he headed toward the door. "If the baby's still asleep, you might ought to come back in case you're needed to help out," he said over his shoulder toward me. "Might as well learn more about the running of the farm you own," he added.

Neither man said another word as I followed them around the barn where they went in a small sized barn door. I headed straight to the house although it wasn't time for the baby to wake up. One thing I didn't want was to be inside a barn with two men while a cow was giving birth. Not that I'd ever seen a cow giving birth or anything else for that matter. The only thing I knew about farm life was what I'd read in books.

My baby was still sleeping peacefully as I had expected her to be. She had put herself on a schedule for which I was thankful. I knew so little about caring for a baby that I would have no idea how to set a schedule for her.

After a short time, curiosity took hold of me regardless of my dislike for the two men. If I was going to run this farm after the men were gone, I needed to learn everything I could – including how to pull a calf. I took a determined breath, went out the door and headed to the barn. I entered the barn as silently as I could. I didn't want the men to know I was there in case I needed to make a quick exit. I heard them talking in one of the stalls. I eased down the hall to where the stall door was open. What I saw shocked me from the top of my head to the end of my toes.

Both men had their backs turned to me as I eased into a shadow near the door. Wilburn was at the cow's head holding onto her halter. Morton was at her rear end. A u-shaped metal bar was attached to the cow's rear end with one long bar that Morton was holding. He had his hand on a handle attached to the bar and was pumping it up and down slowly. Two pale colored feet and inches of legs were protruding from the cow's private area. I couldn't tell if it was a rope or chain that was fastened to the tiny legs.

"Its nose is coming out," Morton said as he gave the contraption a downward pump. "Its tongue is sticking out, but I think it's still alive," he said, as he pumped a few more times.

The calf was slowly coming out. Then all of a sudden, the rest of the calf along with bloody fluids, mucus, and an unbelievable amount of other gross looking stuff gushed out and landed on the hay-covered ground at Morton's feet. Morton tossed the pulling contraption in the hay and bent down over the calf.

I stood there staring in silence – wishing I hadn't been curious enough to come to the barn. What I saw reminded me too much of seeing what had come out of Angie. I felt my insides turn to ice, and my heart started racing.

Don't panic. It's okay, I silently assured myself. *I can handle this. I'm tough. I'm strong.* I would remember what happened to Angie forever, and I had to deal with it. Had to live with what happened the best I could.

"It's alive. A big bull calf," Morton was saying. "No wonder she had trouble having it."

The cow humped up and gave a heave. Another huge glob of bloody, stringy tissue came out and fell on the ground.

Wilburn turned loose of the cow. She turned around and started nosing the calf. Her long tongue came out and she started licking the bloody mucus off the calf.

"Want me to fork out the after birth?" Wilburn asked Morton.

"Naw. Let her eat what she will first. She'll need the nutrients," Morton said, kneeling on the blood-streaked hay as though the mess wasn't bothering him in the lease.

It was all I could do not to gag as I saw what the cow was eating. I had never imagined such a thing. Was it not a type of cannibalism?

It was then Wilburn looked up and saw me. "Don't reckon you've ever seen a calf being born before, have you? You're looking a bit green around the gills."

"No," I said in a voice that was shakier than I wanted.

"Were you awake when your baby was born, or did they knock you out cold?" he had the insensitivity to ask.

"Somewhat," I managed to say. "That thing . . ." I pointed to the contraption lying in the hay.

"Simple tool. It's saved a lot of calves and cows' lives. Most of the time a cow has her calf on her own," Morton said as he rubbed the calf's face and neck with a towel. "Betsy here got bred too early. The bull broke through the fence to get to her. Happens sometimes," he added as though it was a common occurrence. "Mother nature is a powerful force in both animals and humans."

I decided right away that I preferred growing flowers over farming.

Chapter 28

*

Time was passing much too fast as spring made its way toward summer. It was difficult for me to believe how much time had passed since my mother's death. Her urn of ashes was still in the trunk of my car along with the money Jimbo and I had obtained. I had not used any of the money Nokosi Micco had given me to care for the baby. I had used up the cash Jimbo had given me along when he gave me the deed to the house and land. I was being as frugal as possible with the money I'd gotten from selling Mother's house. As for Mother's ashes, I was waiting for a special place to spread them. Until I found that place, they would remain safely hidden away.

I was walking the yard looking at the land and the house trying to figure out what needed done to make the house more suitable to live in when winter set in. As for the land, Wilburn was always planting flowers and shrubbery regardless of knowing he would be gone by next spring. I saw very little of Morton, but I could hear some kind of equipment running from daylight until it was pitch dark. I usually woke each morning hearing the sound of him at the barn. Cows bawling, roosters crowing and hens cackling after they laid eggs. I even learned to identify the sounds of hogs grunting, geese honking, along with the distinctive sounds the guineas made. I wouldn't have anything to do with the barn, land, and animals until the McCrays were gone. The house was a different matter. It was solely my responsibility.

I decided to go ahead and take part of the money I got from selling Mother's house to remodel the kitchen. If it went well and didn't end up costing too much, I would do the downstairs bedroom, and then possibly the rest of the house in time. I'd been told the attic was the main place that needed heavy insulation.

"Might as well do the entire house and get it over with," Wilburn made a point of telling me as he stood in the yard watching me look at the old house. "If you don't have enough money to do it, you can get a loan at the bank. I still have a little pull there."

"I refuse to go in debt," I told him.

"I can understand that since you don't have a paying job."

I knew he was wondering how I had the money to pay for remodeling.

"Hope your husband left you a good life insurance policy," he said, hoping I would ease his curiosity.

"He did, but it won't last long. I have to be careful about what I spend," I told him, although, I didn't consider it any of his business. I wanted him to continue thinking I was well-off financially. Some people took advantage of a woman in need of money. Like forcing her to sell her inheritance to them.

"Morton and I might be able to help you out with the work on the house considering he and I have lived here a long time rent free."

I didn't want either of them to have anything to do with the house, but what he said was true. They had been the ones who were profiting from this place. It would only be right for them to help out. However, there was no question that Wilburn was too old to do heavy work, and Morton spent all his time working on the farm.

"Morton is as strong as a team of workhorses. Me, I'm a bit long in the tooth, but I'm right smart where construction is concerned."

"Thank you for the offer, but I'll see what is going to be needed," I tried to be polite in refusing him. "Besides, Morton is surely working every hour available on the farm. He won't have time for carpentry work."

"I've got an idea he would make time if you asked him."

I didn't know how to take that comment, so I didn't respond.

"My grandboy is a good man with a heart of gold. He did right by Freda, and he'll do right by you."

Now, I understood his offer. He was trying to get on my good side so I would allow them to stay on the farm after a year's time was up. Before I said anything I shouldn't, I heard the baby cry. I left him standing in the yard as I rushed through the kitchen door that I'd left open for that purpose of hearing the baby when she cried.

I took the baby from the play pen I had recently bought for her and put a fresh diaper on her while her bottle of milk warmed up. She stopped crying once I picked her up. It was like my touch had soothed her. I decided that once she was in my arms she felt safe and perhaps loved. I checked her from head to toe to make sure there was nothing wrong with her, and there wasn't. She was perfect in every way. How was it possible that the offspring of two people such as Angie and Hanson Bell could be this perfect?

Looking at little Mitzie made me wonder what my own baby would be like. A wave of disappointment hit me as I realized it was unlikely I would ever know the answer. I had been attracted to Sensi York, and I had wanted a friend in Nokosi Micco, but I knew the feelings I had for them were far from love. I wanted the kind of love my mother felt for my no-account father. The difference was that I wanted him to have the same kind of love for me.

As things stood now, I was going to stay alone forever except for a baby girl that I was trying to become a mother to. It seemed there was no longer any hope of finding her the perfect parents to adopt her. She was stuck with me.

I finished feeding Mitzie and put her back in her play pen where she fell right to sleep. I looked forward to her being able toddle around after me, but that would be several months from now. I was surprised at the protective feeling that came over me when I looked at her.

My thoughts were interrupted by the sound of a vehicle driving into the driveway. I closed the kitchen door and looked out the window as a faded blue Ford car parked in the driveway. Much to my horror, I recognized Aunt Mary sitting in the passenger seat. A man with greasy, slicked-back hair was in the driver's seat. Never had I expected to see such a sight. How had Aunt Mary managed to find me? Who was the strange man with her? I'd never seen him before, but I wasn't taking any kind of chance. I rushed to the cabinet and took out my pistol from where I'd hidden it behind a sack of flour. I was ready to defend what I now had with any means necessary.

Much to my amazement Wilburn suddenly appeared in the yard as Aunt Mary and the man got out of the car. He was wearing a ragged, dirty flannel shirt that was too big for him along with an equally delipidated hat pulled low over his face. He looked a lot like the scary man who had faced me when I first arrived. This time he carried a double barrel shotgun resting over his arm.

"This is private land. You're trespassing," he said in a threatening tone of voice as he pointed the gun at the man's feet. Best you turn around and get your asses off my land afore I take offense."

A feeling of gratefulness came over me.

"Don't you threaten me," Aunt Mary said with a bravado I knew she wasn't feeling. "I'm Mary Smith and this is my husband, Bill Smith. I'm here to see my niece, Millie James."

"No one here by that name."

"You're lying. That's her car. I'd recognize it anywhere."

"No, it hain't. That belongs to my boy. Bought it new, he did."

She made a beeline for the house, but Wilburn was faster. He stuck the long barrel of the shotgun across her chest, stopping her progress.

"Best not take another step," his gravelly voice told her. "It would be a shame if this thing accidentally went off and blowed your feet out from under you."

"Don't you threaten my wife," the man hollered. "We'll sue you."

It was then that Morton appeared. He looked as grubby as Wilburn and twice as fierce. Much to my amazement, he also had a double barrel shotgun resting in his arms.

"You got a problem, Pa?" Morton drawled in a hickish voice different than he usually used. "Did I hear my wife's name mentioned?"

"You did. Got your track-hoe fueled up? Might need to dig two more graves."

"It's in fine working order, but the hogs are mighty hungry. They're ready to eat the hind end out of an elephant." His voice was as threatening as Wilburn's had been.

"I'm looking for my niece," Aunt Mary shouted at the top of her lungs as she had backed up against her greasy husband as though she expected him to protect her. "She stole money from me, and we've finally tracked her down."

Much to my horror, Aunt Mary looked toward the house with determination showing in her body and her actions. I feared she was going to make a run for it again.

Wilburn gave a disturbing kind of laugh. "We might not have to shoot 'em before they visit the hogs. Reckon Millicent will do it. You know how much she likes her guns and killing things. Killing vermin had been her obsession ever since she was the size of pigeon."

I'm not sure if it was fear or fury that came over me. Whatever it was, I wasn't about to hide away like a coward and do nothing. I cracked the kitchen door open, stuck the barrel of my pistol out the crack and fired a shot in the air."

Again, Wilburn chuckled wickedly and said, "That was a warning shot. Her next two shots won't miss."

"Best start running. Millicent likes belly shots. Hurts more. Dies slower," Morton told them.

The man, Bill Smith, was back in the car before Morton's words were out of his mouth. Aunt Mary had to yank the passenger door open and jump in while the Ford was backing up. Gears ground and tires flung up dirt as he floored the gas pedal. Blue smoke boiled as the tires got traction and the car fishtailed as he turned it around.

Through the crack in the door, I could hear the car engine struggling as the old Ford clanged down the rough road. Wilburn and Morton listened for a while before they came to the kitchen door.

"Damn," Wilburn said. "Don't know if that shot was a good idea or not."

"They're lucky I didn't shoot them," I said in a shaky voice. The noise had woken up Mitzie and she started to cry.

"Might ought to let us come in while you tell us what's going on," Morton said.

I didn't like that idea at all, but it was what I should probably do. I opened the door wider, and they both came inside. Much to my surprise and irritation, Morton went to the play pen, picked her up and cradled her in his arms. She snuggled against him and her little eyes closed.

Wilburn stood to the side of the window to keep a watch outside. "Who are they?"

"My Aunt. I've never seen the man before."

"What are they doing here?" Morton asked.

"When my mother died, Aunt Mary tried to claim her house although Mother had left the house to me in her will. She sued me and lost, and I sold the house. It seems she and whoever was with her want to bully me into giving them the money I got from selling the house." I had no doubt that Aunt Mary had run the restaurant into the ground. Jimbo had used my real name on the deed and that was how she had been able to tract me down.

"So, she's after money," Morton said as he eased Mitzie back into her play pen.

"She's always after money. She's never been able to manage anything right."

"Think she'll come back?" Wilburn asked.

"I doubt they'll have the nerve to come back, but most likely she will try to have us arrested and then sue all three of us."

"In that case we'll all three claim there were no guns or pistol shot. You were inside taking care of your baby when they arrived. We'll claim they took a good look at Morton and me and decided it was best they leave. You want to admit that she was your Aunt Mary or an imposter who was after money?"

"What do you suggest?"

"I think you should claim you've never seen the woman before. That she came up with some sort of wild story in order to get her hands on this house and land. Plenty folks have tried it before."

I wasn't sure about their advice. Perhaps I should check with Ronald Watson, but I didn't have time. Morton's cell phone rang. He handed it to Wilburn.

"Hello, Sussie May," Wilburn said as he flipped the phone on speaker so all three of us could hear what she said.

"Wilburn, have you been running off trespassers again?"

"Yep, two of 'em. Barged in here like they owned the place. Think they were scamming for money."

"They're claiming the woman's niece stole her money and she came after it," Sussie May said.

"So, that's what they're claiming?"

"That along with claiming you and Morton held guns on them while someone else shot at them."

Wilburn chuckled. "Had been in the hog pen shoveling shit with Morton when they showed up. Heard the car coming down the road a bit and met them head-on as they were getting out of the car."

"Did you or Morton fire a warning shot?"

"Nope, neither me nor him did. Reckon our looks and smell were enough to put the fear of the devil himself in them. Works most every time. Nearly blew their car engine trying to get away."

"Where was Millie?" she wanted to know.

"She was in the house feeding her baby."

"Did she shoot at them?"

"Why would she do a thing like that? It was me and Morton who put them off the place. You know what kind of trouble we've had since Freda died. By the way, did they tell you the name of her niece?"

"Millie James is what she said."

"If it really was her aunt, she'd know that Millie was married to a York who died and has a baby that's around three months old. If they go to the police, have them ask if Millie James is married and has children."

"Will do, but make sure the three of you keep your stories straight in case Ralph and Pete has to show up," she said and cut the connection.

"Knows you too well," Morton said to his grandfather.

"Known her since she was a twinkle in her daddy's eyes."

So that was why she was slow to respond to me when I called 911 when I first arrived. Then it suddenly hit me. "How do you know I was married to a York who died?"

"Gossip around here travels faster by mouth than it does on the internet. Wouldn't surprise me if folks didn't know what color underwear you've got in your dresser drawers."

I must have given him a surprised look for he continued.

"You'll also find that once you become part of this community, folks will have your back no matter what comes up."

"Ronald Watson is a gossiper," I said.

"Nope. Not him. He takes his fiduciary duties seriously. His secretary and office maintenance people don't have the same professional ethics."

Morton's phone rang again. "That'll be Ralph," he said.

"Hey, Ralph. What's going down?"

"You know what's going down. Two lunatics want you, Morton, and the little lady arrested. What you got to say about that?"

"Did you ask them if she'd ever been married or had children?"

"I did. Sussie May forewarned me about what you said."

"They said no, didn't they?"

"They did. They also said Morton claimed she was his wife."

"Wishful thinking on his part," Wilburn said with a touch of humor. "Where are they?"

"They're here at the police station."

"Can they hear you talking?"

"Of course not."

"Then fib a little. Tell them you've known me and Morton for years, and that Morton has been married to Millie for five years or so. You do know it is okay for a law officer to lie to suspected criminals in order to get at the truth."

"I've heard that," he admitted with hesitation.

"Tell them we plan on suing them for trespassing, harassment, and attempted money scamming, and that they'll be thrown in jail as soon as we drive into town and fill out a warrant. After you've told them that, excuse yourself and leave the room and see what happens."

"Don't tell me how to do my job, you old fart."

"You know I wouldn't do a thing like that, now would I?"

"Nope. You have more sense than to do a thing like that to an officer of the law."

"Right. Call me back later and let me know what happened."

Wilburn grinned as he closed his phone. "Stay with her until she settles down. I'll bring her a little of my good whiskey to calm her nerves down."

"I don't drink liquor," I told him firmly. "And my nerves are fine." I lied. Seeing Aunt Mary has shaken me up more than I realized. I didn't want her and her greasy husband, or whoever he was, anywhere near me.

"We won't let them bother you," Morton assured me after Wilburn went out the door. "Appears Freda's son sent you here for us to look after and that's what we'll do. You're one of our own now whether you realize it or not."

There was something gentle in his words as well as in his eyes. Oddly enough, I believed what he said.

"Would you have fed them to the hogs or dug their graves with a track-hoe?"

"It only takes a little threat to scare bullies away. Although a real man would do whatever it takes to keep his woman and baby from being harmed."

Chapter 29

*

It appeared that Wilburn McCray had played his hand with Aunt Mary and won. Ralph said after he got back to the room Aunt Mary and Bill were long gone. No one had seen hide nor hair of them since. Hopefully, the lie Wilburn had Ralph tell them worked. I hoped so, but I wasn't convinced they would not try something again. Wilburn and Morton must not be sure either because one of them was near me all the time. Wilburn even got me to put Mitzie in her snugly to tend the flowers and garden with him. He claimed the fresh air and sunshine would do both of us good. The fact that the house was filled with construction workers and hard to breathe sawdust made me agree to stay outside every day.

Morton even had me at the caretaker's house for our meals. Most of the time he cooked breakfast, but I always did lunch and sometimes dinner, which he and Wilburn called supper. The house was small, but it was in much better shape than Freda's house.

"It was little more than a run-down shack when Morton moved in here," Wilburn told me. "He spent every dime he made off the farm for the first three years he was here until he practically rebuilt this place from the ground up. You know what I've been thinking. All that sawdust and fibers for the insulation can't be good for a baby to breathe. I think you and the baby out to move into the caretaker's place while the remodeling is being done."

"No way," I told him.

"Don't see why not."

"There's only two bedrooms. Yours and Morton's. That's why not."

"You've seen that little Yurt house down by the creek next to the willow trees, haven't you?"

I had seen something that looked to be a cross between a tent and a round building. I assumed it had something to do with farming.

"That's my own private sanctuary. I spend a lot of nights down there. It's mighty restful for an old man."

"Then perhaps I should be the one staying down there."

"It'd be a fine place for you, but not for the baby. Nighttime would be too damp and chilly for a baby. Yep, the best thing for you and your baby would be to stay in my room. We want to make sure the little darlin' stays healthy. Don't like the idea of her breathing all that dust and bits of fiberglass insulation that hovers in the air. It could give her and you both lung problems."

I was instantly concerned for my baby. Even with the door shut in the upstairs bedroom, I could still detect the impurities in the air.

"I can assure you that Morton will be a perfect gentleman. You don't need to worry about him imposing on you in any way."

"That's not what I'm worried about," I was quick to answer.

"What are you worried about then?"

"I .." I wasn't sure what I had started to say. "It wouldn't look right," I managed to tell him.

He chuckled softly. "Who's going to know?"

"Those construction workers."

"You think they give a rat's ass about where you're sleeping? Besides, you're already eating three meals a day in the caretaker's house."

"The men know it's because I can't cook anything in the kitchen."

"You've usually left the house before they arrive and don't return until after they leave. How would they know any difference?"

He made a point, and I did want to keep my baby safe. I'd never forgive myself if I caused her lungs to be harmed.

"Okay, that's settled. I already have most of my things at the yurt, and you have most of the baby things in the living room of the caretaker house. It won't take any effort to sleep there as well."

Morton appeared shocked to find me in his grandfather's bedroom. I had assumed Wilburn had discussed it with him before he made the offer.

"Where's Gramps?" he asked me.

"He's in the Yurt. He insisted I spend the nights here until the construction work is finished. He said the sawdust and fiberglass insulation could harm the baby's lungs."

"I see," he mumbled. "He does have a point."

"Do you mind us being here?" I asked hesitantly. If he did, The baby and I would have to stay in the Yurt instead of Wilburn.

"No," he was quick to say. "I don't mind you and the baby staying here in the least. You'll be a lot better company than Gramps. I bet you don't snore the way he does. Sometimes I have to take the cotton out of aspirin bottles and stick it in my ears before I can sleep. Wish he would sleep in the Yurt every night."

What he said eased my mind about being there. It seemed like a reasonable solution for all three of us.

It took only a day or two for us to fall into a time-saving routine. Morton got up before dawn and went to the barn to take care of the animals. I slept for another hour since I'd gotten up during the night to care for the baby. Then I'd have breakfast ready by the time Morton returned. We'd sit at the table eating and discussing his day's work until Wilburn arrived. Morton would then head to the fields while Wilburn ate, and I washed up. After the baby woke up and was fed and dressed, I would put her in the snugly and head to the greenhouse and garden where Wilburn was hard at work.

After lunch, and while the baby was napping, Wilburn and I would go to house to check on the progress the workers were making.

"How much longer until you're finished?" I asked the head carpenter.

"We ought to have the kitchen and downstairs bedroom finished in two weeks if things go as planned."

"How much will it cost to remodel the living room while you're at it?" Wilburn asked.

The head carpenter looked Wilburn in the eyes and scratched his chin as if he was thinking. "Let's see now. It hasn't taken us as long as we estimated to do this much, plus we managed to get a good deal on insulation, lumber, sheetrock, as well as utilities." He then quoted a price that shocked even me. It was just a few hundred more than I was already paying them."

"Can't beat that," Wilburn told me. "At that price, you best let them get on with it."

"Okay," I said hesitantly. "I was looking forward to having everything cleaned up and operational, but at that price I couldn't say no."

I saw a couple of the men grin and wink at each other as though they were sharing some kind of silent joke. I suppose they thought I would be foolish if I turned down such a low price.

I began to realize Wilburn was right about Morton being restless at night and having trouble sleeping. I would often hear him stirring around in his bedroom or in the rest of the house. Sometimes I would even hear him going out the door during the night and not returning for hours. I assumed he was checking on the animals.

One night after I had fed the baby and gotten her back to sleep, I decided to go outside to see if there was a light on in the barn. I walked across the yard to a group of apple trees to a where a wooden bench was located. It was pitch dark in the trees causing a chill to creep up my backbone and spread to my chest. I had never left the house during the night before and didn't realize how spooky the dark of night really was.

"I like to sit on the bench and smell the apple blossoms," Wilburn had once told me. I was almost to the bench when a hand reached around the trunk of a tree and took hold of my arm. Fear shot through me. I reacted the way I'd been trained to react. I grabbed the hand holding my arm and delivered a fast front kick to the groin before I twisted the arm and kicked his feet out from under my assailant.

The man's moaning sounded a lot like I'd heard Morton sound. It was that sound that caused me not to stomp him in the throat.

"Da-m-m-m-n," the man moaned letting me realize it had been Morton I had attacked.

"Oh, no, Morton. I'm sorry. I didn't realize it was you. Can you stand up and bounce the pain out?"

A louder moan escaped him.

"I'll help you up," I told him as I grabbed hold of his arm. He was on the ground bent over in a fetal position with both hands cupping his groin. "You'll be all right in a few minutes. It'll help if you get on your feet and stomp about." I'd seen a lot of men get kicked in the groin. Some took longer than others to recuperate. Some rolled on floor the over and over while they puked all over the place. Most of the groin-kicked men wore a protective cup. I could only imagine how much pain a kick to the groin was when the man wasn't wearing a cup.

I was beginning to get really worried about Morton until he managed to sit up. "Why did you do that to me?" he moaned.

"You grabbed me in the dark. I reacted the way I was trained to do."

"Trained to do?" he questioned.

"I went through self-defense training and street fighting in karate."

"I should have guessed," he groaned again. "I may never get to become a father after that kick."

I kind of sniggered at that.

"Don't laugh. Mitzie might want a brother or sister."

His words stunned me more than his hand in the dark had. This time I hadn't been trained in how I should react. "Uh . . ." I mumbled like an idiot.

"Surely you know how I feel about you. I fell hard and fast. Must have been the pistol you aimed at my face that did it."

"Stop joking," I told him.

"A man who's in as much pain as I'm in doesn't joke. Especially about something like that."

I didn't know how to react to his comment, so I said, "If you can get up and walk it will feel better."

"I've heard rubbing the pain out can help. You owe me that much."

I felt like kicking him in the groin again. "Disgusting," I said with feeling.

"I was trying to make a joke, but I don't think disgusting is the correct word I would use."

"I'm not listening to any more of this," I said, as I started to leave.

"Don't leave me here like this, Millie. Stay with me until I'm able to stand up."

"You *can* stand up," I assured him. "Most men don't want to, but it will help."

Again, I took hold of his arm and tugged on it. This time he managed to get to his feet with a few moans and groans.

"Bet I'll never take hold of your arm during the dark of night again."

"Why did you?"

"Because I wanted to touch you. See what you felt like. Hadn't realize touching you would be this painful."

I had to chuckle at that. "I suppose I should say I'm sorry, but I'm not. It'll teach you to say please and may I before you touch me again."

"Please and may I," he said. "Can I put my arm around your shoulders, and have you help me hobble back to the house?"

That was the least I could do for a man I'd put in extreme pain. I had no doubt he would never touch me inappropriately ever again. I hadn't expected the arm he put around me to feel so good, so warm, so right. It was like I'd been waiting for that arm to be around my body forever. Something had to be wrong with me to make a tingling sensation shoot through my entire body. I felt at a loss once we reached the house, and he took his arm from around me.

"I'd say thanks, but I don't think I can manage that magnanimous of a word just yet."

"Understandable," I didn't tell him one of the men I'd injured with a front kick had ended up making love to me. The very thought brought different kinds of chills running up my backbone and settling lower than my chest. "You'll feel better in the morning," I told him.

"Yeah, but I'll be sore as hell, even after some of the pain eases up."

I supposed that was true, but I'd never had one of the men I'd kicked tell me how his family jewels were feeling the next morning. I went back to bed listening to him pace the floor as he continued to moan and groan.

The next morning after Morton and I had eaten, Wilburn showed up as usual. "What's wrong with my grandboy? He's limping on his way to the barn like he's in bad pain."

"Really?" I did my best to sound innocent without grinning. "Maybe you should ask him."

"I already did. You wouldn't believe the look he gave me. Didn't bother answering."

*

A few days later, I made a trip into the grocery store. I was getting lower on baby supplies than I liked. She was in the snuggly on my chest sound asleep. She had come to love being in the snuggly. I thought it might be because the sound of my heart beating soothed her.

I had about half of what I came after in the buggy when I realized other customers were looking at me with some sort of grin on their faces.

"Why are people staring at me?" I asked one of the women I'd talked to before.

"I'd say it's because some of them envy you," she said.

"Envy me? I questioned.

"A lot of them would give their right kidney to have a go at Morton McCray."

I frowned. "What are you talking about?"

"No need to play innocent. Most everybody knows you've been shacking up with Morton. Must say I don't blame you one bit. If I wasn't happily married, I'd give you a run for your money. Have to admit even I've made love to him in my dreams," she kind of laughed a little. "If you tell anybody I said that I'll claim your lying."

"I'm not sleeping with him."

"No need to deny it. The men working for you claim you've got him wrapped around you little finger. They say he can hardly get any work done for trying to stay near you."

My brain was buzzing as I walked away from her. I found it difficult to remember all I'd come after.

Wilburn had been wrong. The construction workers had noticed that I was staying in the caretaker's house with Morton. I wondered if they had also noticed that Wilburn was staying in the Yurt. If so, would they not realize Wilburn had given me his room? Or would they believe Wilburn was giving us privacy to do what they imagined us doing?

I left the supermarket determined to inform the construction workers, along with everyone else, that things were different than they were thinking. If I had too, I'd stand on rooftops and shout out that I wasn't sleeping with Morton McCray. I intended to inform everyone that I was going to run both of the McCrays off just as soon as their contract came to an end.

Chapter 30

*

It had been a long, hot autumn day. Wilburn had convinced me to let the construction workers remodel the entire house. The price they quoted me was way too reasonable for me to refuse. It meant Mitzi and I would have to stay in the caretaker's house for a while longer. I laid in bed listening to the water running in the shower as Morton washed off dirt from a hard day of farm work. The moist air brought the smell of soap and shampoo Morton used straight to my bedroom.

There was some kind of strange force that was keeping me from falling asleep. Instead, I was laying there staring into the darkness thinking thoughts I had no right to think about. I closed my eyes tight and tried not to remind myself that Morton was separated from me by only a thin wall.

It had been weeks, but I could still feel his arm around my shoulder. I thought about the feel of that arm and found myself wishing his arm was still around me. I let my mind go a little crazy as I imagined what he would do if I got out of bed, took off my nightgown, walked a few short feet and got in the shower with him. I could see his eyes widen a moment before he said, *it's about time*. He would put his arms around me and then take me to heights I had only dreamed about.

"Crap," I mumbled out loud. I was letting my imagination run away with me. This hillbilly man wasn't interested in me, regardless of what he'd said after I'd bruised more than his male ego. Actually, he had been going out of his way to avoid coming in contact with me. Not only that, but I was too much of a coward to try something such as I was thinking about. Most likely he would shove me out of the shower and grab a towel to wrap around my nakedness. I couldn't chance being rejected in such a way. That kind of humiliation was something a woman would never get over.

It was obvious my hormones were acting up again. That's what was wrong with me. Hadn't similar happened to me with Sensi York and almost with Nokosi Micco? It wasn't like I'd fallen in the forever kind of love with either of them, I hadn't fallen in love with Morton either regardless of how much I longed to be near him. I told myself the reason I had reacted in such a way to his touch was because I had felt lonely for such a long time. I was realizing that loneliness made me do things I never expected I would ever do.

The shower cut off, and I listened to Morton leave the bathroom and come into the kitchen. He poured himself a glass of water, drank it, put the glass down, took a few steps toward my bedroom and stopped. I then heard his footsteps as he turned around and went to his own bedroom. I was able to breathe again after he was further away from me. Finally, after what felt like half the night, I was able to sleep.

The next morning I found it difficult to look Morton in the eyes. He wasn't looking in my eyes either as he stared at the plate and hurriedly ate his breakfast.

"Best get at it," he said as he jumped up and went out the door.

"Looks like Morton is getting an early start," Wilburn said when he came into the kitchen and sat down at the table to eat.

"Need to make hay while the sun shines," I repeated to Wilburn what he was always saying to me."

"That's a fact. A man can't procrastinate too long, or he can lose out. Morton has always tended to procrastinate when he is uncertain of something."

What he said surprised me. Morton worked before daylight until late at night. The only time I saw him was when he came inside to eat his meals, shower, and go to bed. Often times I heard him get up during the night to go outside to check on the animals. That didn't seem like procrastinating to me.

"Baby sleeping all night long?" he asked when I didn't respond to his comment about Morton.

"I only get up once during the night to feed and change her."

"My boy was several months old before he slept through the night. Morton was the same. Reckon he still has trouble sleeping through the entire night, doesn't he."

"So it seem," I said. "I'm look forward to a full night's sleep," I told him.

"I'm sleeping mighty fine down by the creek in the Yurt. Don't have to listen to Morton snoring."

I didn't comment. I hadn't heard him snoring. I had heard him tossing and turning a lot.

"Well now, Missie. I'm going to head on out to the barn and get an early start on things. The long days of summer will be over soon, and I want to make the best of them before the cold wind blows. Bring the baby out to the garden when she wakes up. She'll soon be big enough to notice the flowers and butterflies if she doesn't already."

I knew it would be several hours before she woke up again. I longed to smell the early morning freshness and see the sunrise over the mountain as it shined it morning light on another mountain I looked out the bedroom window of the house. I left the breakfast dishes soaking in the sink and left the baby sleeping as I headed to the barn.

"Now Gramps, don't start in on that again," I heard Morton say as I came to the open barn door. He and Wilburn were in 'what Wilburn called the cutting-room' dipping feed for the animals into buckets from large sacks.

"My boy, I'm giving you good advice. Besides, I'm getting mighty tired of watching you moon around after that girl."

"Girl is right. She's too young to be interested in someone as old as I am."

Wilburn laughed. "Yep, you're right up there near my age. I'm danged near too old to lift a petticoat, and you'll be too old to do more than that any day now."

"Shit," Morton said with irritation, and Wilburn chuckled.

"You've heard the old saying 'use it or lose it,' haven't you. Wouldn't surprise me if you haven't lost at least of half of it already.

"I've heard an unending rant of things that you keep telling me. It's getting old, Gramps. Mighty old."

"Advice, my boy. Not a rant. I've been around long enough and become wise enough to give you good advice that you ought to take."

"Surely you realize she's not interested in me. I'm too old for her."

"Bull shit. The older the ram, the stiffer the horn."

"Might be true for a ram, but you and I both know it's not true for a man. If it was, you'd be trying to marry a girl her age."

"Nope. I'd be sure to die on my wedding night," Wilburn said with a sigh of longing. "In my opinion, she's mighty interested in you. She's gotten to the point where she can't take her eyes off you any more than you can take your eyes off her. Goodness knows, I've already spent a small fortune paying for those construction workers to remodel that old house in an effort to throw you two together. It's time for one of you to go after what you're both hankering for before I go broke. Why don't you dive in and tell her how you feel about her?"

"There's several good reasons. Like I said, I'm too old for her. She's mighty young. If I admit how I feel about her, she'd think all I want from her is to get my hands on this place by marrying her."

"Is that why you're interested in her?" Wilburn asked.

"Hell no," he was quick to say. "As you know, I've always wanted this place, but I want her a whole lot more."

"So, you're admitting you want to marry her instead of just wanting to get into her bloomers?"

Morton let out a deep sigh before he spoke. "She's the one I want to spend the rest of my life with. I'd given up on finding someone I wanted to be my wife until I set eyes on her. It's ... ah, Gramps, you know how it is when you finally meet the one you want to spend the rest of your life with."

"So, you're saying you're in love with her?"

"There must have been something about the way she tried to protect herself with the baby bottle," he tried to add a touch of humor to his words.

"Then tell her how you feel about her."

"I already did."

"You did?" Wilburn said with surprise.

"I did."

"And she turned you down?"

"To put it mildly. Still haven't gotten entirely over the pain of her rejection."

"My advice is to try, try again until she says yes."

"One thing's for certain, if I get up that much nerve again, I'll say *please* and *may I* while keeping something solid between us."

Chapter 31

Epilogue

I woke up early and looked out the bedroom window as I had a habit of doing each morning. The morning light had barely touched the top of the beautiful, green Appalachian mountain, which meant it was still early. It didn't come as a surprise that my husband's side of the bed was empty. He believed in doing up the work before sunrise.

I got out of bed without changing out of my night grown and padded barefoot into the kitchen to start breakfast. I smiled in relief as I flipped on the overhead light. Instead of going to the refrigerator, I went to the kitchen door and opened it to let the fresh morning air inside.

Feathered layers of morning mist rose from the creek that ran through the valley as it rose toward the heavens. I stood there watching the mist lift upward with fast disappearing fingers as the warmth of dawn consumed the wispy white. I loved the early mornings most of all. It was like having a chance to start life all over again. A fresh new day to enjoy.

I had come to love the peace and safety the mountains brought. It was home, my home. The place I had longed to find. Over the years this place had brought me more love and happiness far greater than I had ever expected to find. It was as though I belonged to these beautiful, craggy hills, narrow valleys, and sweet, pure water that oozed from the rocky craigs.

I laughed out loud.

"What are you laughing about?" asked my husband as he came to the door where I was standing.

"I'm happy," I told him.

"Good to know."

"Yes, it is. You can't imagine how much I longed for a place that felt like home."

"There's no place like home," he said with a grin. "Children still asleep?"

"Yes, and don't wake them." I loved the early morning hours we spent together.

I also loved going to bed with him at night knowing he would be there when morning came. I never dreamed he would be the man I would want to spend the rest of my life with when we first met. Actually, I hated him and resented the air he breathed. Odd how hate can turn into love – and sometimes vice versa.

"When do I wake the children up?" he asked with an innocent grin.

"You wake them up most every morning. You claim early to bed and early to rise makes a man healthy, wealthy, and wise. And it makes children go to sleep early when nighttime comes."

"Truism. If you don't have half your work done by ten o'clock, chances you won't get the other half done. Not to mention I like having my wife to myself when the moon starts to rise."

I was amazed by how much work he did each day as I thought of another truism. A man works from sun to sun, but a woman's work is never done.

"How are you feeling this morning?" he asked as he patted my rounded belly. "Thankful," I told him. "Happy," I added.

"Daisy had her little calf during the night. Heifer. The way you spit out babies we'll need another good Jersey milk cow to be able to keep all the children in milk."

I agreed with having another gentle Jersey cow, but I didn't consider myself as spitting out babies. Giving birth took a lot more effort and pain than merely spitting out.

"Hope we have at least half a dozen. Four boys to go with our two girls. Gramps and I need us some farm hands."

"Three and three," I told him. "Mitzie and Alona love the outdoors, especially Gramps' greenhouse." I had named our daughter Alona Doris after my mother and the name Jimbo had given me.

"Not as much as he loves them."

I smiled at that. This baby boy I was carrying would be named Morton Wilburn McCray, after his father and grandfather. I planned on calling him Morty while he was small and Mort once he was older.

I did keep one secret to myself. I was the only person who would ever know that little Mitzie McCray wasn't my natural-born daughter. I had finally found the parents and home the little girl deserved. No adoption necessary – except for Morton's adoption of her. I even filled out a birth certificate with me as the mother and my deceased husband, Stanley York, as her father. I claimed her lack of a birth certificate came from her being born prematurely from trauma of her father's death– and aid from a mid-wife who failed to fill out proper papers.

As for Nokosi Micco, he was in the past where he and all that had happened in Florida belonged. He never heard of a woman named Millie James. As for Aunt Mary and my father's relatives, I hadn't heard hide nor hair of them and hoped I never would.

As for E.J. Whitley, aka James Boden, he wasn't my blood-related grandfather, but Jimbo made sure his sad, little Robin Hood had her chance to live happily ever after.